SO I WAS TOLD

BRENDA L. WATERS

AuthorHouse™
1663 Liberty Drive
Bloomington, IN 47403
www.authorhouse.com
Phone: 1-800-839-8640

© *2010 Brenda L. Waters. All rights reserved.*

No part of this book may be reproduced, stored in a retrieval system, or transmitted by any means without the written permission of the author.

First published by AuthorHouse   12/30/2010

ISBN: 978-1-4520-9820-3 (e)
ISBN: 978-1-4520-9474-8 (sc)
ISBN: 978-1-4520-9473-1 (dj)

Printed in the United States of America

This book is printed on acid-free paper.

Certain stock imagery © Thinkstock.

Because of the dynamic nature of the Internet, any Web addresses or links contained in this book may have changed since publication and may no longer be valid. The views expressed in this work are solely those of the author and do not necessarily reflect the views of the publisher, and the publisher hereby disclaims any responsibility for them.

AUTHOR'S NOTE

This book is a work of fiction. All work is inspired by the emotions and personal responses to issues that have arisen for many families and in some instances perhaps even from the life of the author. However, any references to actual events, locations, and characters are intended only to give the novel a sense of reality and authenticity. This story should not in any way be construed as real but only as the imagination of the author.

DEDICATION

In loving memory of all my family and friends who have passed away, especially my grandmother, Hannah Waters. You all inspired me to do my best in your own way. You are truly missed, and may you all rest in peace.

ACKNOWLEDGMENTS

It is important for me to give thanks to God for being the head of my life and giving me the inspiration and determination to follow my dream. Without his grace and favor, the writing of this book would never have come to fruition. Being grateful and thankful would not be enough for the many people who helped me and encouraged me on this path.

Without the encouragement of my dear friend Kimberly A. Parrish, my muse, who not only listened to my story but also helped to give it life, I could not have done it without you. It was your determination during those challenging times that kept me going when I was ready to quit. I can't thank you enough and look forward to your help in future endeavors.

I would be remiss if I did not say thank you to Martin Eboma, my friend and neighbor. You helped me stay focused during the times when I had many other things pulling me in different directions.

I must thank my friend Bernetta Jones for all her help in many ways. You were a God send.

To my church family, especially Father John Adamski and Deacon Chester Griffin, a special thanks for all your prayers, inspiration, and guidance.

To Lisa Berkley, the "keeper of the keys", thank you for your patience and cooperation, as well as letting us use the center when we had no other place to go.

Many thanks to my mother, Ernestine W. Smith, for bringing me into this world; you gave me life and a beginning. To my brother, LaVern Anderson, the most kind-hearted and understanding person one could ever ask to share in their life. To my niece, Christina Arnold, you bring me many smiles. Thank you, Godmother LaTanya Renfroe, for always having my back. To my cousin, Precious Fouche Banks, for allowing me to burn your ears off many a day and night during my teenage years. To my extended family, Henry, Truman, Mary, Joyce, Maya and Anjya Thomas, Derrick, Miles and Justin Johnson, Bricca and C. Nicole Banks, Wilburn, Doris, Winston and David Fouche,Twyla McBride and Barbara Ricks, thank you.

To my "sistah and brotha friends" who were there without a doubt: Katrina Norris, Kellie Johnson, Kelsey Fletcher, Cheryl Jacobs, Lenora Lewis, Lynn Crouch, Christy Cox, Juanita Newton, LaQuida Mabry, Melisia Simmons, Leo Spear, Meliza Garza, Brenda Lewis, Brenda Sylvester, Andromeda Oatis, Elsa Willis, Alfreda Johnson, Lee Thompson, Helen Vance, Chavonn Bouquet,Vanessa Bartee, Lou Jean Jackson, Denise Wright, Sandra Martin, Ramona Weston, and David and Doris Coleman.

To my friends through time, Dedra Howard, Arlette Aldridge, Tracey Jones, Johnnie Williams, and Janice Davis, thanks for the memories of our days in college.

Through the countless hours spent talking, crying, and understanding who I am, how to love again; to my dearly departed therapist Dr. Hunt, thank you and may you rest in peace.

I must give a very special thank you to Rebecca Winters, who was always there for me. To some she was just an employee, but to others she was a part of the family.

To my business partner Isaac Gates, thank you for your patience and support.

Many thanks to author Kimberla Lawson Roby for her advice and encouragement when I decided to write this story, as well as her assistant, Connie Dettman, for all the information she sent on behalf of Mrs. Roby.

To my editor and publisher, I cannot thank you enough for all you help and support. I look forward to the next book.

Finally, to all my readers, I thank you for your support. I would love to hear from you, so please e-mail me at blwaters@truelifeproduction.com or visit my Web site at www.TrueLifeProduction.com.

My God bless you all,
Brenda L. Waters

PROLOGUE

One late morning, the snowstorm of the century fell upon Madison, Mississippi. It was the storm people would talk about for generations to come. This was not the fluffy white flakes you see floating and swirling throughout the skies; landing so softly, melting before your very eyes.

On this day, eleven and three-quarter inches of the wettest, thickest snow ever to fall from the heavenly sky blanketed Madison. It was covering and consuming all those poor, leafless trees, which were bending and breaking from the heavy, sodden weight of the snow and ice. You could hear the popping and crackling of power lines. The limbs from the ancient trees were snapping and falling on rooftops and onto the streets. Buses were stopped dead in their tracks with their doors ajar for scrambling passengers to exit, and cars were left in the middle of the streets with nowhere to go. The stoplights were flashing, and most of the stores and homes were without power.

Yet, the arrival of this horrendous storm was little competition compared to the imminent disaster about to befall the house located on 1547 Copperhead Lane.

What storm was this, you ask?

My birth!

CHAPTER ONE

WE ARE FAMILY

The woman who brought me into the world kicking and screaming that windswept snowy day was twenty-four years old and single. Her name is Ethel Lee Collins.

Under her bed in an old shoebox tied with a tattered green ribbon were pictures of Ethel when she was a young woman. She was tall and beautiful, full of life and vitality. Her complexion was the color of honey brown and flawless, except for a faint trace of freckles across the bridge of her nose. Those photographs reminded me of times when I was a child of how I would stand over her as she sunbathed in our backyard and counted the freckles, much to her dislike and protest. I was in awe of Ethel and wanted *so* much to be like *her*, freckles and all.

Aside from her complexion, it was Ethel's eyes that drew you to her. They looked like large amber-colored almonds with a tiny hint of green around the pupils, surrounded by the darkest and fullest lashes imaginable. When she was angry or sad, her pupils enlarged, turning dark and foreboding. When she was happy or excited, they lit up and sparkled like precious jewels, similar to the pendant she wore around her neck. It was a tawny-colored stone with tiny specks of green inside.

Ethel was the youngest of three children born to her parents, John Henry and Elizabeth Marie Collins. She had two siblings, a sister, Martha Louise, and a brother, Nathaniel Louis, who were much older when she was born. When Ethel was almost two, their mother died; Nathaniel was nine, and Martha was eleven. Many people in my family and even in the community thought my grandmother's death was very suspicious and untimely.

It was going to be one of those scorching summer days in Mississippi, yet there was a slight coolness in the morning air when she and grandfather started working in the family garden. They started early, so as not to get caught in the strong heat of the afternoon. Grandmother Marie came rushing into the house from working in the garden looking agitated and acting rather peculiar. She started drinking glasses of water, spilling most of it down the front of her dress and onto the kitchen floor, one minute laughing hysterically, and then weeping and moaning the next.

There were times in the South when the sun and the heat were brutal. I remember days growing up when all you breathed was dirt and hot, stale air. Even the water from the garden hose was warm when you first turned it on.

I don't really remember how old I was when I overheard family members talking about Grandmother Marie's death. When she passed away, she was pregnant with her fourth child. Everybody talked about the children and their strong resemblance to John Henry's side of the family, except Ethel. Martha and Nathaniel looked like twins, if not for their differences in age. It was Ethel who didn't really fit in. Her complexion, eyes, hair, and skin were so unlike theirs. Even the lashes on her eyes, thick, long, and full, were a contrast to Nathaniel and Martha, who barely had a lash to share between the two of them.

The reason she looked different they said probably had to do with that *kickback gene*—some obscure trait that ran in the family. Maybe it was some aunt or cousin she took after, though no one knew exactly. They started whispering how grandfather thought it had nothing to do with kickback genes or some distant relative, but maybe somebody *named* Gene. There allegedly were many fights and arguments about this when grandfather was angry or drunk, accusing her of something or being with *someone*. He made no secret of thinking *she* was having an affair. Whenever he confronted her

SO I WAS TOLD

about this, she always had an answer for him. I don't think he much believed her. She told him not to listen to idle gossip.

The first time my grandfather saw Grandmother Marie, he knew she was the one for him. He wanted to know all there was about her, but apparently my grandmother was not impressed with him. He was determined to win her over and make her his wife.

John Henry was *madly* in love with Marie. To him, there was no woman more beautiful, kind, and smart. Grandmother Marie wanted to marry someone else, but the man's family did not approve of her. They were going to elope, but his family discovered their secret and sent him away. Barely eighteen and heartbroken, she was devastated by her loss, never to see or hear from him again.

Grandfather was the oldest child born to parents who were poor, illiterate sharecroppers who worked from sun up to sun down. For all their hard work, they owned *nothing* and had *nothing*. At times there was barely enough food to feed their family. A thin, patched-up tin roof covered their heads, and a dirty wooden floor was under their feet. They had a roof that leaked when it rained and baked them like a Dutch oven in the summer. Grandfather swore that was not going to be his life. When he went to school, he was determined to learn everything there was to know. He especially loved to read. He was fortunate enough to have a teacher who saw his potential and encouraged his education. The teachers knew children of sharecroppers rarely got an education because they had to work in the fields during crop-picking season. When grandfather was old enough, he left his family and worked on farmlands as hired help, picking cotton and tobacco. He later gained employment on the rail lines putting down studs for the tracks, always working anywhere and everywhere he could until he could afford to buy some land.

He believed if you owned land, you had everything. When he had enough money, he bought his first piece of land and subsequently purchased more until he had over 250 acres of the best farming, dairy, and lumber in Mississippi. This was quite an accomplishment for the son of a sharecropper who became known in the county for his famous vegetable gardens.

Although people often spoke of his quiet nature, grandfather was aggressive in pursuing Marie. When he felt financially stable, he asked for

3

BRENDA L. WATERS

her hand in marriage. They had a decent relationship, but deep down he knew he would never replace the man who broke her heart.

Grandmother Marie was having a hard time with this pregnancy, unlike the other three. There were bouts of severe headaches, strange stomach aches, and pains. She complained of severe nausea sometimes, so bad it kept her up all hours of the night. Often you could hear her moaning while she slept. The doctor said it was just a bad case of morning sickness.

I overheard relatives say she and grandfather argued all the time; he was obsessed with her, but nothing she did pleased him anymore. From what I gathered, I didn't think grandfather thought this baby was his. He was quite certain about the first two, because they looked just like him and his family, especially Martha. I guess he just wasn't taking any chances with more *kickback genes*; he had enough of that with Ethel.

Two days before Martha's eleventh birthday, Marie went into premature labor. She was only six months pregnant. Martha ran as fast as she could to get Ms. Ophelia, the midwife. There wasn't time to get her to the hospital. When they reached the house, Grandmother Marie and the baby were dead. Everyone who knew her was devastated.

A few weeks after John Henry laid his wife to rest, rumors started to circulate about suspicious circumstances surrounding her death. Some of Marie's family wanted an autopsy, but my grandfather protested. In those days, people of color in the South rarely demanded or were allowed autopsies for their loved ones regardless of how suspicious things looked. After grandmother died, the children went to live with their maternal grandparents for a short while. The pressure from Marie's death took a toll on grandfather.

Ethel was five years old when my grandfather met and married Haley Ilene Dodson. The Dodsons were a well-respected family who lived in Madison, Mississippi, and owned several businesses. The girls were beautiful, popular, and very wealthy. Any man who could marry one of the Dodson women was considered very fortunate. Their beauty and wealth brought many a man to court them.

Haley was much younger than John Henry and had never been married. She was considered the prettiest of the Dodson girls but was nothing like my Grandmother Marie. It seemed John Henry wanted the exact opposite of her. Perhaps he thought that marrying someone different would help him avoid the same mistakes.

The first few years of marriage between John Henry and Haley were picture perfect. There was laughter and parties almost every weekend; there were just a lot of good times in their home. During the Fourth of July celebrations, they had the most sought-after party. It start early in the day, and people would drive over from everywhere. There was homemade ice cream and so much food, it was sinful. John Henry Collins felt his life and family were whole again.

It was sometime during the third year of their marriage that things began to unravel. Things changed soon after one of Haley's sisters came to visit, a visit that ended in a lengthy stay. Where there was once plenty of laughter, it was less frequently heard. The hugs and kisses weren't as plentiful as they had been. The summertime parties were no more. No one knew why, but life became very different in that house. My uncle, Nathaniel, went to live with Marie's sister, Rachael Neal- Parker, in Memphis, Tennessee. Aunt Martha was taken in by Mrs. Ida Hunt, a childhood friend, who had promised Marie to take care of her children in the event that something happened to her. One year later, Nathaniel was taken from Aunt Rachael and sent to Piney Grove Military Boarding School. Martha went away to Houston University in Washington DC. After graduating from college, she moved to Los Angeles, California. Neither child returned to their father or that house ever again.

Ethel remained with her father and stepmother until she left for Jamestown State College. All who knew her said she had a good life. She didn't want for anything; she was spoiled actually, or so I was told.

CHAPTER TWO

CARLY

The final school bell rang for the morning classes to begin. The shiny wooden floors glistening with drops of water from the snowy shoes and boots the children tracked in from the outdoors looked like ripples of water on a glassy lake. Here and there were sounds of scampering feet and slamming lockers as children rushed to their classrooms.

The telephone in the Madison High School principal's office rang. Julia Redding, the school secretary, answered and informed Mrs. Helen Watkins there was a call for her on line two.

"Good morning, Helen Watkins, how may I help you?"

"Hello, Mrs. Watkins, this is Mary Stephens, Ethel's co-worker; she is very ill and needs to be picked up right away."

Ethel was a teacher at the elementary school, several blocks from the high school where Helen was the principal.

"Julia, that was a call from Ethel's school; she is not feeling well, and I have to leave immediately to take her home. Mary Stephens was hysterical when I answered the telephone, and I could barely understand a word she said. I had to tell the poor woman to calm down and breathe. You would have thought it was *her*, not Ethel, who was sick."

Looking out, she could see the snow coming down. With a scowl on her face, she grabbed her coat, hat, and scarf, stopped briefly at Julia's desk, and glanced over the report as she headed out the door.

"Oh, Julie, please let Mr. Alexander know I had to leave and he is in charge. If the weather does not improve, I may not be back today."

Helen drove, inching and crawling in the heavy packed snow and ice, to pick Ethel up. Every mile she drove, her anger rose. Apart from Helen telling her to *get in*, their ride home was mostly in silence; with an occasional moan from Ethel as she hugged her stomach. That fifteen-minute drive for her felt like a trip around the world.

The housekeeper, Rayne Matthews, heard a car pull in the driveway while she was cleaning the front room. She stopped dusting and looked out the window and saw Helen's car. Rayne thought something must be wrong or she forgot something important to drive back home in all this snow and ice. The trucks had not cleaned the streets yet, and the snow was falling heavy and fast. Still standing at the window, she watched Helen get out of the car and almost slip from the patch of ice at the car door. Rayne chuckled to herself at the sight and whispered under her breath, "It served you right you old *bat*." She continued to watch as Helen held onto the back of the car, easing her way around to the passenger side. Just as she made it, the car door opened, and Ethel stepped out. Rayne could tell by the look on her face and the way she was hunched over …

She immediately left the window and went to the front door. As they approached, she heard the crunching snow as they made their way up the steps. She opened it just when Helen was putting her key into the lock. It startled Helen when the door opened so quickly, but she was relieved when she saw it was Rayne standing there.

"Oh good, it's you! Take Ethel, *please*, she is sick. I think it's her stomach; she probably has gas or something. She barely said two words to me in the car. You never listen to me, but I told you Ethel did not need all that food. Whatever she wanted, there you were chopping and cooking your heart out. Do you have any idea what an inconvenience this has been for me today? I had to leave school in the beginning of *my* day to pick her up, and now I have to get back out in this mess to get her something from the drug store for *her* upset stomach, because *you* don't know how to tell her no!"

Rayne was holding onto Ethel, helping her out of her coat and boots while Helen was fussing about how she was inconvenienced. Glancing into Ethel's eyes, she could see the fear and pain. She knew then what was happening. No matter how she tried, there was nothing she could do at that moment. No amount of prayer or wishful thinking was going to help; not now.

"Ms. Helen, I don't think you need to go to the sto'. This ain't no gas, is it, Ethel? Baby, you need to tell yo' aunt what is goin'on."

Ethel started to cry uncontrollably. Rayne told her again, this time holding her chin up and looking into her eyes. "Go on, tell her. Tell yo' aunt what *is really* wrong with you."

"I can't! Can you tell her? Please, Rayne, you tell her, tell her for me, please," Ethel said in between her sobbing.

Helen, being unsure of what Rayne was about to say, stopped at the door before she opened it to leave. "Tell me what? What is it that I need to know? Somebody needs to start talking right now. Ethel, pull yourself together and stop all that hysteria; stop all that crying."

Realizing she was not going to get an answer out of Ethel, Helen turned to Rayne and asked her to explain why Ethel was so hysterical.

"Rayne, what is going on here?

"Ethel don't have no gas, Ms. Helen, she's in labor and 'bout to have a baby," Rayne said as she turned from Ethel to address Helen.

Helen looked from Rayne to Ethel, standing in total disbelief. She screamed at the top of her lungs, *"What the hell! Heaven's sake, what are you saying?"*

As she cursed and screamed, everyone's eyes turned toward the twenty-foot ceiling. They were watching as she threw her purse high into the air, barely missing the antique crystal chandelier that hung in the foyer. The Dodson chandelier had been in their family even before Helen was born. No one was allowed to touch it, not even Rayne. Yet, at this moment, all eyes were on it, waiting for it to shatter into a million pieces.

Ginger, one of Aunt Helen's sisters, was in the back room. She stayed home from the family-owned gas station to tend to their ailing father, Hubert Dodson. She heard the yelling and commotion and came running as quickly as she could. Arriving out of breath with her hand over her heart, she said, "Helen, what the hell are you yelling and screaming about? Daddy and I could hear you all the way in the back of the house."

BRENDA L. WATERS

Helen looked at her sister and said. "Your niece is having a baby!"

"A what?" Ginger asked in disbelief.

By this time their father, who was on a cane, walked into the foyer. He could see there was something terribly wrong. "Who is doing all this crying and screaming? What is happening in my house?" he asked.

Ginger, turning to her father, said, "Ethel is pregnant, and about to give birth."

Stepping closer to Ginger, he asked. "Ethel is having a baby?"

Ginger and Helen both replied, "Yes, Daddy!"

"In this house, right this very minute? Nothing like this has ever happened in this family without no husband, no marriage. Lord, I am glad your mother is not here to know about all of this. It would surely have put her in the grave."

He lowered his eyes from hers and shook his head. "Rayne, you take Ethel upstairs to my room and get her out of this draft. Lay her down, for God's sake, and call the doctor." As he left the foyer, he continued to repeat what a sin and shame it was. Rayne gently gathered Ethel in her arms and walked her up the stairs to the bedroom.

As they climbed the staircase, Helen shouted out, "Rayne, after you get that girl in bed, you call Dr. Walker immediately and tell him there is an emergency. He needs to come right now."

Helen and Ginger left the foyer and went into the kitchen to await the doctor. After talking for what seemed hours, they decided they would have their younger sister Haley, Ethel's stepmother, come and get the baby as soon as it was born. Maybe if they gave it to her and have her take it away, no one would know what happened. This would be just another family secret.

Ethel and her baby could not wait. Rayne did not have time to run down the stairs and alert everyone. No sooner had she gotten her in bed and went to call the doctor, Ethel let out a loud horrible scream.

Rayne knew what to do and threw back the covers. She ran to the hall and gathered all the towels she could. By this time, Ethel was moaning and sweating profusely. Rayne looked down and could see blood beginning to stain the sheets. She gathered Ethel into her arms and lifted her off the bed as best she could. With towels in hand, she placed them underneath her and pushed her legs back as far as she could. They both were sweating

SO I WAS TOLD

now, water dripping off their faces. She left Ethel on the bed and ran to gather all the things she needed to birth this baby. Her mother was the local midwife and Rayne was her best student. She knew that baby was coming any minute. With bottles of alcohol, scissors, and a new pack of unwrapped shoe laces, she returned to the room to find Ethel moaning and crying. Her head was moving from side to side, with sweat pouring down her face like a river. Rayne stood by the bed, bent down, and gathered Ethel's face into her hands to steady her.

"Ethel, look at me. I can see the baby's head. Now I want you to hold onto the bed and push as hard as you can. Here, put this towel in your mouth and bite on it so you won't bite your tongue. Baby, I know it hurts, but you got to do it. When I tell you to push, *push!*"

With all her might, Ethel pushed as hard as she could. It felt like everything inside of her was coming out. She could feel the baby sliding and ripping out of her. She felt Rayne's hands inside of her telling her to push while she pulled. Holding onto the bed with the towel in her mouth, she pushed so hard she thought she would pass out. She fell back onto the bed relieved and wet. Then she heard that cry—that loud, full cry—and she smiled. When she looked down, there was Rayne with the fattest baby in her arms, wiping and drying it off. Ethel could see the umbilical cord with the white shoe lace tied around it. She saw the bowl laid to the side of the bed with what looked like a bloody piece of calf liver. She saw Rayne stick her fingers inside the baby's mouth, sweeping around and pulling something out. Rayne then blew several puffs of air across the baby's little nose and mouth Her baby stopped crying after she did this, as if the breath she blew soothed and calmed her. Perhaps by doing so, it let the baby know all was well and she was safe.

Smiling, Rayne told her, "Ethel, baby! You have a little girl! A beautiful baby, with a head full of the curliest black hair I have ever seen."

Rayne then wrapped the infant up in one of the white towels she had at the foot of the bed and placed her into Ethel's arms. Ethel, exhausted as she was, smiled and kissed her baby's forehead. She then opened the towel wider and peeked inside to see her tiny little fingers balled up like she was ready to punch someone. She asked Rayne if the baby was all right. Rayne told her she was and left to bring clean, soapy water to wash Ethel's face and body, and clean linen to change the bed.

BRENDA L. WATERS

Nodding her head at the baby, Rayne asked Ethel, "What you going to name her? She is so pretty. Look at her lashes, Ethel. I think she is going to have eyes like yours. You can't tell right now 'cause they ain't opened all the way, but they sure are shaped like yours."

"You know, Rayne, I never really thought about any names," Ethel said, smiling while holding her nursing baby. She hesitated for a moment before she continued. Looking down at the baby suckling and pulling at her breast, with tears beginning to well in her eyes, she continued: "I think I am going to name her Carly; Carly Elizabeth Collins. I was so young when mother passed away, I don't really remember her, but I always felt that if I had a daughter, I would want her to carry her name, so it could fill that void in my heart. You know Rayne, I was told daddy never thought I was his child. Did you you know that? I want you to swear to me, swear you will never tell this baby who her father is.

While standing over Ethel and the baby, Rayne heard the front door close and the voice of Dr. Walker in the foyer. As he headed up the stairs, Helen spoke to him in a low and stern voice, "Fine, but you know what to do, don't you?"

It was more a statement than a question; Rayne and Ethel looked at each other as Dr Walker entered the bedroom.

After examining Ethel, Dr. Walker told Rayne she had done a good job delivering the baby. He would finish everything else and inform Helen on their condition. Rayne smiled and thanked him for the compliment. Looking back over her shoulder, Rayne saw Ethel and Carly slowly falling asleep. Before leaving the room, she turned and politely asked Dr. Walker what Mrs. Helen was saying about Ethel and the baby.

Dr. Walker shook his head and said not to worry. She was not saying anything of importance. Right now his concern was Ethel and her little girl.

Walking down the staircase, a terrible feeling overcame her. She whispered under her breath, "God help that poor girl and her baby."

After making sure Ethel and the child were resting, Dr. Walker washed his hands in the bathroom sink and went downstairs. He was met by Helen, Rayne, and Ginger.

Helen was the first to speak.

"Well, how are Ethel and the little bastard?"

SO I WAS TOLD

This made Dr. Walker's skin crawl as he replied in a stern voice, "Helen, Ethel and *the baby* are fine. Rayne did an outstanding job in bringing her into the world. If her mother was alive, she would be very proud of Rayne. I think it would be a good idea to let Ethel rest and get her strength back. She lost a little blood and needed a few stitches, but she will be fine in three to four days with some bed rest. Other than that, everything looks good. Rayne, make sure you check on her regularly for fever or excessive bleeding. Right now there is no need in taking them out in this weather to get to the hospital; just let them rest. If the weather allows, I will stop by in the morning to check on them. I have brought many a baby into this world, but Ethel's little girl sure is a cute little something with the same long lashes as her mother's. Well, there isn't anything left for me to do here, so I will be heading out.

"Helen, I'm sure you and your family need some privacy right now, so I will be happy to tell Gloria the bridge party is off tonight. I'm sure she can call the others to let them know not to come. You have more important matters on your hands right now, and with the new baby in the house, you'll need the peace and quiet. Gloria can make up some excuse for you. Besides, if this weather doesn't ease up by this evening, who would want to come out in it?"

Helen looked at him as if he had lost his mind. She glared and said, "Casey Walker, you do no such thing. Not only am *I* going back to work after all this nonsense, but my bridge party will go *on* as *I* planned. I can handle my affairs just fine. You just take care of yours and keep your mouth shut about what happened in my home today. No one is to know; is that perfectly clear? Not even your wife. I do not need or want gossip about this to spread around town, understood?"

There wasn't much that upset him in his many years of practice, but the coldness from Helen shook him to the bone. He shouldn't been surprised knowing the kind of woman she was. She could be aloof, even mean spirited, but he never thought this callous and cold hearted. Ethel might not have been her own flesh and blood, but she was her *sister's* child. Here she was treating her like some stray cat she found on her doorstep that just had its litter, not a living, breathing human being in need of compassion and comfort. He knew the girl wasn't married and the shame this would bring upon herself and the family. His heart felt for the baby, an innocent child born into this den of vipers.

13

He stared at Helen and replied, "Do as you wish, but keep Ethel and the baby warm. Please, check on her in about an hour."

He turned to Rayne and told her to make sure Ethel had plenty to drink. She might not be too hungry, but make sure she had something to eat before the night was over.

Dr. Walker proceeded to put on his coat and hat and left. As he gingerly walked to his car, he turned and looked back at the house. Rayne stood in the window and watched him get in his car and drive off. She closed the drapes and went back upstairs to care for Ethel and her new baby.

Helen glanced at her watch. There was still time for her to return to her office and prepare for the teacher's evaluation and review she was conducting the next day. She turned and walked to the back of the house, where Ginger and her father were watching his favorite game show, to let them know she was going back to the school.

The snow had stopped, and Helen could hear the sound of the trucks plowing and salting the streets.

"Ginger, call Haley and have her come quickly. All the roads and streets should be cleared by now, and the worst of the storm has passed." Helen knew Haley would come if she called regardless of how long or far the drive would be. She knew this was one of the things that irritated Haley's husband the most—the control she had over his wife.

As Helen started to walk out of the house, she stopped at the door. Looking up the stairs, she turned to Ginger and said, "If I had known she was pregnant, that *baby* would have never gotten here." With that she left, leaving Ginger standing in the foyer.

As she arrived back at work, Julia was surprised to see her. A startled Julia responded when she saw Helen walk through the office doors.

"Mrs. Watkins, I thought you were not returning today?"

As Helen walked to her office, Julia proceeded to follow her.

"Mrs. Forbes called wanting to know about the bridge party and if she should bring some wine. I told her you left early to take Ethel home." Stopping mid thought, Julia asked, "Oh, how is Ethel? What was …?"

Before she could ask the rest of her question, Helen cut her off by saying, "Everything is all right, and I need you to call Mrs. Forbes back. Tell her and anyone *else* that calls the party is still *on*, and yes she needs to bring wine, lots of it. A little snowstorm is not going to dampen my plans for the evening."

Helen then closed her door as Julia stood in the doorway with her mouth wide open.

She sat down at her desk and breathed a long sigh while placing her face into the palms of her head. When she uncovered her face, she looked at the photo on her desk of her husband, James Donald, and herself. They looked so happy in that picture. For a brief moment, she smiled, but it quickly faded, "Where is he now? Why does it seem he is away everytime there is a crisis? Why is it always *my* responsibility to take care of everyone? Who takes care of me?"

Helen looked at her phone and dialed home. Rayne answered after the second ring, "Watkins residence."

Helen spoke into the phone as soon as she heard Rayne's voice. "Rayne, make sure my house is clean from top to bottom, and clean up all that mess made by Ethel. Tonight is my card party, and I don't want any sign of the baby or her in sight. Understand?"

Helen immediately placed the telephone back on the receiver and paged for Julia to bring her the reports for the morning meeting.

Rayne hung up the phone and stared at it. She thought to herself, *What a witch. She didn't even ask about Ethel or the baby. She didn't even say good-bye.* That same uneasy feeling came over Rayne again. The same feeling she had when she left Ethel's room. She thought to herself, *There is definitely trouble brewing here tonight.*

CHAPTER THREE

THE PARTY

Rayne was finishing her work. She made certain everything was in place for Helen's party. As she was getting off her knees from waxing the floor, suddenly the door opened and Helen walked in, stopping mid-stride as she looked down at the floor in the hallway. "Hello, Rayne, I see you finished the floors. Is everything else ready?"

"Hello, Ms. Helen, I am just about finished," she said as she stood with her hands on her wide hips, smiling broadly.

"Good, because I don't want any of my club members to have any idea what happened *here* today."

Without a thank you or any other kind word, Helen looked at Rayne and walked away. She knew Rayne wanted a compliment for her efforts, but after the morning she experienced, she was not in the mood for compliments or small talk with the hired help. Rayne felt at least a few kind words was not too much ask for the extra work she did, especially after what they all had been through. Instead she replied, "Yes, Ms. Helen."

It was Helen's turn to host the monthly bridge party with her girlfriends of *high society*. These were not *just* any women friends. They were the esteemed wives of a doctor and lawyer, as well as the president of the state college and the local bank. These were the "tea-drinking" women who knew they were better than the common folk and did their best to remind you of it. When the occasion arose, they did their share of volunteer and community service, but always with an air of privilege. They knew who they were and made sure you knew you were not one of them.

The time was drawing closer for Helen's guests to arrive, however she was not sure what to do with Ethel and her baby. Haley had not arrived, and Helen was becoming extremely agitated. The last thing she wanted to do was explain a crying baby in her home. News had already gotten around town Ethel was sick and had to leave school abruptly. Several people called the house asking about her welfare. This was a small town and it did not take long for gossip to travel quickly. Helen knew having a wailing baby in the house would only add fuel to the fire. The last thing she wanted was her good name tainted with gossip and suspicion.

Ginger explained to Helen she could not reach Haley right away and when she did, Haley told her she would not make it before nightfall.

She asked Ginger what was the hurry. Ginger would only reply, "We'll tell you when you get here."

Haley knew something was wrong. She could tell by Ginger's voice she was not telling her everything. In the pit of her stomach, she felt that feeling like she had better sit down, and she did.

"Ginger, tell me *now*, is daddy getting worse? Is something wrong with Helen? Please, Ginger, let me know. You are making me a nervous wreck, and the last thing I want to do is get in my car and drive all the way up there worried and scared. So you need to just let me know right now so I can prepare myself before I get there. You and Helen do this to me all the time."

Ginger angrily replied, "Everything is *fine!* Just get here tonight before Helen's *damn* party!"

Before Haley could say another word, the phone line went dead. Ginger had hung up on her.

Helen could not take a chance that someone would hear the baby crying and start to ask questions. She decided since the third floor of the house was closed off for the winter, no one would have any idea that someone was up there. This would be the perfect place for her to store Ethel and the baby until her party was over and her sister Haley could come and get her.

She went to her father's room and told Ethel before her guests were to arrive she would be moving upstairs.

"You must be *kidding*, Aunt Helen. You want me and the baby to go *where?* There is no heat up there. Carly and I will freeze to death. Those rooms have been closed off for months. Look out the window—it has started to snow again, and you can feel the temperature dropping. *For God's sake, Aunt Helen, there is no heat on up there.*"

Helen looked at Ethel and the baby sleeping next to her. "And, you want *me* to do *what* about this? Do you honestly think I am going to just leave you here with your baby while I entertain my guest? I have been answering the damn telephone since I got home with people calling wanting to know what the hell was wrong with you, and why a perfectly healthy woman damn near had to be carried out of a building in the middle of a snowstorm. What do you think would happen when all of a sudden, during the middle of bridge, that brat of yours opens its mouth and starts wailing and bawling? Tell me, Ethel, just how should I explain *that?* Obviously, your inability to keep your *legs* shut has also affected your ability to think. Besides, you look strong enough and it will *only* be until the party ends. I'm sure Rayne will make sure you and *her* are comfortable."

As she turned and exited the room under her breath Helen said, "I really don't care if there is heat or not. No one told you to get pregnant and have *that* baby."

Helen Watkins was not about to let this get in the way of her party. She would die before she let them know what happened in her home today. After all, what was more important than her position and good name? What would the school board think, not to mention her friends, to know *her* niece, Ethel, had an illegitimate child? No way. No way in *hell!*

As Ethel lay in bed looking at her daughter sleeping, the fear and concern began to grow within her. Her baby was only a few hours old. How in the world would she be able to keep herself warm, let alone Carly, in a room with no heat?

Every year her aunts closed the two rooms on the third floor for the winter. No one used those rooms anymore, so there was no need to heat them during the winter months. These were the rooms Ginger and her brothers occupied when they were children. With tears in her eyes, Ethel wrapped her daughter as well as she could, hoping that she would be able to keep her warm and safe until the party was over. She heard what her aunt said before she left to go back to school. "If I had known she was pregnant, that *baby* would have never gotten here."

She began to cry, not just for herself, but mostly for Carly. What would the cold do to her? Would her body heat be enough to keep a newborn warm? All the *what if's* began to cloud her mind. Rayne came to the bedroom and helped Ethel up to the third floor. She thought she saw tears coming from Rayne eyes as she took her child from her. "Come on, Ethel, I tried to find the warmest room upstairs. I'm gonna put you and the baby on the other side of the house. It is a little warmer there because of the chimney stack. I can bring you up some hot milk and somethin' to eat in a while, al'right? Don't worry, you and that little one will be fine. I'm gonna heat up some bricks just like my mama used to do in the country when we were li'l. She would put 'em under the cover with us and they did just fine. Sometimes I just don't understand your aunt, but don't worry, I will check on you and Carly when I can. She won't be needin' me all the time with them women friends of hers. She's more concerned about what they might think and say than her *own*. You might not be her flesh and blood, but you the next to kin she's got. I can't imagine what your mama would say if she knew about this and the way she is treatin' you and yo' baby girl. You never took my advice and told Ms. Haley, did you, baby? If only you had, you might not have to be here like this. She and yo' daddy would've understood. You should've told her, Ethel. You should've told her."

Four hours seemed like four days while Ethel was trying to keep her baby warm. Once the last guest had said good night, she then allowed Ethel to return to the main part of the house. At that same time, Haley arrived. Ethel had dozed off but awoke when she heard the familiar voice. She thought perhaps Rayne had changed her mind and called Haley about her and the baby, especially after what Helen had done to her. Ethel knew she could tell her about Helen putting her away so her guests would not see or hear the baby. She knew Haley would save her.

As Rayne entered the room, you could see the heat from her breath fill the air as she spoke. The room was so cold and the hot bricks she brought up during the party did little to keep Ethel and the baby warm. It was only by the grace of God those two did not freeze to death. She spoke to a sleeping Ethel, gently nudging her shoulders to awaken her without disturbing the

SO I WAS TOLD

baby. When she peeled back the covers, the baby's color was fine. Her lips were pink, and her cheeks and hands were warm. She was wrapped tightly against Ethel.

"Ethel, wake up, baby. Your mama's here; Ms. Ginger called her. Come on now, wake up. Give me the baby so I can help you down the stairs. I know she will be glad to see you. I hope you tell her ev'rythin' Ms. Helen has done to you and yo' little one here. Lord, God sure was with you two; it's cold as can be up here. Did the bricks help any? I brung you up another blanket and put it around you. Y'all were sound asleep and I did'nt want to wake you. It wasn't so cold then, but now it's freezin'. I 'm glad her bridge party ended. I don't think you could've stayed up here another minute." Ethel wasn't fully awake, but she could understand some of what Rayne was asking her.

"Mama's here?"

"Yes, baby, she's downstairs with yo' aunts."

As Ethel handed the baby to Rayne and began to stand, she asked Rayne, "Rayne, did Granddaddy Dodson know Aunt Helen put me up here? Why didn't he stop her? It's so cold, and I was so scared. I could have sworn I heard rats or something up here. Every time I nursed the baby, I could hear something scratching, and coming closer. I tried to yell, but it was too cold. I just kicked my feet as hard as I could when I thought it was getting close. Why would she do something like this to me? I could have kept the baby quiet. All while we were up here, she never cried, not a sound. She is such a good baby. I could have kept her quiet in granddaddy's room."

"No, he didn't know. Ms. Helen told Ginger to give him a pill to make him go to sleep right away. She didn't want him to know what she was gonna do. He was snor'n when I passed the back room on my way to the kitchen. He was sound asleep in his chair while Ms. Ginger was watch'in TV. Shhh! Don't worry about that now. The both of you com'in downstairs, yo' mama's here, and that's all that matters. We can deal with Ms. Helen later. Let's get ya'll out of this cold. There's some food left over from the party. I'll fix you a plate and gets you two back in bed."

Before Ethel took her last step off the landing, she saw her stepmother with her sisters in the family room. With all the strength she had, she ran into the room with tears rolling down her cheeks. Her mother was here, here to take her away from all this madness, from Aunt Helen and her cruelty to her and her newborn baby.

BRENDA L. WATERS

"Mama, you're here!" As Ethel rushed to her arms, Ginger stepped in the way. Rayne and Helen were standing behind Ethel with the baby in Rayne's arms. Ginger, the oldest of the sisters, told Ethel that Haley had come for the baby. Ethel did not understand. "What do you mean 'come for the baby'?"

Helen replied, "What don't you understand? Haley has come for that baby and that's that. You cannot keep *it*. Besides, do you know who the baby's father is?"

Ginger spoke up and repeated what their father had said, "Just like daddy said,'Nothing like this has ever happened in this family, ' and you should have--" Helen turned and looked at Ginger with a scowl on her face. The look stopped Ginger in mid-sentence, then she lowered her head in dismay not speaking another word. Ethel looked at her mother, who never uttered a single word; she let Ginger and Helen do all the talking. Turning away, Ethel started to cry, and in a soft tone, barely above a whisper, said, "But she is so little and she needs me."

Helen said, "She needs you for what? What can you give her? I am sure she will be just fine with Haley. She will find a decent home for your bastard away from here, and this mess will be all over and forgotten. Do *you* hear me?"

Ethel cried out, begging and pleading for her baby. As Helen stood next to her sister, looking at the tears as they rolled down Ethel's face, Helen asked, "And who do you think would be here to take care of that baby?"

With the little hope Ethel had left, she replied," I could stay home and take care of her."

"Oh no! No, you have to go back to work tomorrow so that no one will ever know what happened here today."

Not wanting to get in the middle of a family matter but wanting to help Ethel, Rayne said, "I can watch the baby while Ethel is at work."

Helen looked at Rayne with cold hard eyes. "Rayne, I am not paying you to babysit. I am paying you to keep my house clean, to cook, and look after all I tell you to."

Ethel said, "Aunt Helen, I can't go to work tomorrow. I'm too weak. Dr. Walker said I lost some blood and need my rest."

"Oh, yes you can, and you *will* return to school tomorrow. Besides, it is a Friday, and you will have the weekend to rest. So give that baby to Haley so she can go home. She has a long drive, and it is late."

Rayne looked at the Dodson women and wondered, would Ethel's aunts have been so mean if they had children of their own? What happened in their lives to make them the kind of women they were, no compassion and so uncaring? She had worked for a lot of people in this town and elsewhere, but never one like Helen Dodson Watkins. There wasn't an ounce of sympathy in her. If it wasn't for the fact she paid well and Rayne needed the income, she would have quit that day. But if she did, then who would be there to see after Ethel. She knew it would not have been neither Helen nor Ginger.

Ethel cried all night as Rayne sat by her bed and tried to comfort her. All Ethel wanted was her baby girl. She eventually fell off to sleep, thinking about Carly and when she would see her again, if ever.

The next morning Helen and her sister Ginger were up very early. They went to Ethel and told her she could not speak a word about what happened to anyone. Just maybe it would all go away if they didn't talk about it. As days passed, Ethel tried to think of ways to get her daughter back. She told her aunts she would do anything they wanted—just please give her Carly back.

By this time Haley had hired a nanny and decided she was going to keep the baby instead of giving her to a stranger. She interviewed many people until she settled on Regina Hathaway. She came with strong references and appeared to be trustworthy. Haley knew of some of the families Regina worked for. Haley told everyone the baby was from a young girl who could not keep her. She was only fostering the baby until a proper home could be found. After all, it was her Christian duty to look after those who could not help themselves. So what if people wondered why she kept the baby, who would question her.? Not John Henry, who was always away and busy. Carly was good company for her. Haley knew she did not have to explain the baby to him, because Ethel would be too ashamed to tell her father what she had done. She also knew her sisters would never mention it to him, because she was the one taking the problem off their dirty hands. Everything was just perfect. She finally had the baby she and her husband would never have. To think, the baby's name was Carly. That was the name of Ethel's favorite doll.

It was two years after Carly's birth that her birth certificate was filed

BRENDA L. WATERS

with the county. Why did it take so long, and how were they able to name John Henry and Haley as Carly's parents? There were no adoption papers. Whether legal or not, no one was going to ask any questions.

Ethel eventually moved away to New Jersey, hoping to leave all that was in her past behind. She knew her stepmother would always look after her daughter—a daughter who would never know the truth of who she really was. Helen, for her own selfish reasons, persuaded Haley and John Henry to return Carly to her birth home, Helen's house. It was a decision Haley made with a heavy heart, but she knew never to cross Helen or there would be consequences to pay. The day she placed Carly in her sister's care was a day she would forever regret.

CHAPTER FOUR

TRUTH BE TOLD

As I entered the taxi, Mr. Theodore Miles greeted me.
"Hello, Carly, your auntie sure has you dressed up pretty today. What's the special occasion?"

I smiled as I took my usual seat in the back by the window and returned the greeting.

"Hello, Mr. Miles, and thank you. We had our pictures taken today for the school's yearbook."

Several other passengers were riding in the taxi waiting to be dropped off as I got in. Mr. Miles was paid to pick me up every Wednesday from my piano lesson at Miss Katherine's house. Aunt Helen had sewing class on Wednesdays.

We drove for several miles, stopping to drop each one of the passengers off at their destinations. I was the last on his route, since the taxi garage was not far from Aunt Helen's. Just as I was about to fall asleep, I realized we were almost to the house. Rubbing the sleep from my eyes, I glanced up and noticed Mr. Miles staring at me. I yawned and smiled.

"Carly, when was the last time your mother was in town?" he asked. I thought to myself that was an odd question, but I answered him anyway.

BRENDA L. WATERS

"She was here last weekend, Mr. Miles."

This was common knowledge, so I wondered why he was asking me something he already knew. I caught him looking at me rather strangely in his rearview mirror. It made me feel kind of funny inside, like maybe I said the wrong thing. After a few moments of silence, he spoke up.

"Ethel was here this weekend?"

"Ethel!" I replied. "Ethel is not my mother, she's my sister."

Now I knew for sure he was losing his mind. We rode in silence after that without a peep from him. I would try to catch a glimpse of his face in the mirror, but he would never look my way. It was almost as if he was scared to look at me.

As we drove down the street, I saw the house. He pulled to the curb, bringing the taxi to a stop to let me out. When he opened the door, he still had that peculiar look on his face, but it was more like he was scared or something. I looked up at him and thanked him for bringing me home.

"Thanks, Mr. Miles. I guess I'll see you next Wednesday or at church, huh?"

Mr. Miles looked at me as if he had just seen a ghost. It was a look I could not explain but would always remember. As I walked to the front door, I started to wonder what he was talking about. Why did he look at me that way? He didn't even say his usual, "See you later, alligator," waiting for me to respond, "After 'while, crocodile." I thought it was kind of silly to say every time, but he liked teasing me. It was our special bond. As I walked to the house I thought, "what was he talking about?" Why did he think Ethel was my mother?

I looked back toward the taxi as it pulled from the curb and saw Mr. Miles take off his hat and wipe his face with a handkerchief. It wasn't really that hot out, and he had the windows open, so why was he sweating like that?

When I entered the house, I could hear Regina in the kitchen talking to Rayne, but instead of going in to say hello, I went upstairs to my room. I needed to think about what just happened. I stood before the mirror and looked at myself, as if the reflection could give me the answers. Leaning into the mirror, I widened my eyes and stared into them. My Aunt Ginger said you can tell a lot about a person by just looking into their eyes. She would say, "the eyes are the windows to the soul," or something like that. I thought

26

maybe if I stared long enough I could see what *my* soul was saying. After a few minutes of this, all I got was dry, watery eyes, so I decided to take off my dress and shoes and do my homework. That's when Regina realized I was home and called for me.

"Carly, baby, is that you up there? I thought I heard you come in the door, but you didn't come in the kitchen. Come on down, Rayne stayed late today just to make your favorite dish."

I left my desk and went to the door. I yelled down, "Regina, I'm not hungry. I don't feel that well. I'll just stay up here and finish my homework. Tell Rayne thank you, I can have it for lunch or something, okay."

I could hear Regina's footsteps as she stepped on the landing of the staircase. It creaked underneath the weight of her feet. Aunt Helen said if she didn't lose some weight, one day she was going to fall straight through the floor board, and it was going to take an act of God to get her out.

She called up the stairs to me again.

"Baby, I had Rayne make it just the way you like it. You might feel better after you eat something. Come on down and eat just a little bit. The table is set, and we'll be waiting for you."

I sighed and reluctantly closed my book and made my way down the steps to the dining room. As I sat at the table to eat, Regina ran her hand across by face and neck.

"You don't feel hot, what's wrong?"

Shrugging her hand off my forehead, I told her, "I just don't feel well, Regina, that's all."

"Well, aren't you going to thank Rayne for making your favorites for dinner? You know she didn't have to do it. It's not like you weren't taught to say thank you. You need to tell me what is bothering you. Maybe I can help."

Looking up from my plate, I thanked Rayne for my dinner, but I did not respond to Regina's request. I said my "blessing" as I was taught and ate my dinner in silence. I could feel her and Rayne staring at me and then looking at each other. No one said another word until I asked to be excused to return to my room.

After dinner, I went to my room to lie down. All I could think about was what Mr. Miles asked me. If Haley was not my mother and Ethel was, then who was my father? Why had I been told Haley and John Henry were my parents? I just did not understand. Why did they all lie to me?

The last thing I remembered was looking at the ceiling and feeling the tears flow down the side of my cheeks into my neck, thinking and wondering why they had all lied to me!

When I awoke, my mouth was dry and my head hurt. I washed my face, drank some water, and decided to go get some answers.

As I proceeded to walk into the kitchen, I overheard Rayne and Regina talking. I could tell by Rayne's voice something was not right. I stopped and slid behind the kitchen door. Even though I could not hear everything because of the sound of the fan blowing in the kitchen, I did hear this.

"Regina, I think Carly has found out who her mother is!"

I could have sworn I heard Regina say to Rayne, "Why in the world would you think something like that?"

Regina had her back to Rayne and the kitchen door. She was peeling the sweet potatoes in the sink for the pies she was going to have Rayne make. She continued, "Well, Jenny from the grocer said Mr. Miles came in the store looking all strange, and mumblin' something about Ethel being Carly's mother. She said he was *talkin'* really crazy. Saying Ms. Helen was gonna to kill him. He didn't know she did not know, or somethin' like that. Then she said he bought a bottle in the *middle* of the afternoon, and b'fore he even got out the store he nearly drank half of it down. Now you know Mr. Miles drinks, but only on Friday nights, not durin' the week and *definitely* not durin' the middle of the day. Chil', you know Ginger would have his butt if she heard he was drinkin' while drivin' and pickin' up peoples. Old man Dodson himself would shoot him if he wrecked one of 'em cars."

Regina stopped peeling and turned to face Rayne as she stood at the kitchen table flouring and kneading the dough. She wiped her hand on her apron skirt and with the back of her hand wiped the hair that had fallen across her forehead. She wiped the sweat from her hairline that ran down the sides of her cheeks. It was hot in the kitchen, and both Rayne and Regina were sweating. You could see the wet spots down the middle of their dresses, between their breasts, and small patches of wetness underneath their arms. With the fan blowing hot air around, the two women didn't seem to mind the heat as they baked and talked. Rayne continued to flour and knead the dough for the pie crusts. I was going to sneak into the kitchen but jumped back behind the door before Regina could see me. I knew if she did, they would have stopped talking. Rayne looked up from what she was doing and placed both hands on her wide hips while shaking her head.

"Regina, ya'll knew that baby was gonna to find out someday. This is a small town. Didn't you think Carly would find out Ethel was her *mother* not her sister? I always told Ethel she needed to tell Carly 'cause people in this town knew, and one day she would find out the wrong way."

"Well, what did Ethel say when you told her that?" Regina asked.

Looking at Regina, she pursued her lips and said, "You know Ethel. She said okay, but I could tell she was mo' concerned with what Ms. Helen would do or say if she found out Carly was told the truth. I don't understand why she lets Ms. Helen rule her. I just wish she could stand up to her for *once*. You know what happen' when Ms. Helen made her go away for a while that other time."

As Rayne continued to talk, the phone rang. Regina answered. It was Reverend Simmons calling.

By the time they could finish their conversation, Aunt Helen came home. As she entered the house, I stepped from behind the door into the kitchen. They would have to wait until the next day to finish their talk.

Whether they knew I was there or not, I could not tell, but Rayne seemed surprised to see me.

"Carly? Whatcha doin' here? How long you been standin' there?"

Before she could finish asking me her question, Regina spoke up quickly, cutting her off.

"I just took one of the pies out of the oven. You want me to cut you a slice? Jerry brought over some of his homemade vanilla ice cream this morning. I could put some on top!"

"No thank you, Regina. I'm going to finish my homework. Maybe I'll have some tomorrow night."

I turned and walked out the kitchen, pausing at the door to look back. When I did I could see the look pass between Regina and Rayne—a look of fear.

Thinking back, I was ten years old when Mr. Miles gave me that strange look, and asked me about Ethel. It was then I overheard Regina and Rayne talking about Ethel. I often wondered why at times when I entered the room I would get a peculiar feeling my aunts were talking about me. Sometimes I would see Aunt Helen pacing and wringing her hands as she talked to

Aunt Ginger. When I would come in the room, she would look at me so strangely. Aunt Ginger would have this look of sadness on her face. When I asked what was wrong, they would tell me nothing. They were just having an "adult conversation." It was nothing for my delicate ears.

At times when I walked through town, I would notice people whispering as they looked at me. On occasion, if I was close enough I would over hear little things, bits and pieces of conversations about me, but nothing I could put together. Now those things I heard people talking about over the years were starting to come together. Things that didn't make sense at that time made great sense now. My whole life was one big fat *lie*. Haley and John Henry were *not* my parents.

If Ethel was my mother, then who was my father? I wondered if I had other sisters or brothers. I had so many questions, but where would I get the answers? My family had lied to me, so what made me think they would tell the truth now? Could they even remember the truth after lying for so many years?

I remember when I was a little girl and Haley, the only mother I knew, sent me to live with her sister Helen. They say children aren't supposed to remember things when they are young, but I remember what she told me. She said the schools where Aunt Helen lived were better, and she promised me I would be okay, because Regina was coming to stay with me. Haley promised Regina would take good care of me as if I was her own, and we could visit every weekend, holidays, and during the summer, if Aunt Helen allowed.

I was happy in my own little world with just Mama, Daddy, Regina, and me. In my world, that was all that mattered, and it was good for me. Now they wanted to shatter that happiness, and I did not understand why. For years whenever the end of the school year was approaching, all I would think and pray for was time away from Aunt Helen and to be with Mama and Daddy. Regina and I would spend as much of the summer with *my* family as Aunt Helen would allow.

The summer before my eighth grade year, my world fell apart while at Haley and John Henry's. Regina told me she would not be able to return with me to Aunt Helen's house when school started. I did not understand what had I done. Why did Regina have to leave? She told me she loved me

SO I WAS TOLD

and hated to leave me, but her family needed her, and she wanted to be there for them. I understood, at least I thought I did until I went back to Aunt Helen's house. She had changed! She started acting like she was possessed or something. She would yell at me and treat me like I was Cinderella. I am sure you know the story of how Cinderella's stepmother and her three wicked stepsisters treated her. Aunt Helen was all three in one. How long would I have to put up with her evilness? I had to find a way out. By this time, I made up in my mind I was going to write a letter to Ethel, my *real* mother. I was going to tell her I knew who she was and to let her know how mean Aunt Helen was treating me.

Dear Ethel,

I am writing you this letter to let you know I know you are not my sister but my mother Why was I lied to? I am not sure why this was done this way. I truly don't understand. I want to know the truth. I also want you to know that Aunt Helen is *crazy*. She is always yelling at me and said she is going to beat me. Sometimes I just want to run away. She won't let me look at TV during the week. Whenever I get a phone call from my friends, she acts like she has hung up, but I can hear her breathing while she is listening to my call. She won't let me even buy my own "personal things"—you know, my feminine things. She says she needs to do this so she can keep track of how many I am using and *if I am using them*. I *hate* it here! I feel like a prisoner or something. I just want to *kill* myself to get away from her, or better yet, *kill* her. Can you please talk to Mama and Daddy so I can come to live with them? Or, maybe I could come and stay with you. Anywhere except here with crazy Aunt Helen. *Please!*

From,
Carly (your daughter)

After writing the letter to Ethel, (*my mother*), I just knew my time at Aunt Helen's correctional home would soon be over. I was on my way to being paroled from the nut house. I would dream about seeing Ethel drive up to the house, entering the door, and slapping the hell out of Aunt Helen for treating her baby so cruelly and then snatching me out of there. Of

BRENDA L. WATERS

course, she would have me leave all my things because she would buy me new stuff, things that I wanted, not what she wanted me to wear.

A few weeks later, I got a letter from Ethel. Aunt Helen left it on my bed for me to find. I ripped it open so I could learn when I was leaving her house. This was what I had been waiting for. I was so nervous I could barely open the letter. I was so afraid I would tear it before I could get it out of the envelope and read about my parole. I bet this is the way men feel on death row waiting for the governor to pardon them from the gas chamber—all sweaty and anxious with their hands shaking.

Boy was I wrong! When I opened the letter, it was the same letter I had written Ethel. She sent it back to me with all my errors corrected in red ink. What was this, and what was I to do now? All I could think about was I was never getting out of this hellhole. I read the letter again. My mind started racing. I started thinking, *should I run away or would it be easier for me to kill myself, **or kill her?*** The last idea was the best idea. I knew after a judge heard how she treated me, and all the lies told to me, he would understand and take pity on me. He would understand why I did what I did. At this point, it really did not matter. I just wanted out one way or another, dead or alive.

I swear it seemed after Ethel resent my letter, Aunt Helen started treating me worse. Was it possible she knew what was in my letter to Ethel? She started coming up with reasons why I could not go visit Haley and John Henry, really stupid things like she needed to get her teeth cleaned or some other doctor's appointment and I needed to go with her. She would do anything to keep me in *Helen's Correctional Home*. John Henry would call, and I could hear them argue over me not being able to visit like I use to. Everyone knew Aunt Helen did not like him, and keeping me away from them would make him very angry. The feeling was mutual; I don't think he could stand the ground she walked on. No one ever talked about why they disliked each other so much. I guess it must have been something from their past. He only went along with all this to keep the peace with his wife Haley, even though I knew it hurt him when I would not visit. All this was confusing to me, yet no one would explain why I had to stay here. No one!

CHAPTER FIVE

EPIPHANY

It was the end of my junior year in high school when Aunt Helen got sick. She had a heart attack! Can you believe it? Of all the things she could get sick from, it was a freaking heart attack. *I didn't know she had a heart.*

Aunt Helen decided she was going to retire at the end of the school year. Her husband, Uncle J.D., on the other hand, was going to work one more year at the university where he was dean of student affairs. They often talked about retiring the same year when the time came. Retirement for her would mean plenty of free time to make everyone's life a living hell. Just the time spent with her over summer vacations was a nightmare. As usual, Uncle J.D. would be nowhere around to take away some of Aunt Helen's wrath. I felt as if I was a walking target with a bull's eye painted on my back.

For several summers, Aunt Helen's brother, Uncle Joseph, from Florida along with his wife, Thelma and daughter, Barbara Dale, would come to visit. While Barbara Dale, who was named after Aunt Helen's baby sister, could sleep late every day; I, on the other hand, had to get up and clean her house from top to bottom. This was my summer ritual every single day. Aunt Helen would give Rayne two weeks off, so guess who had to take her place? Aunt Helen's sister- in-law and niece were told not

BRENDA L. WATERS

to do anything. This was their vacation, and they were to rest and enjoy themselves. It was like I was an employee of Helen's Country Inn and my pay was room and board. During their stay, for some God-forsaken reason, Aunt Helen felt she had to let them know who was in control of my life and destiny.

She stayed on me from the crack of dawn until she was too exhausted or there was someone else she decided to torment that day. Aunt Helen had this sadistic ritual of making my days so unbearable until her unrelenting demands made me cry. What was even more pathetic, she would not allow me the dignity of crying in the privacy of my room! The most humiliating part was the looks on their faces; I knew they felt Aunt Helen was abusive, but they would do absolutely nothing to stop her. I remember once when Uncle Joseph tried to intervene she turned on him with such a vengeance—it stopped him cold. From that day forward he would leave the room when she would start with me. The really crazy part was when they were gone she would offer to buy me things to make up for her behavior. When other family members visited, she was still mean but did not torment me to tears. I could not wait until my summers would end to return to school. My reports on how I spent the summer were never the sweet, rosy, fun-filled days like most but always brought a look of surprise and raised eyebrows when I handed them in for review.

The summer of my senior year, Aunt Helen's family did not come to visit, and Rayne did not go on vacation. I thought it was going to be the best summer of my life. Instead, I would have taken ten times the abuse of *drill sergeant* Aunt Helen than what I was about to discover. I found out who my father was….it was *Porter Eugene Williams*. Cristan Coleman, my high school friend, was the one who told me. Her father, Samuel Coleman, was Porter's best friend. When she was at their family's grocery store, Cristan overheard Porter tell her father that he was my daddy. She did not exactly hear him say those words, but from what she overheard, she figured out who he meant.

Mrs. Coleman sent Cristan to the store with her father's lunch this particular day. She was dispatched by her mother to spy on her father and Bernice Campbell, who he *suddenly* hired to work in the store that summer. While Cristan's mother was preparing his lunch, she was steadily cursing and mumbling something under her breath, opening and slamming the kitchen cabinet. She couldn't make out exactly what her mother was saying, but she was sure it wasn't a compliment.

When Cristan arrived at the store, *ol' man* Johnson was outside in the blazing sun shining shoes while all the other men who hung around the store were inside, especially Charlie Simpson. She swore he looked as if he was going to pop out of his shirt it was so tight on his fat belly. She decided to enter through the back door to avoid being seen. They did not hear her come in the store, so they had no idea another pair of ears was there to overhear Porter Williams tell them who he thought I was.

"Sam, I know that's my daughter, I know it is. Everyone keeps on saying it's Helen's sister's baby. Look at her, man, she looks like she could be mine and Ethel's. I told you I *had* that back in the day. She was crazy about me. Wouldn't leave me alone for nothing, always finding some excuse for me to drive her here or there, but I knew what she really wanted. Didn't matter to her I was married, and it sure didn't matter to me. I had to cut it off, man, before it got out of hand. That girl was going to cost me my job, let alone my life. I don't put anything past Helen Watkins, not even murder. That's why I don't say *nothin'* to *her* or that child."

Porter's wife worked at the school where Helen was the principal until she could no longer take her mean ways. They had nine children at the time; the older children where hers from another marriage, but the last four were theirs. I went through all my years of school without ever speaking a word to the older Williams kids who had attended school with me. They did not seem to like me, for some reason. I never could figure out why, because I didn't do anything to any of them. They would only stare at me or whisper and laugh when I walked past them in the hall or when they were outside with their group of friends. Only the younger ones were nice to me, except when their older brother and sisters were around.

When Cristan entered the back of the store, she saw Bernice Campbell sitting at her father's desk. She was polishing her nails with a bottle of ruby red nail polish, reading a magazine, and sipping on a coca- cola. It sure did not look like she was doing any bookkeeping like she was allegedly hired to do. She had the radio blasting in the background. That was why Cristan could not really hear everything that was being said between Porter and all the men gathered around him. Cristan was sure she heard the men tell him he was lying as usual and making up stuff in his head. Her father told him

BRENDA L. WATERS

it was only in his dreams. Creeping slowly past her father's office, making a mental note to tell her mother what she saw Bernice doing, all the while trying to inch closer to the front of the store without being seen, she placed the lunch basket down on the store's back counter.

As she tip-toed to the main part of the store, Cristan heard her father say, "Man, you know you can tell some *tales*. You and I both know that gal didn't want nothing to do with you. I don't care who *your* daddy *is*. Everybody here know you married widow Stalling and took all them children of hers because of that money she got from his insurance and war pension. What a gal like her want to do with a man with all them children like you got. You must be crazy!"

"Sam, I'm telling you the truth. I know what she and I did, and I know that child is mines. She would be about the right age and all," Porter said.

The men started laughing and telling Porter he was delusional. There was no way Ethel Collins and her *fine* self would want him; she could have any man in Madison or anywhere else, for that matter. There wasn't any way a single woman like her with her money and class would want him. They kept on laughing at him and calling him a liar. Besides, everyone knew Carly was her sister, not her daughter.

As soon as she tried to move closer to hear more, the front door opened, and in walked ol' man Johnson. He was wiping the sweat off his forehead with a dirty rag; it looked like the one he probably was using to spit shine the shoes he was polishing. The men stopped laughing at Porter and exchanged greetings with him. Cristan continued to move towards the front of the store where the men where. No sooner did Cristan take a step than out walked Bernice, blowing air on her wet nails from her father's office. She stopped in her tracks when she saw Cristan tiptoeing towards the men in the front room.

"Cristan Coleman, just what do you think you are doing? Why are you here in the back of your daddy's store, and why are you tiptoeing around? Who are you spying on, young lady? I am sure your father would like to know just what you are doing."

Cristan thought to herself, "*And, I am going to tell my momma exactly what you are doing, Miss Thang. We'll see just how long **you** last this summer.*"

"Oh, Ms. Bernice, you startled me. I brought *my* daddy's lunch and was just about to go tell him it was here, but he was talking and all, and I didn't want to disturb him right away, you know."

SO I WAS TOLD

"Uh huh! It looks more like you were eavesdropping on grown men's conversatin' to me! You know, it ain't real ladylike to be spying on men's talkin'. You might get your delicate little ears burned if you ain't careful. Don't no man like no nosey woman. You need to remember that, young lady."

She then started talking loud enough for the men to stop talking and turn toward them as they walked into the main part of the store.

"Sam, Samuel, Cristan is here with your lunch. Wasn't that nice of Mrs. Coleman to have her bring it all the way down here to the store for you? It sure smells good. I hope she made enough for *us*."

Cristan told me while that painted hussy Bernice was calling out to her father, she was pushing her in the middle of her back toward the front of the store. The men were in front of the deli counter; some were sitting on the stools while the others, including Porter, were standing in front of them. Mr. Coleman was behind the counter slicing meat for the deli case. Mr. Simpson was trying his best to suck in his stomach, but the more he did, the redder his cheeks got. When she turned and walked out, Cristan swore she saw a button pop off his shirt.

Sam asked Cristan how long she had been there, but before she could answer, Bernice spoke up and told him she had just gotten there when she saw her in the back of the store. She turned and winked at her as she reached into the cooler and got another coca- cola before she walked back to his office, popping her gum and about to swish her way out of that tight red skirt she had on as all the men's eyes were planted squarely on her gyrating hips.

Cristan father spoke up and told her to go on and get back home. He was sure there was plenty she needed to do around the house to help her mother or some girlfriend of hers she needed to see to gossip about some boy or something. There was nothing but grown men in the store, and she did not need to be hanging around.

"Okay, Daddy, but can I get a push-up from the ice cream cooler before I go?"

"Yeah, but only one; them things cost money, you know. Go on get one and get home."

"Yes sir, thank you, Daddy. I'll tell Momma you and *Ms. Campbell* got your lunch."

BRENDA L. WATERS

As soon as Cristan walked to the front door where the ice cream cooler was, she heard all the men burst out laughing. Some were falling over themselves and hanging off each other shoulders as they were pointing and laughing at whatever Charlie Simpson was saying. The only ones not laughing when she looked back where her father, ol' man Johnson, and Porter. She noticed Mr. Johnson standing up, and all the men fell quiet when he started talking. She could see Mr. Williams' eyes grow darker and larger as he was listening to him, but she could not hear what Johnson was saying. Then all of a sudden, Porter was screaming, calling Mr. Johnson a liar. He had the old man by the shoulders with his fist raised, ready to strike him. The other men stepped back and did nothing. It was her father who jumped across the deli counter and was holding onto Porter as his face turned as red as Bernice Campbell's nail polish. He was cursing and spitting at ol' man Johnson as her father was trying to calm him down. She had never seen Mr. Williams that angry before, and it scared her. The other men stepped further back as her father swung Mr. Williams against the counter and told ol' man Johnson to leave the store. It scared her so much she stopped looking for the ice cream, and all the while her hand was in the cold freezer drawer. The cold air mixing with the heat was making a cloud around her hand and spiraling up her arm, but she did not notice the cold, only the speed and fury coming at her as Porter was storming out of the door. If she had not moved quickly enough, he would have knocked her into the cooler head first. He was mad, really mad. His face was distorted and red. He was cursing and calling ol' *man* Johnson a liar and an old fool. Porter looked back and told him he didn't know what the *hell* he was talking about and if he wasn't a decrepit feeble old man, he would have kicked his *ass* right then and there in the store.

"Don't you worry, old fool, I will ask my old man and find out the truth. You don't know a damn thing. It ain't nothing but a filthy lie, a filthy lie, I'm telling you, and you better keep your lying ass tongue in your old mouth or you'll lose it, brother. *You* better be glad Coleman held me back or I would have killed you, you *motherfucker*. You hear me, do you hear me?"

With that he took off down the street, running as fast as he could. Cristan said her father ran out the front door after him, but Porter was long gone by the time he made it to the door. He turned back and told Cristan to go home. She could not get home quick enough to tell her mother all that happened in the store and what she thought she heard. She could care less about Bernice Campbell. She had something better to spill.

She came running into the house, out of breath and sweating, while trying to remember everything that was said and done from the time she entered the back of the store till she left running out the front door home.

"Momma, Momma where are you? You are not going to believe what happened at the store with Porter Williams, Daddy, and them."

Mrs. Coleman was coming indoors with a basket load of laundry in her hands. When she got to the top of the stairs, she thrust the basket into Cristan's hands and told her to start folding the towels and sheets while she gets the other load for her to iron.

"Cristan, calm down, girl, before you have a fit. You are all out of breath and sweating. What did you do, run all the way home? Did you give your daddy his lunch? Was that bitc ... I mean, was Ms. Campbell there doing the books like your daddy hired her to do?"

"Yes, I mean *no*. That's not what I want to tell you. I think I heard Porter ..."

"Cristan, stop right there. I am not interested or concerned about what Porter Eugene Williams or any of your father's other low-life friends have to say or do. For all I care, they can go jump in a lake, and you should not be interested in them either. They are grown men, and whatever they were talking about, I am sure had nothing to do with you. I've told you about eavesdropping on grown folks' conversations. It is not nice to gossip and do those kinds of things. Besides, I sent you there to see if Ms Campbell was at work today, not to come home with some nonsense about your daddy and them men. Now, was she there, and what was she doing? What did she have on today? Oh, before I forget, Carly came by to visit, you just missed her. She probably is just down the street."

"Carly was here! Momma, I got to go, I got to tell Carly what I heard. I'll fold and iron all these clothes when I get back, I promise. I got to catch her before she gets home."

Cristan placed the basket down on the kitchen floor, and before her mother could protest or ask more about Bernice Campbell, she was gone out the front door and running down the street, yelling after me.

She did catch up to me that afternoon, and what she told me changed my life forever. When I found out that Porter Williams *could* be my father,

I decided to write Ethel another letter. I wanted to know if what Cristan Coleman told me was true. I told Cristan she was a big fat liar, and Porter Williams could never be my father. She must have misheard them or was making it up because she was jealous of me. I told her I would find the truth, and when I did, I would make her eat every dirty lie she told me. From that day forward, she and I never spoke a word. I hated Cristan Coleman, and I hated all the lies I had been told.

After several unanswered letters or every excuse she could conceive, Ethel eventually called; it was two days before I was to leave for college. Ethel said what I had been told was true, Porter was my father.

Ethel explained, "Carly, sometimes Aunt Helen would send me with Porter to run errands when she couldn't. One afternoon she was running late and needed me to pick up some things for her bridge party. When she told me Porter was taking me, I had a sick feeling in my stomach. I never felt comfortable around him, because of the way he looked at me, his eyes burning into me. I swear sometimes he would stare so hard I thought they changed colors. The way he did it made me so uncomfortable I would feel the hairs stand up on the back of my neck and arms.

"Rayne was home with me on this particular day, and I was going to tell her how I felt about Porter when his car pulled up to the curb. She looked out the window and saw him get out the car. He leaned back on the door, lit a cigarette, and took a long drag. I closed my eyes and in my mind kept repeating, *don't go out there, don't get in that car.* Just tell Rayne you have a headache and ask if Porter could go and get the items without you. Just don't get in that car with him, not today.

"When I opened my eyes, I saw Rayne looking at me, and I felt foolish, so I ignored my feelings and went about to do what Aunt Helen told me. I remember walking to the front door and slowly opening it. It was a little past noon, and the sun was high in the sky. It shone brightly in my eyes, making me squint. When they finally adjusted to the light, I saw him by the door, staring at me. He took one last drag on his cigarette and flicked it to the ground, grinding it with the heel of his shoe. Honey, he was standing at the door looking like a vulture, all slick and shiny, looking at me like a man on death row and I was his last meal. I tried not to make eye contact as I walked to the car. I just wanted to get in the car, do what I had to do, and get back home."

Ethel then took a deep breath and told me about another time before that day, where she came out of a store and there was Porter and his friends standing on the corner, talking and laughing hysterically. When he saw her, *he* stopped laughing. The closer she came toward him, the more intently he stared. When she reached the corner, all the other men stopped talking as well. It was Porter who spoke first. "Hello, Ethel, I didn't know you needed to come to the store today. I surely would have been happy to give you a *ride,*" he said. She remembered hearing fat Charlie Simpson snicker as the others tried their best not to laugh. She looked at Porter, half smiled, and kept on walking. As she passed, the men began to laugh even louder. It made her skin crawl, because she knew she was the butt of their joke.

She then continued to tell me what happened *that* day.

"As I reached the car, Porter opened the door. I stooped to enter, and he touched my arm to help me inside. 'Ethel, you look very nice today. What is the name of that perfume you are wearing?' he asked as he took a whiff of my hair. Carly, he was so close I could feel his hot breath on my neck.

"I told him, 'Porter, could you please step back? I can't get in the car. Besides, have you ever heard of being in someone's space? You are in mine, thank you. I would appreciate it if you recognize this fact'."

"He just leered at me and then he said, 'Oh! My apology, Ms. Ethel, I meant no harm. I just wanted to compliment you on your fragrance, that's all. It must be your favorite, because I smell it sometimes after you leave the car. As a matter of fact, I smelled it on one of your handkerchiefs you left on the backseat the other day. It's very nice, very nice indeed, but I won't mention it again if it makes you uncomfortable.'

"I didn't say a word. I just got in. Looking back at the house, I saw Rayne peering out the window as we drove off, and I thought I saw a strange look on her face, or maybe it was my mind playing tricks on me. All I wanted was for Porter to stop the car and turn around, because at that very moment I felt like jumping out and running inside the house to tell her how scared I was. But I told myself I was being foolish and needed to stop thinking this way. This man ain't crazy enough to try anything with me. I am Helen Watkins' niece and he would have to be out of his mind to touch me. Aunt Helen would have him skinned alive; don't be silly. So I sat back on the seat, closed my eyes, and counted the minutes I would return home and finally be away from him. After we picked up the linens from the cleaners and the last of the things needed

BRENDA L. WATERS

for the party, we were on our way back to the house when Porter told me he had to make one quick stop. I said to him, 'Mr. Williams, I need to get these things home for Aunt Helen. Couldn't you do that after you drop me off?'

"At first he didn't answer me. I thought maybe he didn't hear what I said, because he had the radio on and it was blaring, so I asked him again this time, trying to shout over the music, 'Mr. Williams, can you do whatever it is you have to do after you take me home?' That's when he looked in the rearview mirror and told me his stop was on the way back to the house and it wouldn't take long.

"We started driving down an unfamiliar street where there were abandoned buildings. As he pulled into an empty garage, he told me he needed to get some tools for a car he was working on. I looked out the window and noticed there was no one around or inside. It was dark and damp, and I could smell the oil and dirt in the air. The heat made the smell nauseating. He got out of the car and left me sitting in the backseat. I watched him open a box on a shelf and rumble around inside of it. Apparently he could not find what he wanted, because I saw him go into another room in the back, but this time when he came out, he had a towel in his hand, along with a box. Then he started to walk toward the car. The look on his face is one I will never forget. 'Don't look at him, look away,' I told myself. What should I do? Then I remembered the magazine I brought to read later, so I opened it, pretending to read. I needed to do something. That's when in the pit of my stomach I had that same uneasy, sick feeling. I could feel my hands starting to sweat; my heart beating faster. He leaned into the window, 'Ethel, it is hot inside that car. Wouldn't you like to get out? I still can't find what I need, so it might take a minute,' he told me.

"'Be calm and just pretend you are reading your magazine and whatever you do, do not look up and don't look at him,' I told myself. 'No thank you, Mr. Williams, I am just fine. How much longer do you think it would take? I have to get home,' I asked.

"Suddenly I heard what sounded like the car door open. When I looked up from the magazine, Porter had his hand on the door, and it *was* opening. I looked into his eyes and he looked possessed, evil. Before I could scream, he was pushing me down on the seat, his hands grabbing at me. As he pushed my dress up with one hand, his other was inside my panties, tugging and pulling at them, ripping the material. I started kicking and pushing back as hard as I could, but he was lying on top of me, and he was heavy. His breath smelled horrible from the cigarettes and what smelled like alcohol and peppermints. I remembered trying to feel on the floor with my free hand because I thought there was something on the floor like a pipe or crowbar when I got in the car. He must have known what I was trying to do, because he grabbed my hands and held them to my chest. Carly, I could feel him unbuckling his belt, unzipping his pants. He pushed my legs apart and... Oh God, he was inside of me. I heard myself screaming at him as I tried my best to push him off; screaming, 'Stop, please, please, you have to stop. Porter, please don't do this. This is madness. I am Helen Watkins' niece.' I knew I was saying this out loud, but I couldn't hear anything coming from my mouth. I knew I was saying it, but he wouldn't stop. He kept telling me I wanted it. I wanted him. He was sweating and grunting, grinding himself deeper inside of me, thrusting and shoving as he was talking to me.

"'Relax, girl! You feel *so* damn good. I knew you would. The way you walk with them big-ass hips, your butt swaying in them tight-ass dresses. I love to watch you walk."

"Carly I begged him, not to do this."

"Please Porter, please, think about what you are doing, think about what--" He took his hand and covered my mouth.

" Shh! Hush up girl, you know you want me. Just relax, baby, enjoy this."

"I was crying, begging him, but it did not matter. Porter just kept on talking and hurting me."

"I'm good baby, you know I am. You want this just like I do."

"I tried to bite his hand. He pulled it away from my mouth and for one moment as he raised up I thought he was going to stop, but instead he became angry."

"Stop fighting me bitch, stop moving or I am going to...'"

BRENDA L. WATERS

"I could hear the air from the slap before it hit me. I turned my head before it struck my face. He hit the side of my head, and for an instant I thought I had passed out. My brain kept telling me to scream, scream as loud as I could, but who would hear me? There was no one around. I kept thinking, *please just let me die right here, now, God, please*! I could hear him moaning and grunting, mumbling to himself like a mad man. Then all of a sudden he started pushing inside of me harder and faster. In my head I could hear me screaming over and over, "please, let me die. I can't take this," as the tears streamed down my face.

Then he gave one last thrust and fell limp on top of me. He didn't move for awhile. When I realized he was no longer moving, I thought the bastard was dead, that God heard my prayers and killed *him* after what he did to me. I tried to push him off of me but he was too heavy. If I did not move, somehow he was going to crush me with his dead weight. After what seemed forever with me pushing and shoving, he slowly got up. He looked me in the eyes, laughed and cursed as he said, 'I knew it would be like this. You are *one* special girl. Did it feel good to you, baby? Ha, ha, go on tell me, you know it did.' He was saying this as he was running his hands through his slicked back hair. Now I understood why he had the towel. He took it and wiped himself off and then tossed it on me.

"'Here, use this and wipe yourself up. It's a little messy down there.'

"My mind was blank. It felt like my soul was leaving my body. I saw his mouth moving, but I could not hear what he was saying. That's when I felt the towel as it landed on my thighs. It was wet, slimy. My head felt like it was in a wind tunnel, and all of a sudden I could hear him. 'Wipe yourself, it's a little messy down there.' He was pointing to where he had just been—where he had just *violated* me. I remember slowly rising up as he was backing out of the door. He was standing and stretching. He ran his hand through his hair again and was smiling at me. That bastard was smiling at me like he was my lover and this was something I wanted to do. I took the towel and turned myself away from him. As I rose up from the seat, I could feel *it*, *feel him*, seeping from my body, so I took the towel and placed it between my legs and the car seat. I could feel the searing pain, the humiliation all at once, thinking this did not happen to me. I kept repeating this over and over in my head as he walked away. That's when I noticed him go into the room where he got the tool box and towel and come out with two coca- colas in

SO I WAS TOLD

his hand and placed them on the hood of the car. He took out a flask from his back pocket and poured some liquor into his bottle then threw the flask onto the front car seat. He drank from his bottle, and reaching for the other one on the hood, he handed it to me.

"'Here, drink this, I know you are thirsty. It got pretty hot back there. Go on, drink it, I didn't put no booze in it.' When he reached into the car to hand me the bottle, I saw him look at the towel between my legs. It was bloody and messy, but I held onto it for dear life.

"'Give me that towel, Ethel. You cleaned up like I told you? I don't want any mess on them leather seats.'

"I smacked the drink out of his hand and moved as far away from him as I could. I was not going to let him touch me again. He became angry and reached into the car to grab it from between my legs as he said, 'Girl, let go of that damn towel. What's wrong with you? You're acting like a child, not some grown woman. Don't be acting like you never had no lovin' before! You ain't no virgin. I know all about you and that boyfriend you had back when you went away to college. Oh yeah, I overheard your peoples talking about it one day. They didn't see me, but I heard them clear as day. All the time you walking and acting like you don't know nothing about being with a man. Bet he wasn't as good as me. Ain't no man as good as Porter Williams. That's why *all* the women here want me, that's why *you* wanted me. I see how you look at me. I know when a woman wants something from a man. You were looking at me like that when you came down them stairs from you auntie's big ol' house. You like me being next to you and smelling you. That's why you put on all that perfume. You want me to smell you. Go on, fix yourself up so I can take you home. We can do this again some other time. Once a woman been with me, she always comes back. I knew you wanted some of this when you walked out that door.' He said this to me as he grabbed his crotch.

"That's when I felt the tears begin to fall, and I turned my head and tried not to cry. I was not going to cry in front of this animal. I finally gave him the towel and did my best to fix myself up. I took out my compact and fixed my makeup. I didn't know what else to do Carly. I ...," Ethel hesitated before she continued.

"We left the garage and drove away. I remembered looking out the window as we rode home and thinking to myself, *this was a dream. This did*

45

not happen to me. In a few minutes I was going to wake up and thank God this was just a horrible nightmare. But there was no use in me pretending or praying this did not happen. *He raped me.* What made matters worse, he kept talking as if nothing happened, and I kept thinking, *Why is he talking to me? I must be losing my mind. He's talking and laughing, singing to the music while I sit back here in agony and shame. Doesn't he realize what he just did to me? He is acting like I wanted this."*

Ethel then told me the rest of the story. When he brought her back to the house, Porter told her to keep her mouth shut. He knew just what to say and how to make it look like she came on to him. He threatened her and told her Aunt Helen would throw her out of the house. How he would lie and tell her they were secret lovers and what a whore she was and what a shame and disgrace she would be to her uppity family and the community. He would make it so she would have to leave her home and her job. He told her with his help she could make a fine living on the streets. She said Porter whispered this into her ear as he helped her with the bags out of the car. He then left without another word. She too was silent. She was afraid of Aunt Helen and what she would do if she ever found out what happened. Ethel said she was afraid she would *believe* him and not her.

Months went by, and her period did not come. She said she wasn't always regular and she wasn't going to worry. But as the days and months went by, she knew. In her heart, she knew. Who could she tell? She waited so long. Ethel said she only told Rayne when she was too far along for an abortion because she knew no one else would believe her. She swore Rayne to secrecy until she could figure out what to do. Maybe she could tell Aunt Helen she was going to take a leave of absence from teaching at the elementary school after the Christmas break, perhaps ask for an extended leave; go somewhere and have the baby. She would figure out how to explain the baby later after she had it.

Ethel said it helped that she never showed during her pregnancy. Her hips got a little wider and rounder and her breasts a little fuller, but she told everyone this was from all the eating she had done during the holidays. But as life would have it, it didn't work out that way. Rayne told me years later Aunt Helen asked her if Ethel ever said who my father was. Being very loyal to her friend, she kept what she knew to herself. Aunt Helen could not prove Porter Williams was my father, she only had her suspicions. She felt there was a striking resemblance to him, to the Williams family. Where my eyes were dark brown and his light, they were shaped the same. We even had the same nose and chin. There was only one other man she knew who had these features, and that was her husband, J. D. Aunt Helen swore there was a nasty rumor around town that J. D. was my father. Maybe she didn't trust her husband or thought by spreading this nasty rumor, this would make Ethel or Rayne tell her what she wanted to know, who my daddy was.

All I cared about it was my senior year and soon I would be leaving to go to college I did not care where, only how far away it would be from here. I was so ready to go ... so ready to get away from *her!*

It was at the end of May, and my graduation was in just a few days. I was planning to spend the summer with my mom and dad, Haley and John Henry, but Aunt Helen had other plans. It was fine, because I knew I was going away to college very soon. I had the grades for several scholarships to pay my tuition and everything. I just kept thinking about my great escape.

Aunt Helen gave me a great graduation party. I guess she was feeling generous, but believe you me, it made me nervous. I had not heard from some of the schools I applied to. Unlike some of my friends and other students, I did not waste time sending my applications and referrals, but my mind starting playing tricks on me ... maybe Aunt Helen never mailed them off, or better yet, bribed the post office to destroy them, anything she could do to keep me in arm's reach.

Ethel was supposed to come to my graduation, but she called the morning before to say she was not coming after all. I was hurt, but I never let anyone know. I had no idea what was going on with Ethel and her new husband Jeff. I found out later he had left Ethel and was filing for a divorce. This was typical of Ethel to put her needs above mine. It didn't matter. In a few weeks, I would be at someone's university, not in this house any longer.

CHAPTER SIX

BOY MEETS GIRL

Hooray! I was finally off to Amherst State University and paroled from The Helens Watkin's Institution for Lunatic Relatives. For the first time I was on my own, and campus life was starting out great. As I sat on the front steps of Grandford Hall with my best friends, Terri Scott and Cheryl Higgins, we joked and talked about all the crazy things *they* did in high school. Because we had the same middle names, we were known as the three Beths even though their lives were so different than mine. We made a pledge wherever one went to college, all would go. It was great having them to guide me through this new life I was experiencing. They were the sisters I did not have growing up; we shared everything. I did have other friends in school, but Terri, Cheryl, and I were inseparable. Our friendship began from the time we started kindergarten through high school, and now here we are together in college. We considered ourselves the female Musketeers; *one for all and all for one.* Terri claimed she liked the book, *The Three Musketeers*, because it was written by a black man. I thought she liked it because it was about men, period! If something had to do with the male species, she was interested in it. Cheryl always said this was why Terri was determined to

BRENDA L. WATERS

make the cheerleading squad in high school, so she could hang around the husky, sweaty football players.

Sitting on those steps reminiscing about their *activities*, started a wave of uncontrollable laughter. Terri started hiccupping we were laughing so hard. Cheryl was telling the story how they snuck out of their houses and went to a nightclub. Of all the places to choose, they picked the *Pink Pearl*. Being only sixteen at the time, they got fake IDs to be admitted. Cheryl found the extra set of keys and took her parents' car. It was easy to do because they always went to bed early, and their bedroom was on the other side of the house. All she had to do was stuff her bed to make it look like she was in it and climb out her bedroom window. It was a good thing she paid attention to her father when he worked on the car, because she knew how to turn the odometer back so he would never know it had been driven. She met Terri halfway down the street, who bribed her little brother to secrecy. With a set of clothes, they changed in the car as they drove to the club.

Fifteen minutes later they were there and having a ball. Terri began drinking, dancing, and flirting with every guy in the club. Although the other women were not too pleased with this, things were going just fine until Terri and Cheryl went into the ladies room. Several of the women came in, not knowing they were in the bathroom stalls. They could hear the women talking about them. As they listened, one of the ladies called them every name in the book. Well, that was all it took for Terri to come bursting out of the stall, earrings and shoes flying. Before she knew it, Terri was sitting on top of the woman with a hand full of her hair, banging her head into the bathroom floor; fist swinging, hair pulling, and clothes getting ripped off.

While Terri was sitting on top of the woman beating the crap out of her, the next thing she knew, she was lifted off and thrown over some man's shoulder. He carried her out of the bathroom and slammed her into a chair. When she looked up, whose eyes did she look into? Her cousin *Malcolm*. They both were surprised to see each other, but not as much as he was. Malcolm was bartending that evening; listening to the men discuss the woman in the tight green dress, talking about her fine body and what they would do to her if they could get her home. He thought there was something familiar when she walked in, but couldn't figure it out. So when he realized it was Terri's eyes he was staring into, he was not only shocked

50

but also pissed off, especially hearing all the things the guys had said, and him thinking the same things as well. The sheriff was called, and everyone got hauled off to jail, including Cheryl and Terri. They couldn't leave until their parents came to get them. You can't imagine how long they were on punishment. I swore Terri looked like she had grown a couple of inches before I saw her again.

Now I, on the other hand, could not go out the front door without my bodyguard. You would have thought I was the president's daughter with secret service. Every step I took, there was my bodyguard, AuntHelen. If she couldn't watch over me, she would enlist the services of Uncle J.D. or whoever else was around. She was determined to keep me under her finger until I left for college. There wasn't going to be anything to interfere with her plans for me. Aunt Helen monitored my phone calls, and if there was company over, we had to be close enough so she could hear our conversation. When Terri or Cheryl would visit, there were no closed doors. We couldn't even sit in my room and listen to records without the bedroom door being wide open. Talk about someone being paranoid, that was Aunt Helen. She allowed me to befriend Terri and Cheryl because they had come from *proper families* and were going to college like me.

The best part about being on my own was there was no one telling me when to go to bed or no one asking me, "Is that a boy you are talking to on the telephone?" Not only *could* I talk to boys, but I could do so all night if we wanted to. There was no one around to tell me who I could befriend—like the time Aunt Helen told me I couldn't go over to Shannon's house because her mother was never home and she had no house rules. They were not the type of people she felt were *acceptable*. Only she knew what was acceptable, because I apparently did not have a clue. All I knew was Shannon was nice, and her parents were together. Her dad was a deacon in their church, so they couldn't have been too bad. So whenever I asked her what she meant by not *acceptable*, she would never give me a definitive answer—just that crazy look of hers—and tell me *case closed*.

At the end of my first semester, I had a 3.75 grade point average, better than Terri and Cheryl, but then I didn't party as much as they did. They were more interested in pledging a sorority and dating upper class fraternity brothers than studying. One evening, after much persuasion, they convinced me to hang out with them at the campus sandwich shop. Much

BRENDA L. WATERS

to my surprise, the inevitable happened, I met a boy. When we entered the place, I noticed him from across the room, sitting with some guys as they were talking and laughing. With a quick glance, I noticed him looking in my direction. When we found a table, I immediately grabbed one of the menus, holding it to my face as I pointed him out to Cheryl. Out the corner of my eye, I could see him getting up from his table and walking in our direction. I didn't want him to think I was talking about him, so I turned my back and told Cheryl I thought he was cute. She asked me who I was talking about, because all she could see was this gorgeous *chocolate brown* man walking in our direction. There was no way I was talking about the same guy; he wasn't *yellow* enough for me, because she knew I was attracted to light skinned men. Reaching our table, he stopped and spoke, and when he did, out of his mouth came the most heavenly voice I ever heard.

"Hello, ladies, how are you doing this evening?" We all said "hi". He then turned and looked right into my eyes.

"I'm Richard Tate, but all my friends call me Rick, and you are?" For one precise moment, I forgot exactly who I was. It wasn't until Terri kicked me under the table I realized I had not spoken.

I looked at him and stuttered, "I'm Carly, Carly Collins."

He leaned into me, just inches from my face. "Hello Carly, Carly Collins. That is definitely a pretty name for a very a beautiful lady."

Now I can't possibly tell you how many times and ways have I heard that before, but there was something very different in the way he said it—not just some pick up line to impress me. Suddenly I could feel everyone's eyes on me. When I turned, sure enough, Terri and Cheryl were leaning into our conversation in stunned disbelief. As they realized Rick had stopped talking and was looking at them, they closed their mouths, looked at each other, giggled, and excused themselves from the table.

"We're going to get something to drink; be right back," they said. Before I could tell them not to leave me alone with him, they were gone; so much for friendship. I could feel panic rising within me. What am I supposed to say now? My warden, Aunt Helen, never left me alone with a boy, so what was I supposed to do? Perhaps he saw the fear in my eyes, because he just sat down and started talking. About what I don't know, and who cared? All I could see was his beautiful lips, so full and moist. Every now and then, he would smile at me and lick his bottom lip.

52

So we sat and talked for awhile, with him periodically asking if I was hungry or thirsty. I couldn't eat or drink in front of this man; my stomach was in knots and doing summersaults. When I could not take it anymore, I told him I needed to go to the ladies room and excused myself. What he did next nearly floored me. He got up from his seat and pulled my chair out. Oh, how I wished my Aunt Helen was here to see this. She thought boys today were animals and barbarians. They had no home training, she would say. Boy, would I love to see the look on her face if she saw him behaving like a true gentleman.

I went to the bathroom not to do anything, but just to look in the mirror and make sure it was me I was seeing. The hysterical giggles started as I thought, *Oh, my God, this man is talking to me.* He came over to be with me. There were a couple of girls in the bathroom having a cigarette. They stopped smoking and looked at me as if I had lost my mind. Clearing my throat, I fixed my lipstick and hair and walked out like I owned the place.

As I approached the table, I noticed Rick talking to one of the waitresses, the one with way too much makeup and about to spill out the top of her uniform. The closer I got, Rick stopped talking, with his eyes locked on me like radar. I guess he was looking so intently she had to turn her head to see exactly what he was starting at. When I got to the table again, he stood up and pulled out my chair. I could see the *hate* and *disbelief* in that girl's eyes. She asked him if there was anything else he needed.

"No thanks, I have all I need," he said without glancing her way.

Boy, oh boy, did girlfriend huff off! If looks could kill I would have been D.O.A. -dead on arrival. It was getting closer to midnight, and my friends were nowhere in sight, so Rick offered to walk me to my dorm. The doors were on automatic locks, and if you were not in by 12:30 AM, you were locked out until they unlocked at seven o'clock in the morning. After getting over the initial shock, we talked all the way to my dormitory. From that point on, we started seeing each other every day, between classes and in the evening until we left for Christmas break. I did not consider Rick my *boyfriend*, because I never had one before. I really liked him, but I wasn't sure if I was ready for that kind of commitment.

He called every day over Christmas break and warden, I mean Aunt Helen, asked me if that was my boyfriend. There was no way I was going to tell her my business. It would have been suicide. She would want to

BRENDA L. WATERS

meet him, probably have the secret service do a background check, get his blood type, you name it, she would have done it. Boys and I, as far as she was concerned, were never to mix. God forbid when she saw him what she would say. Even though he was the most delicious black man I had ever laid eyes on, I knew he would be a big problem. The problem, amongst many my Aunt Helen had, was that she was color struck. If you were not "light bright almost white," I knew not to bring you home. She was of the brown paper bag era, where you could not be darker than the brown bag to be accepted, and she lived up to it. Most of her friends were very fair or had a light-brown complexion. Thinking back, that might have been one of the reasons she was not so friendly with Mrs. Patterson, the mortician's wife. Even Uncle J.D., her husband, was fair with light eyes. If you didn't know better, you would have sworn he was white. He possibly could have *passed* if he wanted to. Sometimes I wasn't so sure about him myself.

When I returned to school, it was Rick who decided it was time we became more than friends; he wanted something serious. We were best friends, so why couldn't we take it to another level? I knew what he meant, but I was afraid to make more of the relationship. Being the great guy he was, he offered to wait until I was ready. Need I say the wait was not that long, because Rick was the first man I had sex with. No, I shouldn't say sex, but made love with, for it truly was love I felt for him. He assured me the feeling was mutual and he too was waiting for the right person. Rick told me his parents both were virgins when they got married. His mother wanted him to wait until he found the right woman to marry before he had sex, because she felt it was the most precious gift you could share with someone, but she understood what it meant to be a young man in this day and age. She told him to just be careful and true to the young lady.

It wasn't something we planned, but something that just happened. We missed each other more than we thought over our break, even though we talked every day. Outside of Terri, Cheryl, and a few other friends I made on campus, Rick and I spent all our time together. He was very serious about school and me. We would spend hours talking about our future and how life would be when we graduated and got married. He was going to be a lawyer and have one of the largest law firms in the country. Richard Harrison Tate was the captain of the debate team, and a very persuasive,

54

eloquent speaker. He was the reason they were the regional champions and on the way to the nationals.

I can't be sure when I got pregnant. We tried to be careful, but sometimes we would get so caught up and ... I would always be thankful when my period would come. Like Ethel, I wasn't very regular, so this particular morning when I woke up feeling nauseated and queasy, I thought it had to be what I had eaten the night before or hopefully my period. Being in college and living in the dorm did not lend to the greatest or healthiest food choices. My friends and I would stay up to all hours in the morning and eat whatever we could get our hands on. The morning I woke up sick, I called Rick and told him how badly I was feeling. First he wanted to know if I was all right, and then he said, "That's what you get for making me go to the store last night to get you that nasty, greasy burger." We both thought it was the thing that made me sick; perhaps I had food poisoning. This went on for several days, and then it stopped.

It wasn't until the next month when my period did not start I realized it was not something I had eaten, but maybe something *we* did; I was pregnant. My Aunt Helen's curse had found its way into my life. Even though she would test me every opportunity she had, we never talked about boys and sex. She thought if you didn't talk about sex, then it wouldn't happen. There were cute boys that I liked in high school, but I knew better than to show any interest or bring them home to my aunt's house. What was I going to do now?

Telling Haley was out of the question. She was the only mother I knew, and I did not want to disappoint her or John Henry. They were so proud of me because I did not fall into that pregnancy trap but graduated from high school and went to college. Not knowing what to do, I thought about the only person who might be able to help me, maybe someone who could understand my situation; I called Ethel, my biological mother. I asked her to send me money to have an abortion. I felt so trapped and confused. The only saving grace was Rick, who was always there for me. When I realized I was truly pregnant, it was difficult to tell him. This definitely could end both of our dreams. It was just like Ethel, who could never be there for me; she did not disappoint. Week after week she would tell me to wait. She would send the money. How long did she think I could wait? Time was not my friend.

Exams were finally over, and school was out. Everything was a blur. I don't know how I made it through my exams. My plans were to go home for the summer to Haley and John Henry. The first morning home from school, Haley fixed me a great breakfast. Ten minutes later, it all came up. The look on Haley's face when she found me in the bathroom told me she knew. When I spoke to Ethel, she tried to talk me into having the baby and giving it to her to raise as her child. Rick, on the other hand, wanted to get married. I just wanted all of this to go away. I did not want to get married, and I was not going to have a baby and let Ethel raise it as if it was her child. Its life was not going to be a lie. I had been to hell and back with my aunts, and no other child deserved that kind of life. That was not an option. I would not do to any child what had been done to me. I would rather die.

Perhaps a higher power or maybe the universe understood my dilemma, because I lost the baby. Maybe it was just as the doctor explained how the body knows when something is not right with it. When this happens, it will do everything it can to correct itself, given time. The doctor told me I could have other children. Haley assured me the pregnancy was going to be our secret, Ethel, her's and mine. No one was going to know, especially Aunt Helen

After several days of bed rest, Haley thought it would be good for me to spend time with Ethel in New Jersey before returning to school. Ethel and I talked about telling the family I knew she was my biological mother. She agreed, however when it came time, she could not go through with it. As usual, she changed her mind. Ethel asked me not to say anything. She thought it would make Aunt Helen have another heart attack and cost Haley too much pain. At that point, I agreed to leave everything alone and just go on with my life. I knew the truth,, and that was all that mattered. I also knew that Ethel had no *backbone* when it came to Aunt Helen and her stepmother Haley.

It was the end of summer and time for me to return to school; another semester getting closer to graduation. Rick wanted to be with me, but I couldn't face him at that time. When he found out I miscarried, he was so hurt. He begged me to let him come to New Jersey, but I told him to give me time; I would see him when summer ended and I was back at school. It was a risk, because I wasn't sure if Rick would be there. That was the summer I grew up. I put away all my childhood fantasies and dreams and decided to get on with my life and to make the most of the opportunities ahead of me. I was given a chance to start anew and on the right track. Ethel and Haley were a blessing to me during this time. They did everything to keep me away from Aunt Helen.

Returning to school in the fall, as I was walked to the sandwich shop in what had to be ninety degrees of the most unbearable heat, I decided to stop and pick up my mail from the campus post office. Amongst the packages was a letter from someone named C. Allen. *Who is C. Allen?* I thought. I turned the envelope over several times, wondering who this person was or thinking perhaps someone else's mail was placed in my box. Then it dawned on me maybe it was Cristan Coleman. She and I had not spoken since the time she told me who my father was; perhaps she and her high school sweetheart, Anthony Allen, had gotten married after all. Opening the letter, not knowing what to expect, and reading the first few lines, I realized it was not from her. Again I looked at the envelope to make sure I was not reading someone else's mail. Nope, it said Carly Collins, and it was from someone named C. Allen. Nothing could prepare me for what I read next, so much so I had to sit down on the concrete bench. The strangest thing was that I didn't feel the heat anymore. As a matter of fact, I could feel my body temperature drop, almost as if I had stepped into one of the coolers in the store where they kept the meats and soda. I could not believe what I was reading as my vision began to blur and tears fell from my eyes. I could feel them roll under my chin. As I continued to read, my tears were dropping and staining the letter. Oh God, not another secret. Here is something else I was not told. When will this nightmare end?

Dear Carly,

My name is Christian. We met some years ago at your mother's house. At the time we were introduced as cousins. I know we did not get off to a good start, but maybe we can start over. I was told a few days ago that you were not my cousin, but my sister. I know this may come as a surprise to you, because it was truly one to me as well. I knew that I was adopted, but I did not know I had a younger sister. There are so many unanswered questions. Hopefully we can meet again and get to know each other. I must say, I will never understand why our mother gave me away.

I am in school in Florida and hope to see you again. We have so much to talk about. Maybe we can keep in touch. I really would like to get to know you. It would be nice to have a little sister. Right now I'm sure you are wondering how I found you. Martha Thompson, our aunt, gave me your address. I hope it was okay, and I hope to hear from you soon. Love Always.

Your Brother,
Christian

I folded the letter and put it back into my pocket. I didn't know what to think or do. I'll wait for Ethel to get home from work, and then I will call her. I walked slowly back to my dorm room, recalling the letter in my mind. It was as if each word, each letter, was burned into my brain. People passed me by and spoke. Did I say *hello* or answer when they asked me a question? I don't know. I couldn't think. Everything felt heavy; my feet, my arms, even the door to the dorm. The stairs appeared longer. I made it to the top, now which way to my room?

When I entered my roommate, Emily Proctor, was at her desk reading. She looked up, and the smile on her face slowly faded as she looked at my face. Pushing back her chair from the desk, she quickly walked toward me with a look of concern. Her eyebrows were furrowed as she spoke. "What's wrong, Carly? Have you been crying?" Putting her arms around my shoulder, she gently guided me to my bed. She sat down next to me, still looking at me with concern and curiosity. I was in such a daze I couldn't remember if I answered her. I do remember handing her the letter and watching her read it. As she read, she would glance up at me. I could see the confusion in her face. It was then I started to cry again. I was glad she was there.

After she read the letter, she placed it on the bed, turned to me, and took my hands into hers and said, "Carly, it's all right to be sad and angry about this. I don't know what I would do if I got a letter like this from someone."

As she tried to comfort me, more tears came. Slowly I spoke, trying to think and measure my words carefully. How did I feel? "I am not angry I have a brother; that's a good thing. What I am upset about is finding out this way, once again from a stranger."

SO I WAS TOLD

Getting up from the bed, I became agitated. I walked over to the dorm window facing the lake. "Emily, I would be glad when all the lies and secrets end. Maybe then I will know and understand who I am. I was just so afraid that there will always be some surprise around the corner waiting for me, one lie after the other, more letters from strangers."

Turning from the window, I saw she was reading the letter again. I could tell she wanted to ask me some questions but felt too embarrassed. Emily did not seem to be the type to pry or be nosey; maybe this was why we got along so well. I told her before the night was over I was determined to know everything. I was going to find out the truth, if there was such a thing with my family.

Placing the letter back into the envelope, Emily sighed and said, "Carly, I'm not agreeing the way you were told was right, but now you know. It's a good thing too because sometimes people can meet and start dating and then find out that they are related. It happened back home to someone my parents knew, and it was devastating. Trust me, you are not the first and won't be the last to find out about family. Well, it's done now. You know, it took a lot of courage for him to write. I bet he is just as confused as you are. So, what are you going to do? I mean, look on the bright side, you now have a big brother!"

I took a deep breath, nodding my head as I turned, and walked out the door to try to call Ethel. I glanced at my watch and figured she would be home by now. Thank God no one was at the payphone at the end of the hall. I could at least talk privately. The phone rang three times before she answered.

"I have a collect call from Carly Collins. Will you accept the charge?"

I could tell by her voice she was happy to hear from me. I didn't make it a habit to call too often. "Hello Ethel."

Before I could tell her why I was calling, she started talking. "Hello, baby, I am so glad to hear from you. You know I had the worst day. I am so sick of my job and all those stupid people I work with. Hearing from you just made everything all the better. I should quit that job and do something else with my life. How are you feeling? How's school? Why haven't I heard from you sooner? Do you know how long it has been since we talked? I tried calling you the other night, but that phone stayed busy. Do any of those other girls do anything else but talk on the phone? I mean, what if it was an emergency

59

BRENDA L. WATERS

and I needed to reach you? You should really tell someone about this. I just gave up trying to call and figured if something was seriously wrong then the school would contact me. Are Terri and Cheryl back yet? You know I saw their parents at church Sunday before I left Madison and they were just a talking about their girls and what they had been doing all summer. Not a single word about their studies or their grades, just what new boy one of them was seeing and his uppity family or who was pledging what ..."

She was just going on and on. I realized if I did not speak up, I would never get a word in. I had to shout for her to hear what I was saying. *"Ethel, will you please be quiet? I have something important to ask you. Why do I have a brother that I know nothing about?"*

There was a long silence on the other end of the phone, so long I had to be sure she did not hang up.

"Hello! Hello! Ethel, are you still there? If you are, then tell me *please* is there anything *else* I need to know, because I don't think I can take any more surprises. I've had way too many in my short life, so can we be honest here for a moment?"

I could hear Ethel crying softly. She then blew her nose. Deep down I knew she would be hurt when I told her I knew about Christian. I guess she thought she had done everything she could for us not to find out about each other. Yet, these things always have a way of becoming known. She told me everything, all about him, his father, and what my aunts did to them.

Ethel called Haley weeping and wailing. Haley could barely make out what was wrong with her, but she did make out the part when Ethel told her I knew I had a brother named Christian.

"Ethel, how in the world did she find out? Who told the child?"

She replied, "It was Martha, mother. Martha told Christian the truth. She told him all about it and where he could find Carly. Mother, Carly hates me now. How could Martha do that? What possessed her to ruin my life? What have I done to her? It was just pure evil, evil. She always was jealous of me and what I had. So now I guess she has gotten even. It didn't matter to her who she hurt with all this, as long as she comes out looking good. As if she did the righteous thing. Why did she do something like this? After all this time, why now?"

SO I WAS TOLD

"Ethel, I want you to calm down. Let me handle this. I will call you back. Go and get yourself together. I will call you later and check on you."

No sooner did Haley hang up the phone from Ethel than she immediately called her sister Helen. "Hello! Helen, this is Haley. Helen, you are not going to believe what Martha did."

Helen replied in her usual sarcastic voice when she was annoyed, "No! Surprise me, Haley!"

Haley could barely get the words out quick enough.

"Martha called Carol Beth, and they got together and told Christian that Carly was his sister."

What Haley said stopped Helen from reading her magazine. She asked Haley to repeat what she said. "I beg your pardon, what did you just say?"

Haley, shouting as if she was deaf, repeated, "You heard me, Helen. Martha told Christian about Carly."

Helen threw down her magazine and rose from her chair. The anger began to surge within her. "That bitch! That church-going, bible-waving bitch. She knew the agreement. They were not to *ever* know. That woman has hated me since she was a child and I know this gave her immense pleasure in finally having something to crow about. How did Carly sound when Ethel spoke to her? What did the boy do, call or visit her?"

"No, Martha told him she was in college and gave him the address. He wrote to her. I don't have to tell you what this means. I am sure Carly will be calling one of us soon."

Helen told Haley not to worry, she would handle it and Martha also.

I knew my aunt and grandmother were expecting me to contact them right away, but I decided at the end of the week I would skip classes on Friday and go home. I wanted some answers. Emily let me borrow her car; she really was a great roommate. All that week, she stayed in the room with me to make sure I was okay. I think she was a little concerned I would do something to myself. I had to admit I was in a bad mood and feeling distress.

As I pulled into the driveway, all those old feelings flooded me. I thought about this house and what a prison it was. I thought back on the horrible way my aunt treated me. What was she going to say now? I mean, now that the secrets were coming out. My family didn't tell me much, and other

61

things were not to be mentioned, ever. Getting out of the car and walking up the driveway I noticed my grandmother's car in the garage; Haley was there. They must not have heard the car pull up. As I entered the house, I saw them in the great room drinking tea and having what appeared to be a deep conversation. Apparently, Haley was not at all happy about what Aunt Helen was saying. I overheard Aunt Helen asking why Martha brought this up after all these years. What would possess Carol Beth to tell Martha about him? As Aunt Helen was speaking, Haley rose from her chair and walked to the mantle. She took a silver-framed picture from it and looked intently at the photograph of Ethel. In her thoughts, she appeared to be remembering something.

It was so long ago, and Ethel was just beginning her life in college. All the plans they made for her would soon be gone. Gone because she thought she was in love. What did this great love get her? Nothing but a swollen belly and what could have been the end of everyone's hopes and dreams. If it wasn't for Ginger and Helen, her life would have been ruined. So, what if the boy wanted to marry her? He was not their type of people. She was going to finish college and forget all about that boy. Ginger got the adoption papers signed by Judge Harrison, and with the papers, in hand Helen and she made Ethel sign her son away, a son in which their family would never speak of. Ethel was barely a woman when she got pregnant with Christian. She had just started college, and everyone was excited about her future, especially Haley. She was determined not to let anyone or anything ruin it no matter the cost.

She placed the silver framed photo back on the mantle. Helen had stopped talking, and she too appeared to be in deep thought. She rose from her seat, and taking her tea cup walked to the window, pulling back the curtain, she sipped her tea. She remembered that time also. Ethel was doing something they always wanted her to do, going away to college, getting a good education, meeting new people, and maybe even finding a husband. She was still so young and inexperienced, and Haley was worried about her being away from the family, but she taught her well, raised her to be a lady at all times. So when she came home for winter break, Helen was the first to notice something was wrong. She wasn't herself. There was something different about her. She wasn't that young woman who went away. She wasn't the same girl who couldn't leave home without that raggedy doll

Haley gave her when she first married Ethel's father, the one she named Carly.

It wasn't long before Helen knew why she was so different. As Ethel was getting out of the tub, it was Helen who saw her stomach. She didn't know Ethel was in the bathroom when she opened the door. Their eyes met; then Helen's drifted down her body. Ethel didn't know what to do or say. She reached for the towel to try to cover herself, but Helen grabbed it first and threw it on the floor.

Stepping toward her, she told her, "Get out the tub, Ethel."

Ethel slowly stepped out of the tub and stood in front of her aunt. Helen backed out the door and called for Haley to come up the stairs immediately. She wanted her to come to the bathroom. As Haley walked up the stairs, Helen could hear her fussing, demanding why she had to stop what she was doing and come right away. From Helen's tone, she thought the house was falling down.

"What do you want, Helen? Daddy needs me in the cellar to help him store the canned fruits, and you are yelling at me like the house is on fire."

As she entered the bathroom, Helen told her to look at her daughter.

"Look at her, Haley, take a good look. This is what she has been doing while away at school wasting *my* good money. Just take a real good look. What are we going to do now, *sister?*"

Haley looked confused. Then she looked at her stomach and at her breast. She placed her hand to her mouth and stepped forward, asking in disbelief, "Ethel, baby, are you pregnant? How did this happen?"

Angrily, Helen spun around and looking at her sister. "Haley, why would you ask that foolish question? You damn well know how it happened. I just want to know who it happened with, and how far along she is. Go tell Ginger to call Dr. Walker and have him come over here. Ethel, you go to your room and put on some clothes. Don't you come out that room until I say so, understand me?"

After the doctor arrived and examined Ethel, he told Helen her condition. "Well, I'd say the girl is about twenty some weeks along. She says she feels fine, no morning sickness or light headiness. I want to start her on some vitamins right away. Now don't let her gain too much weight right off, ladies. She's got a small frame, and I don't want the weight to keep

BRENDA L. WATERS

her down. Either you or her mother needs to bring her to my office in two weeks to get another check up; I will know more then."

As he was about to put on his hat and coat to leave the house, Helen spoke up and asked, "Forget about the weight and nonsense. Is she too far along for an abortion? If not, I want to send her to Texas tonight. I can arrange everything with J.D.'s family there. They will now what to do, and no one will have to know about this mess."

"No, Helen, an abortion won't help you now. She is too far along for that, and you know what can happen to her if she gets into the wrong hands. No respectful doctor here or there would do such a thing to a healthy girl like her and that baby."

"I don't give a damn if the doctor is respected or not," said Helen. "I want this matter taken care of, *pronto*."

"Stop all that foolish talk. The girl is young and strong and can have a healthy baby come fall, so put that thought out of your head. We talked, and she told me she loved the young man and they planned on getting married. Apparently he's there on a scholarship and will graduate in another year. According to Ethel, he is being recruited by some companies up north for a position when he finishes."

"Helen, maybe Dr. Walker is right. Perhaps we should talk to Ethel and see what she wants," Haley responded. "I mean, if he thinks she is too far along for--- He did say they were in love and he wants to marry her."

"Your sister is right, Helen. Let the girl have her life. Yes, she made a mistake, but she is not the first and won't be the last in this situation. At least the boy wants to do the right thing. With her mother's and your help, her life won't be over, so help them both out, until they can get on their feet."

"Oh, and just how should I go about helping them, *doctor?* Let me guess before you waste your time telling me. You think I should take my hard-earned money and support them, don't you? Well since you are being so generous with your opinion and such, why don't you cough up the first installment! No, no, sir that is out of the question."

"Please, Helen, you and I both know you have enough money in this house to support them while they get started. She is a good girl, so help her, help them. Ethel can always return to college after she has the child.

Go ahead and let them get married and finish school; at least the baby will have a name."

With that said he left the house, leaving both she and Haley to decide Ethel's fate.

When Ethel was eight months pregnant, Helen decided to send her to New York to live with her father's cousin, Carol Beth. That's where she had her son, naming him Christian, after his paternal grandfather. When the baby was four months old, Ethel returned to her Aunt Helen's home, leaving her son behind. Carol Beth persuaded her to leave the child by telling her he was too young to travel and promising to drive him south when she got settled.

While Ethel was back at Helen's house helping Rayne hang up clothes one day, Ginger called her into the house and said she needed to talk to her. It was she and Helen who advised her it would be best for everyone if Carol Beth adopted Christian. This would give her a chance to go back to college. Besides, she just begun, and this would help to get her back on the right track. Ethel cried and pleaded with her aunts not to take him from her. She loved her son and the man who gave him to her. She told them Carol Beth was not his mother, she was, and she had no plans to give up her child. Not now, not ever!

Their decision was final, not open for discussion. As far as they were concerned, she had no choice. If they were going to pay for her to finish her education and take care of her, she was going to do what they wanted. Besides, they had made all the arrangements for Carol Beth to keep him. Ethel fell to the floor devastated. How could they just give her baby away? What about Robert Bradley? They were going to get married after he graduated. Helen told Ethel if she did not sign the papers she would make sure Robert lost his scholarship and get put out of school. If she cared about him and that bastard she had, she would sign them. Ginger, the one aunt who Ethel thought would be on her side, told her to get up from the floor and to stop all that crying. It was in her best interest. That summer day, Ethel did as she was told. Her baby boy was gone. She would not be there to watch him grow up and become a man. She was forbidden to see him or have any contact—that is, if she wanted Helen to pay for her tuition to finish college, and to make sure nothing happened to Robert Bradley. She did love him, but she feared Aunt Helen more.

Several years later, another baby was born, another baby taken away, *so I was told.*

CHAPTER SEVEN

ON MY OWN

There were times when it was hard for me to believe I finally made it. For someone whose every move was monitored and designed, this was heaven. When I left for college, I swore I would make every effort not to return to Aunt Helen's home. Now, it is my graduation day from Amherst State University. With that little glitch in my first year, the following years were trouble free. Richard and I didn't last another semester. The only good thing from that heartache was a decision to never allow my life to be sidetracked from my goals. I wasn't ready to be anyone's wife or mother. Besides, what role models did I have in my life to prepare me for that? All I was told were lies and was kept from the family secrets. With a degree in business administration and a minor in photography, it was my year. Where could and would I go? I wanted some place new, where I knew no one and they didn't know me. This would be my chance to take control of my life. So, I stepped out in faith—faith developed and molded in the church I attended back home. I knew God was with me and would guide my steps. I also believed he had forgiven my mistakes.

After I graduated college, I moved to Dallas, Texas. This was pretty far from home, and I knew I wouldn't have to worry about surprise visits from anyone. As a graduation present, Haley had given me money to help with my living expenses until I found employment. One afternoon as I was scanning the paper for possible job opportunities, the phone rang. I answered. I almost didn't recognize the voice on the other end. Back then there was no caller ID, because if it had been, God only knows I probably would not have answered.

It was Aunt Helen and she was actually in a good mood. *This must be the beginning of her senile dementia*, I thought. She, along with Haley, had decided to buy me a car so I had a way to make my interviews, a brand new Honda Prelude. I waited for her restriction to go along with the offer, because I knew there had to be a catch. I waited and waited. I guess it was so long she asked, "Are you still there, Carly?"

My aunt was the greatest "Indian Giver" I had ever known. She had no problem with giving you something and taking it back.

I responded with much enthusiasm. "Aunt Helen, are you serious? I don't know what to say. Thank you. That would be a great help to me. With a car I could come home to visit you and Mother, especially during the holidays." I knew this is what she wanted to hear, so I poured it on. I wanted her to think she still had control over my life and could dictate my comings and goings. Did she really think I would actually return to her on my own accord? No way, no way in hell. The only thing I had to do was figure out a way to make sure she did not go back on her offer.

After I got off the telephone, I asked God to forgive me for that little lie. I promised I would do something good for someone to make up for it. For that fib I guess he decided to make me sweat. I could not find a job. I had it all planned out when I graduated. I would walk into one of those grand skyscrapers in downtown Dallas in my blue suit, black pumps and resume in hand; expounding on my exceptional school record, and be hired on the spot. The business world would be overwhelmed by my intelligence and academic brilliance and beg me to join their company. I would be offered whatever I wanted since I excelled in the majority of my classes with straight A's and had great references from my professors. I must have been out of my mind to think I was going to get a job after one interview. Or better yet, maybe all those years living with Aunt Helen really did make me crazy. It took me five months to find a job—five long, disappointing months of pure hell, doors slamming, and people looking at me as if I had grown a third eye.

On many occasions when asked about my work experience I would be so tempted to say, "No, I do not have any business experience. I just got out of college, fool!"

How am I going to get any experience if you don't hire me? I would say this over and over in my mind with a frozen smile on my face, taking rejection like it was my middle name. I was told my grades were excellent, but some work history would be helpful. Work history! How could I have a work history and maintain a grade point average of almost 4.0? Obviously these idiots did not understand what it took to maintain high grades, because if they did they would know my head was in a book instead of someone's toilet after too much partying at some stupid frat party. Where was *affirmative action* when I needed it! I guess for some, five months might not have been a long time to find work right out of college, but for me it was an eternity. If I did not find a job soon, this would be the perfect opportunity for Aunt Helen to rise up and take control.

As I was lying in bed sleeping, I dreamt, the phone rang and Aunt Helen asking, "Carly, this is your aunt. Have you found a job yet?"

Of course my response would have to be, "No, Aunt Helen, I haven't."

Then she would ask with the pitch in her voice rising, "Well, are you looking?"

With all due patience, I would try to control my breathing and reply, "Yes, Aunt Helen, I am looking and going on interviews every day."

Then she would want to know how I was dressed, and how my hair was styled.

"Aunt Helen, I wore the Jones of New York navy blue suit with the Aigner black pumps and I carried the briefcase you and Uncle J. D. gave me for graduation. Yes, my hair gets done every week."

Now she would make it my fault.

"Well, Carly, what seems to be the problem? Do they know you graduated number one in your class? Are you showing them your references from college, Reverend Simpson, and others?"

This is when a strong shot of liquor would have done me good. The sad part is, I don't drink, but talking to Aunt Helen surely could start me down that path. So I told her what I had been hearing over and over.

"Aunt Helen, I was told I need business experience, and yes they have reviewed my references."

BRENDA L. WATERS

"Are they crazy? How on earth do they expect you to get work experience if they don't hire you! Any damn fool knows how difficult it must have been to maintain your grade point average and try work at the same time. You are a bright and intelligent girl, Carly, but you are not Einstein."

After a long sigh and pause she continued, "Well dear, it appears to be a difficult task for you to secure work. Perhaps it would be best to drive home in that new car I bought you. It's just good money being wasted paying your apartment rent. I am sure I can find something for you to do here at the school, or perhaps J. D. could find you work at the college."

Ahhhhh! I immediately awaken in a sweat with my mouth feeling like I ingested an entire bag of cotton. Talk about an incentive. I was more determined to find something, anything that would keep me from going back home. God must have heard me or got a glimpse of that nightmare, because I finally found a job. I was hired as an office manager for one of the largest department stores in Dallas. I made it my plan to work as hard as I could and make something of this experience. I would arrive early and leave late. My desk would be cleared every night and all calls returned before I left. Obviously, this worked in my favor. An employee, Alicia Simone who worked in window displays for the store got fired. Rumor has it, she was pregnant with Brock Martin's baby, the store owner's son, who was very married with a whole lot of children. What is it with men who have a lot of kids? Why do they keep making more, either with their wives or someone else? This was the eighties, and birth control had improved considerably.

I applied for her position and got the job. This was my opportunity to shine. A neighbor, who lived next door in my apartment complex, majored in art design and gave me the greatest ideas for displaying merchandise. In exchange I had to babysit her pet poodle whenever she went out of town. *I hated that dog, and he hated me.* Not only did I have to dog sit, but I also had to make sure his meals were cooked. This animal did not eat regular dog food. Instead, I was left with a menu to prepare for this creature. Once I tried to feed him dog food out of a can, and that animal nearly bit my hand off.

Finally my hard work and creativity paid off. With all my new ideas for the store, I was promoted to Senior Department Manager of Merchandise and Cosmetics. This was fantastic! Our store was huge and noted for its

SO I WAS TOLD

quality of products. We carried the most expensive creams and powders in the city. Can you imagine a cream for you face that cost $200 per ounce? I would watch the women who came into the department and purchased not one jar but the whole line. Some of them needed to bathe in it to combat the lines and wrinkles they had. They would expound to the clerk how well it worked and what an improvement they had in their skin: how everyone noticed and complimented them. It was hilarious to watch the women's faces behind the counter as they smiled and nodded in agreement. Remember, the customer is always right.

To say I was excited with my new position would be an understatement. This became the job of my dreams. Here I am, Miss Carly Collins, in charge of a department in the most glamorous and expensive store in Dallas. So what if I was not working in my major. I loved the clothes and the perfumes, everything about fashion.

When I worked in window displays, the results were phenomenal. Because of the dynamic promotions, the cosmetic department tripled its revenue for the first time in six years. It definitely got me noticed.

When I was promoted, I made sure every client who came into cosmetics left with their makeup perfected, new ideas for their hair, and samples of the most expensive perfumes. I became a fashion icon. I made sure to stay up on the latest styles and trends no matter how outrageous they were. This was the eighties, and everything was outrageous. Of course, this fresh approach wasn't always received with fanfare from the other departments. I stepped up the game, and they had to get on board. The vice president of the store was very pleased with my work and what I had done for my department as well as the company.

My first year as a senior manager, I put on a spring and winter fashion show in order to display the new colors for the year in makeup and apparel. This was something no other manager had ever done, especially a woman of color. You see, green does not discriminate, especially when you are making it for someone else.

At the end of the Christmas holiday, the company president paid us a visit. He loved the idea of the fashion show and wanted it continued every year as the focal point of the season. This was something no other department store in Dallas offered their customers. I finally felt secure in my job.

BRENDA L. WATERS

Although I knew what to do in my business life to make things happen, I just couldn't bring that magic to my personal life. I would date occasionally, usually with someone my friends hooked me up with. Needless to say, their taste was truly different than mine. They would tell me I needed to dummy down. There were a lot of good, hard-working men out there, and I should not be so picky. Picky is one thing, but desperate is another, and to seriously consider some of these men, I had to be desperate. After Richard, I didn't want to commit to someone. I needed to work on me.

It was the end of the season, and a new shipment came in from Paris. I was working late one evening when I heard this voice asking if I was all right. He said the mall was closed and wanted to know how much longer I would be working. I sure hoped looks went along with that voice, it was heavenly. I looked up from my desk as he walked in. I blinked twice and cleared my throat. I always made sure I looked nice in public, but since I thought no one was around, fixing my hair and makeup was not necessary. It was late, for God's sake, and I was tired. Hair and makeup was last on my agenda. A hot bath, some food, and a good book were my plans for the evening.

Into my office walked this big, beautiful man. He introduced himself with his hand outstretched, "Hello, I'm Mitchell Thompson, head of security for the mall. One of my officers called in sick, and I took his shift. Sometimes it helps to get back on the floor to see how things are going. Sitting in my office and taking meetings all day can become tedious."

He stood there for what seemed a very long time with his hand out to me before I realized I was staring at this man and didn't utter a word. Perhaps he thought I was a deaf mute, because he said his name again.

You know how you hear that tiny voice in your head telling you to say something and make it sound intelligent? Whatever you do, do not say something stupid. Well I heard that tiny voice but could not reply. With his hand still extended, all I could see was the most perfect set of white teeth and dimples.

After coming around, because I must have slipped into a mild coma, I replied, "Oh, please forgive me, I'm Carly Collins. I'm over this department and needed to get some inventory registered. I understand your dilemma. I was short staffed also. You know the grunt work never ends for us po' black folks."

Oh God, I thought to myself, *did I really say grunt work and po' black folks, and why did I say it in that old southern singsong way like I was just off the plantation?*

There goes that tiny voice again. "Didn't I tell you to say something intelligent, something clever? This man is going to think you are an imposter and arrest your butt." Someone over a major department with my educational background would not have said something stupid like that. Obviously he did not hear me or did not care, because he was still standing there smiling and I was not lying face down on my desk being handcuffed.

I took his hands as he said, "Yes, I know who you are. It came across my desk about your position. Quite something for a black woman here in Dallas, let alone this store. You must be proud of yourself. I can see why they gave you the position. Not too many department heads stay late to work like you do. I should know, I am aware of everything that goes on in the mall."

Actually, I was very visible in my department. It wasn't beneath me to work the counters when needed. Sometimes it was funny when there was a problem and some of our affluent white customers would ask for the manager and I would show up. This happened once with a customer, and boy did she get angry. She thought we were playing a trick on her, and she demanded to speak to the store manager. The store's regional vice president was in that day and came to my little old department to check on things. When he introduced himself and asked what the problem was, she was more concerned in telling him the trick she thought was played on her when she asked for the manager than what her complaint was. I just stood there with a smile on my face as he explained who I was and how I was his top employee, what a fantastic job I did and how the store and the department needed me. He assured her, whatever her complaint or problem, she was in the right hands with me. After that, the store made sure employee and customer alike knew who Carly Collins was.

Mitchell, I guessed, did not see or care if I looked a mess, because he asked me out for a late dinner. I was taught when an opportunity comes, you grab it. Well that one date led to many more. As time passed and the more we got to know each other, there was still something about him that just did not feel right. We got along great and did some wonderful things together. We even had a few similar experiences, except he grew up in a stable family knowing who his parents were. Like me Mitchell was an only child. He wished he had brothers and sisters when he was growing up. His mother had a difficult time with his birth and was advised not to have another. His parents thought about adopting but never did.

He was a fantastic lover, and I enjoyed his company. Even though he wanted marriage, I think what changed it for me was his lack of interest in church or God. That lack of faith I finally realized is what bothered me the most. I didn't have a church home myself, but I did make an effort to visit other places of worship on Sunday. No matter how disappointed I was with the sermon or the constant begging for money, I sometimes felt spiritual renewal at the end of the service. Have you ever been to church and left with absolutely no idea what the sermon was about? Yet you definitely understood when that gold plate came around for the third time asking for your tithes or "love offering" for the minister. Will someone please explain to me what is a love offering anyway? Back home, the ministers worked and supported their families with a job. On Sundays they put on their collars and continued their work for the Lord.

Mitchell would attend sometimes when I asked, but he never seemed to care one way or the other. We talked about religion, and he seemed to know who God was, but it wasn't important. His family did not attend church on a regular basis, only when one of his aunts or grandmother visited. There goes that gut feeling I am talking about. I mean, I'm not a saint, but I do know church is important no matter where you go. I made it a point to try to find a house of worship; where people knew me and if something happened at least there would be someone to say a kind word over me. Mitchell, on the other hand, had no interest in church. One Sunday after service we went to lunch. While we were waiting for our food, I thought this was an opportune time to bring up religion.

"Mitchell, what did you think of the service and the sermon this morning?" I asked.

In between bites of the bread, he shrugged his shoulders and said, "It was okay."

"Just okay!" I responded. "What about the pastor and the message in his sermon?" This was one of the few places I attended where I truly enjoyed the minister and the parishioners. That little plate only passed once, and there was never any mention of a *love offering* for the minister. It was my understanding he did take a salary from the congregation, but a modest one. His home and transportation were paid for by the board, but he did not drive nor live in anything elaborate.

I noticed Mitchell did not appear all that enthused with the choir or the service. He responded when it was called for, but other than that, he just sat there with this dazed look in his eyes. I truly believed he was asleep with his eyes open. The only time I saw a reaction was when one of the women screamed out and appeared to faint. Even then he really did not seem to care. He watched as the church mothers in white came and fanned the woman as she lay in the pew. So, I guess I should not have been surprised by his response.

When I pushed him further about it and everything that was said, he put the bread stick down, took my hands into his, looked me in the eye, and said, "Carly, he is only a man, just like me, with all the same weakness and faults. That minister is not God, and he is not telling me any more than I can read on my own. I don't need some man to tell me how I should feel or what I need to know about God. Don't be surprised if you read or hear something about what he has done or some outrageous scandal that happens in the church. Everyone will get all bent out about it and poof, that's the end of it. Some folks will go and some will stay. Those who left will just latch on to some new minister telling them the same nonsense. Organized religion is not for me. I like to think of myself as a *spiritual* person. I don't need to go to church all the time and hear the same stuff over and over."

I need to clarify I `am not one of those women who go around spouting off about wanting a good Christian man, blah, blah, blah, but it would have been nice to have one in my life who at least had a little more feeling for God than this. What is with this, "I am a spiritual person?" So, if you believe in God and going to church, it makes you less spiritual than someone who believes in some higher power, but just doesn't want to call it God or go visit him? It's like people who are *non-denominational*. Please explain to me what that is all about. I mean, even Jesus knew he was a Jew, so why don't they know who they are? Why not be Baptist, Methodist, Catholic, or something? I soon realized this was going to be a problem for us somewhere down the line. Don't ask why or how, it was just my gut talking again. I think he kind of sensed something also. We eventually started drifting apart. Sometimes it was good, and sometimes it was only two people taking up some space.

BRENDA L. WATERS

About nine months after I got my second promotion, I received a call with devastating news. My Grandfather, John Henry. died. I had to return home, for I knew Haley would need my help with the arrangements. My boss was really great and told me to take my time returning, not to rush, my job would still be there. Sometimes good work pays off when you need it. It wasn't one of those situations where people have emergencies and crisis in their life then find out they have no job to return to. I told my staff this every meeting we had. "Work hard and don't abuse your sick time. People will notice when you do a good job."

I went home. Only a few people knew I was his granddaughter, because secrets and lies were the backbone of my family. My grandfather had three children, and I was the product of his youngest and most-loved child.

When the limo pulled up to the front of the church, many people were still outside waiting for the family to arrive. I could only wonder how many were inside if this many people were out. I knew grandfather was a well-liked and respected man, and he and Haley did a lot for the community. I just didn't expect this. As the limo finally stopped and we started to exit the car, Uncle Nate was the first one to exit, I was the last.

Do I look that good, because I saw many mouths open and drop when I walked in. It appeared as if time stood still, and no one ever changed. They all had the same hairstyles, dressed in the same style of clothing and makeup they wore when I lived there. Even woman my age looked as old as Haley. They resembled a small town where possibly inbreeding was the recreational activity. You know, where no one new from the outside moved in and people ended up marrying their cousins or having children with their wives' sister, etc. Very eerie! It was sort of like the twilight zone or a time warp where nothing changed.

I made it a point to sit on the front row opposite of the immediate family. No, I didn't sit with Haley, Uncle Nate, and the rest of the family, and no one seemed to notice or care. I could feel all eyes on me and hear murmuring from the back of the church. I wanted to stand up, turn around, and yell and scream at these inbred morons to stop looking at me. So instead I sat there and read the obituary. *Oh my God!* I cannot be reading this right. I must be going into shock or something. My vision started to blur, and my throat choked up. I could feel the tears well up in my eyes. In black and

SO I WAS TOLD

white it read, "He leaves behind a *granddaughter*, Carly Elizabeth Collins." I asked the lady with the God-awful hat sitting next to me if I could read her obituary, because I must be delusional and could not possibly be reading this correctly. There it was again; my mind was not playing tricks on me. No wonder people were staring at me and whispering. The lie had finally been told. The secret was out for all to read and talk about, but why hadn't anyone told me? There were other names listed as well, not just my Aunt Martha, Uncle Nate, and Ethel, but many more. There had been rumors John Henry had outside children and grandchildren from them. I guess Haley didn't know, or if she did, at the time she didn't care. It was her name on the will and insurance policies, not theirs. As I read the names, I wondered who these people were and what they had been told. Who did they all belong to, and who were they told were their parents? It takes a funeral for stuff to finally come out. What's done in the dark will be shown in the light, or something like that. It never fails. Go to a funeral or wedding and you are bound to find a new cousin or sister you never knew you had.

Remember Mitchell? He and I attended his best friend's wedding. It was a beautiful ceremony. After a few drinks at the reception, the father of the groom decided to acknowledge the best man of the groom as his other son, not his cousin, as all were led to believe. Of course, this led to a lot of cussing and fighting, which added another dimension to the festivities.

One thing I knew for sure, Haley was not going to address this, not now and not here. None of that was going to take place at her husband's homegoing. But there it was, all in black and white. Maybe she too was tired of all the secrets and lies, tired of all those things never spoken.

A few days after we laid grandfather to rest—it felt so odd to call him that—I decided to finally let it go. Now, I had it all here in black and white. This obituary was definitely going in my Bible for safe keeping. When it was time to write mine, I wanted it to be correct. My life had been one fat lie, and I was not going to leave this earth without the truth being known. I didn't care if it would never be spoken. It was going to be in black and white, just like grandfather's.

I decided to take my manager's offer to stay awhile and help Haley tie up any loose ends. I loved Haley, she was my mother in all the ways she could be. All the bad and horrible memories I had were not because of her, but Aunt Helen and Aunt Ginger. Haley was just as much a victim. I was twelve years old when my Aunt Ginger died, and no one would tell me how much she played a part in the drama of my life or Ethel's. What did it matter now anyway? She was dead and took whatever I needed to know with her.

The week before I was to return to Dallas, a woman who sat with Haley said she was celebrating her twenty-fifth wedding anniversary. She wanted me to come to the celebration with Haley. Although I needed to get back to work, I felt it was important for me to be with my step-grandmother. Her husband was dead, and another woman was celebrating twenty-five years with hers. She told me I would probably get to meet family I had never seen before because she was family also. The woman was my biological grandmother's younger sister, Donna. She told me this would be a good chance to connect with family I knew nothing about. I guess she felt this would give me closure. Apparently, Haley told her about my life.

When the anniversary party came, there were so many people there that I didn't know where to start trying to figure out who was family or who was guest. These were faces and names I had never seen or heard. I was introduced to people who I found out were Ethel's cousins and second cousins down the line. There were aunts and uncles who knew about me, but I surely didn't know them. They too had heard the stories and whispers when they were growing up. I wondered what they had been told, truth or lies! My Grandmother Marie was one of ten children. Although most were dead, they had large families, with lots of children, grandchildren, and some even with great-grandchildren. My grandmother's older sisters got married as young as sixteen and had several children. This was why this celebration was so large. No one gave theirs away to be raised by others as their own. Everyone here knew who they belonged to good or bad.

CHAPTER EIGHT

SORRY I...

Things were finally returning to normal for Haley after grandfather's death. I knew I made the right decision staying with her a while longer. It was a great idea for both of us to attend Donna's anniversary party. Initially, Haley had feelings of apprehension about attending since it was so soon after loosing her husband, but in the end it turned out for the better. We had a great time listening to the stories from friends and family about relatives. I never got bored hearing things we knew were being repeated over and over each time with a tad more exaggeration. Driving home, we laughed and wondered how the story would change the next time it was told and for whose benefit. It was good to hear her laugh and chuckle again.

After making sure she got to bed and all the doors and windows were closed and secured, I turned in for the evening. I had no idea of my exhaustion until I was chin-deep in a hot tub full of lavender soapy bubbles. With eyes closed, images and thoughts of my life flashed before me. If I had a hundred diaries, it probably wouldn't be enough to fill them all with the story of my life. The warmth and smell of the lavender lulled me into a peacefulness I had not felt in some time. Before long, I could feel myself slowly falling to sleep.

BRENDA L. WATERS

Suddenly, I awoke realizing I was freezing. My once-warm cocoon now was frigid, and so was I. It was only by the grace of God I did not drown. Perhaps the sleep or maybe the realization of my possible demise gave me clarity. While drying off, I knew what I had to do no matter what the consequences. The decision was made. I was going back to Dallas, but not to the same job, not even to Mitchell. He called daily and sent the loveliest flowers to the service. He even wanted to come and be with me, but I told him not to. This was my time to share with grandmother. I had to admit there were some nights it was good to hear his voice; stirring up feelings I did not want to have being so far away from him. I realized loving him was not the same as being *in* love with him. Our lives were going in two different directions, and no matter how we would try, I knew it would end badly if I did not break it off now. The last thing I wanted to do was burn a bridge with someone who cared for me, because you never know the day you may have to cross it again. This was one of those life lessons I learned from watching my Aunt Helen who did not only light the match, but also poured the gasoline; leaving piles of smoldering ash from the bridges she burned.

What was I going to say and how could I say it without sounding like I was out of my mind? A woman had to be crazy to want to end a relationship with a man like Mitchell. *Lord, you have to help me with this one,* I thought to myself. *I don't want to be harsh or too evasive, yet I have to find a way to explain myself to him.*

What logical or rational excuse could I have for breaking this man's heart? We didn't have a fight or disagreement over small issues, such as leaving the top off the toothpaste or wet towels in the middle of the bathroom floor. He did not snore or take all the covers; he had good hygiene and did not expel gas in the middle of the night. Mitchell was sweet and considerate, thoughtful to a fault. He laughed at my silly jokes and in the evening would give my aching feet the best rub down anyone could ask for. He had all the qualities someone would consider a good catch. The problem was my heart was no longer in it. Good catch or not, I just wasn't fishing anymore!

I decided the next time he called I was going to tell him how I felt. It would be better to do it while I was here. Being a coward, I knew I could not face him and say the things I needed to say. Besides, if he held me and started kissing me, I could never summon the courage to end it.

Perhaps his ears were burning, because no sooner did I step out the bathroom grandmother told me there was a call for me. Trying to whisper as she handed me the telephone, she said, "It sounds like a good-looking man." She winked and left me standing in the hall. I laughed at her ability to know what the man on the other end of the phone looked like. Mitchell must have heard her attempt at whispering, because he told me, "Tell her she was right about how good-looking I am." Instead of being the jubilant, happy woman hearing from her man, I said the one thing men hate to hear. *"Mitchell, we need to talk."*

Taking a deep breath as I sat down by the telephone with the towel wrapped tightly around me, I began the hardest conversation to have with the man who loved me. "I want you to listen to what I have to say, and I hope you will understand how I feel right now. It's just so much has happened to me in my life, and coming home to bury grandfather just brought everything to a head. I'm coming back to Dallas to make a fresh start, beginning with *not* returning to the store. I don't quite know what I want, but I know I need more than what I have right now, and that includes our relationship. I know we care for each other, but it's just not going anywhere for me *anymore.*"

I could hear him breathing on the other end, but that was all I heard from Mitchell. He made not a peep or sound while I was talking, just slow, steady breathing.

"Do you understand what I am feeling or trying to say?" I asked. "I know you might think I am not making a lot of sense right now." At first I thought he hung up on me, because there was no immediate response.

"Carly! What are you saying?", he asked. " You're right, you are not making any sense right now. Where is this coming from? I know the death of your grandfather was difficult, and now everyone knows you were his granddaughter. I mean, look, why don't you come back to Dallas before you make any more decisions or changes and let's talk face to face. I know at times things were tense or maybe I took you for granted, but you know I am crazy about you and want us to work on this. Don't do something irrational or spontaneous right now. You need some stability, and I want to be there for you. I know you are not happy about the way I feel about this *God thing* or going to church, but is that enough of a reason to want to end our relationship? Really Carly, has it come down to this? Is this a rational reason to walk out on me? Let's not end a good thing over something as *silly* as this. Don't end it like this, not now, not this way."

BRENDA L. WATERS

My heart was breaking with the sound of desperation in his voice. I knew this was something he never expected to hear. I didn't want to be that kind of person who uses people or stays in situations just because they are too afraid to leave, or remain with someone until they hope something better will come along. I believed in myself and knew this was the right thing to do. I felt it in my gut and spirit. I had to make him understand.

" Mitchell I know this is not what you may want, but having a belief in God is important in my life and I want it to be that way for the man I am with. This is who I am and what I believe in. I am afraid if I compromise on this, what else will I give in to?"

Mitchell hesitated and then asked, "Carly, is there someone else? Did something happen to make you feel this way?"

I could hear the strain in his voice. I knew the things I said were out of left field, and I could not rationally explain myself to him. Yes, I blindsided him, but only with the best intentions for both of us.

He continued, "I just don't understand where all this is coming from. Baby, I'm confused. Look, why don't you get some sleep and think on this some more? We can talk again in a few days. If you feel the same way, then I won't try to convince you otherwise. Just remember, I love you and want to be with you. Goodnight, Carly!"

Before I could reply, Mitchell hung up. I looked at the phone for what felt like forever. Finally after hearing the irritating recording, "If you'd like to place a call, blah, blah, blah ..." I hung up. It did not matter if we spoke tomorrow or tomorrow's tomorrow, my mind was made up. It was over with work *and* with Mitchell.

After a few more days with Haley, I kissed her good-bye and drove back to Dallas. If she had her wish, I would have stayed with her and found work there. I was no longer that little girl from Mississippi. My life and needs had changed, and I had outgrown my small town. When I got back to Dallas, I looked up some old contacts for leads on jobs. Deborah Hill, my college buddy, came to mind. She heard about my grandfather's death. One thing I could say about Deborah, that girl got around—in a nice way, I mean. She was the most popular girl on campus, and everyone wanted her in their sorority or functions. Her party-planning skills and coordinating major functions on campus were legendary. Deborah came from a long line of women who catered some of the most elaborate soirees in Dallas and in other cities. It all started with her great-grandmother from Louisiana and was kept within her family for generations. If anyone knew about who was doing the hiring and firing in Dallas, it was Deborah Hill.

"Hey, girl, it's Carly. I just got back from Mississippi and thought I would check in. Yeah, everything is fine. Grandmother was good, and I promised to call her more often than I had in the past. Some family and a few of her friends promised they would check on her and let me know how she is getting along."

Deborah said something I had long forgotten about my Aunt Helen that made us both laugh out loud.

I replied, "Yes girl, the one and only she- devil, I believe, is developing a soul. I don't know, maybe the heart attack has softened her some, and she's thinking it's time to make amends before she standing before you know who."

Deborah laughed and said, "No offense Carly, but from the things you told me and what I remember about your aunt, well someone needs to give St. Peter the heads up. There is going to be a *long* line of frustrated people waiting behind her to get in. He is going to be standing at those pearly gates for quite awhile talking to *that* one. Can you imagine that scroll with her life's history written on it hanging from the clouds with all the nonsense and havoc she has caused in her lifetime? Poor Peter better have on some good reading glasses and comfortable sandals. I don't care if he is in heaven, his eyes are going to go bad and his feet will hurt after standing there reading about her life." Both she and I laughed until our stomachs were aching from all the things Aunt Helen said and did. After we stopped reminiscing, I told her why I was calling. "Deborah, seriously, I need to talk to you about my life. I am ready for a change, a new beginning." Before I could continue she asked.

"Is the rumor true that you and Mitchell broke up?" She didn't want to say anything at first, but she thought she saw him out the other night at a local jazz club *with* someone else. They looked very *friendly*. She apologized for being the one to tell me this, but she thought I should know. I told her I was okay with it and was glad he moved on and hoped the best for him. I would always love him in some way and would have a place for him in my heart, but he wasn't the one for me.

Deborah chuckled. "Are you a lesbian, honey? Only a woman who liked other women would have dumped a gorgeous man like him."

BRENDA L. WATERS

Sarcastically, I told her to *step to hell*, and that the only thing another woman could do for me was my hair. She told me not to worry, because the sistah he was with had nothing on me. I thanked her for that but steered the conversation back to work. I knew she wanted more details about Mitchell, but I wasn't biting.

"Deborah, really I need your help in finding me another job. I want something entirely different. I want something adventurous, maybe something where I could travel abroad. Got any leads or know someone I could talk to?"

She paused and asked, "Carly, what are you doing this weekend? I am giving Justin a surprise birthday party, and I know there are going to be plenty of people you can talk to. Come to the party and I'll hook you up with maybe a new lead or a new *man*. Now that you are single again, no telling who you might meet. Be at the house before eight o'clock and wear something cute, but not too cute. You can't outdo the hostess now."

We both laughed, and I agreed to come. Besides, even if it didn't work out with a job, Deborah gave the best parties with the most delicious food in the world.

The party was as I imagined. Deborah outdid herself with the Polynesian theme. For all you knew you thought you were on some tropical island. The girl even had sand flown in for a beach. It was out of this world, and as she said, everyone that was somebody would be there. I had never seen that many people for one person's birthday party in my life. I realized when I got there this was her husband's fiftieth, so that explained all the hoopla. Deborah always did like her men older. Even when we were in college there were rumors she dated not just the seniors, but perhaps some of her college professors. She used to say the guys her age were boring and she was so much more mature than they were. I guess it wasn't only the maturity she was looking for when she married Justin, it did not hurt that he was also one of the wealthiest black men in Dallas with his construction company. They did not have children of their own, but the kids from his first marriage called her, Mom.

She kept her word and introduced me to several people, including her good friend Victoria Peterson. Victoria worked for American South Airline and told me they were hiring. She had been with the company for many years and knew just about everyone there.

Victoria told me she would call Sarah Polanski in human resources on Monday to see if Steven Majors, the senior director of marketing and designs, was still in need of a junior director for his department. She felt with my background I would be an asset to the company, and Sarah owed her a favor.

"Victoria, I really appreciate this. I never thought about the airlines, but I think it would be a great opportunity. You know with your help, and a push from the man above, I can do this," I said. "Thank you."

For the rest of the evening I was feeling great. It had been a long time since I felt this renewed and exhilarated. It must have been showing, because I caught the eye of the good-looking *brother* I noticed when I first walked in. I guess he was not with the woman I saw him talking to when I entered, because she was leaving, and leaving without him. The next thing I knew he was smiling and walking over with two glasses of champagne in his hands. *This is going to be the best champagne I ever drank*, I thought, smiling at him as he walked my way.

Sure enough, at the end of the week, just as Victoria promised, I was in Steven Majors office. I knew the interview was going well, because he took no calls when his secretary rang his office. He said he was impressed with my resume' and references and wanted me on board. Like Victoria, he agreed I would be an asset to the company and his division. Two weeks after I interviewed, I was the new junior director of marketing and designs for American South Air Lines.

There was intensive training and meetings within the next few months, which did not leave much time for a social life. The handsome guy I met at Deborah Hill's party turned out to be not so great after all. After the second date, I understood why the woman left without him. The *brother* had been married three times and had about six kids from all the women combined. Not only that, he was in-between jobs, as he explained it to me over dinner one evening. What he really wanted to do was start his *own* business. He was just having a difficult time getting it off the ground. That's where he needed a good woman with a smart head on her shoulders who could assist him with starting up his company. She could become a partner and they could make a fortune. I wasn't exactly sure how this fortune was to be made, because the minute I got the drift, Mr. Big was hitting me up for the *start-up funds*, I immediately tuned him out. Fine though he may have been, no man was that good looking when they started asking for *my* money.

The following day, while at work I got a call from Deborah Hill. She wanted me to join Justin and her that Sunday at their church. She remembered me telling her how frustrated I was about not having a church home. I was tired of visiting different ones. They were having a well-known guest speaker that Sunday who went to Wharton Business School with her husband, and she thought I would enjoy the service and meeting him. It was one of the larger black churches in Dallas, with a very popular minister. Everyone who was somebody or thought they were attended.

Growing up, my family was Methodist, and as a child I attend service on a regular basis, not because I wanted to, but because I had no control over whether I went or not. The only time I remembered liking church was when I attended the Catholic Mass with one of my school friends. How this happened I do not remember, because Aunt Helen thought all Catholics were strange; she would not have approved of me attending their church. So, it must have been on some rare occasion when she was out of town, or better yet was feeling most giving because she had destroyed someone's happiness that week.

The first time I remember meeting and spending time with someone Catholic was with a distant cousin named Sister Theresa Bailey. I remembered seeing her in her nun's habit and smelling like ivory soap when she hugged me. I wondered if her face hurt from being pinched by the habit and if she ever got tired of wearing the same black dress. She entered the convent when she was fourteen, where she received her education and became a nun. The rare occasions when we were together gave me such a sense of peace, a special feeling of being with God. Maybe it was the serenity of Sister Theresa or the quietness of the convent that influenced me when I visited her there. This is what I needed and searched for when I went to church.

When I asked about God, she would tell me that to truly experience him sometimes you had to just be quiet and still, find that special place, and let him in. She found that comfort and peace many times just walking through the convent gardens and feeling the slightest touch of a breeze across her face. I remembered those words and tried to hold onto them whenever I was at my lowest.

Seven months flew by while I worked my butt off in my new job. Again, fate was with me, and I was given the greatest boss. Steven was a God

SO I WAS TOLD

send. We sometimes would spend our lunch hour together talking not just about work, but sports, families, and why I did not have a *love life*. His wife Veronica just had their fifth child, but you never would have known it by the way he acted. Each birth of a baby for him was the greatest experience. He was a hands-on father and worshipped his wife. During the summer, he would bring most of the kids to work with him way before it was popular. His daughters were more interested in becoming pilots than his sons, no matter how hard he tried to convince them it would be *cool* to fly airplanes for a living. The boys were more interested in things he wanted his girls to do, and his daughters were the biggest tomboys imaginable. He often asked me for advice on how to make his daughters more ladylike, especially his oldest daughter, Mary Margaret.

"Carly, what can I do about Margaret? She is now fourteen, and I cannot for the life of me get her into a dress. Each Sunday we have the biggest fight about her putting one on for church. My wife has bought her some of the prettiest dresses, and she absolutely refuses to wear them. Veronica has just given up and told me it's now on me. I am the man of the house, and maybe I can influence her. Influence her how?"

I couldn't help but laugh at Steven and the look of desperation on his face.

"Steven trust me, you are making *way* too much about this. Give the girl some room and let her make this decision. What are you concerned about? Do you think her wearing a dress is going to make her more or less a lady? Ladies are made by who they are, not what they wear. When I think about it, I didn't much like dresses either at that age. Now that's all I care to wear. It's just something that happens, I guess. I'll talk to her if you want me to. Maybe I'll take her shopping with me the next time I go and get a feel for what she likes. Besides, nowadays kids wear jeans to everything. Trust me, just you being a good and caring father who shows her how a man should treat a woman is far more important than what she wears. These are some troubling times for young girls."

Steven was quiet and listened to me as I talked. I could see by his facial expression he was soaking this all in. Besides, I don't know where he thought this child would get the idea to be more *feminine*. The last time I saw Veronica, she didn't quite look the *girly* type to me. But then again, sometimes that's not necessarily easy with a bunch of children demanding

BRENDA L. WATERS

your time as well as a husband. We finished our lunch and left his office for our weekly team meeting.

As we were walking down the hall, we passed a man who caught my attention. I had seen him a few times in the building, but I didn't know the department he was in. Steven almost bumped into him from looking at me while he continued talking about his daughter and the dress drama. Our eyes met, and we smiled at each other as we passed by. I casually turned around to see where he was going and saw that he too had turned back, although I guess not to see where I was heading, but rather to look at my behind in my leather skirt. I chuckled to myself, *gotcha*. I guess he figured out what I was thinking, because he smiled and winked back.

"Steven," I asked, "you know just about everyone here. Who was that good-looking guy we just passed?"

Turning around in a circle, "What guy?" he asked.

"I'm talking about the guy you almost knocked over, because you were looking at me while we were talking about your daughter."

Steven smirked and replied. "Oh, you mean the good-looking guy that passed us in the hall. The one you almost swallowed whole ... that guy? Didn't think I caught that, did you?" Holding on to my elbow, he leaned in and said, "Carly, you *cannot* have five kids and not know what is going on around you. It's utterly impossible and potentially hazardous." Letting go of my arm as we continued to walk, he said, "That's Carl Yates. He's in the finance department. As a matter of fact, he just got a major promotion last year. So I know he is doing very well. Not only that, I don't think he is married nor has any kids if I remember correctly."

Steven continued, "You know what that means, don't you?"

"No, Steven, enlighten me," I replied sarcastically

"It means *no* interruptions," he said as he laughed out loud. "Carly, can I ask you something personal? I don't want to pry, but why don't you have a man in your life? I know you come to work early and leave late. There are no photos on your desk of anyone. You never, ever talk about a man or what you did over the weekend. I mean, I don't get it. You are a young, attractive woman, who dresses really nice, and always have on great-smelling perfume."

I laughed when he said this, but I could tell he was truly serious.

He continued, "What's the deal? You do like men, don't you? I hope I

88

SO I WAS TOLD

am not crossing the line here, but I feel we have become close enough where I could ask you this, right? I know I am your boss, but I am really concerned, and so is Veronica. Actually, just the other night over coffee she--"

Before he could finish his sentence, I said, "You know Steven I've started to ask myself that same question."

"What?" he asked with a puzzled look on his face. "Do you mean if you like men?"

"No, silly," I responded. "Why I don't have someone in my life? I was consumed with changing my career and just thought *he* would fall into place when everything else did."

"Don't you want to get married and have a family?" he asked. "Right now I know I have probably crossed way over the line of propriety."

I laughed and told Steven not to worry I had no intention of filing a sexual harassment suit against him. Who would believe it anyway? Everyone at American South Airlines knew about him and his love affair with his wife. If you walked into his office, it looked like a shrine to the *holy family*. There are pictures of children of every age in sports activities plastered on all the office walls, not to mention his desk and bookcases as well. I think there is even the sonogram of the last baby framed beneath the picture of the youngest child missing his two front teeth on his desk.

I assured him I was confident everything would someday fall into place. "Who knows, maybe Mr. Right just passed me by," I told him as we walked into the board room for our meeting.

For several weeks thereafter I would see Carl in passing. It seemed we were always going in the opposite directions. If I was pulling into my parking space, he was leaving out of his. Well, it was just my fate one late Friday evening I decided to leave a little later instead of rushing out of the office to beat the evening traffic. If you ever spent any time in Dallas, you would know the Friday night traffic on the connector was brutal. I guess my soon to be new friend (and possibly more) Mr. Yates had the same idea. As I was walking down the hall into our courtyard to wait out the traffic, he was coming from the outside in. There we were finally in the same place at the same time. He politely opened the door for me to step through, and instead of continuing; he stopped and touched me on the arm.

"Hi," he said. "How long do you think we can keep missing each other? I have been trying to figure out your schedule so I can be in the same vicinity at least to say hello, but my plans have not exactly worked out. Perhaps someone has finally heard my plea and here we are." He was smiling while he said this to me. Here was my chance, and I had no desire to say something stupid like I did when I first met Mitchell long ago. No, I was going to do better this time.

I smiled back. "I am glad that someone finally heard you. I'm Carly Collins."

Smiling into my eyes, he took my hands into his. They were large and warm. "Nice to meet you finally, Carly Collins. I'm Carl Yates.

After that, it all pretty much was a blur. He turned around, and we both went into the courtyard and talked. It began to grow dark, and we noticed the evening lights coming on in the building. He asked me if I was hungry and wanted to join him for dinner. I politely declined, and I guess he was confused or so he appeared to be.

"I'm sorry, perhaps I am moving a bit too fast," he said. "It's Friday night, and I am sure you have plans. I just didn't feel like doing the singles *thing tonight* and hang out at the bar eating alone. It's getting pretty old, and having dinner with you just felt right."

I thought to myself, *He's right. This is not the time to be coy or acting like you got someone. Go ahead and go out with this man. He is fine, got a good job, all his teeth, and he is interested in me.* Besides, I did not want to hear Steven's mouth if he found out I let this opportunity pass by. Steven talked consistently about how he met Veronica and knew from the first date he was going to marry her. On and on how it was fate and all, but I guess he had a point, because less than a year after they met they were married and just recently had their fifth child.

As we stood in the courtyard into my head popped this song from church, "Do Not Pass Me by Oh Gentle Savior." I don't know what made me think about that song. I figured it was an omen and it was telling me I needed to go out with this man. I told Carl dinner would be great and he was right the *single* happy hour scene was getting old. I too was tired of seeing the same faces and refusing the same people over and over again. He laughed hysterically because he knew exactly what I meant. Many a Friday night he would see the same guy hit on the same woman who turned him down the week before. One thing you had to give him, he said, either the guy was stupid or had a heart of steel to endure that kind of pain and rejection over and over again. We both laughed and decided to have dinner in downtown Dallas. Carl knew about one of the best steak houses in the city and wanted to share it with me. I asked him if I could follow him in my car to the restaurant, even though he offered to drive and leave mine parked in the garage. He said he didn't have a problem bringing me back to get my car. Apprehensively I told him I could follow him.

In my mind I was thinking the man is all that, but I was not taking any chances. You always read or hear on the news how everyone thought he was such a good guy, but then they turn into some stark raving lunatic and the girl is never seen or heard from again. Besides, they don't put twenty-something-year-old black women on milk cartons when they are missing.

He must have read my mind and told me not to worry. He would be on his best behavior. Besides, there were cameras in the garage and he was sure his buddies in the security office were watching at that precise moment. As a matter of fact, he turned and waved into the camera. Right on cue, a voice sounding like it came from the heavens above told us both to have a nice evening. We laughed as we walked toward his car and he helped me in.

After dinner and the best steak I ever had, Carl ordered a brandy for himself. He asked if I wanted something, but since I had wine for dinner I did not want to take any chances of losing my cool. As the dinner progressed, he was getting better looking and I could visualize our wedding and lots of babies. He politely excused himself from the table to go to the men's room which gave me a good chance to get a good look at *his* backside. Yes, women do look at men's behinds as well as what is in front, and from what I saw going, I could only hope the *front* would be better. When he returned to the table, he was smiling and appeared to be in good spirits. He paid for the dinner, and we left the restaurant.

The drive back to the office was full of conversation and laughter. Carl could talk on anything. He pulled into the garage next to my car, got out, and opened the door for me. When I stood up, we were nose to nose. Inching closer, he looked into my eyes and smiled. I just knew he was going to kiss me, but he didn't. He asked for my keys and opened my car door.

Standing in front of me, he asked for my number and said, "We have to do this again very soon."

I replied, "I would like that."

We stood there for a few moments in that awkward silence.

"Goodnight, Carly," he said as he lightly kissed me on the cheek. "I had the best evening, and from now on that restaurant will be my favorite place, our place, okay?"

CHAPTER NINE

FALLING

So the love affair began. Even though both of our jobs were very demanding, we managed to communicate through memos at work and talked late night on the phone. Friday night became ours. Then Saturday, then Sunday... I was falling and falling hard.

It was on one of our Saturday dates Carl asked me if I wanted to attend church with him that Sunday. This came as a happy surprise. I decided not to push the whole church thing from my experience with Mitchell. I had gone to service with some of my girlfriends from time to time; what a pleasure it was going be to attend with Carl. I wasn't quite sure where he and I were headed, but it was refreshing to have someone I could share my faith with as well as other entertaining things we were doing.

After nine intense months of dating, Carl told me how he felt. He wanted more from this relationship. We had not been intimate, and I was trying to hold out as long as I could. It was difficult, but I was determined not to appear too easy. We often took weekend trips together but never shared a hotel room. He would always book separate rooms with adjoining doors but always respected my privacy. In fact, I found myself being more

BRENDA L. WATERS

tempted than him. Yet it was refreshing not to be hounded by someone to be intimate without establishing a solid friendship first.

One of my girlfriends always joked about the ninety-day rule. She swore this was tried and true. Her theory was to give a man ninety days, just like he was in the probationary period at a job. It would take just about that amount of time for his true identity to be revealed. The first thirty or so days, he will be on his best behavior trying to impress you, but after that ninetieth day, when he is comfortable with you, watch out! If by then he hasn't gotten *any*, either he will just give up and you never hear from him again or the frustration will set in. The stories he told to impress you in the beginning now became the lies they really were.

I decided to take her advice, even though I stretched the time a bit longer. It wasn't that difficult because our jobs sometimes took us away from each other. I have to give Carl some credit; he did hang in there for those long nine months on his best behavior, a real gentleman. I decided to give him a chance and let the relationship become intimate, and I am glad I waited, because it was worth the wait. I never felt more connected to someone in my life. I knew he was the one for me and thought he felt the same. He was devoted and loving, considerate, spiritual. He was all the things I asked and prayed for. My checklist was looking good, as well as that column of more right than wrong. Finally I felt all the pieces of Carly Elizabeth Collins coming together. I even ordered a subscription to some bridal magazines, just in case. It got to the point where he and I were practically living together. If he didn't have half of his things at my place, the other half of mine were at his. It was nice sometimes when we didn't do anything but lie around drinking coffee and reading the Sunday paper. We were a couple, and it felt good.

There is truth to when you ask for something, be specific. It was toward the end of the second year of my relationship with Carl I started noticing changes in him. They were small at first but became increasingly noticeable as time went by. Questions I asked in the past that didn't seem to bother him now appeared to be a burden to answer. He started lying, and may I say not doing a very good job with hiding it. His pleasant, easygoing personality became more irritated, and I noticed he was sleeping less. When I walked into the room, he would abruptly hang up the phone. There became more, "Baby, I'll be back, I got to make a run or see someone about some business," than before. He was coming home later, and instead of giving me a hello kiss or pat on the behind, he would jump right into the shower. He was agitated some nights and ill at ease. If I inquired what was wrong, my head was nearly taken off. This would follow with an excuse and flowers the next day, always something to do with work or someone in the family needing something from him. There were more weekend trips out of town, all business-related, of course, and I believed him. I knew how demanding his position was and heard the rumors about someone in his department getting a promotion; we all believed it to be Carl. I was evening planning on giving him a huge party when it happened. I had absolutely no clue what was happening to him or us.

Like some women, I started to think maybe it was me. I had been passing subtle hints about marriage and didn't hide the books on wedding planning I was getting in the mail. So naturally I figured Carl was getting cold feet. Maybe the idea of settling down with me was something he did not plan. I remember a conversation I had once with a male friend whose logic about marriage consisted of having to live with the woman first before he could marry her. That way he was ready for all the *little surprises* when they came along. He felt this was the perfect way for him to see the *true* person he was marrying. After listening very intently to him, I politely told him that was a bunch of bull. I did not understand what he meant by the *true* person. From all the people I knew who had this same idea either, they broke up or the marriage failed within the first six months.

Even though Carl and I spent the majority of our time together in his home or mine, shacking up was not an option. Sharing my time and my love with Carl was a given, but not the bank account without a license. Don't get me wrong, Carl was a generous man. He felt it was his obligation as my man to make sure I looked good all the time. My money was mine, his was ours. I used to tease him when he gave me my weekly allowance. Sometimes when he left town he would leave money for me under the coffee cup with the sweetest card telling me to have a great weekend with my girlfriends on him.

As time went by, Carl's behavior grew worse. I felt it had to be another woman. This explained the late night calls and the way he would get off the phone when I came into the room, new business trips, and his distance with me. I am not the type of person to snoop or look around, but I started to

BRENDA L. WATERS

look for clues to the changes in his behavior. Something had to be wrong, and I eagerly wanted to find out. There must be another woman. That would explain his behavior and attitude. The question was, did I want to know? My Aunt Helen would tell me when you look for trouble you are going to find it. When you are nosey, you better be prepared to lose that nose.

Cleaning out his closet one Saturday while Carl was away, I decided to pay back the favor and have a wonderful surprise for him when he returned home. His closet was a mess. To say Carl was not the most organized person was an understatement. It drove me nuts, but it was his things, not mine. While he was away, I thought I would surprise him with a closet makeover. I hired an expert who assured me they could redo his closet with new shelves, drawers, shoe racks-- the works. While rearranging the closet, I took some of his shirts and suits to the cleaners. He owned French cuff custom-made shirts and some of the most expensive suits and ties you could imagine. It wasn't until I got to the cleaners and the little woman behind the desk started going through his pockets that she found the little packets. At first I thought they were those wrappings of powdered aspirin wrapped in wax paper. Some were even pieces of foil crunched up with traces of fine white powder. There were so many of them and all in different pockets of his pants and suits. I guess the expression on my face said it all. When I looked up, the little woman behind the counter holding a handful of these wrappers placed them in my hands. I had found out there was another woman, and one I could not compete with. Her name was *cocaine*.

I drove home in fear the lady from the cleaners would call the cops and they would be knocking at my door any minute. I started making phone calls to some of Carl's friends' wives or girlfriends that we traveled and hung out with. If Carl was doing something, I prayed to God they would tell me. Trust me, if the shoe was on the other foot and it was happening to them, I would sing like a bird. I can handle many things, but drugs and infidelity were deal breakers for me.

By the third phone call, I reached Shelly Hudson, the wife of one the guys Carl played golfed with, and found my answer. To my surprise, Gregg was in drug rehab because of his cocaine habit. Shelly was packing up that weekend to move back home to her parents house with the kids. They had lost everything–the house, his job, all was gone. We talked for hours with her pouring out her heart and telling me about Gregg and what she suspected about Carl. When I told her what I found in his pockets when I took his clothes to the cleaners, she confirmed my worst nightmare. Carl was hooked on cocaine. I told Shelly how his behavior had changed. He was even having trouble at work, which he blamed on his new co-worker, Martin Sykes. He and Carl were up for the new vice president position, and Carl swore the guy was trying to sabotage him every chance he got. Being the devoted girlfriend, of course I took his side because I knew how corporate America worked against most of our black men.

Shelly told me Gregg had a $3,000 a week habit. She said almost all of Gregg's friends were using. He even tried to get her to try it, assuring her it was harmless and only a very weak person would get hooked.

Now the question became, what was I going to do about it? Should I walk away or stay and confront him? If I decided to stay, what should I say to him? What are my options? This was new territory for me. I loved this man, and now I felt helpless.

As I lie in bed, I could not sleep, so I sat up and began to pray. I prayed so hard my head pounded from the confusion and the stress. Thoughts began to race through my mind. Was Carl as addicted as Gregg? He had not lost his job; as a matter of fact, he was up for another promotion. Maybe Shelly was wrong about him. Perhaps he was not hooked like her husband. Maybe he was the stronger one and cocaine was something he could give up. Just because a man drinks on the weekend or when he's at a party does not make him an alcoholic, does it? Isn't alcohol a drug? Yet, if you saw a man drinking, would you assume he was an alcoholic? Besides, what would it say about my love for Carl if I just up and left him? This might be the time he needed my support the most. When he came home, we would talk this thing through and seek counseling if necessary.

Carl's flight arrived on time, and I was there to meet him. As he walked up the jetway, I could not believe this was the man Shelly described. He was handsome, intelligent, professional; not a common drug addict. This was not a man with a cocaine habit. He was the last to deplane, and the flight attendants were walking with him. They were talking and laughing, yet when he looked up, he only had eyes for me. One of them actually stopped talking to follow his gaze. When she saw me, I don't have to tell you she was not too happy. I thought to myself, *Honey, if you only knew. If your pretty little*

BRENDA L. WATERS

feet were in my shoes right now knowing what I was about to do, you would not be smiling and feeling like he is all that and then some.

Carl put down his bags and scooped me up in his arms. He gave me the most passionate kiss, not caring who was watching. Putting me down, he whispered into my ear how much he missed me and the things he planned on doing to me to prove it. It scared me, but I tried not to show it. All I could think, was this coming from a true feeling of love and missing me, or is he high! I had spent the weekend reading as much I could find on cocaine and addiction—the extreme highs and then when they crash how ugly and awful it could get. Carl met all the signs of an addict. He was good about hiding it from me and from everyone, so I thought. Months later, I found out the reason for that business trip. Carl was making major mistakes at work. His boss gave him the assignment as a last chance to redeem himself. He was not going to get the promotion of vice president of finance. It was only because of his past accomplishment he was hanging on by a string.

I convinced Carl to go to dinner instead of cooking for me. I even told him it was my treat. He wanted to know what he had done to deserve the royal treatment so he could keep it up. All the time I spent with him I don't remember ever paying for anything. While at dinner, he was so talkative. I sat and listened patiently. Obviously he did not notice my silence but rather took it as my interest in him and what he was saying. I nodded my head and smiled at the appropriate times, yet if you asked me what he was talking about, to this day I could not tell you. My own thoughts were only how to bring the subject up and let him know I knew his secret. I asked the waiter to place us in a private place, just in case there was a scene not too many people would notice. Carl, on the other hand, thought I was trying to be romantic. The waiter accommodated us by seating us with the ability to pull a curtain around ourselves. Even though you are in a public place, it gave you the illusion of being in your own private space. This was perfect, and I knew it was a sign I was doing the right thing by bringing us here.

"Carly! Baby, where are you?" he asked. "Did you hear me? I asked you twice about your weekend while I was away. Are you all right?"

He put his fork down and placed his hand on top of mine. "Baby, what's wrong? You have this serious look on your face. What is it, Carly? Tell me."

I hesitated, and before I knew, the tears started to flow.

SO I WAS TOLD

"Carl, I know. I know all about it. I spoke to Shelley, and she told me about Gregg. She told me about *you*. I want you to know I wasn't snooping or anything, but I wanted to surprise you when you got home and had your closet made over. I saw all your suits and shirts you probably were going to take to the cleaners and decided to do that for you. I know how busy you have been lately and just thought this was something I could do for you … I mean because of all the wonderful things you do for me."

I could not finish the sentence. By then I was crying hysterically. I looked up and saw Carl looking down at the table. His napkin was in his plate, although he was not finished eating. I had not touched any of my food. How could I eat? I was scared to death of what I would say, what he would tell me. My stomach was in knots. Finally, after I pulled myself together, Carl looked up.

"Are you going to leave me?" he asked. "I want you to know I am not addicted. Okay, on occasions I tried cocaine, but only because the boys were doing it. Then sometimes I took a hit or two because I needed to be on my toes at work. Carly, you just don't understand what I have been going through. They are constantly on my back. I am not their golden boy anymore, so when I found myself slipping or getting tired, I would take a hit or two just to give me back that edge, but I swear to you, I am not an addict. You believe me, don't you?"

In my head I kept replaying the look on the face of the woman at the cleaners when she placed all the wrappings in my hands until they spilled out and onto the counter top. This was not just a sometime thing.

"Carl, I want to believe you," I said, "but I know what I saw. What I held in my hands from just a few of your suits lets me know this is not something you can pick up and put down when you want to. Whether or not you want to admit it, you are hooked. You were high when you got off the plane, weren't you? Tell me the truth, please do not lie to me. Look me in my eyes and tell me the truth."

It is funny how your emotions change. Just looking at Carl when he came off the airplane my heart was so full of love for him; yet less than a few minutes ago, this love turned to anguish and I could feel my heart aching. It was aching so much, because I did not want to be here or have this conversation. I did not want to hear the truth to where I could not control the tears, even though I tried to tell myself not to cry. Now sitting

BRENDA L. WATERS

here across from this man, this man who I envisioned me spending the rest of my life with, having babies with, all I felt was anger and disgust and disbelief. Carl was sitting across from me fidgeting like a child, playing with the silverware, anything, I guess than look me in my face.

I asked him again, "Tell me, Carl, were you high on cocaine when you got off the airplane?"

He sat there for a few minutes in silence. I could see his shoulders slump for a moment, and then he straightened himself, cleared his throat, pushed his plate aside, and placed both of his hands on top of the table. He looked me in the eye and said, "I am not an addict, but if you want me to tell you this, then I will. What is it going to take? What must I do to prove to you that I am not what you think I am? What happened to Gregg is unfortunate, but he is not *me*," he said as he pointed to his chest. "I am not weak or strung out on this stuff like you think. I feel for the brother, but I am not him. So, to answer your question, no I was not *high* when I got off the airplane. I was happy to see my woman and wanted everyone to know it, especially *you*."

In my heart I wanted to believe him, but my gut was telling me he was lying. If he loved me and this was not what I thought it was, then I wanted him to prove it by getting some help before it became a problem.

He held my hands in his. "Carly, do you believe I love you? I just don't love you, I *need* you in my life. I knew you were the woman for me the day I passed you in the hall. I knew then just like I know now you are the most important person in my life. I don't want to lose you, I can't lose you. So, if drug counseling is what you want me to do, then I will do it. I'll do it for you. Just don't leave me, not now."

I knew he could tell by the expression on my face I was not buying what he was saying. All the books I read said to be prepared for the lying or denial. Which one was it for him? He got up from the table and sat down next to me as he gathered me into his arms and hugged me tightly.

"Baby, I am not an addict. I can stop anytime. If you can forgive me and trust me again, I will prove myself to you."

He kissed me lightly on the lips and hugged me tightly again.

"All right, Carl, I will not leave you if you promise me you are going to call someone right away and start therapy. If you say this is *not* serious and you are not dependent on it, then I want you to get professional help before

SO I WAS TOLD

it does. I do not want us to end up like Shelley and Gregg. I don't want to see you strung out and in rehab or something worse. She said he really went downhill, hit rock bottom. Promise me this will not happen to you, to us! Promise me, Carl."

"Baby, with all the love I have for you, I promise to go to therapy. We can get through this. I'll show you."

Carl contacted a drug counselor that Monday and started weekly sessions. He did not want me to go to his therapy sessions in the beginning, and I respected his wishes. After the third month, he invited me to meet his counselor. I liked him right away. His counselor told me his story of his drug addiction. It was heartbreaking hearing how he lost everyone and everything that meant something to him. He was beginning to reconcile with his ex-wife and children, so he understood the damage drugs can do in one's life.

Carl was getting back to himself again. People were noticing the changes, and I thought within time we would probably start talking about settling down and making our relationship permanent. He told me he loved me, but was not ready for marriage or a family right away. He was being considered for a position in another department which came with a promotion and a raise. Carl said he wanted to concentrate on making it happen, for him and for us, before he made that kind of commitment.

Steven came to me about a new position in Atlanta and wanted to know if I was interested. As much as he loved having me work with him, he knew this would enhance my career within the company. This is what I loved most about Steven, he always looked out for me. I thought about the offer and what this would mean to Carl and me. I decided not to give him an answer right then, but asked him if I could think it over. What I really wanted to do was wait to see what was going to happen with Carl, with us.

Carl did not get the promotion. He was beginning to dislike what he was doing and began to grow resentful of my accomplishments. He heard about my job offer from all the gossip in the company. This was a new division, and my name was being tossed around for the junior vice president. My achievements proved too much for him. He said he needed a break, some breathing room and I reluctantly agreed I knew this was more about Carl and his issues than me or our relationship, but I did have my pride.

BRENDA L. WATERS

Begging a man to love or be with me was *not* in my DNA, no matter how I might have felt about him.

Everyone was talking about Atlanta. Some were calling it the new *Mecca* of the south. People who moved away and went north were returning to the south because of Atlanta. This might be good thing, I thought. Perhaps what I needed to get over Carl.

As Steven and I sat in his office, discussing the position, his phone rang.

"This is for you," he said as he handed me the telephone.

"Hello, Carly Collins. What … When did it happen? Yes, yes I will be there as soon as I can. Thank you for calling." I could feel the blood drain from my face and Steven must have noticed too.

"Carly, what is it? Who was that?" he asked.

"That was my aunt's housekeeper. My Aunt Helen has died. I need to leave. I have to help my family with the funeral arrangements."

"Go and pack. We can talk about this when you get back. I'll make all the arrangements for you to take the next available flight to Mississippi. Don't worry, you'll make that flight," Steven replied.

I thanked him and went back to my office to get my things. Walking down the hallway, it felt like the walls were becoming smaller, closing in on me. It was a strange feeling. I wasn't sad or hurt, and I don't remember crying. I just felt numb. I kept playing the phone conversation over and over in my head, Aunt Helen was dead.

CHAPTER TEN

GOOD-BYE, AUNT HELEN

While getting dressed in my bedroom, I noticed the clock on the old dresser. I heard a knock at the front door. Glancing back, I realized it was noon and Mr. Patterson from Patterson and Son's Funeral Home had arrived. It was time for me to say farewell to Aunt Helen. At exactly 3:13 PM three days earlier, she took her last breath at Our Lady of Mercy Catholic Hospital. That cold, cruel heart of hers had finally stopped beating.

No one understood or really could explain why she had been mean to so many people in her life. It had to take a lot of years to build up that much venom, or perhaps she was just born that way. Apparently there wasn't much crying when everyone found out she was dead, not even from her own husband. He didn't seem shaken or surprised about her sudden death. Maybe he felt the same way I did—that she never had a heart. Whenever I asked Haley why Aunt Helen was that way, she never gave me a good explanation. She only replied Helen had her *reasons* or her heart was hardened by things that happened to her when she was younger. Haley had a way of eluding questions at times when she did not want to discuss Aunt Helen or anyone else. She would say, "Just pray and let God." My aunt's life as a young woman will forever remain a mystery. At times I wondered what it was that made Uncle J. D. fall in love with her. Forget falling in love, what was it that made him *stay* with her all those years? In his case, it wasn't just her meanness but rather indifference, treating him like a piece of furniture whenever he was home. I guess his being away helped him cope.

I know I should be sad because she raised me for the better part of my life, but all I felt was numbness. The only person who showed the slightest bit of sorrow was Rayne, the housekeeper. I wonder, is it still considered a *homegoing* when you going to …? There was no doubt in my mind she was sitting right next to the devil in the fiery pit. Poor old Lucifer, I bet he wondered what he did to deserve *her*. The image of Aunt Helen and the devil together made me laugh. I could envision him sitting on his mighty throne, pitchfork in hand and Aunt Helen cursing *him* out, telling him to get his lazy, hot, red ass off that throne and clean up the place. Asking him did he honestly think *she*, Helen Watkins, was there to serve *him?* Oh hell no! She was not about to spend the rest of eternity in his nasty, hot, smelly pig sty with all those wretched souls weeping and wailing, asking why they were there, to wait on his ass? She was going to do this her way or no way at all.

Fastening the last button on my blouse, I started thinking about all the lives she destroyed before leaving this green earth. The walking wounded included Ethel, Haley, my grandfather, Christian, Martha, and Ethel's brother Nathaniel, to name a few. I could go on. Even the students at the high school despised her. They, too, felt she was mean and evil to everyone. There was never a kind word or the least amount of encouragement from her toward them or her staff.

Out of all who knew her, it was my Aunt Martha who felt she was soulless, the most vile and evil person to walk the earth. She never talked much about her, but when she did, it was never kind or favorable. Whatever she held against Aunt Helen, she never talked about it.

It was Aunt Helen who took away both of Ethel's children and made her life a living hell. All the mean things I heard about her growing up became reality. An example of her craziness, she would spontaneously order me to take a pregnancy test, even though I had never had been on a date or had sex. She hid them in various rooms, and depending on what level of the house she had me cleaning, she would pop up like a jack in the box with that damn thing in her hand. With her face in a pinch like she smelled something unsavory, she would thrust the box in my hands.

She would say, "Carly, take this to the bathroom and use it. When you are finished, leave it on some tissue paper on the sink. I left a timer in there for you to set, and you better pray to God it doesn't tell me something *you* will regret, young lady!"

With that, she would disappear, and I swear to God, I didn't know how she heard that timer from wherever she was slithering around in the house. When she saw it was negative, she would thrust the wet, pee-soaked plastic tube in my hand and walk past me. I was left standing in the hall wondering what she was expecting to see.

All of this coming from the most churchgoing, God-fearing, righteous hypocrite you ever wanted to meet. She was in service every Sunday, sitting in her reserved pew with a feeling of entitlement because of all the money she donated to the church, just a clapping and singing.

I finally finished dressing and taking one last look in the mirror. I tried to make myself cry. Placing my mourning hat on with the veil, I left my room and proceeded down the stairs. With each step I took, my mind wondered about the service and who would be in attendance. Mr. Patterson was standing in the foyer and looked up as I came down. Now he seemed sad, but then he was the mortician, and it was his job to look that way. I know he couldn't be all that put out by her death because she was so terrible to his wife, Mable Patterson. Aunt Helen never invited her to her monthly bridge party. She and her friends did not consider her good enough to be in their company, even though her husband owned the largest funeral home in Madison.

Setting in the limousine as we headed to the church, I started to think about Aunt Helen and what made her the way she was. I wonder what made her tick, what fueled all that venom and anger. As we pulled up to the church, I was startled to see so many cars and people lined up out the door. Many from near and far came to say their final good-bye to Aunt Helen. I pulled my veil a little lower as I stepped out the limo. Mr. Patterson gently took my arm as he led me into First Corinthians AME church. Rev. Simmons was at the door to meet me. He took my hand in his and led me to the front of the church where Aunt Helen's casket lay. To my left and right were family and a few of the women in her bridge club. Haley was too ill to attend. Her doctor advised her not to leave her bed no matter how much she felt it was her place to bury her sister. It took all we had to convince her

BRENDA L. WATERS

to stay home with the assurance Uncle J.D. and I would give Aunt Helen a proper burial.

Proceeding to the casket with Rev. Simmons still holding my hand, I glanced at him through my veil. Not even he seemed truly saddened by her death. He leaned down and with a whispering voice said, "Not to worry, for she is in a better place. Be glad she is at home with the Lord."

Now, that is when I almost lost it. I wanted to tell him I didn't think it was *the Lord* she was probably with right now. Rev. Simmons was not exempt from Aunt Helen's *hit* list. There were many Sundays she would call his home, telling him what she did not like about his sermon and what he needed to do about something or someone in the church, always reminding him how much money she tithed. If it wasn't for her donations and the various funds she helped organize, that church would have fallen apart years ago.

As I stood there looking down into her silver steel metal casket with the pale rose satin taffeta crepe lining she requested, many memories came to me at once. It was at this moment, my eyes did become watery and sadness filled my heart. The funeral home did wonders with her hair and makeup. The floral displays and various cards and messages were heartwarming. I have to admit; they even managed to make her look peaceful, even youthful somehow. Her mouth was etched in a smile and her hands gently folded across her chest, not looking dead at all, but as if she was sleeping. Perhaps she was finally at rest, at peace.

As I turned to take my seat in the pew next to Uncle J. D., I caught Rayne's eyes. She smiled at me as if to say all was well. Only Rayne and Haley could truly understand what Aunt Helen meant to me.

As the service progressed and several people from her school, the church, her clubs, etc., spoke, Rayne left to make sure that everything was ready to receive family and guests at the repast. She squeezed my hand and kissed me on the cheek as she rose to leave. Uncle J. D. was holding my other hand so tightly as if I was his lifeline, or maybe it was out of fear she really wasn't dead. I squeezed his hand back and gently placed it on his lap. He did something I never knew him to do in all the years I was in his home. He placed his arm around me, gently kissed me on my cheek, and smiled as he patted me on my hands. There was sadness and relief in his eyes. I think we all felt we could breathe a little easier with Aunt Helen gone.

SO I WAS TOLD

Although the service was long and many people spoke, there was very little emotion. There was no sniffling, weeping, or wailing; asking the Lord why it was she that had to go. Rev. Simmons said his last words of praise and the casket was closed. As Uncle J. D. and I proceeded down the aisle, there standing in the back of the church was my mother, Ethel. I could see she had been crying with her makeup smeared and tears staining her cheeks. As we drew closer, I reached out and embraced her. Ethel held me so tightly I could feel the air being squeezed out of me. She placed her head on my shoulder, and we stood there for what seemed an eternity holding onto each other, not saying a word. Uncle J. D. gently placed his arms around both of us as we walked to the waiting limousine.

There was silence in the car as we drove to the cemetery. With me looking out one window and Ethel the other, only our hands entwined, Uncle J. D. rode up front with Mr. Patterson. The interior window was down, and I could hear them engaging in small talk. I wasn't paying much attention to what was being said, only to the murmur of their voices. I glanced at Ethel, who seemed lost in her own thoughts. I gently squeezed her hand. She squeezed mine back. She and I had travelled a long and difficult path, yet through it all we somehow survived. With many scars and maybe wounds that would never heal, we survived.

Looking out the window, there were people on the streets who stopped and stared as the hearse and limousines passed. Some came outside of their shops, while others paused mid-step to watch and whisper as we traveled to the end of Helen Evangeline Dodson Watkins' reign.

A fine mist started to sprinkle as Aunt Helen was slowly lowered into the ground and the last bit of dirt thrown on top of the casket. Uncle J.D. and other family members headed back to the house, where Rayne had prepared a meal for the family and visitors. Ethel and I lingered at the graveside as the funeral director placed the flowers on her grave and his staff removed the chairs. Mr. Patterson waited patiently until we were ready to leave. Without a word, we both turned and walked to the car. I glanced back as I heard the caw of a black bird fly overhead. Somehow I felt that was the soul of Aunt Helen floating on the wings of that bird. I smiled and turned toward the car as Mr. Patterson helped Ethel into the limousine.

Rayne greeted Ethel and me at the door as we entered the house. I heard laughter and the clink of silverware from the many people who had gathered. Some faces I remembered from the funeral others were people who were strangers to me, yet all knew Aunt Helen. Uncle J. D. was off in a distant corner surrounded by people from the university who came to pay their respects. Other family members and their children were scattered throughout the house. I was exhausted and only wanted to lie down. As I was heading up the stairs, Rayne stopped me and told me I had a call from Detective Raphael Ramirez from the Dallas Fort Worth Police Department. He wanted me to call him as soon as I returned from the cemetery, because he needed to speak to me about my car and an important case. She tried to get more information, but he would go no further. Rayne took his telephone number and told him she would have me return the call.

Rayne asked, "Carly, baby, you ain't in any trouble, are you? I didn't like the way he sounded on the phone and all. He wouldn't tell me what this was about, only you needed to call him right away. You would tell me if there was a problem, now?

To the best of my ability, I tried to assure Rayne I didn't know who Detective Ramirez was. I was tired and needed to lie down for awhile, but would call him after I got up.

"Rayne, don't worry," I said. "I'm sure it's nothing. I left the car at my condo; perhaps someone broke into it. There is nothing I can do from here anyway. I'll be down in a little while and I will call him. "

Rayne kissed me on the cheek and told me she would check on me later as I proceeded to climb the stairs. I walked down the hallway and past Aunt Helen's room. I stopped and peeked in the room to look around at all the things left out as if she would return home that evening. Her combs and brushes were still on the vanity, along with her nightgown and robe, laid across the bed. There were still fresh flowers in the vase by the window and the curtains pulled back and tied by their sashes. Her closet door was slightly ajar. There were pictures of Uncle J.D., and her mother and father on the nightstand by the bed. Her Bible lay open with a red leather bookmark resting on the last page she must have been reading before she went to the hospital. I could still smell a faint trace of her favorite perfume in the air, a trace that would slowly fade away, yet forever etched into my memory.

I slept longer than I thought. When I went downstairs, many of the guests had left, along with a considerable amount of the food and beverages. Thank God Rayne put a plate aside for me; I was famished. It just dawned

SO I WAS TOLD

on me I had not eaten anything since the night before the service. I did not have much of an appetite that morning, but now all I could think about was eating. As I sat down at the kitchen table, Rayne reminded me to call the policeman in Dallas. After swallowing the last bite of the pecan pie, I went into Uncle J. D.'s study to call to Detective Ramirez.

I was greeted on the phone by a deep and unfriendly male voice.

"D.F.W.P.D., Sergeant Henderson, how may I place your call?" he asked.

"Hello, this is Carly Collins returning a call to Detective Raphael Ramirez."

"Hold on, ma'am, I'll transfer you," he said.

After a short pause a man answered the phone.

"This is Detective Ramirez. How can I help you?"

"Detective Ramirez, this is Carly Collins. You left a message for me?"

"Hold on, ma'am, let me get the file. I'll be right with you." He placed the telephone upon the desk, and I could hear the sound of his shoes as he walked away. There was a squeak of what must have been a file drawer opening and the slamming of the drawer as he closed it. I could hear his feet as he walked back to the desk. It made me wonder how big of a man he was and the size of his feet to make that kind of noise. I heard the ruffling of paper and the faint murmur as he spoke to someone near the telephone. He was telling them he had me on the phone and to stay close.

"Ms. Collins, I have a report that your car was involved in an arrest made from an undercover operation. There was some suspicious evidence found in your vehicle, along with Mr. Carl Yates, who said he had permission to have your car while you were out of town. Mr. Yates is in police custody awaiting arraignment. Your car was impounded for evidence. Ms. Collins, we need to speak to you in person about this matter. When will you be returning to Dallas?"

Undercover operation ... evidence ... Carl ... this could only be one thing and one thing only-- *drugs*. My head was spinning, and I had to keep the panic under control. My worst nightmare had come true with Carl. From the moment I stood at the cleaners with the evidence in my hands, I was sure this day would come. No matter what he told me and the lies I

BRENDA L. WATERS

believed, I knew it would happen. Why didn't I listen to myself? Why did I believe he had changed? What about the therapy? Was that a lie also?

"Ms. Collins, are you there? I need to know when you are returning to Dallas," he asked.

"I'm sorry, Detective. What is this about? What do you mean my car impounded, and Mr. Yates arrested? When did it happen and where?"

"Ms. Collins, I'd rather not go into any details over the phone, but when will you be returning to Dallas?

"Am *I* in some kind of trouble, Detective Ramirez?" Why do you need to know my itinerary? When I'm returning?

"Ms. Collins, let me assure you this is a very serious matter. *Presently* you are not under suspicion, but my department and the FBI need some information that perhaps you may be able to assist us with."

"Again, and for the *final* time Ms. Collins, when will you be returning to Dallas?"

"I will be home tomorrow afternoon *detective*. My flight should get in around 3:30, and I can come directly to the station if you want. Will you be there? I want to cooperate as *much* as I can. Is there anything else?"

"Yes, ma'am, make sure you are on that flight tomorrow. One other thing, this would not be a good time to leave the country. Thank you for your cooperation, good day Ms. Collins.

Standing in the hallway staring at the telephone, all I could hear was the rapid beating of my exploding heart. What had Carl dragged me into?

CHAPTER ELEVEN

OH WHAT A DAY

After meeting with Detective Ramirez of the D.F.W.P.D., I realized it was time for me to move away from Dallas. There was nothing left for me here, and Atlanta was the place to start anew. My crazy cousin, Taylor Marie Thompson, lived there and had been trying for years to get me to relocate. She always said Dallas was a place for retired people. She swore Atlanta was the place to be and it had the best-looking men she had ever seen at least for the South. Before I returned to work, I decided to visit her. Although I had not yet told Steven I was interested in the position, I decided as long as I was in Atlanta I would look for a place to live. One thing for sure—it was only a matter of time before I was going to leave Dallas.

Staying with Taylor was a *trip*, but I had the time of my life. I had forgotten how much fun she was and how much I missed being around her. With all her craziness and silly antics, it helped to take my mind off Carl and all that had happened. Although I was truly enjoying myself, the time had come for me to return to work. This would only be for a short while, because I decided with or without that new job, I was moving to Atlanta.

"Taylor, girl, if you don't hurry and get me to the airport, I am going to jump in that seat and drive myself. I need to be on that flight back to

BRENDA L. WATERS

Dallas so I can talk with my boss about the job here. I need to let him know something by tomorrow in order for me to be considered for the position."

"Carly! Pleaassse! Will you stop being so dramatic? Girl *not* only will I get you to the airport on time, but you will be able to have a drink before your plane takes-off, and I don't have to tell you, *you really* need one, Uhhhh! Anyway, I want to make one more stop at Saks before I drop you off. I have to buy those *kickin'* shoes we saw, now that I've found the perfect dress to wear with them. Besides, wasn't *I* the most patient cousin when *you* wanted to shop in Neiman Marcus for three hours?"

I looked at my cousin as if she had grown a third eye right in the middle of her forehead.

I shopped for three hours! No, it was more like Carly holding Taylor's bags as she piled on dresses, pants, whatever she could find on sale that was still too expensive and way too tight for her behind. Yes, Neiman Marcus is my favorite store and I did some damage, but not at all like what she was trying to make it out to be. Besides, I needed to budget two months salary for all the new furniture I was going to purchase for the condominium I wanted in Buckhead.

As usual, Taylor believed she was not only the best driver in Atlanta, but also the fastest and knew this city down to a science.

"Look, your flight does not leave until 4:35 PM; it is 3:00 right now. I assure you, we are going to be at the airport in no time. Just relax! Here, you stay in the car and I will run into the store and buy the shoes. It won't take that long, have some faith. I do this all the time and haven't been late for a flight yet."

I was not only late getting to the airport, but there was traffic I swear backed up at least five miles in both directions on I- 75/85, one of the major freeways in Atlanta. Apparently dear cousin Taylor had forgotten about the Braves game that afternoon. It was the playoffs, and everyone and their mama were in town. It had been awhile since the team was in a winning series, and no one wanted to miss out on this event.

As we pulled up to curb side check-in, I decided not to look at my watch anymore. Taylor was right, she got me to the airport approximately thirty minutes before my flight was to depart, so technically she was not wrong and I was not late. The only problem, she forgot I still had to check my bags and make it to the gate. With a quick air kiss and a wave good–bye, I was left standing on the curb with bags in hand and my ticket between my lips.

This was not going to be my day. Why of all people did I have to get the oldest and slowest skycap to check- in my luggage? Wasn't there mandatory retirement or something? He moved at a snail's pace, and the glasses on his eyes with the right amount of light could start a small fire if he wasn't careful. After what felt like an eternity standing in line, he finally got to me.

"May I have your ticket please? How many bags do you need checked?"

"I only have the one bag to check, please."

"Where you headed?"

"Um, I am going back to Dallas."

"Well, I hate to burst your bubble, pretty lady, but your bag ain't gonna make that 4:30 PM flight. I can get it on the next one to Dallas, but they might not get in until after midnight."

"*Fine*, just as long as I get on the plane I can get the bag later."

"Well, now just hold on a minute, no need in getting all upset about it. You're the one late, *not* the plane."

I thought to myself, *I am sure he is expecting a huge tip for all this profound wisdom he's mouthing off. I am not late, Taylor made me late. This would not be the case if she didn't have to buy those damn shoes from Saks.*

"No, no I apologize, I'm not angry. I just really need to get on that flight. I have so much to do when I get there, and I am just a bit upset with my cousin for not getting me here sooner."

"Uh huh, I know, little lady, I know. Here's your ticket. Your flight is out of Concourse D, Gate eleven. I sure hope you make it; don't know how, with you wearing them high heels and all. Good luck!"

He was right. How in the world was I going to run to catch a flight wearing three and a half-inch sling back heels? Even though they made my legs look fabulous and really worked with my outfit, running was out of the question. *I know! I can get one of the electric carts. That would cut down on the walking, running time. Those things can move pretty fast If I'm lucky, I can get him to call the gate and tell them I am on my way.*

With the biggest smile and the most syrupy, sappy voice, I asked, "Sir! Would you be an angel and do me a favor? You are absolutely right. I can't run in these heels. Do you think you could have an electric cart pick me up

BRENDA L. WATERS

and take me to the gate? It can get there a lot quicker than me trying to run in these shoes."

While I was talking, granddaddy *four eyes* stepped from behind his counter and began staring me from head to toe, with his eyes resting quite comfortably on my bottom. Oh, no he did not just lick his lips. Obviously he needs his glasses adjusted. He could not possibly think he has a chance with me. This old man would give me worms. Just the thought made me shudder … yuck!

I asked again, because he did not reply.

"Excuse me, could you arrange for an electric cart to meet me at the top of the escalator at Concourse D?"

"For you, pretty lady, I can do anything you like, just ask. Let me call my buddy Fred, he should be working the gates. I'll see if he can have a cart waiting for you when you get to the concourse. There ain't much I can do about the plane, though, if you don't make it on time. The next flight to Dallas won't get out of here until eight forty-five PM. I hope you make it, but if you don't, my shift ends around five thirty. Maybe I'll stop by the gate to see if you are still here."

Clearing my throat, I thanked him for his assistance while slowly backing away.

"Thank you so much. I really appreciate you doing this for me, but I do not want to miss this flight. Just calling your friend Fred would be a great help."

Great! There were no long lines through security checkpoints. I barely made it down the escalator to the train when the doors began to shut. I almost landed on top of the people standing in the doorway as I eased myself to the back of the train and held on for dear life. Why did my flight have to leave out of the last concourse and the last gate? I hope gramps called his friend with the cart because there is no way I am going to make it to my gate.

Thank God for small miracles. As soon as I got to the top of the escalator, there was Fred with the electric cart. There was only one small problem. It seemed he had the *only* electric cart, because every blue-haired old lady was on this cart with him. There barely was enough room for me, let alone my garment bag. I don't have to tell you the looks I got when Fred jumped off the cart and helped me on. He was younger than gramps, but only slightly.

SO I WAS TOLD

He too looked me from head to toe. Introducing himself with the broadest smile, I noticed he was missing a few teeth, but obviously he did not seem to mind. With an outstretched hand, he helped me on board.

"Hi, I'm Fred. You must be the lady Larry radioed me about. He said to look for the prettiest lady out here with some red high heels. Well I guess that must be you, because you sure are cute with those red shoes on. Here, let me help you up."

This did not sit well with *Miss Grace*, one of the blue haired ladies who I had to sit next to. She was watching us both while holding her bag with a dog's head sticking out of it.

"Excuse me, young man, if you could stop with all *your* socializing, I need to catch my flight and you are wasting time. I'm sure that young woman doesn't need all that help."

"Yes, ma'am! As soon as everyone is seated, we will be on our way. Don't you worry; I will get you to your gate on time. Just hold on."

I guess it just wasn't meant to be. Not only did he have to stop at what seemed like every gate on the concourse, but he also had to go to the opposite end first. Just my luck, miss blue haired, *meany* was the last one off the cart, and it took all he could to help her down. The poor man really struggled trying to help all three hundred pounds of "Miss Grumpy Grace" down with her doggy bag and whatever kind of small snippy creature she had inside.

By the time Fred was able to turn the electric cart around and make it to my gate, I could see the plane slowly backing out of the ramp. The gate agent was closing the door and her assistant was packing up her tickets. Flight 285 to Dallas Fort Worth was history, and I, Carly Collins, was stuck in Atlanta.

Don't get me wrong, I love Atlanta. There is absolutely nothing wrong with the city. I was moving here very soon, but sitting in Hartsfield Airport waiting for four and a half hours for the next flight with no guarantee I would get on was not how I wanted to spend my evening. Besides, this now sets me back on all of the things I needed to do before work tomorrow morning. If it wasn't for Taylor and those ugly shoes she just had to have at that very moment, I would be sitting comfortably in first class with my second drink and maybe having a decent meal. What makes matters worse, I know my cousin, and those shoes will be back at Saks by the end of the week.

115

BRENDA L. WATERS

Maybe I will go to the airline's VIP II Lounge; being an executive does have some privileges. I'll ask for directions, because no matter how many times I have been here, I am still not familiar with this airport.

As I approached the agent at the desk, I could see her talking loudly on the telephone. "Gayle, child, let me tell you about this fine brother I saw last night at the club. Not only was he tall, he had a body to die for. He was wearing all black with one of those really tight sheer T-shirts. Yeah, yeah one of those muscle shirts. Well, that is a good name for them, 'cause you could see every muscle and cut in his body. He didn't have a six-pack, honey it was more like a twelve pack. Did I mention those jeans he had on his tight ass?"

Now I know girlfriend saw me walk up to the desk. Why did she turn her back to me? The telephone cord was almost wrapped around her body.

I politely asked, "Excuse me, could you tell me where I might find the VIP II Lounge?"

Did Miss Thing stop talking and turn around? Oh no! She kept right on talking as if I wasn't there

"Uh huh, that's what I said. Girl, he brought me a drink and told me he worked for BellSouth. He said he was some kind of engineer."

I cleared my throat and thought maybe it was my imagination. This heifer did not just look me up and down and turn her back when I asked her a question. Yep, that's it! It was all in my head.

Again I addressed her, "I'm sorry, I know that's really an important conversation, but could you take a moment, and give me some quality, not to mention appropriate customer service? I would really appreciate it, and I know your supervisor would be so pleased as well."

Well that did it, because she whipped around so fast my eyes blurred. I could see in her eyes she wanted to use that fabulous "B" word, when I pulled out my badge with my name and credentials. After she read it and realized who I was, that phone call ended very abruptly.

"Girrrlll, I gotta go."

Without a good-bye, Miss Chatty slammed down the phone and gave me the phoniest smile. She apologized, and explained she did not see me walk up to the desk.

I stopped her midsentence and told her all was forgiven and in the future try not to make it a habit of not *seeing* the valuable customers who were *essential* to her income. She then directed me to the lounge. I chuckled to myself as I descended the escalator to board the train. *Now that must be a miracle.* She can read minds. I thought she said she did not see me, let alone *hear* me ask where the lounge was located. Thank God it was on the same concourse as the next flight for Dallas.

As I entered the lounge, I was met at the door by the concierge. She too was on the telephone, and I could tell by the smile on her face and the way she was leaning onto the desk this was not a business call. But, unlike Chatty Cathy, she hung up when she saw me enter. With a warm smile, she politely introduced herself as Yvette and asked for my garment bag to hang behind the desk. She handed me the ticket and asked if she could be of assistance. I told her I missed my flight to Dallas and would have to wait four and a half hours for the next one. Yvette smiled and said she was sorry that happened but encouraged me to make myself comfortable. She took my cocktail order and proceeded to open the inner doors, letting me know my drink would arrive shortly. I thanked her and made a mental note of her name to make sure her supervisor was told of her excellent customer service. It did not matter that I worked for the airlines, this was the kind of employee we all could use in the company.

No sooner did I step into the lounge a heavy, grey haze of tobacco, cigar, and pipe smoke smacked me square in the face. My lungs started to burn, and my eyes felt like they were frying in my head. How in the world did people smoke, let alone be in a room filled with the foulest-smelling odor in the world? There was no way I was going to spend four and a half hours in this room in my new Chanel outfit. It would cost me a fortune to have the cleaners get the smell out. I proceeded to walk backwards out of the lounge, covering my mouth with the back of my hand. I almost walked over Yvette, who was escorting an elderly gentleman into the lounge.

Yvette politely asked, "Ms. Collins! Is there a problem? Your eyes are watering and you don't look well. If you stand right here I can get someone to assist you. I just need to seat Mr. Fredrickson at his table."

I responded between my coughing and trying to catch my breath, "Thank you, Yvette! Don't worry, it's all the smoke. I will have to speak to operations about the ventilation in the lounge. It is dangerous in there!

Mr. Fredrickson chuckled and told Yvette he could find his table.

BRENDA L. WATERS

He smiled and apologized, "I guess I am just as guilty," as he pulled out the biggest, fattest cigar I have ever seen. "But I do understand what you mean about the smoke. I have complained about it myself, but what can you do? Sometimes there is a price for guilty pleasures."

He then took my hand into his and kissed the top of it, giving me a wink as well.

I laughed and told Yvette when she got back to her desk I needed my garment bag. I was going to take my chances at the gate. With a few good magazines and newspaper, I could probably make the time go by.

What is it with all these old me hitting on me today? I mean, it's nice to get noticed, but could it be done by someone at least half their age? Mr. Fredrickson was kind of cute and sweet. He had a head full of white hair and a tan that said he spends quite a bit of his time in the sun. From his clothes and shoes, he looked like old money. It amused me how he gave me that sly wink after he kissed my hand. Just thinking about it made me laugh out loud.

I found my way to the nearest newsstand and proceeded to buy every magazine and newspaper I could carry. The latest *Essence, Ebony, Vogue, W, People*, etc., you name it; I bought it, especially if it was about fashion. There were days I missed my job at the department store, because I no longer got the discount on the latest cosmetics and designer outfits. Now I had to pay full price for my Chanel, Calvin Klein, and St. John's.

Walking for what seemed a mile down the concourse with my bags in hand, I found the perfect place. There was not one person in the entire gate area. I could sit and read or watch the planes come and go with total peace and quiet. Besides, my feet were killing me. When I bought these designer shoes, I was told no matter how long you wore them your feet would never hurt, just like walking on air. So untrue! If the sales clerk feet had my day in these shoes, she would have amputated them by now; they were throbbing. I was afraid to take them off, because I did not think I would be able to get them back on. What the hell! I would take my chances. With no one around, I could lean back and give them a nice rub down.

I took a seat facing the window and had the best view of the airplanes arriving and departing Atlanta. The heat from the sun shining through the window felt wonderful on my face and aching feet. It was like my own personal sauna. I sipped from the bottle of water and laid out my reading material. As I began reading I realized this was the first opportunity I could sit and think for some time; my mind began to wander.

I started to reminisce about the telephone conversation and meeting I had with Detective Ramirez. Deeply within my thoughts I remembered feeling like it was the longest flight I had ever taken. The closer I got to the airport the more apprehensive I became. I remembered the detective telling me to come directly to Dallas and not to leave the country. I thought that was rather odd to say, unless the police department had investigated me and knew my work took me out of the country from time to time.

What had Carl done, and how did it involve me? Regardless of what Detective Ramirez said, I had seen enough cop shows to know they say one thing and do another. The next thing you know, you are face down in the streets, arms pulled behind your back with your butt up in the air exposed for all to see. My flight arrived on time, and as soon as I exited baggage claim to get a taxi, I saw a door open from a shiny black car. Out stepped the most handsome man I ever-laid eyes on; he was tall and gorgeous. I noticed he was walking towards me as if he knew who I was.

As he approached, taking off his sunglasses, he called out my name, "Ms. Collins? You are Carly Collins, aren't you? I am Detective Raphael Ramirez with the Dallas police department."

He was showing me his badge as he introduced himself to me. I was startled to see him here at the airport, but tried to maintain my cool.

Clearing my throat, I replied, "Yes! I'm Carly Collins. You did not have to meet my flight, detective. I had every intention of coming to the station. I was just about to get a cab."

"Well, I can save you the fare. My car is right here, and we can talk on the way to the station. I want to assure you, Ms. Collins, you are not under investigation. Mr. Yates confessed, but we need to put some of the pieces together. My team has been handling this case for some time. Here, let me take that bag. It looks heavy."

Handing him my luggage, I noticed the way his muscle rippled under his jacket when he lifted it and placed it in the trunk. Thank God he did not drive a standard police car, but a black Impala. This must have been his car. I could not believe the police department would issue this kind of vehicle to their officers.

He must have noticed me looking at the car when he said, "Don't worry, Ms.

BRENDA L. WATERS

Collins, I thought it would be best to pick you up in my car than a squad car. I did not want you to feel embarrassed or have everyone staring at you. Besides, the back seat of a squad car is not designed for comfort or very clean. I hope you don't mind."

I smiled while thinking, mind, is he kidding? If he had a broken-down Pinto I would go with him.

"No, detective, I don't mind. As a matter of fact, I appreciate you thinking about me. You are right, I have never been in a police car and have no intention of breaking that record."

Taking my elbow and hand he helped me into the seat. As he walked around to get into the car, he took off his jacket. Yep, I was right! There was a body there to die for. I was so going to enjoy this ride to the police station.

On our drive, we talked about everything but Carl. When I asked him about the case, he said he would prefer to discuss that at the station where he could have someone there to assist him with my statement. Again, he assured me I was not under suspicion. They had been watching Carl for some time and knew I was not involved. So we talked about the Dallas Cowboys and other football teams. He was surprised I knew so much about the sport, even though we disagreed on who we thought was the best quarterback and wide receiver in the league.

He parked and walked me into the station. Checking into the front desk, he asked one of the female officers to take me to his office and ensure I was comfortable while he checked on another case.

His office was so tiny; I don't know how this hunk of a man could possibly fit into it. I sat in the chair across from his desk and noticed all the awards and plaques on the wall. Amongst all the scattered papers, next to a coffee mug that looked like it had never seen the inside of a dishwasher, I noticed a picture on his desk of the cutest little girl with a beautiful woman kneeling beside her. I picked it up. The child had to be his. She had the same eyes and smile as he, but who was the woman? She was African- American and gorgeous; she must have been a model or something. You could tell even with her kneeling next to the little girl she was tall and slim, model slim. She too had the most beautiful smile, and from the picture, she was very happy. Hmmm! So Mr. Beautiful is into sistahs. When he walked into his office, I was startled and almost dropped it on the floor. As he came around his desk, he took the photograph out of my hand. He looked at it, smiled, and placed in its original spot.

120

SO I WAS TOLD

I apologized for snooping around on his desk, but I noticed the picture and could not help but admire it.

"Is this your family? Your wife and daughter are beautiful. There is no mistaking that she is your child. I'm sure I am not the first person to say this. How old is she in this picture? I'm guessing, but about four years old? So how long have you been married?" I asked before he could answer.

He looked at the photograph for a moment and I thought I caught a glimpse of sadness in his eyes.

"Yes, this is my daughter Isabella and you're right, she was four years old when I took that picture. She is six now, going on thirty, if you know what I mean. That was her mother in the picture. She died a few months after I took that photograph--a hit and run accident. Never found the assailant or the car. It was just a blessing Isa wasn't with her when it happened. It took some time, but she now is coping better with her mother no longer being with us. My sister Sara lives with us to help me with her. Isa is my joy. You have to forgive me. I can talk about her all day."

Feeling badly for their loss, I could not help but feel some joy there was not a wife in the picture. One of my girlfriends used to say wives are off limits, but girlfriends are made to be moved. From what I could see, there weren't any other pictures on his desk or walls, so maybe there was no future Mrs. Ramirez on the horizon.

Detective Ramirez sat down at his desk and took out his notepad. He asked me about Carl Yates and our relationship. At the time of the drug bust, Carl told the authorities he knew I was out of town. He said Carl broke down in tears and assured them I knew nothing about this or him having my car. He knew where I kept the spare keys for my house and car and stole both of them. Presumably, he had been staying in my house while I was gone. He told the neighbors he was "house sitting" for me while I was taking care of my family. The neighbors were not suspicious because they knew him and had seen him at my home. Only Phyllis, my next-door neighbor, would have been suspicious but she had been out of town for awhile taking care of her ailing mother.

The detective said Carl was driving my car when he went to buy drugs. This is why I was being interrogated about the situation. When he was arrested, there were one hundred kilos of cocaine in the trunk. The car was impounded and searched; actually, it was dismantled piece by piece. From what Detective Ramirez told me, criminals can find some of the most ingenious places in a car

BRENDA L. WATERS

to hide drugs. With the magnitude of the amount of contraband found, they had no choice but to strip the car.

Detective Ramirez wanted me to look at some photographs of people involved in the drug operation. He wanted to know if I recognized any of them and from where. He handed me the book, and after several pages of not knowing anyone, I came across a photograph that made me gasp. He asked me if I knew the person. The tears clouded my eyes and started to drip down my cheek. He handed me a Kleenex and asked me how I knew the suspect. After I wiped my eyes and blew my nose, I looked up and told him the man in the photograph was Carl's drug counselor. I met him a couple of times when he was suppose to be in therapy. I was so sure he was legitimate; he had all the plaques on the wall and the awards. The office looked like a therapist's office, and he talked the talk. Carl finally let me go with him several times as his support. Once I felt Carl was doing better and off the drugs, I did not feel it was necessary for me to go with him any longer. I was so proud of him, knowing he had kicked his habit, but now to realize I was made a fool of broke my heart. I began to bawl like a baby. I could not hold it in any longer. This was the man I knew I was going to marry and grow old with. I had the names of all our children picked out. I had envisioned us together as a family with people admiring my beautiful children and handsome husband. All those dreams I had are now a nightmare.

Detective Ramirez handed me a glass of water. I drank some and thanked him. I just could not believe this was happening. He told me the man in the picture was indeed a licensed drug rehabilitation therapist, but he also was over one of the largest drug organizations in Dallas. They had their suspicions about him but never could prove anything. With Carl's arrest, he agreed to give up his therapist.

"Ms. Collins, at this moment he and his lawyer are down the hall trying for a plea bargain if he gives up state's evidence against Dr. Conrad Benjamin."

My eyes must have popped out of my head when he mentioned Carl. It never dawned on me to think he would be here in the station.

I replied, "Carl is here in the station as we speak? Does he know I am here?"

Detective Ramirez told me he did. He was called into the interrogation room to speak to Carl's attorney, and informed them I was down the hall when we arrived

"Did he ask about me?"

Detective Ramirez said he did not. I put my head down, closed my eyes, and felt the tears welling up again. He must have known how hard this was for me, because he came from behind his desk and placed his arms across my shoulder. He told me he knew this was difficult. He spoke to people in the condo Carl used to own. They only had positive things to say about me. They too assured him they did not believe I knew anything about Carl selling drugs

I told him I had no idea this was happening. Carl and I no longer worked in the same building and I made it a point not to talk or be told anything about him. I had no idea how bad things had become. This was a man on top of the world who had everything going for him. Now he was a criminal facing federal charges for drug trafficking and possibly spending the rest of his life in prison. This was too much for me to handle. I asked Detective Ramirez if there was anything else he needed. I was exhausted and wanted to go home. I wanted to take a long, hot bath and go to bed. He told me we were through for now and he was very sorry for what he had to put me through. If I would just give him a moment, he would call me a taxi to take me home. He apologized again about my car and told me the department would pay for a rental until I could find a replacement.

He left the room and returned after a few minutes. My taxi would be there shortly and he would walk me out. As we left his office, another door down the hall opened. It was a door I would have to pass to exit the station. Out stepped a man in a grey suit with a briefcase. He was talking to a police officer who was escorting a man out the room in handcuffs and shackles. As the man shuffled out the room, he glanced down the hall towards my direction. He stopped. I was paralyzed. It was Carl, my Carl in those handcuffs and ankle shackles. He saw me, and even from that distance I could see the tears in his eyes. He lowered his head and mouthed, "I'm sorry." As the police officer assisted him down the hall, he looked back at me one last time. I could see the tears streaming down his face. He continued to shuffle further down the corridor, then he was gone. The man in the grey suit must have been his attorney. He gave a nod to the detective and me as he proceeded to follow Carl and the officer.

There were no more tears; I was cried out. Ironically, when I first got the message about Carl, I was so angry, angry enough to kill, but after seeing him like this, my heart broke. It was pity I felt now; deep, sorrowful pity.

Detective Ramirez asked me if I was okay and if I wanted to wait in his office until the taxi arrived. I told him no, I was fine. It was the initial shock of seeing Carl that got me so upset. I did not expect to see him. He said he understood, and if I did not mind he wanted to walk me out. He thanked me for my cooperation.

As we walked out the front door of the station, my cab arrived. Detective Ramirez took my suitcase and placed it in the trunk. He helped me into the taxi and shook my hand, placing his business card in my palm. He smiled at me and told me if I ever needed any assistance or just needed to talk to give him a call. He closed the door and tapped the roof of the taxi. As we pulled from the curb and traveled down the street, I looked out the back window and saw him still standing on the curb looking in my direction. I turned, around opened my hand and smiled. He had put his personal number on his card.

Startled by an overhead announcement I checked my watch and realized I had a few more hours before my scheduled flight departed. Perhaps it was the heat from the sun or just sheer exhaustion but the next thing I knew I had fallen sound asleep and drifted into the most exquisite dream. It was about Detective Ramirez and me holding hands as we walked along a beautiful sandy white beach. We were smiling and looking into each other eyes. He pulled me into his arms lowering his head to kiss me, then all of a sudden there was this smell, this awful horrible odor. It was so strong it almost made me gag.

Slowly opening my eyes and looking down at the floor is when I saw them. There were two huge, dirty, ugly black work boots with only who knows what covering them. As my eyes drifted upwards I noticed the filthy dirty blue work pants with stains I did not want to know about. Over the top of the pants hung a huge stomach, so big it was stretching that poor little button until I thought it was going to pop. The shirt was no better than the pants and shoes with its own dirt, and sweat stains, grease and what looked like old food. More importantly was the smell. I know recognized it. It was a combination of dirt, sweat, never seeing a bar of soap, and jet fuel. If you ever smelled jet fuel, you will understand what I mean. As my eyes adjusted to the light, I saw the toothpick sticking out of his mouth. His nails were so dirty they looked like a French manicure with black nail polish instead of white. His hair was not only unkempt, but probably had not seen a barber's shears in a lifetime. This *thing* was standing over me. I must have scared him, because *he* jumped when I screamed. I grabbed my purse and held it to my chest. I looked around and there wasn't anyone else there, except him and me.

It spoke, "Hi! You sure are pretty when you sleep. I looked up and saw you through the window when I was fueling that plane out there. I told my buddies I was going to come up here and meet you and tell you just that. They didn't think I was going to do it. See, there they are down there."

He then went to the window and waved down. He even gave a thumbs-up sign. When he turned from the window to face me not only had he not seen a shower in a while he hadn't seen a dentist either. He had all his teeth, but they were the color of corn. I didn't think teeth could get that yellow or be that big.

I politely asked him if he could step back. I knew he could tell I was getting nauseated from the look on my face.

He was the most peculiar man I had ever seen, with eyes that looked like a cat. I swear if he had whiskers he would look just like a big old lion. I guess I was staring at his face so long and intently I did not hear him until he stepped closer.

He asked, "Are you all right? I was talking to you asking you your name and you kind of *blanked* out on me. I bet you are still kind of asleep, aren't you? I get like that myself when I've been in one of those real hard sleeps and then wake up. Sometimes in the break room I'll take me a little cat nap and when I first wake up I have no idea where I am. It might take me a minute to pull it all together, you know what I mean? That's probably how you are feeling. You were sleeping kind of hard there! You should be more careful doing that because you never know what crazy person might be out here."

I thought to myself, did he actually say *cat nap?* There, that proves it, my assessment was correct. I shook my head and replied, "I'm sorry! You are right, I guess I fell asleep. It's been a long day. What did you want to know? Oh, my name … It's Carly Collins."

He answered, "Carly! That is a pretty name. It fits you. My name is James Jones Stokes. Nice to meet you. You waiting for a flight or something? Are you leaving or waiting for someone to arrive because the next plane coming into this gate won't be here for another two hours or so? I know because I have to refuel it when it gets here. It's booked for somewhere in South America, but it has to stop in Miami first. You mind if I sit down here?" he asked as he pointed to the seat next to mine. I told him no, but my

BRENDA L. WATERS

head was screaming, *Hell yeah I mind. Go take a long, long hot bath with some soap, see a dentist and a barber, then maybe I'll think about it, fella!*

Just as I was about to reply who should I see walking down the concourse, but Victoria Peterson. It was Victoria's recommendation that helped me get this position with the airlines. I jumped up so fast and quick to get her attention I knocked all my belongings out of the seat next to me. My purse flew open, and everything went everywhere. James was down on his knees before I could tell him he did not have to do that, gathering my belongings from under the chairs and aisle. Kneeling on all fours, I swear he looked even more like a great big old dirty cat.

"I think I found everything that fell out. You sure have a lot of stuff in this bag. If you needed to you could use it for a weapon or something. Why do women carry so much stuff with them?" He replied as he stood with my bag, stuffing everything back inside,

Before he could finish his question, I politely told him, "James, thank you for helping me, but I really need to speak to that woman over there. It was a pleasure meeting you, and you have a great day, okay!"

I hastily gathered all my magazines and garment bag and walked as fast as those three and a half inch heels could move my sore and aching feet. As I was leaving to catch up with Victoria, I thought I heard him ask, "Say, can I have your number or something? I mean, can we talk or maybe go out?"

I politely waved good-bye and ran as quickly as I could to catch Victoria, all the while thinking to myself, *What did I do to deserve this day? From missing my flight to the "cat-eyed" man, could it get any worse?*

I caught up with Victoria. It was great seeing her again and catching up on old times. Victoria told me she finally put in her resignation from the company. She and her husband decided to adopt a baby. The adoption was in the final stages, and she was going to stay home to take care of her new baby girl. Seeing I had a couple hours before my flight to Dallas, Victoria invited me back to her office where we could finish our conversation.

I finally made my flight to Dallas. Thank God I remembered to call for a limousine to pick me up at the airport. On my way home after my second glass of white wine in the limousine, I decided I was going to visit Haley before I moved to Atlanta. It would be good to spend some time with her. She was getting old, and any time I could spend with her was important to

SO I WAS TOLD

me. In the morning I would meet with Steven and discuss the new position. I am moving to Atlanta.

The drive to Jackson, Mississippi was a long one, but with my brand new BMW and the surround sound system the time went by quickly. It was Whitney Houston, Luther Vandross and me on the highway.

I pulled up to the house, and no sooner did I get out of the car than the front door opened and there was Haley waiting with her arms open. It was good to be home. It's funny, I never thought I would feel that way after leaving, but it truly felt good to be there and in my *grandmother's* arms. I was tired and she knew it, so after some small talk, I went to my old room. Nothing had changed from the time I left it to venture out on my own. The same curtains at the windows, the same quilted bedspread folded back on the bed, even Ethel's doll I had when I was a little girl was propped up in the rocking chair by the window. I was too exhausted to do anything, so I kicked my shoes off and lay across the bed, just to get some rest before I unpacked.

The next thing I knew, the most pleasant smell was waking me out of my deep sleep. When I came to my senses, I realized it was morning. I had to have been exhausted, because I was still in my street clothes. Grandmother must have peeked in on me, because the family's handmade quilt was laying across me. Oh, how I loved that quilt and the story told about how it was made. She told me it was made from old scrapes of cloth and materials handed down from generation to generation in the Dodson family from the beginning of slavery. Knowing her ancestors had worked on this quilt, adding their own piece of history to it, was inspiring. What began as a quilt for a baby's crib now was able to fit a king-size bed. Grandmother said she was going to teach me one day how to quilt so I too could add to the story.

Each distinctive smell brought back memories. There were plenty of fond times of Haley and me in the kitchen cooking all my favorite foods for breakfast. There would be grits with eggs and hickory-smoked bacon fresh from the butcher. A pot of the strongest black coffee percolating on the gas stove. When I was little, I would stand and watch the coffee bubble up in that tiny glass bulb on the coffee pot's lid. Grandmother said that's what gave the coffee the deep, rich flavor. All I know, you can't find a cup of coffee to match it today. Breakfast would not be complete without a plate of homemade buttermilk biscuits with honey or canned jam sitting next to the pitcher of fresh-squeezed orange juice. I was truly at peace and excited to be with Grandmother Haley. As I settled in at the breakfast table, she pulled up a chair with her cup of coffee, staring into my eyes and holding my hand. She told me to tell her everything going on with me.

"Carly, I know you better than you think. I want you to tell your grandmother what is happening in your life and don't tell me, 'nothing, everything is fine'. I know there is more to you just wanting to move to Atlanta. You loved Dallas. You blossomed there and became the beautiful woman you are. So you better start talking, because I'm not moving from this kitchen table until you do."

I sat there in silence as she continued, "Baby you know you can tell me anything. I am here for you. Whether it's good or bad, it makes no difference to me. Once you let it out, it no longer has any claim on you, honey. So, tell me, we can sit here all day if needed. I love you for wanting to come home to see me before you moved to Atlanta, but this is more than just a friendly visit, isn't it?"

With that, I decided to tell her everything. We talked about Carl and Detective Ramirez. We laughed until we both were wiping tears from our eyes about the day I had in the airport trying to get to Dallas with all the men hitting on me, especially the "cat-eyed" man. We talked about my past, present, and want I wanted for my future. We even talked about Aunt Helen and Ethel and how they affected my life, all the secrets and lies I was told.

Once I started talking, it seems I just could not stop. In between bites of food and crying into my napkin and laughing, I think grandmother had a least four or more cups of coffee. The hardest part was telling her about Carl and how hurt I was. Haley knew how I felt about him and the dreams I had for our future. She hugged me tightly when I cried about the pain and deception, stroking my head and telling me all would be right. She said the pain would pass and I would realize it was his loss, not mine and just to let it out so it no longer could claim me and keep me from finding love again.

So we sat and talked. I don't think there is a therapist in the world that could do what my grandmother did for me that morning. I was blessed for sure.

My planned short stay in Jackson turned into two weeks, and it was the best time I had in a long time. Haley needed help with getting rid of John

Henry's belongings. It had been over a year since he died, and Haley had not touched a thing. She too felt it was time to let go, so we packed up his belongings. Some things we gave away to the few remaining friends he had. What was left, we donated to the church and the Goodwill.

Before we knew it, the week had come to an end. With the time spent working in the garden picking vegetables she was going to pickle and can, baking cakes and pies she still made for the church Sunday dinner, the experience felt new. Even though these were things I had done with her as a child with all the complaining and groaning, I was too happy to be here with Haley helping her. She even kept her promise and taught me the art of quilting.

It was time for me to leave. I made a promise to grandmother to keep in touch more and let her know how I was doing in Atlanta. With hugs, kisses, and tears, I left with a basket full of "goodies" she packed for me. There was no way I could deny her. The word no was not acceptable. Although it did not matter to her, I gained at least ten pounds eating all that down-home cooking while I was there. When I told grandmother I probably would have to buy a whole new wardrobe when I got to Atlanta, she laughed it off and told me I was too skinny anyway. She said those extra pounds did me good, "Besides, bones only look good on a skeleton."

As I drove into Atlanta, I was met with the beautiful skyline of the city. My excitement was an understatement. I could not wait to become a part of this town. My cousin Taylor told me so much about the places to visit. It was required I visit the *King Center* and the birth home of Rev. Martin Luther King Jr. Then there was the house of Alonzo Herndon, the first black millionaire in Georgia, not to mention all the malls for shopping and most importantly, the numerous nightclubs where she swore some of the finest men hung out. If you wanted to party, Atlanta was the town to do it in. She told me it was going to be her job to make sure I was at all the right places, meeting all the right people.

Before I knew it, it was Monday morning, and here I was stuck in the famous Atlanta traffic. I guess Taylor forgot to remind me about that. Just as I was passing the Grady curve, the telephone in my car rang. Who would be calling me at this time and for what? No one had this telephone number. I could not remember it myself and had to contact the dealership in Dallas

BRENDA L. WATERS

to get it. The sales agent who sold me the car wrote it down on the back of his business card, along with his own number in case I got *lonely* in Atlanta and wanted to talk to someone. As he handed me the card and expressed his concern, I glanced at the picture of his lovely family framed on his desk; wife, kids, and even the family dog. I am sure from the look on my face he knew I was not going to get that lonely.

"Ah, is this CC?"

"Pardon me, I think you have the wrong number."

"Is this Ms. Carly Collins?"

"Yes it is, and.."

"Well hello, pretty lady. I bet you have no idea who you are talking to. This is James Jones Stokes. I met you at the airport—you know, when you were waiting for your flight to Dallas when you were sleeping."

I took the phone from my ear and looked at it. No, this was not happening to me all over again. This man was not calling me. How on earth did he get the this telephone number? I very politely asked, trying to control the rage, "Hi James, how are you? May I ask how you got this number and why you are calling me?"

James laughed. I guess he felt what he was about to tell me I would find amusing. "Do you remember when you dropped your purse and I helped you find your things? Well, after you left the gate to go meet with your friend, I was walking away and saw a card lying on the floor by your seat. I picked it up and it was a card from a BMW dealership in Dallas. There was a note on the back with your car's telephone number on it. I tried to catch up to you, but you were gone by the time I got to the end of the concourse. You know what? I felt it like it was meant for me to find the card with your number. The last thing I asked you as you walked away was could we stay in touch, but you must not have heard me. You just waved back and in a flash you were gone. Yep, it was fate or something, I just knew it."

I had to find a way to let this him know: first, this was not fate, second if I was desperate and he was the last man on earth …

"Mr. Stokes, thank you for finding my card. I could not find it and had to contact the dealership to retrieve my telephone number, so knowing you have the card and number is a relief. You never know what *raging maniac* could have found it and contacted me. While I was driving to Atlanta

I just could not imagine what I did with that very personal and private information."

"You are here in Atlanta?" he asked. "See, that is what I am talking about, *fate*. I just took a chance to call hoping you would be in your car there in Texas. I never thought you would be here in Atlanta. How long are you going to be here? Can we get together, maybe this evening when I get off work? We can go to Piccadilly's for dinner or something."

"Thank you for the invitation, but that would not be possible. Mr. Stokes, I am flattered by the fact you would like to take me dinner, but I have to be honest with you. I just got out of a relationship, and right now I am not interested in dating anyone just yet. So, I hope you would not be offended if I ask you not to contact me again, and if you still have that card, *burn it*."

With that I hung up my phone and immediately called information to find the nearest BMW dealership to have my number changed.

After I hung up and calmed down, I had to laugh. When I thought about him that day at the airport and with him calling me, I began to laugh hysterically. I must have looked a sight, because when I glanced over, the woman driving in the lane next to me was looking at me as if I had lost my mind. I just shrugged and sped off.

I pulled up to the main headquarters of American South Airlines. Entering the gate for the executives, I turned down the lane and found my assigned parking space. There it was, my name on the sign, "Carly Collins, Junior Vice President of Marketing." I parked my BMW and exited the car in my new St. John's two-piece suit, and the sharpest black patent leather Feragamo three-inch heels Neiman Marcus sold. With my leather briefcase in hand, I entered the building.

Welcome to *Atlanta*. Welcome to the new *me*.

CHAPTER TWELVE

WISHFUL THINKING

Standing on the balcony of my condo, I was taking in the moment with coffee in hand, watching the traffic flow beneath me. There were couples walking their dogs, people jogging, businesses opening; city life everywhere.

I have been here almost a year and a half, but had never taken the time to enjoy this city. I loved my position with the airlines, and my support team was a joy to work with. My boss was wonderful, although I had my trepidations at first when I met her. It had been several years since my superior was a woman, and there are times when women working in close proximity can be worst enemies. It had been a *positive* experience working under the leadership of Sheila Montgomery; I could not ask for a better boss. She expressed to me in our first meeting that her door was always open.

The constant traveling in and out of every time zone imaginable was difficult and grueling, yet exhilarating at the same time. I wasn't expecting this much responsibility and travel when Steve told me about the position, but now that I was here, I could honestly say it was fulfilling. The trips to develop some of our new markets like Bangkok, Tokyo, Buenos Aires, and Johannesburg were interesting and rewarding.

BRENDA L. WATERS

A few days after one of my business trips to Bangkok, my cousin Taylor and I meet for dinner at a popular restaurant in Atlanta.

"Carly, what have you been up to besides work? When was the last time you went out on a date? What happen to that good-looking cop you met when your man Mr. Carl went to jail?"

"Are you talking about Detective Ramirez?"

"Yes, the one that you never got up the nerves to call."

"Well Taylor, a few months into my new position I was in California on a business trip. While I was there I decided to give him a call. He was very surprised to hear from me. Raphael told me how much he had wanted to talk to me but under the circumstances was not sure *I* would want to communicate with him. After all, he was the man whose investigation led to Carl's prison sentence."

"*What?*" Taylor screamed so loud that every patron in the restaurant turned to look at us.

"I can't believe this. You did not tell me. What did he have to say?"

"Raphael assured me his interest in me outweighed the past. Carl committed the crime, and his sins were not mine."

"So how long have you guys been talking?"

"The first phone call lasted from sunset to sunrise. I could have bought a brand new pair of Jimmy Choo's for that phone bill, but it was worth it. Every time I tried to end the call, Raphael found a way to keep me on the phone. Since then we have talked about so many things, including the situation with Carl and what happened at his trial. He did tell me Carl was remorseful about his involvement with the drugs, and stuff. Raphael told me he felt badly for him. He was saddened how someone that successful and bright could get caught up in something so destructive. He felt, unlike the other thugs and gang bangers he arrested for drugs and crimes, Carl did not have to go down that road. He was smart and had achieved much in his life, but there is always that thin line between a genius and criminal."

"Carly, I am not interested in the jail bird; what's really up with you and the cop?"

"Talking to Raphael was easy. He made me laugh and smile when he told me stories about his daughter Isabella, who really has him hooked. She is beautiful and smart, and little boys were trying to call her on the phone. It was a blessing his sister was there with him, because many times he wanted

SO I WAS TOLD

to wring their necks when they rode their bikes and skate boards past his home yelling out her name."

"Don't care about Isabella either, what about you and the man?"

"Well he asked if my travels ever brought me back to Dallas. I told him I had been back a few times for meetings but always left the same day. I could tell by his question he wanted to ask me more, but he did not push it. We talked about my job and Atlanta. He seemed pleased when I told him I had not gotten out much or wasn't *dating* anyone. He too was not involved, because of Isabella and his work took up most of his time. I realized how long we had been on the phone and recalled I had an early flight the next day. I told him I had to go

"He then asked, 'Carly? I feel we have gotten to know each other pretty well, and I would like for this to continue. Would it be all right if I came to visit you in Atlanta? I have to take some time off in a few weeks and Sara wants to take Isabella to visit her grandparents in Miami for her school break. Do you think …?'

"Before he could finish I answered, 'You want to come and see me in Atlanta? Is that what you are trying to ask me? I love talking to you on the phone, but it would be *so* much nicer face to face. Let me know when you can make it so I can rearrange my schedule.'"

Taylor placed her fork down and asked, "So what you are you saying, Carly, is this man you have not seen in ages, but talk to almost every night is finally coming to see you? Girl, we got to get out of here. We got to make plans for this momentous occasion. Come on, let's get the check and go."

It was about midnight when I left Taylor's. On the way home I thought to myself, the weeks cannot go by fast enough for Raphael to get here. Our conversations were not lengthy every time, but when we did they were exciting and engaging. I found myself thinking about him at the oddest times and places. I would be in a board meeting, or sitting at my desk, and his face would pop into my mind or maybe bits and pieces of our conversations. I wondered had he changed any. I hoped not. I mean, he was *fine*. The only thing is sometimes the imagination can make the reality a lot more than what it is. Had I changed any since he last saw me? I don't think I have. I let my hair grow, I have lost a few pounds, but in places I could afford to. One thing I did find time for was the gym, but I had slacked off a few days. What if I was not what he remembered me to be? What would I do then?

135

I arrived earlier than normal to the office and waited for my meeting to begin. I suddenly found myself lost in thought about Raphael and me.

"Carly, are you all right?"

I heard my name called and realized it was Sheila asking me about the projections on the next deadline for the new office in South Africa.

I told Sheila I was fine, took a sip of my water, and headed to the conference room for the monthly department meeting.

At the end of the meeting, Sheila stopped me before I left the room.

"Carly, is there something we need to discuss? You were not yourself today. Is everything all right? The one thing I can count on is you are always on top of your game, but today you seemed distracted. I noticed how quiet you were; usually you are the first with the questions and the last with the suggestions."

"Sheila, really it's nothing. I'm fine. I think it is just a little jet lag from the last trip. I haven't been able to catch up with my sleep. Rest assured, tonight I am turning in early and getting all the sleep I can. I will be back to myself in the morning."

Sheila replied, "Good! Get some rest, Carly. I depend on you and want you to be at your best. Everyone is talking about you in this company, and I want you to go to the top. You are an asset and have the ability to do things many of us aspire to achieve. On a personal note, I want you to know you can come to me to talk. You remind me of myself when I started with this company—all work and no rest. It is good to be ambitious, but you need a balance as well. It took me a long time to realize that but I have a husband who reminds me of what is truly important. Find time for yourself. Get out and enjoy this city. Meet someone and start a life. We can have it all if you know how to juggle. Now get out of here and go home. I will see you in the morning."

Sheila's words stayed on my mind until all I saw were the back of my eyelids. If I was not talking to Raphael, I was fantasizing about him all hours of the night. I scratched off the days on my calendar until his arrival; he would be here in a week, and I wanted to be ready.

I made an appointment with my hairdresser Robin to get a fresh perm and color. I found her by accident while shopping at Neiman Marcus. We both laughed while standing in the mirror with identical dresses. Robin was petite with slimmer hips but bustier than I. She had a gorgeous haircut, and

SO I WAS TOLD

I complimented her. We both thought each other looked nice in the dress, but I had to admit it was made for her. She and I started talking across the dressing room, and that's when I found out she was a stylist. Robin said she would love to do my hair. As we left the dressing room, she gave me her business card.

Because Raphael was arriving on Thursday afternoon, I called Robin to make an appointment that Tuesday.

"Robin, I know this is last minute, but I really need to get my hair done, Raphael will be in town on Thursday, and girl, I really need you to do your magic."

"Who is Raphael? Is he someone special?"

"I will explain when I see you, but you have to schedule me first thing Thursday morning."

"I will call my first client and reschedule her; she owes me a favor anyway for being two hours late for her last appointment."

"Thank you, Robin. You don't know how much this means."

Thursday could not come quick enough. In a few days I would be seeing my Raphael, and nothing could calm the butterflies in my stomach. I was anxious, nervous and giddy.

I arrived a few minutes early for my appointment, and Robin was excited to see me. She had me change into a smock. As she began to apply the perm she inquired, "So, Carly, who is the lucky man that got you up this early to get your hair done?"

"His name is Raphael. We met in Dallas a few years ago."

"Okay, tell me more."

I told her the whole story about how we meet. She thought it was amazing and wanted to make sure I looked gorgeous when he saw me. Robin swore Atlanta was a cliquish town and the competition was fierce for a man. She thought the ratio was seven to one for every single black woman to a single *straight* black man.

Robin was engaged to be married at the end of the year, so she was very happy to be out of dating scene. She met her fiancé Charles at the grocery store late one night. It was one of the few stores that stayed open twenty-four hours. She had a craving for Haagen-Daaz ice cream. When she got to the freezer section, he was standing in the door with his hand on the last carton of her favorite, *rum raisin*. He looked at her, she looked

137

BRENDA L. WATERS

back at him, and he handed *her* the carton of ice cream. That was two years ago.

As I left the salon with my new hair color and style, I felt very pretty. I headed to my favorite store at Phipps Plaza for some last-minute shopping. Before heading to the airport, I stopped home to change into the black dress I had just purchased for this special occasion. Raphael's flight was due in at 6:41 PM. Shopping always seemed to calm me when I was stressed—that is, until I get the bill the following month and wonder what in the world was I thinking! Thank God I had a job that could afford me some indulgences.

I watched the aircraft as it taxied to the gate. In just a few minutes he would be walking off the plane and standing in front of me. After so many late night phone calls, endless notes, we were about to be face to face. My palms were beginning to sweat. One minute I was sitting down, and the next I was up pacing, looking out of the window. Pretty soon someone was going to call the police or security thinking there must be something wrong with me.

"Why am I acting like a schoolgirl instead of the mature, high-powered executive that I am? Why? I'll tell you why! I am scared out of my mind, that's why! I have fantasized so much about this moment, I feel like I am going to pass out."

They opened the door to the jet-way to allow the passengers to deplane.

Now, I have to think quickly! Where should I be standing when he comes out? I can't stand too close to the door because that would make me look too desperate. I don't want to be too far away either; not to give the impression that I was not excited to see him.

As I craned my neck to look down the jetway, I did not see him. Raphael had told me he changed some but refused to send an updated picture. Since he wanted to be that way, I did not send him one of me either. He would just have to rely on his memory, like a good detective.

The wait seemed like an eternity until I saw the first passenger coming through the door. I started to pace again, thinking maybe this was not a good idea. What if Raphael and I were disappointed when we saw each other again?

What if he was not the man I remembered? It was a good thing he reserved his own accommodation. While I was pacing with my head down,

SO I WAS TOLD

I heard a man's voice say my name. I stopped abruptly, turned, and standing before me was Raphael.

Raphael dropped his bag and pulled me into his arms; it felt good. It seemed like we were glued to that spot, neither one wanting to let the other go. He bent down and grabbed his bag while holding my hand. We then moved through the crowd to the other side of the concourse for privacy. I could not take my eyes off of him; he had really changed, but for the better.

The Raphael I remembered was clean shaved with short hair. He wore a button-down white shirt, sleeves rolled back off his wrist, with a tie mostly undone. He had on khaki pants and black laced-up shoes. His tweed sports jacket was thrown over the back of his chair. As handsome as he looked then, he reminded me of a typical cop.

This man standing before me had long, dark, shoulder-length hair that fell across his chiseled face. His dark, heavy brows and long, thick black lashes were accentuated by a rich, bronzed tan. Across his cheekbones you could see where he might have been sunburned or chapped by the wind. There was a faded scar across the corner of his right eye. Above his full, luscious mouth was a thin mustache and a goatee below his lip that flowed into an unshaven jaw line. When he pulled back his hair, I noticed a small gold hoop. He was wearing a faded blue jean shirt opened at the collar with a custom-made jacket, designer jeans, and a pair of black alligator cowboy boots. I noticed both women and *men* checking him out as they passed us by.

I began to feel nervous, a bit uncomfortable by the way he was staring at me as we walked down the concourse. My mind started racing.

I wonder what is going through his mind. Is he disappointed? Am I the same woman he remembered? We only saw each other that one time even though we kept in touch.

"I'm glad to finally be here." Raphael whispered. "You look beautiful, just the way you were when we met." He then leaned over and kissed me lightly on my cheek.

For a moment I could not get my mouth to move. I told myself to breathe, to relax. This man just told you everything you wanted to hear.

I replied with a smile, "I'm glad to see you as well. You changed some since the first time I saw *you but* I like your new look."

As I reached out and touched his unshaven cheek, I said, "I *really* like it."

Raphael chuckled and said, "Uh yeah, just a bit. It's something new for now."

Pulling out of the airport, I entered the freeway and drove to mid-town, where Raphael's and had made hotel reservation. While we were stuck in traffic, I asked him, "Do you think you would be more comfortable staying with me instead of at a hotel? *You will have plenty of privacy and the comfort of home.*"

Raphael laughed aloud when I made this dramatic point. He resisted at first, but after much persuasion, he relented.

"I would love to stay with you if it is not an inconvenience."

Glancing at him, I replied, "I would not have offered if I thought it would be any trouble."

Raphael looked at me and smiled, while nodding his head. Driving through town, he commented on the skyline.

"I came here briefly years ago for some training exercise but did not have an opportunity to get out and enjoy the city. Some of my buddies back home said that for every church building in Atlanta, there probably was a strip club to match it."

The traffic was nauseating, so I decided to take the street route down Peachtree Road to get to my condominium.

"Carly, did we not just turn off another Peachtree something? I know this is the fifth Peachtree you have crossed over since we left the airport."

"Sweetheart, there are probably one hundred and fifty different Peachtree streets in Atlanta. If you didn't know your way, you could get lost for days."

We started talking about his daughter Isabella and how she was growing into a young lady. The way he smiled, you knew he was a proud father. When I asked about his work, he changed the conversation. Maybe he thought the subject of Carl, my ex-boyfriend, would come up, and he did not want to discuss this.

We arrived at my condominium. Pulling into the courtyard, we were met by the parking valet.

"Hello, Ms. Collins, would you like me to park your car in the garage or leave it out?"

SO I WAS TOLD

"Hi, Stuart. You can leave it out. I am going up with my guest, but we will be coming back down soon. Thanks for asking. By the way, how is school coming along? You should be finished with your finals. Have you heard from any medical schools yet?"

"Yes ma'am, I got a letter of acceptance from Morehouse yesterday. My folks are thrilled. I'm pretty excited myself. Thank you for asking."

"That's wonderful, Stuart. I'm happy for you."

When we entered the building, I could tell Raphael was impressed. Crossing the lobby to the elevators out the corner of my eye, I saw the concierge lean over and watch us walk to the elevator.

When the doors opened, there were several people inside. There stood the little white-haired woman the size of a small child who lived down the hall with her yapping terrier; my neighbor across the hall, who on every opportunity asked me out; and the fashion model *wannabe actress* who never speaks to anyone who lives on the floor above mine. When my neighbor saw me, he folded the newspaper he was reading and greeted me.

"*Hello Carly! How are you?* I haven't seen you in the building lately. I asked Karen when the last time she saw you. Been keeping busy? You know there is a great play in town this weekend ..."

Before he finished, I politely introduced him to my houseguest. There was no way he did not notice Raphael. Even the little white-haired woman noticed him, and so did her dog. She and that animal stared up at him the entire time we rode the elevator to our floor. I believe not only was she smiling, but so was her dog. The fashion model-actress nearly caused a major wind storm by the way she was batting her false eyelashes at Raphael. He smiled and said hello. I thought she was going to pass out.

"Hi, Duncan, good to see you too. This is my friend Raphael."

Raphael turned and extended his hand. When Duncan took it, I could tell Raphael gave him a firm handshake. He smiled and said, "It is a pleasure meeting you."

With that, he turned facing the elevator doors and firmly placed his hand on the small of my back. The remainder of the ride was in silence. Duncan resumed reading his paper. The model-actress stopped batting her lashes. Only the little white-haired lady and her dog remained staring up at Raphael. When the door of the elevator opened, Raphael stepped back to allow the others to exit.

BRENDA L. WATERS

Entering my home, he stopped in the center of the great room and looked around. He walked to the full-length windows, which gave him a view of the city. The luxury of being on the top floors not only gave me more space, but also a breath-taking view every morning and night. Sometimes at night when I could not sleep, I would stand on my balcony, and it almost felt like I could touch the stars they were so close.

He said, "Your place is really nice. When you told me you moved and bought a new home, you did not tell me about all this. I can see why you had to have it. The view is unbelievable."

He stepped from the windows and walked towards me.

I replied, "Glad you approve. Come on, let me give you a tour. You are my first official overnight guest. I want you to know where everything is so you can make yourself at home while you are here."

As we walked throughout my home, he complimented me on my artwork. I had a mixture of African, Asian, old, and contemporary art scattered throughout the house. My floors were hardwood with Persian rugs in the dining and great room. I grew up in a home with the most beautiful hardwood floors. My Aunt Helen thought it was a crime to cover them.

Raphael and I walked throughout the house as he admired the décor of each room. He felt there was a nice feminine- masculine balance. I thanked him for the compliment but could not take all the credit. My interior decorator was a man, and he made many suggestions when he was furnishing the home. I showed him to the bedrooms I thought he would be most comfortable in. It had the same view from the balcony as the master bedroom.

I saved the kitchen for last because Raphael told me how much he liked to cook. Walking into the kitchen, he stopped, turned around and nodded his head in approval. He ran his hands across the Jenn-Air stove with the chef's hood. He admired the dual oven with the confectionary setting, and the wide doubled door Sub-Zero refrigerator and freezer. I also had a separate ice-maker and wine cooler built into the lower cabinets. The middle of the kitchen had an island with a dual eye range, but was mostly a grill with another larger chef's hood. To the right of the grill was a separate stainless steel sink and cutting area. I think this impressed him the most.

SO I WAS TOLD

All the countertops were 3 ¼-inch-thick, dark gray granite with marbling. My cabinets were a deep rich cherry wood with open-faced doors for my china and stemware. To the left of the refrigerator was my empty walk-in pantry and storage room.

He asked with a chuckle, "Do much cooking, do you?"

I laughed and told him, "I think I made toast in here once. Only the coffeemaker gets the most usage."

There are some men I think who would have been intimidated by my home, but Raphael did not give me the impression he was one of them. He admired its beauty and complimented me, saying how my home reflected my accomplishments and my own personal beauty.

"If I may impose, I would love to cook you dinner tonight. I want to show you what a kitchen like this can do. Do you like steak, seafood? I make a mean surf and turf! Is there a market around here? I don't mean a supermarket, but a fresh market. I did not notice one when we were driving. All I saw were grocery stores."

Opening the refrigerator, he looked inside, closed it and laughingly said, "We might need to stop at the grocers, also. Don't eat much, do you? Let me see, I saw a bottle of V-8 juice, some old lettuce, a spoiled tomato, and a sickly, withered cucumber. Maybe a stick of butter and a couple of bottles of champagne. Oh yeah! What's with the nail polish and the bottles of French milled body splash?"

I laughed and told him I had been traveling quite a bit lately and did not have time to go the store, but since he was here we could do just that.

"To answer your question, there is a great market called the DeKalb Farmer's Market. I think you will find everything you need there. On the way home we can stop at the grocers by the house. Oh, by the way, I need to go to the mall to pick up a package. You wouldn't mind stopping there with me, would you?"

He replied, "Not a problem, ready to go when you are. I want to see and do as much as I can while I am here with you. So far, I understand why you like Atlanta. It's a beautiful town."

The sun had set as we finished our meal. Wiping my mouth and sitting back in my chair, I sighed. He had prepared dinner for the two of us. We decided to have it on the balcony off the great room. The evening weather was picture perfect. There was not a cloud in the sky, and the Atlanta skyline was coming alive with all the lights shining brightly like tiny diamonds on a black velvet canvas.

"I complimented him on his *chef's* skills. Raphael, that was the best home-cooked dinner I've had in a long time. Where did you learn to grill a steak like that? The meat was so tender." I took a sip of my red wine and continued, "Not to mention the lobster. At first I wasn't so sure about eating it after I saw it *alive* and knowing what you were going to do to the poor creature. You just don't think about those things when it comes to you on a platter all steamy with a bowl of butter next to it."

He laughed. "Yeah, I thought you were going to have a heart attack when you saw them crawling out the sink. I wish I had a camera for that moment. Isabella would have loved to see it. She would have laughed and called you a *scaredy pants*. I remember the first time I brought lobsters home for Sara to cook. When she took them out of the bags and put them in the tub of wine, Isabella thought they were her new pets to play with. The child is fearless. She wasn't afraid of the claws or anything. As a matter of fact, I had to keep my eye on her. She kept putting pencils and her little fingers into the tub trying to get them to clamp their claws. Isa especially loved what she called their "itty bitty" eyes and the way they moved around on their head. She rolled her eyes around in her tiny little face trying to imitate them. I remember Sara and I laughed so hard when she did that. She called Isabella her *langosta diminuto*—tiny lobster."

I tossed my napkin across the table at him and laughingly said, "Well, Isabella would have been absolutely correct; *scaredy pants* I am. I wanted to ask, why did you put them in wine? But I got a little distracted and lost my train of thought when that really big one tried to escape the sink."

"I can't take credit for that little trick. Sara told me wine gets the lobsters drunk and keeps them from tensing up when you put them into the boiling, scalding pot of water." I shuddered when he said this. Raphael laughed when he saw my face and response.

I said to him, "Remind me in the morning to give PETA a call. I am sure they would *love* to meet you."

"Oh, sweetheart, not just me, don't forget you did *eat* that poor, defenseless lobster. Lest we forget, I think this meal was called *surf and turf*! Hint, hint!

"Okay, you got me there. We'll keep this our little secret. But, I will have to admit, I may think a little differently about lobster the next time I have one. Would you like some coffee?"

"Yes, thank you, and while you are doing that I can ..."

Just as he was about to finish his sentence, I heard the telephone in my office ring. I left strict instructions I was not to be contacted unless it was a dire emergency. I pushed back the chair and excused myself from the table.

"Raphael, I have already put coffee in the pot; just push the start button and it should be ready in no time. I don't think we got anything for dessert when we were at the Farmers Market. You know, there might be some cookies around somewhere.

"Don't worry, it will be fine. Go, take your call. I can sit here and enjoy this beautiful night."

As I walked through the French doors, I stopped and turned to look at him standing at the balcony rail. I nodded my head, smiled and said, "Thank you, God, *you* did good!"

After what seemed an eternity, I left my office with my head pounding from the conference call. I felt bad for leaving him alone for all that time while I was talking with my overseas team in South Africa. I decided I would make it up to him somehow. Perhaps I could get tickets to the Hawks game. After the sumptuous dinner he prepared, it was the least I could do. No wonder I am alone and single. I thought to myself, *all work and no play makes Carly a dull girl any day.*

As I turned the corner, entering the main hallway, it was that sweet smell that stopped me in my tracks. A strong essence of vanilla with a slight almond flavor wafted through the air. I closed my eyes and breathed in the aroma deeply. I walk down the hall with my eyes closed, just allowing the smell to guide me. When I entered the main room and opened my eyes, there were floating white vanilla and almond scented miniature votive candles, each placed in its own water-filled vase on the hardwood floor leading to the master bedroom and bath. I followed the candles to the bathroom and found more candles surrounding my sunken marble-topped Grecian tub. There were candles everywhere. A trail of red rose petals extending from the bathroom door led to the foot of the tub where the finest man in the world was kneeling. He was stirring my favorite almond scented bath oil in the steam-filled water. A bottle of my favorite champagne rested in an ice bucket with two glasses next to it. He was shirtless with his back to me as I entered into the bathroom. I noticed the way the muscles expanded and contracted in his bronzed back and shoulders as he continued to stir the water. He had on his button-front blue jeans and no shoes.

I cleared my throat as I entered the bathroom. With the slight turn of his head, he looked up and smiled. A wisp of his long, black hair fell across his chiseled face, covering his dimpled smile. He straightened himself up and turned to face me. I watched intently as he smoothed his hair back behind his ears and then wiped his wet hands down the front of his pant legs. I noticed how hard and tight his chest and stomach muscles were. Obviously, this man spent quite a bit of time in the gym, or he was blessed with extraordinary genes. Whatever way he got them, it did not matter. I was just glad he was here.

He walked toward me with his hands outstretched for mine, and I noticed the first two buttons of his jeans were undone, causing the front of his pants to slightly open. There was just a whisper of a fine dark line of black hair underneath his navel leading downward into his pants. It was obvious there was nothing underneath those jeans but him. As he walked towards me, I could feel the heat in my body rise. I lowered my eyes, and in a moment I saw his feet in front of me. He placed his hand underneath my chin and slowly lifted my head with his fingers. I could see his mouth coming closer to mine. He licked his lips first; then very gently with only the tip of his tongue, he traced mine.

A sigh escaped my parted lips, and with that breath, he placed his mouth over mine. He kissed me all the while still holding my chin delicately with his fingers. He pressed his lips into mine, with his tongue searching and seeking my own. He increased the pressure as he lowered his hands down my back and gently cupped my bottom. He pulled me so close I could feel *him* grow between my legs, along with the intensity of his own body heat. He pulled from my mouth and lowered his head to my shoulder. Raphael moaned softly as he rubbed my lower back and kneaded my bottom. He raised his head off my shoulder and placed tiny soft kisses behind my ears, down my neck, and underneath my chin. I felt my body sway as if my legs were about to give out from under me. He must have sensed this and lowered his arm around my waist to support me. He chuckled and told me not to worry. He said, "Baby, I got you."

I leaned back and looked into his eyes. I asked, "When and how did you do all this? Was I gone *that* long? Raphael, I am so sorry I left you, but I had to take that call ..."

Before I could finish, he pulled me close and kissed me with an intensity that let me know he did not care how important or how long my conference call was. He had me now, and that was all that mattered. As he was kissing me, I felt his fingers on the buttons of my blouse, unbuttoning each one until my blouse slipped off my shoulders and fell to the floor. He unlatched my bra and pulled it from my body, letting it slip and fall at my feet. He kissed one shoulder, leaving a trail of wet marks across my body, until he reached the other shoulder. I felt like a teenager getting her first hickey. I giggled from the way the hairs on his chin and face tickled. He pulled back from his kisses, rubbed his chin, and asked, "Need to shave?"

"No," I replied.

He then knelt down in front of me and unzipped the back of my skirt. He lowered it down over my hips and helped me step out of it. Standing there with only my panties on, he gently pulled them down my hips and lifted each leg out. When I was completely naked, he picked me up and carried me to the tub, gently placing me into the water. He thought of everything. While I was in the steaming scented water, he sat on the edge of the tub and poured champagne for him and me. He placed the glass into my hand, and with a dimpled smile, he said, "Thank you, Carly, for insisting I stay here tonight. I will do all that I can to be the best house guest you ever had."

I smiled and told him it was my pleasure and I would do everything I could to make sure he enjoyed his stay. With that we clinked glasses and drank our champagne. Raphael took the glass from my hand and placed it back next to the ice bucket along with his. He then reached into the tub and with my bath sponge proceeded to wring the scented bath waters down my back and across my shoulders. Taking the soap from the dish, he lathered the sponge and started to rub my body. I giggled when he washed under my arms and between my toes. I asked him if he was going to join me so I could return the favor.

"No, this is all for you. I took a shower while you were in your office. I had a feeling from the way you sounded on the phone it was going to be a

BRENDA L. WATERS

while before you would be finished. Your timing was perfect. I heard you coming down the hall as I was pouring the bath oil."

"But Raphael, when did you buy the candles and everything?"

"I bought them while you were on the other side of the store buying some lotion. I told the sales clerk what I needed and requested that she place them behind the counter. That's why I went back to the store and told you to wait at the curb with the car. When you opened the trunk, I placed them inside. I brought them in with all the other bags and groceries from the market."

Raphael leaned into the tub and kissed me. He dropped the sponge, and I could feel his hands travel up my legs and over my knees as he slowly parted my thighs. With his thumb and forefinger, he stroked me. He wanted to look into my eyes as he brought me to a climax as he sought and toyed with my clitoris. I had never felt this intense pleasure in my life—not with Mitchell, not with Carl, not with anyone. I could feel my body begin to quiver and shake. As I was about to scream out, he placed his mouth over mine and kissed me deeply. I could do nothing but hold onto his shoulders as he allowed my release. When I was done, he lowered me back down into the water, with his hand holding the back of my head. He rinsed my body, and I stepped out of the tub.

Raphael told me not to move as I stood there shivering in the cold. He returned with a large, fluffy white heated bath towel and placed it around my body. Gently picking me up, he carried me to the bed and unwrapped the towel. He rose from the bed and returned with a bottle of almond scented bath oil he had warmed while he was bathing me. Pouring the oil into his hands, he rubbed and kneaded my body with the skill of a masseuse. As he stroked and kneaded me, he kissed each area he finished. He gently turned me over, and instead of placing the warmed oil in his hands; he poured it down my body. When I thought he was done massaging me, I turned my head and saw him wipe his hands on the bath towel. He looked down at me and knelt by the bed, his face only inches away from mine. With a smile he asked, "Are you hungry?"

I replied with a smile, "Starving, but not for food."

He laughed aloud and told me I needed to hold that thought, because he had something special for me. He rose and left me lying on the bed unable to move and with no desire to do so. I heard him in the kitchen opening and closing the drawers. I listened as he walked toward the bedroom. Entering the room with a large glass pie dish, one large spoon, and napkins, he sat on the bed as I slowly rose up, pulling the bath towel around my naked body.

"Hmm! What is that? It smells heavenly. Is it for me?"

He told me to close my eyes and open my mouth. When I did so, he placed the smoothest, creamiest custard I ever tasted in my mouth. There was a hint of coconut and rum with a caramelized topping. I licked my lips and asked for more. He obliged. When I opened my eyes, he was staring at me. I smiled and asked, "What is this? It's delicious; so rich and creamy. It melted away as soon as you placed it on my tongue."

"It was my mother's recipe for flan, my favorite dessert as a little boy," he said. "My grandmother taught her to make it when she was a young girl in Havana. It's an old family recipe from Cuba."

I thought to myself, *I never liked custards when I was a child. It was the least of my favorite desserts.* I don't know if it was truly the dessert or the man who prepared it that made me want more.

Raphael placed the dish on the bed; leaning on his side, he took a bite. Some of it dropped on his chest. As he began to wipe it off, I stopped him. Looking into his eyes, I pushed him back and told him, "Honey, let me take care of that for you."

I moved closer to him, and with the tip of my tongue, licked the flan off his chest. He sighed and closed his eyes. When he attempted to rise up, I pushed him back down. This time I dipped my fingers into the dessert and placed sticky droplets from his chest to his navel. As I licked the creamy custard off of him, I could see the muscle in his jaws tighten as my tongue touched his body.

When I reached the top of his open, unbuttoned pants, he rose up and grabbed me by my shoulders. He pulled me up onto his body and kissed me deeply. When I tried to pull away and move back down his body, he stopped me. With one swift move, he flipped me over onto my back. He untied the knot I made with the towel and opened it, exposing my body to him. He never said a word as his fingers moved down my body.

Finally he said, "Carly, I want you. It's important for you to know I have not been with anyone in some time, and I never was the kind of person to just screw around. I have a daughter to raise, and I want to be around to do so. Since Isa's mother's death I don't ..."

BRENDA L. WATERS

He stopped talking and moved off the bed walked to the window and peered out. Running his fingers through his hair, he turned from the window and said, "I don't want you to think I have been a saint or monk since my wife died. I have dated and been with someone, but it was not serious. I was careful and made sure I was protected."

He then proceeded to walk back to the bed with his arms folded across his chest. "I did not come here to do this, I swear. I just wanted to see you and spend time with you. You have been on my mind so much; Sara got tired of me talking about you and told me to do something about it. I did not want to intrude or make you feel pressured. That's why I made reservations at the hotel."

I slid off the bed and walked toward him. Standing in front of him, I looked into his eyes and undid the remaining buttons of his jeans as I slowly pushed them down his slim hips, removed each pant leg until he was free from them. Taking him by the hands, walking backward, I led him to the bed. He gently laid me down as he rested his body on top of mine. He cupped one breast in his hand while gently stroking and suckling the other. He made me sigh with each pull and tug on my nipple, then proceeded to do the same to the other. I reached out to touch him but he moved my hand away and shook his head. He raised his head from my breast and proceeded to kiss me down my body as he held my hands over my head. He rested at my navel, gently using the tip of his tongue, tracing around the edges. With his leg, he parted my thighs and moved his body to the end of the bed. Kneeling at the foot of the bed, he softly kissed the inside of my thighs and with each kiss moved closer and closer to where I wanted him the most.

His mouth and tongue were soft and hard at the same time. I never felt a sensation like this before. With each stroke of his tongue, he followed with a gentle kiss. The pleasure was more than I could take. Raphael must have sensed how close I was to climaxing. He raised his head, and where his mouth had been, he inserted his fingers. With each thrust of his hand, the feelings intensified. It was more than I could bear. He knew I was about to climax again. Without stopping, he moved onto the bed, his fingers continually pulling and thrusting inside of me. His mouth found mine, and with this kiss, my body convulsed and shook. I could not stop. I pulled from his lips and clung to him. He held me tightly until my body stopped quivering. Raphael then gently laid me down upon the bed. My breathing

SO I WAS TOLD

was deep and hard. My hair was damp, and my body felt cool. When I opened my eyes, he was leaning over me smiling.

I could not speak, but I knew what I wanted. I reached for him. I could feel his hardness within my hands. I grasped him firmly and proceeded to stroke and knead him until he was full and pulsating. I could feel the blood rush into him as he grew longer and heavier. He lay back onto the bed and moaned deeply. Raphael placed his hand over mine and said my name, but then he did something that surprised me. I knew he was about to *release*, but he stopped my hands. He slowly opened his eyes as he rose from the bed. He pulled me into his chest and kissed me.

"Carly, I want you more than I have ever wanted any woman, but this is not the way I wanted this to happen. I did not come prepared, and I will not have you without protection. God knows this is taking all the strength I have not to do this, but right now we have to stop. I am going to take a long, cold shower and sleep in the guest room tonight. "

He kissed me on the tip of my nose and left the bedroom. I lay back down and thought about what had just happened. My body still tingling from the pleasure this gorgeous man gave me. As I was smiling with my eyes closed, reminiscing, I heard the shower in the guest room come on. With a loud cry, I heard him curse and scream. I laughed hysterically into my pillow. He really did take a cold shower, silly man!

Later in the evening, as I drifted off to sleep, I heard the knob on my door turn as the door gradually opened. I rolled over, and when I did, I heard a voice call my name.

"Carly? Are you asleep?" I slowly opened my eyes and saw Raphael standing in the doorway. The nightlight in the hall cast his shadow behind him. As my vision cleared, I saw him slowly enter the room and walk towards me . He had on his robe, and as he approached, he took it off leaving it on the floor in a pile at the foot of the bed. Raphael climbed on top of the bed like a sleek black panther ready to pounce on his prey. There was a wicked smile on his face, and his eyes were emblazed with a hungry passion. I stared into his eyes as he slowly crawled closer to me. As he was coming toward me, he said in a deep, sexy voice filled with passion and desire, "*I want you now*. I thought taking that shower would help, but as I lay in bed, all I could do was think about you laying here in your bed your body so soft, so sexy, *and so wet!* I thought about the way you felt, your smell, the way you taste. I know I told you I wanted to wait, but I can't. I need you too badly."

He threw back my covers and kissed me passionately, his hands caressing my body. With one smooth move, he parted my legs with his and …

Ring! Ring! Ring!

I rolled over and looked at the clock it was 5:00 AM. What was that horrible noise? I realized it was my telephone ringing. I picked up the receiver right before it went to my recorder. I answered half asleep and with a yawn.

"Hello."

"Carly!"

I did not reply right away. The voice on the end of the phone shouted my name.

"CARLY!"

I answered, fully awake: "Who is this?"

"What do you mean who is this? It's your cousin, Taylor. That's who!"

"Taylor, are you aware that it is 5:00 in the morning?"

"Duh! Yeah," she replied.

"Okay! First question, why are you calling me so damn early? Second, where are you with all that noise? I can barely hear you."

"Yes dear, I know its 5:00 in the morning. I am in my aerobics class. How do you think I maintain this gorgeous body? Besides, I have a new instructor and girl, he is fineeeeee! It's worth getting up at 4:15 to be here for him. Forget about *me*, I want to know, where is *he?*" She asked with a whisper, "Girl, is he there?"

"Is he where, Taylor, and why are you whispering?"

Taylor asked, whispering again, "Is *he* there? You know, there *next* to you?"

I rose up in the bed. At this point, I realized I was fully awake.

"Taylor, to answer your question, no, Raphael, is not here in bed with me. He is down the hall probably fast asleep in the guest bedroom. Now, more importantly, I just want you to know I was having the most delicious, fabulous dream, and just about to get to the really good part when it was interrupted with this damn phone call."

"Why is he in the guest room? Did you have a fight? He's ugly, isn't he, not the way you remembered him, right! Girl, I told you to get a picture of him before you got all tied up in him coming."

SO I WAS TOLD

"No, *we* did not have a *fight*. We had a beautiful evening. As a matter of fact it was more than that. He's ... he's wonderful, sexy, gorgeous, and has a body to die for. We made out. Well, not so much *we*, but rather he did things to me, and ..."

"Okay, let me get this right. This beautiful, sexy man whose body *you* saw last night, who did things to *you*, but not *all* things, is down the hall in another room in another bed! I'm confused! Wait, girl, did you start your period or something? God, I hate that. You know that happened to me last week with David, and I was so pissed."

I pulled the receiver from my ear and looked at it. Placing the telephone back to my ear, my cousin was still explaining to me her sexual misadventure with David. At this point, I knew I had to interrupt her or this was going to go on for hours.

"Uh, Taylor! Stop! No, I am not on my period. We did not do *it*, because *we* did not have any protection. Raphael was concerned about this and wanted our first time to be right, you know what I mean?"

Taylor asked, "Is there something wrong with him"?

"*No!* We are being responsible adults, Taylor. Besides, I am not on any birth control, and the last thing I want is a problem. I am sure he feels the same way."

"Carly! What century are you in? You mean to tell me you don't have any condoms? Girl, I keep those things on me. I mean in my purse, in my gym bag, my desk at work, everywhere. You have to be prepared at all times for these kinds of moments. Besides, you mean to tell me *he* did not have any either? What planet are you two from? I don't know any man who doesn't have a jimmy for his johnny at all times, somewhere on him. Did he check his wallet? Did you check yours? Forget that, don't you have some Saran Wrap? Any plastic?"

"Taylor, I love you, but you are *insane*. Why would I have condoms? Do you know how long it has been since I had sex? If I did have them, I am sure they would have turned to dust the minute I used one, and to answer your question, no, he did not look in his wallet. What is this thing with the Saran Wrap? "Ouch!"

"Look! We, I mean *he*, stopped before things got too far along. It was difficult, but I respect him for it. Any other man would not have done so. He was looking out for me and for himself."

153

Taylor replied, "Humph! If you say so, but if he is going to be there all week, you better get to a drug store *today*. By the way, is he still that fine?"

"Fine is not the word."

Taylor chuckled and asked, "How tall is he?"

Hum, I guess about six-foot-two, maybe six-foot-three. Why?"

"How big are his feet?"

"His feet, what about his feet?"

Taylor asked again, "How big are his feet? You have seen his feet, haven't you?"

I replied, "Yes, Taylor, I saw his feet. I guess he's a size twelve or thirteen. I don't know, they looked like big men's feet. What is it with the height and shoe size?"

Taylor asked, "How are his thumbs?"

I replied with a smile, remembering his hands, "Oh, he has nice thumbs."

"Well in that case, dear cuz, when you go to the drug store today, make sure you buy *Magnums*! Got to go, my future baby daddy just came in to start the class. Love you! Call me later. Smooches!"

The week was going by so quickly. It seems like I just picked him up from the airport. We got a chance to go to a basketball game at the Omni. The Hawks were playing the Chicago Bulls. My neighbor down the hall got us courtside seats for a sold-out game. We both had a great time watching the game, and I think Raphael was impressed that I understood the game of basketball. Now football, on the other hand, was not my sport, though it appeared to be his favorite. He told me the next time I was in Dallas he would take me to a Cowboys game. He swore you never saw football until you saw the Cowboys play. After the game, we hung out in Buckhead and went to some of the clubs he had heard about. When we both realized the music was too loud and dancing was not on our minds, we decided to leave and spend the evening somewhere quiet so we could talk. As we were getting into the car trying to figure out where to go, we both agreed my place was best. We could sit on the balcony and have a bottle of wine. It was intimate, quiet, and had a great view.

While we were driving home he asked if there was a drugstore opened on the way. That's funny; I was thinking the same thing. I needed some things, and Raphael said he was out of his razors and other items he forgot to pack. While driving down Peachtree Street, we pulled up to a store that was about to close. We went down separate aisles. A young woman was stocking the shelf when I discreetly asked her where the birth control items could be found. She told me they were just around the corner, on aisle three near the end. I thanked her and with the bath oil and cotton balls in hand I turned the corner. To my surprise, there was Raphael with not only his razors, but also a rather large box of condoms in hand. When he looked up and saw me, we both burst out laughing. We laughed so hard that the young lady who helped me peeped around the corner and asked if everything was all right. We both shook our heads and laughed some more.

I said to him, "Well I guess it's true great minds do think alike. I think I will leave this up to you, but may I suggest the *Magnums* instead."

He looked at the box he had in his hands, placed it back, and picked up my suggestion. Holding hands, we left the store with the products and the biggest smiles on our faces.

The night before he was to leave, I made reservations at my favorite restaurant in Midtown. It was small and quaint, but had the best Italian food. It was perfect. While at dinner, I noticed Raphael was rather quiet. I asked if there was something bothering him. He smiled.

"It had be a long time since I have had this much fun and hate for it to end. But, some things may change rather abruptly in my life when I return to Dallas. What I told you about Sara taking Isabella to my parents' home in Miami was partly the truth. Isa is on her break from school, but there is more to it. I wanted Sara and Isabella to go to my mom and dad to stay for a while. Sara has temporary custody of Isabella while I am away.

I frowned and cleared my voice. "Away, what do you mean away? Raphael, are you in some kind of trouble? What is this about?"

He could tell by the concern in my voice I was scared. He took my hands and held them tightly. "No, I am not in trouble, I have a new assignment. This explains my new look. I wanted to see you before I go undercover to help the FBI with their efforts in busting the Mexican drug cartel. I was selected by the bureau to infiltrate a new and dangerous crime family."

While he was here in Atlanta the FBI and police department were

BRENDA L. WATERS

setting him up to be portrayed as a "dirty cop." Only his captain and partner knew he was going undercover. The rest of the police department was told he was under review by their internal unit for suspicious behavior and was on extended leave. To ensure his safety, only a select few knew what he was doing. The FBI and his superiors made sure his name and picture were never connected with the drug sting that arrested Carl. It was because of his work with the drug bust that he was selected to work with the bureau.

Tears welled up in my eyes. What is it with me? As soon as I think I have found the right one, they have to leave. I asked him while pulling my hands from his, "You mean they could not find anyone else to do this? You are right; you do have a child to think about, but what about us? Maybe I am being a little selfish here, but I am not going to let some foolish pride stop me from telling you this really meant something to me. *You* mean something to me. Don't I count in this, or were you just lying and this is about you having a last fling in case you don't make it?"

I realized that was the wrong thing to say the minute it came out of my mouth, but I was scared and angry. "Raphael, I did not mean that. I hope you know that. I'm just …"

"Carly, you don't have to apologize. I know who you are. I'm the one who is sorry. When the FBI came to me about this, you were just a thought, a mere fantasy. But since that first phone call from you months ago, and me being here with you, this is the hardest thing I have ever had to do. I gave them my word, and I want to do this. If this turns out the way it should, it will help me in my future. Not just for me, but for my family, even for ---

I could tell he wanted to say more, but he stopped short. He pulled back in his chair and asked if we could leave. He summoned the waiter and paid the bill. When the waiter returned with his credit card, he rose and helped me from my chair. We left the restaurant without saying a word. He gave the valet the ticket for my car, tipped him, and when we were both buckled in, he raced from the parking lot. We drove home in silence. When we made it to the garage, he pulled into the space, parked the car, and we exited. The night doorman greeted us and opened the door. Raphael pushed the button for my floor, and when the doors shut, he leaned back on the wall with his head down, his legs crossed, and his arms across his chest. I stood there with my back to him, watching the numbers go by as we made it to my floor. When the doors opened, I could not move. I felt his hand on the

156

SO I WAS TOLD

small of my back as he gently guided me out of the elevator, took the keys, and opened the door.

It was dark inside; I had forgotten to turn on a lamp. It probably was a good thing, because I did not want this man to see the tears that were beginning to fall from my eyes. As I was about to walk down the hall, he stopped me. He turned me around to face him. My eyes had barely adjusted to the darkness, but I could make out his face from the little light shining in between the closed blinds from the full moon. His face was so beautiful. I raised my hands and caressed his cheek. He took my hand from his face and kissed the inside of my palm. He held my hand to his mouth for a moment as he pulled me into his arms. He bent down and placed his head on my shoulder and said, "Carly, I am sorry. I am so sorry I came here. I am sorry for all of this. If I knew this was going to mean so much to me, if I had any idea you were going to affect me like this, I would not have come here, I swear to you. Please forgive me. I just did not know. You were not real to me. You were just an idea, my 'what if.' I can't begin to tell you what I am feeling. The only thing I know I can do is show you."

Before I could reply, he raised his head and kissed me. I could not stop the tears. He kissed each tear that fell from my eyes while holding my face in his hands. Between the kisses, he begged me to stop crying and told me he would be all right and will return to me.

A fury and hunger seem to possess us as we began to tear off each other's clothes. We fell against the wall and knocked over the vase on the hall table. On our way to the bedroom, we left a trail of clothes along the way. Making it into the bedroom, Raphael picked me up into his arms and laid me across the bed. He kissed me and caressed me all over. I could not get enough of him. I needed to feel him, to taste him, to have him. I reached for the drawer on the nightstand, opened it, and handed him the little gold wrapper. He pulled back from me. Taking the foil packet in his hands, with a swift pull tore it open. I watched as he unraveled the thin wrapper down himself and before I could take my next breath he was inside of me. I was ready, and so was he. He made love to me that night like no man ever had. As we drifted off to sleep, he held me tightly. I could feel his breath on the back of my neck with his arm around my waist, holding me. If only I could keep this moment, but for now it would have to be a memory to hold until

BRENDA L. WATERS

he returned. I said a prayer, asking God to protect him and keep him safe not just for me, but for his beautiful little girl—his love, his life.

A cool breeze moved across my face and woke me. The bed felt cold; I realized I was in it alone. I reached over to where he had been and it was bare. The memory of last night filled me as I lay there, unable to move, knowing this could be the last time we spoke or saw each other again. I replayed the conversation over in my head. It did not make it any better trying to rationalize his decision. The only thing I knew I could do was to pray for his safety and that of his family. I felt the breeze again and this time noticed the French doors to my bedroom balcony were open. As the curtains swayed in the breeze, I saw him standing on the balcony. The sun was beginning to rise over the horizon, and the sky was coming alive with its magnificent shades of purple, orange, and blue. He was standing there with his jeans on, shirtless and shoeless. He was holding onto the balcony with his head down into his chest.

I sat up in the bed and pulled my knees up to my chest. Raphael on my balcony with the sun rising was my moment to keep forever. He lifted his head and turned his face toward the sky. His long hair falling down his shoulders and moving in the wind made my heart skip. When he lowered his head, I saw him raise his hand and place it on his forehead, to his chest, across each shoulder. I then realized why he was there and what he had been doing. He was praying. When he turned to enter the room, he saw me through the parted curtains and he smiled. He came through the doors and stood at the side of the bed. He removed his pants and climbed back into the bed, pulling me down beside him. His body was cool from being outside, but it felt *so* good. He shivered slightly, and as he turned over, he snuggled closer, pulling me into his body until his was wrapped around mine. He moved my hair and kissed the back of my neck. I yelped when he slid his legs between mine and I felt his ice cold feet. He chuckled and apologized for putting them on me.

As his body temperature began to rise, so did mine. I wiggled closer to him until my bottom was snuggled into his crotch. I could feel him become aroused and his heart beat faster. Every time I moved, so did *he*. Raphael placed his free hand upon my hip to still me. He whispered something into my ear in Spanish and then kissed it. When I asked him what he was saying, he laughed and told me if I didn't stop moving, I would surely find out.

I laughed and turned over onto my back with him at my side. He took my hand into his, pulling it towards his mouth and kissed each finger. He stopped at my middle finger and asked me about the ring I had on.

"What a beautiful ruby ring. I noticed you had it on the day I met you, and since I have been here you have never taken it off. It looks very old."

I pulled my hand away from his lips and held it up in the air. Looking at the ruby ring, I began to sit up in the bed with Raphael down by my side. He was looking up to me when I told him what I knew of the ring.

"This ring belonged to my Grandmother Marie. It was given to her by a man who loved her deeply, but she could not be with him. She was married to my grandfather at the time with children. I don't think she and my grandfather were getting along, or maybe she was no longer in love with him, I don't know. Back in those days, there was no such thing as divorce. I believe the man she loved was also married and had a family of his own, but he told her if she ever needed him, she was to send this ring and he would be there. It was found by my Aunt Martha in a box grandmother hid with a letter he had written to her about how much he loved her and wanted to be with her. Ethel, my mother, gave it to me one day out of the blue. She told me the story, but I don't know if it is true or not. So much of my life has been lies and stories; sometimes I don't know what to believe. Ethel is one to exaggerate at times, so who knows. It is a beautiful ring, though. On the inside is an inscription."

I took the ring off and handed it to Raphael. He looked inside the ring and said aloud the inscription, *Forever.* "What a beautiful thought, *Forever.*"

He took my hand and placed the ring back on, and kissed it.

I sat there looking at my hand. I looked down into his face, bending over, I kissed his lips. Pulling me back down into the bed, he held me. Quietly we both drifted off to sleep, knowing in a few hours he would be leaving to return to Dallas, returning to a life of uncertainty for him and for me.

Over the intercom, the gate agent was calling for the remaining passengers to board.

"This is the last and final call for all passengers to board flight 752 for Dallas Fort Worth."

BRENDA L. WATERS

Raphael and I were standing at the window looking at the plane as the few remaining passengers were scrambling to make the flight. He picked up his bag and turned to board. We walked holding hands toward the door with the agent checking the boarding tickets. There were a few people ahead of him as I stood by his side. I touched his arm and stopped him. A man standing behind him grunted and walked around him. Raphael stepped out of the line, placed his bag down, and hugged me. As I pulled from his embrace, I began to remove the ring from my finger. Reaching for his hand, I placed my ring into his palm and told him. "Here, this is for you. Keep this ring and only *you* can give it back to me. So I am going to hold you to keeping it safe, because you know how important it is to me."

I did all I could not to cry as I continued to tell him, "Don't be a hero and do whatever you have to. If you can, call me or write. Give Sara my number at home and work and tell her if she or Isabella needs anything to contact me."

He took the ring from his palm and placed it on his little finger. He kissed the ring and then pulled me into him. He kissed me long and hard.

The gate agent asked if he was ready to board, because she needed to close the door. All the passengers were on board.

He picked up his bags and walked to the door, handed her his ticket, and proceeded down the jet way. He stopped mid-way, turned, and looked at me. He smiled, turned, and continued toward the plane.

I walked to the window and stood watching until the aircraft left the gate and taxied down the runway. There was no one at the gate except myself and the gate agent who was preparing for the next flight to arrive. I stood with my hand on the window and watched the plane and the man I ...

I said to myself, "No, Carly, don't think it, don't say it."

I turned from the window and left the gate.

CHAPTER THIRTEEN

AM I GROWN YET?

In one week I will be thirty years old. Just the thought of it makes me want to pull the covers over my head and stay in bed forever. I have to get it together. All I do is work and think about *him*. It has been a month, and I have not heard from Raphael, and there is no way I can contact him. I spoke to his sister Sara a week ago, and she too had not heard a thing. Before he left, Raphael and Sara explained why he was leaving to Isabella, without divulging too much information that could put her life in danger. When he finished, Isabella hugged him, then said, "It's okay *Papi*. You are doing something good for all of us by putting the bad people away forever, just like the stories you tell me. Then it will be safe for "Tia Sara" and me-for everyone. I will keep our secret and won't tell anyone, not even my friends, okay."

Raphael was on his knees when he was talking to her. When finished she hugged him tightly around his neck and gave him a big, noisy, wet kiss on his cheek—their special kiss.

Sara told me to not worry and be strong. She was putting her faith in Isabella, and I should too. There is something to say about the undying faith of a child, because Isabella was keeping her strong. I thanked her for the

BRENDA L. WATERS

support and promised to keep in touch. I again reminded her if they needed anything—anything at all—to call me.

After we hung up, for a moment I did feel better, but unlike a child, I knew the danger he was in. There was nothing I could do. This was a horrible feeling. Once I got out from under the claws of Aunt Helen, I swore I would always have control over my life and destiny.

So how am I going to spend this birthday? Right here! Right under these covers, with maybe a pint of ice cream and cake feeling sorry for my miserable self. Aunt Helen told me once when I did something, thinking I was *grown*, that until I turned thirty years old, I was not grown at all. Well that day is coming, and I still don't feel it. I feel just like that same sad little girl that day after she whooped my butt.

I began to feel a big cry coming on. As I reached for the Kleenex, the telephone rang.

"Hello."

On the other end was my cousin Taylor.

"Carly! What is *wrong* with you? I can hear it in your voice. Girl, are you over there crying or something? Please do not tell me you are over there in bed sobbing. What the hell are you crying about? It is a beautiful day. Saks and Neiman Marcus are having the most fantastic sales starting today, and you are over there in your fancy home boo-hooing into those six hundred threaded sheets, about what?

"Oh, let me guess! It's about *him*, isn't it? *Carly, honey*, you have to get over *him*. *Look*, the guy was all that and then some, but you should have known someone who looked as good as did would not want to be tied down to just one woman. Girl, he probably hooked up with someone as soon as he got on that plane. You should be glad you got to spend some time with his fine ass, *and* got a piece of his *ass as well*! You know what I mean?"

Taylor continued, "Men come and men *go*. You just got to be ready when the next one flies by, that's all. Get your sticky paper out and be ready, honey, because somebody will be buzzing by just so you can snatch him up. That's *my* motto and *you* need to embrace it, *but you can't do it if you are over there with the covers over your head, crying.* Get up! I know exactly what we are going to do today. I will call the girls, and we are going to drive out to Chateau Élan and spend the day getting *beau-ti-fied*. Then when we are all fine and done we are going out clubbing tonight. We are going to meet some

SO I WAS TOLD

good-looking brothers and have a great time. When *was* the last time you were in a club? Don't answer—probably since the time of the *disco ball*.

"Un-uh, oh no cousin, you are *too* young to be doing nothing. How are you going to find or meet someone if you stay locked up at home or work all the time? All you do is go to work, get on an airplane, get off the airplane, go home, and then do it all over again. Oh yeah, in-between you do get your hair done and go shopping. I don't know *why*, because no one sees you but the flight attendants and the people at the hotel. I bet you don't even go out to eat when you're working, do you? All you do is go to your dull meetings and then back to your room and order room service while you watch TV, right?"

I stopped Taylor before she continued and told her if she was trying to cheer me up, she needed to work on it. If I wasn't going to cry, I surely was about to now after she told me how pathetic my life was, regardless of how successful I am.

I did not tell Taylor or *anyone* about Raphael and his assignment. I thought it would be best if I gave the impression he never contacted me after the time we spent together. I knew this would make sense to my cousin and most people. Taylor is right about one thing—a man as good looking as Raphael would not have a problem drawing attention from anyone he wanted. It just *pissed* me off; Taylor did not think someone like me could hold onto him. What is it about family being the ones who know how to throw the daggers, and how deeply to twist them just enough to draw blood, but not kill you? They have to save something for the next time, don't they?

I know Taylor loves me and has my back, but this was more about *her* than me. She's had plenty of heartache with one man after the other, so this tough *act* is nothing more than that, an act. I am five years older than Taylor, and unlike her, I am not interested in marriage or a family. If there is any clock ticking for me, it is only the one by my bed. If it happens, it happens; if not, then so be it. So listening to Taylor, I tried not to take her unsolicited advice to heart. It actually made me chuckle because if it was her and not me who was with Raphael, *she* would have jumped, screaming from the top of her lungs, off my balcony if she thought he had dumped her.

"Taylor, you are absolutely right. Chateau Élan is a wonderful idea, and since it is my birthday next week, *you* are going to treat me. You make just as much as me being the high-powered investment banker, dearie.

"Oh, by the way," I asked with a chuckle. How are your finances? It would be more fun to take a limousine than drive. We can have champagne on the way, and since this was *your* grand idea, you can call everyone and tell them to meet here; let's say eleven-thirty."

She agreed to make all the arrangements. Since she knew one of the top executives of the company, she could get us in without a reservation at the last minute. She just wanted me to get out from under the covers and get ready.

"Taylor," I said, "I want the *royal* treatment."

I hung up the phone laughing, because I knew the look on her face. If there was one thing I could say about my cousin, she did have a big heart. She would give you the shirt off her back if you needed it; just don't expect it to be her expensive designer one.

Stepping out of the limousine with Taylor and her girlfriends, we entered Chateau Élan. This truly is a beautiful place, so serene and peaceful. They have the finest spa, a beautiful golf course, an exquisite winery and restaurant, as well as a four-star hotel. With the combination of French provincial mixed with a bit of Southern charm, it makes a fantastic getaway. This is exactly where I am going to bring my team on our next employee appreciation day. I have to make a point to thank my cousin for the idea. After signing in, we all went to the lounge and changed into our robes and slippers.

This is heaven! Lying here in the steam room, I am letting go of all my fears and worries about Raphael. Just as the steam is releasing all the toxins from my body, I am going to do the same with my thoughts. Taylor told me this was my day to enjoy, and that is exactly what I am going to do. After this magnificent steam, I am going to have my entire body exfoliated, oiled, and massaged; whatever, this place has to offer I am getting it. Taylor let me pick and choose what I wanted. I basically told them whatever is on the "a la carte" is what I wanted. My goal was to leave refreshed, shiny, and new.

The best part of it all is being here with Taylor and her wacky girlfriends. I never thought I could laugh so hard or be so shocked by three women in my life. There is Lennox Hickson, Taylor's partner at the investment firm. She is divorced and has two little boys. Her ex–husband is a former NBA basketball star who she found out was *gay* in the worst possible way. It took

SO I WAS TOLD

her a long time to overcome the deception, but now they are good friends. She can talk freely about the situation, but that kind of hurt doesn't go away easily.

Then there is Ava Anderson. She is an attorney with a small but promising law firm. Ava is one of those people who has what they call *book smarts*, but when it comes to common sense, absolutely none. It's a good thing she is a tax attorney, because she would have made a lousy defense or prosecuting attorney. If you have a sad story, please don't tell Ava. She will take in any stray dog if she could, and I just don't mean the four-legged kind either. Her taste in men would have all of us rolling our eyes. Taylor would have to come to her rescue many a night when they were out. Ava is all of our *pet* project. She is a beautiful person, but God help her when it comes to men.

My favorite friend of Taylor's is Katelyn Jackson. She is an executive with Coca-Cola and oversees their philanthropic department. She comes from a very wealthy family in Atlanta, what we like to call "old money." Her father is a retired obstetrician-gynecologist and is a descendent of one of the original families who founded downtown Decatur, a neighboring city of Atlanta. There is a wing at the Emory University Hospital dedicated to him and his family; so, I guess I don't have to tell you Katelyn's father is white. Her mother is black and a Spellman College graduate. Her parents met when her mother was doing a fellowship in neurosurgery at Emory. From what Katelyn told me, it was love at first sight. It was difficult at first with his family, but they grew to love her mother and accept her as part of their family. When Katelyn and her brothers, Michael and Justin, came along, her father's family was overjoyed. One thing her mother made sure of was that Katelyn and her brothers knew and understood regardless of their mixed blood, they were black. It was important for them to understand their heritage and foundation.

Like me, Katelyn was all about business. She could have been a fashion model with her beauty and height, but she was not stuck on herself. Her mother and father instilled in them to always help those who are less fortunate. On the holidays before they had their own family dinner and gift giving, they all would spend time at a shelter feeding the homeless. Her dad would even see some of the pregnant woman there to make sure they got some kind of prenatal care.

BRENDA L. WATERS

When Dr. Jackson practiced medicine, twice a month he volunteered his services at his office to women without income or insurance. Many of these women would never have seen a doctor or gotten any care without his assistance. He felt it was what he was supposed to do. Medicine for him was not about the income and prestige; it was truly about helping others and bringing life into the world. For Katelyn, overseeing a department within a major corporation whose mission is to help others was her destiny. Since her arrival, the company's charitable endowments had doubled. Her good looks and charisma made writing those fat checks painless.

While having our manicure and pedicure, we sipped on champagne and ate strawberries dipped in chocolate. Taylor thought it would be a good idea to keep the limousine for tonight since she wanted to *club hop*. That way we would not have to worry about enjoying ourselves and figuring out who needed to stay sober to drive. I don't know why she thought this would have been an issue, since we all knew I would have been selected as the designated driver whether they asked or not. There was no way I was leaving my life in the hands of one of these women after a few drinks.

On our way back to the city, we decided to go to the new club down the street from the Fox Theatre. Taylor went there last week for happy hour and said she had the best time. All the movers and shakers of Atlanta were there. There were times my dear cousin was the biggest snob, but I loved her anyway. From the art world to the jocks, everyone was hanging out at Jazzy's Jays.

After that, we went to a club in a strip mall on Piedmont Avenue that had live entertainment. This was Taylor's favorite weekend hangout. She dated one of the owners and had carte blanche. Even though they were no longer an item, they still were good friends. As a matter of fact, she was his son's godmother.

Taylor was right, this place was jamming. I never saw so many Mercedes and BMWs, not to mention hair weaves, in all my life. Yep, she was on the money, looks like a few celebrities and politicians were here tonight. As we entered the club, there was barely standing room, least of all a table that could accommodate us. I peered across the room as a group of people were leaving.

"Taylor, I see a table over by the bar. Grab everyone, and I will go over to claim it. You were right, this place is fantastic. I had no idea it could hold this many people. From the outside it looked so small."

Taylor replied, "If you got out more, you would know there are many fabulous places like this in this city. Isn't it fun? Have you ever seen this many gorgeous men in *your* life? Look over there, now that is what I am talking about. *Girl*, I think I just felt my ovary release an egg. He and I would make *pretty babies together.*"

"Taylor, hold on to your ovary and your egg. I think I saw a very large gold band on a very noticeable ring finger. "

Taylor did not seem to mind, because the next minute she was pinching my arm about someone else. I had to admit there were some handsome men here tonight. Black, brown, white, tall, and even some vertically challenged. A few caught my eye, but I just wasn't interested. I did not share this thought with Taylor, because the last thing I wanted to hear was her mouth telling me how foolish I was.

Winding my way through the crowd, I made it to the table just in the nick of time, before another group of women got there. As I took my seat, I politely told them some friends of mine were on their way over. I suggested that we could share the table if they could find additional chairs. I guess that didn't fit her needs, because instead of being grateful for the offer, she looked me up and down, rolled her eyes, and stomped off; weave flowing behind her.

You see, this is what I mean about women being their own worst enemies. It was a good thing Taylor and her crew did not over hear me make the offer. It was hard enough to meet a man by oneself, but a whole table full of women would have been impossible. For Taylor, that would have been just too much competition. No one liked a good fight better than Taylor, but she was also pragmatic when it came to a *whole* lot of single women and a *few* single men.

The hostess finally arrived to take our drink orders. We noticed several men at the bar look our way when we entered.

Once seated, several drinks as well as a bottle of champagne were sent over to our table. From the looks we were getting from other people they noticed as well. The waitress returned to our table with a note she handed to Ava. Apparently someone from the bar sent it over. Trying to figure out

BRENDA L. WATERS

whom amongst the many attractive men sitting or standing at the bar had sent her the note, all eyes fell on Ava.

The waitress said, "The gentleman over *there* wanted me to give you this." She leaned in and politely asked, "Do you want it?"

Ava took the note, read it, and asked the waitress to point out the sender. It didn't take long for us to follow her gaze. There standing at the end of the bar were three of the scraggliest misfits you could imagine. Each one looked worse than the other. Even I had to imagine how they found their way into this place. All the other men here were good enough to walk down a runway, or grace the cover of some men's magazine.

Lennox grabbed the note from Ava and read it out loud as the rest of us tried to compose ourselves.

"Hey, sexy lady! I saw you when you entered. Would you mind if I joined you at your table? A beautiful woman like you should not be alone tonight. You need a *real* man by your side. Just say yes, and I can be him."

Lennox handed the waitress back the note and said.

"Please tell the gentleman the lady said, *hell no.*"

While Lennox and Ava were squabbling over the note, and Lennox's rudeness, Ava went on to tell her, "You should never judge a book by its cover. Just because he is not as good looking or well dressed as some of the men here tonight doesn't mean he did not have a good heart or isn't a nice person."

Lennox proceeded to tell Ava as she handed the note back to the waitress, "Good book or not, that ain't the one you need to read, not tonight, and not while I have a living breath in my body."

Taylor leaned over to me and asked while she was adjusting her eyes to see who sent Ava the note, because one of her contacts had fallen out on the table, "Carly, does that guy look like a great big cat, no, like the lion from the Wizard of Oz to you? He has the *strangest* eyes. Even with my one good eye, I can tell they aren't normal. I swear his eyes look just like that great big old black cat Katelyn has. You know, the one that doesn't like me. She then proceeded to tell everyone to be careful with their drinks and bags, and to help her find her contact somewhere on the table.

The minute she said cat, I realized who he was. He had cleaned up a bit, but it was *him*. I quickly turned my head and with a whisper, I told Taylor to stop.

"You are not going to believe who that is. Remember I told you about the *cat-eyed* man at the airport. You know the one who confiscated my car dealer's business card and called me. Well that's *him* and he has *eyes* for Ava."

Taylor looked at me and then over at Ava, who was still squabbling with Lennox about the note, and burst out laughing. I kicked her leg under the table. "Stop laughing." Just as I was about to tell Ava about him, he appeared at the table. Ava and Lennox stopped arguing. Katelyn, Taylor, and I turned and looked up at him.

His hair was combed, but he still had not seen a barber. Instead of the smelly, stained work clothes and boots, he had on washed-out khaki pants that needed ironing with an orange polo shirt, and an orange and brown tweed jacket that he probably had since high school.

Looking directly at me, he blinked and said, "Hey, don't I know you?"

All eyes turned to me. He continued, "Yes, I do. I didn't know it was you. You hair is different and you lost some weight. It's me, James Jones Stokes. You know, from the airline. That day I met you, I didn't know who you where. My buddies told me you were the new bigwig with the company. I don't read those newsletters they put in our boxes about the company and stuff, but they do, so they knew you. Had I known that, I would have spiffed up a bit before I came up to meet you."

"It was nice seeing you again," I said as I extended my hand. I introduced him to the rest of the group. As he went around the table shaking everyone's hands, he stopped at Ava, held her hand longer, and asked her if she would like to dance.

Ava smiled. "I would love to."

Lennox tried to hold her in the seat with her hands under the table, almost tipping over our glasses when Ava stood up. James grabbed Ava by the arm and helped her steady herself. Ava gave Lennox the meanest, nastiest look possible, turned and smiled at James, thanking him for helping her as they walked to the dance floor.

Lennox looked at me and then Taylor and Katelyn, took a huge sip of her drink, swallowed, coughed, and asked for someone to please explain Ava.

BRENDA L. WATERS

"When I get home, I am going to call her mother to make sure Ava really is a part of the family and not adopted." We all laughed hysterically. Several men took James' idea and asked the rest of us to dance.

When our evening ended, the limousine driver dropped everyone off at my front door. We kissed and hugged and made a pact to do this more often, especially me. Taylor decided to spend the night with me since she was in no condition to drive. She was very pleased with herself tonight. She exchanged numbers with several of the men there and had a confirmed lunch date that afternoon.

I met several men who did their best to persuade me to let them take me out. I took their numbers instead of giving them mine and told them *I* would be in contact. The last thing I wanted was to go through that old dating game. My head and heart just were not into it. I needed more than this merry go round of clubbing and serial dating. This was Taylor's world and she lived happily in it.

While we were getting ready for bed, out of the blue Taylor asked, "Carly, when was the last time you spoke to Aunt Ethel? Her moving to Chicago with Uncle Nate was the best thing she could have ever done. I think we should pay them a visit. I spoke to Brenda, the next doors neighbor recently, she said his health was poor and she was not sure if he would be around much longer. Brenda is the granddaughter of Mrs. Hunt."

I replied with a frown, "Taylor, I know who Brenda is. This is my family as well."

"Anyway, Carly, you know Brenda and I keep in contact. She recently told me Uncle Nate's kidneys were beginning to fail. The dialysis was no longer working effectively because of his poor health and other problems. I know that your relationship with Ethel is strained, but she is your mother and he is our uncle. We should go to Chicago to see them. We don't know how much longer he has, and you should check on your mother."

"Taylor, I do not need a lecture on my relationship with the family, especially with Ethel, but I agree we should visit Uncle Nate if his health is failing. After I get back from my business trip to Paris, I will meet you in Chicago. We could spend the weekend with him ."

Taylor was pleased. As she left the bathroom with me sitting at my vanity, she turned and thanked me for agreeing to go. As she exited, she

170

SO I WAS TOLD

stopped at the door and said, "Besides, this would be a great time to do some shopping on *Michigan Avenue*. The holidays are coming, and nothing is prettier than Chicago during the winter. I'll get my fur out of storage, or maybe I'll buy a new one while I am there. If there is one thing I hate about Atlanta, it's that it never really gets cold enough for me to wear any of my *dead* animals."

I threw my face cloth her way and told her she really needed a crash course in sensitivity training. "Good night, Taylor. You are going to be the first and last in my prayers tonight. Love you, see you in the morning."

Taylor put her hands to her lips and blew me a kiss. I heard her singing as she walked down the hall to the guest bedroom.

My plane touched down at Charles de Gaulle airport in Paris. The company limousine was waiting to take me to the Four Seasons-George V Hotel. As I checked in, I was told there was a message for me in my room. The desk clerk handed me my key and welcomed me to the Four Seasons. Riding the elevator, I wondered what message would be in my room rather than the front desk. If there was something I forgot or Sheila felt I needed for my presentations, the package or information was always left at the front desk upon my arrival.

Handing the bellman my key, he opened the door and ushered me in. There were more than two dozen Chrysler Imperial red roses arranged in the most exquisite Waterford crystal vase. When the light from the window shone on the vase, a multitude of colors filled the room. The bellhop handed me my cosmetic bag and proceeded to take my luggage from his carrier and place it in the closet. I walked to the desk and smelled the rich, heavily fragrant roses. Looking down on the desk, there was a note addressed to me. When the bellman was finished, he handed me my key and wished me a pleasant stay. I thanked him as he closed the door. Sitting on the bed I opened the note.

It read:

Hello Carly,

I hope you like the roses and the other treats I sent you. Sara told me you would be in Paris for work and your birthday. I want you to know I am all right, and I am so sorry I cannot be with you to share this day. I know you are wondering why I have not been in contact with you more than I have. One day I will be able to explain all of this to you, but now I am still asking for your patience. It is difficult for me to contact my family as well. Sara tells me how strong and helpful Isabella has been through all of this. I have you to thank for that, as well as Sara. Isabella told me you sent her the doll your mother had as a little girl. Thank you. I know what it meant to you.

Please know I think about you every waking moment. I miss not being able to hold you, love you, to just be with you. Yet, where I am and what I am doing does not afford me the opportunity to be vulnerable. It could cost me too much. The times we have talked affected me truly. The deeper I get into this, I cannot take the risk. It may be a while before I can contact you again, please be patient. I know it is a lot for me to ask, but please know you mean everything to me.

Hopefully this will be over soon and I can return to my family, to my life with all of you. For now, know you are in my heart and my soul. Enjoy your stay in Paris and your birthday.

Carly, I love you! Please wait for me!

Raphael

I folded the letter and placed it back into the envelope. Walking to the window, I looked out over the city and imagined what it would be like to be here with Raphael. He told me he loved me and to wait for him. I smiled and placed the letter over my heart. Closing my eyes, I breathed in the smell of the roses. I turned from the windows and taking my makeup bag into the bathroom, I stopped at the door. Leading from the door to the tub was a trail of red rose petals. Next to the tub was a bottle of French champagne and one long-stem champagne glass. On the edge of the marbled tub was a bottle of my favorite almond bath oil. I laughed aloud and shook my head. He had not forgotten a thing. The only thing missing was him.

CHAPTER FOURTEEN

IT COMES IN THREES

My flight touched down mid-morning at Chicago O'Hare International Airport. It had been a long and exhausting flight. My trip to Paris was wonderful. There is something to say about French cuisine and the people.

It is amazing to me how small most French people are, especially the women. Yet everything is made with real butter, not margarine. Perhaps their ability to remain petite with all the riches of Paris has to do with everyone walking or ride bicycles. I understand why it is called a place for lovers. As you walk throughout the streets, you see couples everywhere kissing or holding hands. Young, old, gay, or straight, it did not matter.

I asked my waiter one evening, while dining on the hotel terrace, what was it about Paris that makes people fall in love.

He laughed and said, "Mademoiselle, it has to do with the freedom of Parisians to enjoy good food, good wine, and good sex, no matter if you are young or old."

I laughed and told him I had to agree. I never ate a better meal or enjoyed a bottle of wine more than I had here in Paris. Now about the last part, I had to leave that to another time perhaps.

He smiled, bent forward, and whispered to me as he nodded in the direction of a very handsome, yet older distinguished man sitting across from me, "Mademoiselle, that might not be a problem either. I could not help but notice Monsieur across from you this evening while you were dining. He could not take his eyes off of you. We Parisians have an eye for beauty, *tally vous?* If you like, perhaps I could send a message to have him join you for café." He said this with a sly wink.

Clearing my throat, I thanked him for the offer, but told him my check would be sufficient. I was returning to the States and had a late flight to catch. Smiling, I told him, perhaps another time.

"Oui, Mademoiselle. Another time perhaps, indeed. I hope you have enjoyed your stay with us. I will have it momentarily."

As he turned from the table to leave, I glanced up and noticed the gentleman across from me smile and nod his head.

I gave him a nod in return, smiled but shook it back and forth to tell him, "No thank you."

He smiled, shrugged his shoulders, and continued to enjoy his dessert and coffee.

Exiting the restaurant as I passed my waiter, I thought to myself how much of that was a "setup" for me without me knowing. I think Taylor is right about my naiveté. Ah Paris, what a great place.

Taylor was on time and at the curb waiting for me. I heard the car horn and saw her standing outside the door waving in my direction. It was freezing cold in Chicago. I surely hope Taylor brought more than one of her "furry" friends or bought a new one. My cashmere overcoat was not going to do the trick. Gladly, I did not have to stand out here in the cold waiting for her.

Pulling my luggage to the curb, Taylor opened the trunk and met me at the back of the car. She seemed stressed, not herself.

"Hey, Carly, I am so glad your flight from Paris was on time. I went by Uncle Nate's house, and as soon as I pulled up, there was the ambulance there and Brenda was coming out of the front door. He had collapsed and was unresponsive. Brenda thinks it is his kidneys. She went to the hospital in the ambulance with him. I told her your flight was due in and once I got you, we would come directly to Mercy General. Girl, I

SO I WAS TOLD

don't know what we would have done if Brenda was not over there when it happened.

"Taylor, where was Ethel while this was going on?"

"I don't know, Carly. I asked Brenda the same thing. She had not seen your mother in a couple of days. That was not like her to leave without contact information."

It bothered me as to Ethel's whereabouts, but right now, I, like Taylor, was concerned about Uncle Nate.

I swear I think Taylor broke every speeding violation and ran every light to get to the hospital. I had to tell her several times this was Chicago and she was not accustomed to driving on snow and ice, however she got us to the hospital in one piece. The front desk told us he was immediately taken to ICU.

Taylor and I both were in our own thoughts. Mine were mostly on Ethel and why she was not there when Uncle Nate collapsed. She could be forgetful or unconcerned about me, but that was not the case with her big brother. Once they reunited when they were older, no matter where he was, he contacted his baby sister. They did not always agree on her lifestyle, but Uncle Nate was there to help her and vice versa.

We exited the elevator to the dim lights and the quietness of the floor. Except for the sound of machines beeping, and the humming of the respirators, there was little to no talking. We passed a few beds with family sitting with loved ones. One lady was by the bed of an elderly gentleman. She was holding his hands and praying on a rosary. The look on her face as she prayed told me this was someone she loved dearly.

Taylor and I reached Bed 4, and there was Uncle Nate with many tubes attached to his frail body. This was not the robust man I knew as a child who would swing me around on his arms or buy me my favorite popsicles on those hot days in Mississippi. I barely recognized him. While the nurse was taking his vitals, Brenda stood next to the bed. He had slipped into a coma. Brenda told us his kidneys had completely failed, he was in respiratory distress, and his heart was very weak. The doctors did not feel he was going to make it through the night. While Taylor and Brenda were hugging, Taylor told her how grateful we both were for her kindness and care of our uncle. I walked over to his bedside, bent down and kissed him on his cheek as I held his hand. I whispered in his ear that Taylor and I were here with him. For a moment, coma or not, I could have sworn he squeezed my hand. I felt a peace overcome me and told him to rest. I stepped back from the bed to allow Taylor a moment with our uncle.

Turning to Brenda, we hugged and I too thanked her for her goodness. I told her I felt badly for all the times I did not make a point to come visit Uncle Nate and now it was too late.

She assured me my uncle knew I loved him and was grateful for my financial support. Even though I was not there physically, I made sure his life in Chicago was comfortable. Without the money Taylor and I sent to Brenda for him, she could not have done all the things he needed with his home and hospital care. He loved to hear about Taylor's adventures and was proud of our successes. His only sadness was neither of us married or had children, but he told her he understood why we didn't, especially me.

Brenda needed to leave and make a phone call to check on her family. She had left them a note telling them what happened to Uncle Nate.

Taylor and I sat on either side of Uncle Nate's bed, holding his hands. Suddenly, we heard him take what sounded like his last breath. The machines started chiming and going off. Several nurses rushed into the room. We stood at the doorway holding hands. One of the nurses turned to us and said, "I am sorry. There were orders in his chart not to resuscitate."

As she left his bedside and the other attendants turned off the machine, she touched my arm. Taylor and I started to cry.

When Brenda returned her face was sullen, her eyebrows were furrowed. There was a deep sadness in her eyes. I thought perhaps one of the nurses had told her about Uncle Nate, but I soon found out I was terribly wrong.

"Carly, I have some terrible news to tell you, to tell the both of you. Your mother is downstairs in the emergency room. She has been seriously injured. I'm not clear on all the details, but when I called home my son told me when he arrived home there were several police cars and an ambulance in the driveway. They were taking your mother out on a stretcher and the police were taping the house off. I think she was attacked and shot. My son said one of the other neighbors heard several shots and called the police. When they looked out the window, they saw the front door open and maybe someone running from the house or that direction. I just don't know what to say. When I was coming up to tell you I met your uncle's nurse and she told me he just passed. I'm so sorry. It all seems like a dream. I can't imagine who would want to hurt your mother."

I told Brenda to stay with Taylor while she spoke with the doctor and started making plans for his body to be moved.

I paced back and forth, trying to think who would do this to Ethel and if she was still alive. She arrived at the house after they left. "Who was there with her, and how could this have happened?"

Ethel and I did not have the best relationship, and over the years, we had become more distant. There could not be two women on the face of the earth who were more different than she and I. Yet, this was my mother, and I wanted nothing hurtful to happen to her. It's funny about family. We can be our worst enemies and fight like cats and dogs, but the minute someone from the outside says or does something against a family member, watch out. It is almost like that right to abuse one another is only a family's right.

The elevator door opened, and I rushed to the emergency room. It was packed with people with different complaints and concerns. There were women holding their coughing children, a man with a bloody towel on his head, and several people who did not look ill but were sitting there watching the television. It was on the news channel, and they were talking about a recent home invasion with a shooting. I glanced up toward the television as I made my way to the triage desk.

Sitting behind the desk was a middle-aged gray-haired woman. The window was half opened, and I could see people being brought into the examination rooms on stretchers. As I stepped to the window I said, "Excuse me, I was just told Ethel Collins, my mother, was brought in by ambulance. She was attacked and possibly shot?"

Looking up from her paperwork, she asked, "Who are you inquiring about?" The badge pinned to her blouse said she was the ER coordinator, Betty Lawson.

I told her again I was the daughter of the victim. I asked if she could bring me inside to see her.

She smiled politely then said, "Please take a sit in the waiting area. The attending physician will speak to you shortly."

"Thank you, Mrs. Lawson."

BRENDA L. WATERS

After what seemed like an eternity, the doctor finally came out to speak with me.

"Hello, Ms. Collins, I am Dr. Wong. I am going to get straight to the point. Your mother is in critical condition. We have her stabilized for now and will send her to surgery very soon. Your mother was severely injured from the gunshots. She was very fortunate none of the bullets hit any vital organs. Apparently, from the extent of the bullet entries, she fought her assailant even though she was injured. I feel she will survive, but there will be some permanent scars and a long healing process for her. We have her heavily sedated at this time.

"Can I see her?"

"Ms. Collins, I don't think that would be a good idea right now. Your mother has sustained some severe injuries to her head and face aside from the bullet wounds. I don't think you would want to see her this way. Besides, as I said, we have her heavily sedated to keep her calm and stable until we can operate. Once she is out of surgery and in her room, you will be able to see her. We have rooms here in the hospital for family members to stay overnight. We can arrange these accommodations .You can speak to Mrs. Lawson there at the front desk. If you will excuse me, I need to get back to your mother and have her papers ready for her transfer. Ms. Collins, I just want you to know your mother was very fortunate." As he stood to leave, he shook my hand and asked, "Are there any questions I can answer for you at this time?"

"No, but thank you for asking, and I appreciate all you have done to help her."

As Dr. Wong turned and walked away, he stopped and spoke to the police officers who were standing across the room looking in my direction. Whatever he said, the younger officer nodded his head and patted the doctor on his back. The police officer, along with a man wearing a black fedora and overcoat, walked toward me.

I stood up as they approached. The man in the black hat and coat extended his hand and introduced himself to me as Detective Phillip Randolph. He was tall but slightly overweight. His coat was unbuttoned, and I could see the top of his stomach slightly extending over his belt buckle. He pulled out his badge, and it was a gold shield to identify his rank. He then introduced me to the younger police officer standing next to him as the one who found Ethel. The police officer was standing with his hat in his hand. He extended his hand and shook mine. I embraced him and thanked him for finding and helping her. I don't think it was too often he got a hug or compliment for doing his job.

The detective asked me to take a seat.

"Ms. Collins, how long has your mother resided at that residence?

"I would say about a year."

"When was the last time you saw or spoke to each other? Do you have any idea who would have hurt her?"

"Ethel and I were estranged and had not spoken in some time. I just arrived from Paris on a business trip and was here to check on my sick uncle, who just passed away in ICU on the fifth floor. I have no idea who would have hurt her this way."

"Do you know if there was any money or valuables in the home? From what I gathered from the neighbors and those around the crime scene, people in the neighborhood thought your uncle kept a large amount of money in the home, and there were possibly some other valuables as well. There was no forced entry into the house, and whoever did this had to be let in or had a key."

"I knew nothing about that. My cousin and I send money to assist with his social security income to pay for his care. I assumed he kept it in the bank like most people did. It wasn't until last year he became bedridden and needed around the clock care. "

"Brenda Harris was your uncle's caregiver, correct?"

"Yes, she is a registered nurse in geriatric care and saw to his medical needs. Ethel moved in to assist her with my uncle's care. She is a retired schoolteacher and works part time at Bergdorf Goodman's."

"Again, do you have any idea of your mother's whereabouts at the time your uncle was taken to the hospital?"

"No!"

"How was your mother's relationship with her brother?"

"She was very devoted to him and will be heartbroken when she finds out he has passed away.

"Detective, I don't know why Ethel was not in the house when my uncle left. I can only assume she was at work. Apparently she was not missing, because no one called from her job to inform anyone they had not seen her. We all will have to wait until she's able to tell us."

BRENDA L. WATERS

The detectives shook my hand and thanked me for speaking with them.

I sat there in silence for a few seconds. Mrs. Lawson came to tell me they were about to move Ethel.

"Ms. Collins, would you like to see your mother for a few minutes before they take her up for surgery?"

"Yes, but I thought the doctor said ---"

Mrs. Lawson patted my hand and told me not to worry about what the doctor said, this was my mother and I should see her before she goes to surgery.

As I entered her room, the orderlies were waiting to move her. Attached to her body were many machines and monitors, emitting disturbing sounds. I was horrified and speechless to see her laying there. She looked so helpless. A nurse was assigned to accompany her to the operating room.

I leaned in with my head on the cool steel door, and the tears began to fall. I felt a hand on my shoulder, and when I turned, it was Mrs. Lawson. She turned me around and held me in her arms as I cried like a baby. I could not stop the tears.

"It is good to cry. Let it all out."

I could not believe this was my mother being taken upstairs. Mrs. Lawson smoothed my hair with her hands as she walked me over to the chairs to sit until I got myself together. Out of nowhere, she handed me a Kleenex to blow my nose and wipe my eyes.

She asked, "Baby, did you say you had some family here in the hospital with you? Do you want me to contact them?"

"Oh no! I have totally forgotten about my cousin, Taylor. I left her upstairs waiting for the funeral home to pick up our uncle's body."

"Lord, child I don't know why all this fell in your lap right now, but God must have wanted you here. Your uncle is in a better place, and thank God he did not live to know what happened to his sister. Now, for your mother, she has the finest doctors in the world taking care of her. If she is going to survive, it will be because of them. Baby, the Lord was with you tonight, whether you believe it or not. He had to know what was going to happen to make you come here to Chicago to see about your family, and then for that police officer to be in the area right when this happened to your momma. Just have faith; the Lord knows what he is doing, even if we can't make head

SO I WAS TOLD

or tail out of it. It's not our place to questions these things, honey. We just have to be strong and accept them for how they come. You know what I mean? Now wipe your eyes and come on, I will take you upstairs. I'll call and have a room for you and your cousin to stay. It has everything you need for the night. There are two beds, some gowns, and slippers with toiletries in the room. I doubt if you both get any sleep, but at least you can rest until your momma is out of surgery. I'll make sure your room is on the same floor she will be moved to."

While this sweet woman was talking to me, I thought to myself, *Sometimes angels are sent when we truly need them.* This definitely was one of those moments. The warmth of this woman and her concern enveloped and soothed me. I believed what she said about Ethel, but the part about God ... well at this moment, I was not so sure; I was not so sure at all."

The surgery was longer than expected. Several nurses kept Taylor and me updated on her condition. Even though I was trying my best to be strong, poor Taylor was losing it. Eventually she cried herself to sleep curled up in the waiting room chair. I told her to go to our room, and once Ethel was out of surgery I would come and get her. Taylor was exhausted, but she reluctantly left. I stood looking out the windows over the hospital grounds as I watched the ambulances come and go from the emergency room. As I turned from the window, I saw one of the doctors from the surgery enter the room. He was removing his surgical cap and rubbing his eyes as he spoke.

"Ms. Collins, I wanted to come see you before I left. The surgery went longer than we had anticipated, but your mother pulled through fine. She is a fighter. We removed two of the bullets, but we had to leave one in because there was swelling and it was to close to her spinal cord. We did not want to risk permanent injury by trying to remove it now. I am confident it can be remove at a later date, once the swelling goes down. We will be able to determine more definitively from the x-rays. Now, for the other injuries; there was severe damage to her right eye socket. She was very fortunate Dr. Lee was on duty tonight. He is one of our top ophthalmic surgeons, and he was able to save her eye, though her vision may be slightly impaired. Her left eye is heavily bruised, but did not sustain as much damage, and once the swelling has left, there should be normal vision. Her nose was broken, and her chin and jaw fractured in several places. Your mother lost several

BRENDA L. WATERS

teeth and will require implants or dentures at a later date. She sustained a concussion from the fall but only has a hairline fracture to her skull. She will be heavily sedated for the next forty-eight hours. I want to keep her immobile until we can see about the remaining bullet. Your mother was very lucky she received immediate attention. Had it been a few minutes later, I could not say I would be here telling you all this. Try to get some rest. I know that will be difficult, but she is in good care. We have the best trauma and post-op care staff here at Mercy General. *Good night.*"

With that, he turned and left the room.

For the first time tonight I felt relief. I must have had been holding my breath while he spoke, because all of a sudden I felt light- headed. I stumbled to the chair and grabbed the armrest as I sat down. With my hands in my face, I began to pray and thank God."

When I made it to the overnight room, Taylor was asleep in one of the beds. I could see a glass of water and an empty medicine cup on the nightstand. One of the doctors or nurses must have given her a sleeping pill. With the covers pulled up almost over her head, she reminded me of that bratty little girl who would follow me everywhere when she came to visit me as a child.

I pulled a chair to the window and looked outside. There was nothing to see but other medical buildings and the skyline. Every so often I could hear the sound of an ambulance or police car siren as they entered the hospital. Sleep was not coming easily to me tonight. One of the nurses knocked at the door to check on us.

"Ms. Collins, I just wanted to check and see if you were okay. Is there anything I can get for you, or would you like something to help you sleep?" Taylor had told her about our uncle and Ethel.

"No, thank you, I want to stay awake to see my mother when they move her from recovery to her room."

"You should try and get some rest. It probably will be morning before you can see her. With the extent of her injuries, they will keep her sedated for a while. They will no more by then. Try and get some rest. You'll need your strength.

She turned and left the room, closing the door behind her.

I could hear the sound of Taylor's easy breathing as she slept. Turning toward her, I saw she had kicked the covers off. I walked to her bed and placed the blanket back on her, tucking in into the corners. She moaned and turned over, curling up in a tight ball, with her knees pulled up and her hands tucked under her pillow. Pulling a chair up to the bed I stayed there the remainder of the night. As the night wore on and early into the morning, a nurse knocked and entered the door.

"Ms. Collins, I just wanted to let you know that your mother has been transferred to her room down the hall."

I looked at the clock on the wall. It was 5:30 AM. Taylor was still asleep as I arose from the chair, stiff and sore. Quietly, I walked to the bathroom to freshen up before I went to see Ethel. I heard the ruffle of covers, and Taylor awaking, speaking as she yawned.

"Good morning. Boy did *I* sleep. I haven't slept that good since I… come to think of it, I don't think I have ever slept like this. "

Taylor stopped mid-sentence as I turned to face her.

"I'm sorry, Carly. You know I was hoping this was all a bad dream. Have you heard anything about your mom?"

"Yeah, the nurse just left. They've moved her to the room down the hall. I'm on my way to see her right now. I spoke to the doctor last night. He was pleased with the surgery, but they had to leave one bullet in because it is too close to her spine. She was pretty messed up. Not only did they shoot her, but whoever did this beat her badly. They busted her eye and broke her jaw. I just don't know who would do something like this. The police said there was not forcible entry, so Ethel had to know who it was or they had a key. When you talked to Brenda, did she ever tell you someone else was living in the house?"

"No, Carly, nobody. I am positive if Brenda thought something was wrong she would have *said* something or *done* something about it. She loved Uncle Nate like he was family. There must be more to this. Maybe they forced Ethel into the house or surprised her. Once your mom is able, I know she will tell us everything.

"Give me a moment to get up and get dressed. I want to go with you to see her. Then I'm going to meet with Mr. Swanson at the funeral home. Brenda and I made the arrangements for the service this week. Are you going to call your brother?"

Through all this anguish, I had totally forgotten about Christian. How was I going to explain this? Over the years he tried to reach out to Ethel, to

BRENDA L. WATERS

make some kind of connection with her, but she always gave some pathetic excuse why they could not get together. She even stood him up once when he traveled to see her. Ethel never showed up at the airport to pick him up after they made plans to spend a weekend together. There was so much he wanted to know about her and his father, so many questions, like myself, he did not have answers to. I knew this hurt my brother, but he would try to find some way to rationalize her behavior toward him. He said he understood her better than I gave him credit, but I knew deep down inside it carved away a bit of his soul every time she let him down.

"Yeah, I will call him right after we see her. It's still early in Seattle. I don't want to wake him out of a sleep to tell him all of this right now. Why don't you go on and get ready. I need to call my office and let them know what is happening and make arrangements to stay here a few days longer."

As we entered Ethel's room, there were two nurses at her bedside. One was checking her bandages while the other was changing her I.V. fluids. Her face and head were heavily bandaged. I could see the thick gauze covering the one eye, and it appeared her mouth and jaws were wired shut. The nurse told me they took the breathing tube out of her as soon as they brought her into the room. Her nose had been broken and reconstructed, thereby allowing her to breathe on her own. She looked so small and fragile as she lay in the bed with all the tubes in her body and the bandages wrapped around her like a living, breathing mummy. Her hands were exposed on top of the covers that were tucked underneath her. Looking closely, you could see her chest rise and fall as she slept peacefully.

Taylor asked the nurse, "Is she in pain?"

"No, she is still sedated right now. She probably doesn't feel anything. I can't say the same when she does come to, but we will monitor her around the clock. She will get meds for any discomfort. Right now we just want her to lie still and rest peacefully. She is being fed through IV. She is going to receive nourishment this way for a few weeks until her jaw and chin heal. The doctor did a good job repairing them. There should be no scarring, from what I understand. She was lucky to have those surgeons on call when she was brought in. They made a good team. For the records, she is lucky to be alive. If there is anything you need, just push the call button. Would you like for me to have the kitchen bring you up breakfast? They should be making the morning rounds soon."

SO I WAS TOLD

We both told her no thanks, and thanked her for looking after Ethel.

I walked to the bed, and looking down at her, wondered who would want to hurt her this badly, and why?

Ethel was smart about most things in life except men. She had been involved or married to so many men that I could not keep track. Her latest husband was not only twelve years younger than her, he was her former student. It seemed like each new husband or fling got younger and riskier as they came.

I sat at her bedside as Taylor apprehensively approached. Looking down at Ethel, she took her hand and began to cry softly.

"Ethel, I am so sorry this happened to you. Please get better and recover. You don't deserve this, and I want you to heal and help us find the bastard who did this to you. Get better, Ethel, get better soon."

Taylor bent down and kissed her forehead. Wiping back a tear, she squeezed her hand and left the room.

I was all alone with the silence of the room and only my thoughts to keep me company. At least when I called Christian I could tell him she was alive and recovering. I just could not tell him who did this or why this happened to her. That was going to be the hardest part of it all.

After leaving several messages at my brother's home, his girlfriend called me back.

"Hello, Carly, this is Phyllis. I got your message about your mother and uncle. I am so sorry! Unfortunately, your brother is in Argentina with the woman's basketball team. They are there on a cross-cultural tour and are not schedule to return until the end of the month. I will try to contact him as soon as we hang up. Carly, I am so sorry about your family. Is there is anything I can do? Would you like me to come to Chicago for the service since Christian cannot be there? It's funny, but right before he left for Buenos Aires, he spoke about your uncle and tried to contact your mother. He was very concerned about her. It is almost as if he must have known something was wrong."

"Thanks, Phyllis, but no, you don't have to fly here for the memorial. Taylor and I decided to have Uncle Nate cremated. When Ethel is better and can travel, we will have his ashes scattered over the family garden back in Mississippi. I know that is what he probably would have wanted. Like my grandfather, he too liked to garden."

185

BRENDA L. WATERS

After speaking with Phyllis, Taylor and I discussed our uncle's memorial service.

"Taylor, have you spoken to Trey, Uncle Nate's son? When was the last time anyone saw or heard from him?"

"I don't know, Carly. Uncle Nate's neighbor saw him about a month ago and he was in bad shape. She thinks he is back on the streets, *using again*. It is so sad. With all his effort to get Trey clean, he was always in and out of rehab. It worked for a while, but I guess he just couldn't fight those demons.

"Well, we will just have a small memorial service here for his friends and neighbors. We can't wait around to see if Trey shows up. I am sure by now he has heard that his father has passed."

I returned to Ethel's bedside and noticed she was becoming restless.

"Ethel, Mother, it's me ... Carly. You are in the hospital and everything is okay. Taylor is here with me. They are taking good care of you, so just rest and get better. Don't try to move or say anything, it will be all right. Just sleep."

Ethel drifted back to sleep. Taylor and I thought it would be a good time to leave and finalize the memorial service arrangements. We only knew a handful of Uncle Nate's friends, but we wanted his memorial to be right. He deserved that much.

We were standing on the steps of the funeral home. Many people from the neighborhood, his church, and his fraternal organizations came to pay their respects. It stopped snowing, and the temperature was rising. It was a lovely morning with the sun glistening off the newly fallen snow.

As we began to leave, Brenda and her daughter Bernetta stopped us on the steps. Hugging us, Brenda replied, "Carly, Taylor, this was a wonderful service for your uncle. I know he is proud of what you girls have done for him. Many of his friends were here from the neighborhood, from everywhere. He would be tickled to know they all came to see him. You know he never thought anyone really cared about him. No matter what I said to him, he would always shake his head and tell me I was wrong."

Looking up into the sky, Brenda commented on how the snow stopped falling and the sun was out.

"You know your uncle loved to watch the snow fall. He said that was the one thing he did not like about Mississippi; there just wasn't enough snow."

Bernetta replied, "Yeah, I used to think Mr. Nate was nuts about snow. I don't care how much fell; he just loved it, especially at Christmas. He loved to watch the kids on the block make snowmen. He would have mama make us hot chocolate with marshmallows to warm us up after we finished playing. He just loved the snow."

Brenda asked, "Are you going back to the hospital?"

I replied, "Yes, right after I drop Taylor off at the airport. I called this morning before the service, and her nurse said she is awake and better. They are still giving her pain medication, but she is coherent. Hopefully, her doctor will be there when I get there so I can get some answers about her progress and when he thinks she will be released."

"Good, I will come by later and check on you."

Driving to the airport, Taylor was unusually quiet.

"Hey girl, you all right?"

Taylor turned from the window. I could see she had been crying.

"Man, Carly! This has been brutal. I mean, we were celebrating your birthday and I suggested we come here, and now --"

"Taylor, don't go there. It was meant to be. Look, Uncle Nate was so sick and he was not going to get better. It was his time. As for Ethel, now that's another story, but she is on her way to recovering. Once she is able to tell the police what happened, we can move on from there. Trust me. Everything is going to work out."

Pulling up to the curb, I helped Taylor with her bags and kissed her. Just like my cousin, her sadness does not last long. As I watched her walk into the terminal, a tall, good-looking *brother* was helping her with her luggage. There was Taylor with the biggest smile, flirting outrageously. She looked back, winked, and waved good-bye. It was good to see her back to her old self. I am sure tonight when she calls I will get an earful.

Several days after Ethel was discharged from the hospital, I returned to Atlanta. In a few weeks, she would be strong enough for us to meet in Mississippi to say our final good-bye to Uncle Nate.

It was a beautiful day. Spring had come to Mississippi, and everything was in bloom. The sun was high, but it was not hot. There was a slight breeze in the air, and the petals from the Bradford Pine trees were falling and swirling like snow. Standing in grandfather's garden, we were there to remember Uncle Nate and scatter his ashes. Grandmother Haley was there, much to our objection. She had been extremely ill and was just recovering. She fought all of us when we asked her to stay in bed, yet her stubbornness won out. My Aunt Dale accompanied her to the carport, where she sat.

The plastic surgeon did wonders with Ethel. You had to look closely to notice the scarring around her eye. She still needed the cane to steady herself, but she was doing well. The detectives had questioned her about her attack, but she was not cooperating. It wasn't clear if this was because she did not remember or if she was protecting whoever did her harm. All I know is Ethel would not talk about it. Taylor and I both tried relentlessly to persuade her to say something. Her doctors said they could not find any medical reason for memory loss. If this was what she was experiencing, they could not say conclusively. Only time would tell.

My brother could not make the service. Again, he was out of the country, but I think it had more to do with Ethel. When she learned I had invited Christian, she swore she would not attend her brother's service. She was not ready to meet her son and did not want to do so under these conditions. I think it was more out of fear and her own demons about what she did to him than her sorrow over Uncle Nate's death. With a lump in my throat I tried to explain to Christian the kind person his mother is. *How could a mother deny her child?* Christian said he understood, but *I* don't

After the minister finished, I scattered Uncle Nate's ashes over the garden. People started to leave after extending their condolences. I stayed behind to thank the minister for all he had done. In a distance I heard screaming. Turning, I saw people running toward Grandmother Haley. I could see her slumped over in her chair with Aunt Dale trying to help her. It was all in slow motion. This could not be happening. By the time I reached grandmother, she was dead.

CHAPTER FIFTEEN

IN GOD WE TRUST

"Carly, these projections are fantastic. If you keep this up, I just might be able to retire earlier than I planned. The board will *love* this. You know, they have been on me about finding my replacement in the event that I seriously consider leaving. I am really happy with all you have done with this project. We should be up and running in South Africa in no time."

I asked quietly, "Sheila, do you think it hurts when you hit the ground? I mean, when it happens, do you think maybe your mind leaves your body before you hit that *cold, hard concrete?*"

"When *what* happens, Carly? Why would you ask me something like---"

I could tell by the sound of Sheila's voice as she entered my office she did not see me standing at the windows. She was too busy reading the report and expounding on my success to notice me leaning against the floor to ceiling window panes looking down into the darkness.

The window felt cold against my body. I was so high up it felt as if I could reach out and touch one of the stars glistening in the night sky. The street below resembled a replica of a miniature toy city with all the cars moving to and fro and the stoplights flashing.

BRENDA L. WATERS

I turned and faced her as she continued to speak, slowly and precisely, as if I was a child, her face etched in concern.

"Carly, honey come here, come on?"

I saw Sheila walk toward me with her hand outstretched. She touched my arm as I turned back toward the window, this time pressing myself even harder against it.

"Come on, Carly, let's sit down on the sofa. We can talk about the report later. This is *not* you talking; it is the grief you are experiencing."

Holding my hand, she led to the sofa as we sat facing each other.

"You know, Carly, I told Craig I felt you came back to work too soon. You just buried your grandmother and here you are in your office. You haven't given yourself enough time to *grieve*. I told you, you did not have to come back so soon. You need time to think and regroup."

"No, Sheila it's my fault! I should have told grandmother everything about Uncle Nate and Ethel's shooting before I arrived for the service. If only I had flown home earlier and spent some time with her, that may have softened the impact, but Aunt Dale asked me to let her do it. She wasn't sure how much of it Haley would have understood anyway. Aunt Dale said in the few weeks before the memorial she was regressing more into her childhood. It's just I was *so* afraid my Aunt Martha would have found a way to tell her before she could. She hated Grandmother Haley and would have relished in being the one to tell her about Ethel."

I got up from the sofa and stood again by the window.

"I am so sick and tired of grieving and feeling loss, of being so damn *angry*. I didn't grow up having this big, warm, fuzzy family, but what I did have is now dying around me. It's like I can't hold onto anyone. It is not just my family, Sheila, but someone *dear* to my heart is missing, and I know in my soul I am going to have to prepare for another loss."

"Carly, you have to believe that the Lord only gives ..."

Turning from the window, I stopped Sheila before she could continue.

"I know! He gives us only what we can handle. What doesn't kill you only makes you stronger. Oh, yeah, this one's my favorites; just put it in *God's* hands. What else do you have for me? I have heard it all from everyone and everywhere."

Placing my hands over my ears, I leaned my head against the window

190

SO I WAS TOLD

and said, "I don't want to hear that anymore. God isn't listening to me. He has opened his fingers, and I am slipping through."

Sheila got up from the sofa. I could hear her walking toward me. She gently placed her arm around my shoulder and led me back to the sofa.

"Carly, I want you to stay right here. I am going down to my office to get something for you to see, all right? You will be here when I get back? Promise me!"

"Sheila, I'll be here. Don't worry. I am not going to do anything *crazy*, regardless of what you are thinking right now. Oh, by the way, I hope you are bringing that bottle of tequila you keep hidden in your armoire with you."

Sheila chuckled and said, "Yeah, I'll bring that too."

Kicking off my shoes, I lay back on the sofa and waited for Sheila to return. My mind was racing just thinking about everything. I felt a wave of anger overcome me as I thought about Ethel and her insane stubbornness in not telling the police who shot her. No matter what I said, she was determined to stay quiet. The police had no clues, and they knew she was their only hope in trying to find out what happened. Ethel moved back into the house, and with the care of Brenda and her daughter, Bernetta, she recovered quickly. I would visit and arranged my flights to return to Chicago instead of Atlanta to spend time with her when I could. Yet, no matter what we did, she did not budge. Brenda felt perhaps she was severely traumatized and just wanted to forget it all; I knew better. She was protecting someone, and the thought of it angered me to no end. It wasn't rational to want to protect someone who could harm you this way, but then again, when was Ethel rational.

I heard Sheila in the hallway speaking to the cleaning lady as she entered my office.

"Good night, Mrs. Hancock, you have a pleasant evening and congratulations on that new grandbaby of yours."

I sat up as she entered, and in one hand was the bottle of tequila and in the other was the picture of her family she kept on her desk. Sheila handed me the photo and walked to my armoire where I kept my ice bucket and glasses. Filling two glasses with ice and tequila, she returned to the sofa. Handing me my glass, she sat down and told me to take a good look at the picture. It was a photograph I had seen a thousand times in her office.

After taking a sip, Sheila leaned back and started to speak.

BRENDA L. WATERS

"Carly, I want to tell you a story about that photograph you are holding. You know or have met just about everyone in it. What you don't know is, there would be no smiling faces looking at you if I had let my soul die, or lost my faith. I have told you so many times how much you remind me of myself when I was starting with this company. Like you, I was smart, eager, and determined to go as far as I could. Then I met Craig and fell in love. We got married. The game plan was to have a career and family. I had it all sorted and planned out the way it was supposed to go. Well, it didn't work out that *way* for a long while. After the first year of marriage, Craig and I decided to start our family. I came off the pill, and bingo, I got pregnant. We were overjoyed. Craig had just gotten a big promotion, and we moved into a brand new five-bedroom home with a big screened-in porch. Everything seemed perfect."

"Three months into the pregnancy I miscarried. I don't have to tell you how sad my husband and I were, but the doctor assured me all was well and I could get pregnant again. I miscarried again! Carly, I miscarried *two* babies and had one still birth. Do you have any idea what that did to me, to Craig? A part of my soul died each and every time I heard the doctors tell me how sorry they were. You see, as far as they knew, and from all the medical tests and exams they gave *Craig and me*, there was no medical explanation why I could not carry a baby to term.

"My husband was so supportive and loving, but when I looked into his eyes, I could see the pain and hurt."

Sheila got up from the sofa and walked to the window. Looking out with her back to me, she continued to talk, "At this time all of our married friends had children. If there was one thing my husband wanted, it was kids. After all he had done for me I really wanted to give him a child. It would kill me to see him laughing and playing with our friends' children, all of them calling him Uncle Craig, but not one to call him daddy. We would leave their homes and come back to ours with only the dog and cat to greet us. No child's laughter or toys to trip over in the night. No hugs, sticky wet kisses, or painted pictures taped on the refrigerators doors."

Sheila turned and walked over to the armoire to pour her another drink.

"You want me to freshen that up for you, Carly?"

SO I WAS TOLD

I was listening so intently to her story I hadn't touched my drink. I had never seen or heard Sheila speak like this before.

"I'm telling you this, because I want you to know I understand how you are feeling about God right now. I understand the sadness, anger, the loss and disappointment."

Walking back to the sofa Sheila sat down and continued.

"It got really bad for a minute. Craig was wonderful, but me, on the other hand, I was miserable. Every time my husband reached out for me, I pulled away. I didn't want him to touch me, to love me, because I was afraid. I did not want to continue to hurt him. Don't get me wrong, he loved me, but having a family of his own was important. One night we were in bed and he turned to me. I knew what he wanted, but I pulled away *again*. It was too much for him. He got up, put on his clothes, and left. He didn't come home until the morning. I just knew he had been with another woman. No man, I don't care how much he loves you, is going to keep accepting rejection from his woman, especially in the bedroom.

"I was furious and out of my mind with worry. I accused him of going out to find someone to take care of his needs. I wasn't meeting them, and he wasn't going to convince me he did not have someone there waiting to replace me. Craig swore that was not the case, that he drove around the city to clear his head. Before he could finish, I slapped him and walked out the room. I knew he was lying to me. He had to be, after the way I continually rejected him. He was a man, for God's sake, a man who loved making love.

"Carly, I was blind with anger and disgust. I felt even *more* of my soul disappear that morning. Here I rejected my lover and accused him of being unfaithful, even slapped him, because of what I was feeling. We didn't speak to each other for the remainder of the week. Whenever he tried, I walked away or slept in the other room. I deliberately came home as late as I could to avoid him. It wasn't until that Sunday when we went to mass one of the nuns who worked at Grady Hospital in the labor and delivery unit stopped us before service began. Sister Cecilia hugged Craig and thanked him for sitting and rocking the babies the night he did not come home. The nurses were so surprised to see a man come to the nursery to volunteer with the little ones left by their mothers who were not able to keep them because of drugs. He changed the babies' diapers and fed them, rocked and told them stories. He did this until the early morning hours. Afterward he went and

BRENDA L. WATERS

got all the nurses coffee and donuts before he left. She asked him if he would come again.

"Do I have to tell you how I felt at that moment? I think I cried enough tears to fill Lake Lanier. It was so bad Father Patrick took us both to his office so I could pull myself together. I think the church thought I had lost my mind or someone had died. Even Sister Cecilia didn't know what to do. Craig reassured everyone I was okay. Father let us stay there until service was over. When he came back, I told him what happened and why I was so hysterical. I remember Father standing over Craig with his hand on his shoulder. He gave him a pat on the back, and then he hugged me. He told me even in our darkest moments, our deepest despair, God is there. He loves us and just as Craig was holding those babies, God was holding me every time I thought he abandoned me. I just had to stop fighting him and let myself feel his presence and love. You know, Carly, it was at that moment I decided I needed to *heal*. I needed to get my *soul* back and fill it up with the love of God. I had to love me again. I apologized to Craig and to God for becoming this person who only thought about herself and *her* pain. Now I want you to think for a moment about the losses *your* mother has experienced.

"Though they might not have been the same as mine, her children were taken from her. She, unlike you and I, just wasn't strong enough to let go and let God fill her up. She is a lost *soul*, honey, that's all. As for the others who have died and gone, be glad for them. Dying only hurts those left behind, not the dead. They aren't grieving, angry, or sad. It's *us* who are here, the *walking wounded*, that feel the pain. Go on now. Take a long look at that good-looking family in that photograph.

"That Sunday night after I made a fool of myself at church, when my husband turned to hold me in his arms, I did not pull away. I gave myself with all the love I could to him. Nine months and two weeks overdue, I gave birth to Craig Jr. One year after that, his sister Elizabeth came. Ten years after Elizabeth was born, just when my husband and I thought God was done, *he* sent us the twins. I think that was his way of letting me know exactly whose hands I was in.

"I had not one complication with any of those babies. Not a day of morning sickness or pain, no prolonged bed rest, nothing. It was as if God made me over again and gave me all new parts. The doctors were even amazed. As a matter of fact, I would not be surprised if I'm in some medical journal

SO I WAS TOLD

somewhere. I'm telling you this for a reason. Give yourself time, Carly. Let go of the pain and anger. God has not let you slip through his fingers, and even if you feel he has, his other hand is underneath to catch you."

Sheila then hugged me and helped me up from the sofa.

"Come on, it's late, and I want you to go home. I don't want to see you in this office for the remainder of the week, but I do want you to do something for me. I want you to go to church with Craig and me this Sunday. Craig is assisting Father, and I want you to share this with us. I know you will like our little church. It is a wonderful family.

"We are finally getting another priest at the church and he is visiting this Sunday. Since we have grown so much within the past ten years, the powers that be felt Father Patrick could use an assistant. What is so special about this priest is that he is a young black man who grew up *and* went to school in our parish. Now he is coming back to lead his flock, and he is a dynamic speaker. The kids in the church love him, as well as some of us older parishioners who remember when he was just a child. I know you will enjoy the service.

"So what do you say? Will you join my family this Sunday? After church we can go to C. J's. new bed and breakfast he and his wife opened in the Highlands for brunch. Please, Carly, come and join us. It would mean so much to me."

I hesitated for a moment. "Okay, Sheila, for you I will come. Just tell me where it is and the time. You know it's been a while since I stepped into a Catholic church. I hope I remember all the things you do."

"Don't worry about that, Carly, I know God will be glad to see you there. Now come on, put your shoes on and get out of here. I'm coming right behind you. That man of mine is home, and I don't plan on keeping him waiting too long. The twins are at a sleepover, and we have the house to ourselves."

As we were leaving my office, she turned and walked back in to retrieve the bottle of tequila we had been drinking. Laughing, she placed it into her bag.

"Trust me, Craig and I will find good use for this tonight."

Sunday arrived, and I met Sheila as she was standing at the church doors. Craig had gone ahead of her. As we entered in together, we were greeted warmly by the usher. Walking down the aisle I noticed there were people kneeling in the pews, some had their heads bowed as if they were in deep prayer. Others were sitting quietly with their rosary in hand. Moving closer to the front of the church, I could hear the music director giving instructions to the choir. Sheila's husband was standing on the altar talking to the priest. I noticed he was dressed in a robe similar to what the minister was wearing.

As I glanced around, I saw the older women of the church stylishly dressed and wearing their large, fancy hats. The younger generation, some dressed in the latest designers, intermingled with those clad in blue jeans and sneakers. Some of the men dressed in suits and ties were sitting next to others wearing T-shirts and tattoos. I thought the people in this church would make the best ad for the clothing line United Colors of Benetton. This was so unlike what I experienced growing up in the church, but when the choir stood and I heard that first note of, "Pass Me Not, Oh Gentle Savior," I knew I would like it here.

Fr. Raymond, the visiting priest, gave the sermon. He preached about the life of Job and all the trials and tribulations that afflicted his poor soul. Did he somehow miraculously know I was going to be here this Sunday? Listening to what he was saying, I felt like it was my life he was talking about. It was as if no one else was present, and he was *only* speaking to me. He talked about Job having everything he loved and held dear to him taken away, being stripped to his bare bones and soul, yet never once losing his faith or devotion to God. He talked about there not being Oprah or even a Dr. Phil he could turn to to save him in his deepest, darkest hours. This brought resounding laughter from the congregation.

No, Job, he said, only had his unwavering *faith* and *belief* in God, and it was because of this his life was restored in great measure. I could feel myself become emotional when he talked about the unconditional love of God. How that love can carry you through those times of deep despair. Again, he lightened the moment by saying it didn't hurt to also seek *professional help*, along with *spiritual support* when the road gets rocky. Sheila reached over and squeezed my hand when he said this. There were moments in his sermon when I felt overwhelmed. I began to understand and feel what Sheila had said about your soul sometimes needed to be refilled. I was glad she asked me to come. After the mass ended, I introduced myself to the new

SO I WAS TOLD

priest and thanked him for his wonderful sermon. He told me he was happy if what he said could reach just one soul; then he knew he did his job well. He shook my hand and told me to come again. I assured him I would.

"So what did you think of Fr. Raymond and our little church in the *hood?*" Sheila jokingly asked as we were seated at the table for brunch.

"I really liked it. I have to admit I felt a bit foolish sitting there dabbing my eyes one minute from crying and then in the next moment laughing hysterically at something funny Fr. Raymond said. I agree, he is a dynamic speaker. I can see why he is so well received. He puts you at ease. I got to tell you Sheila, the few times I attended a Catholic church I don't think I ever heard a minister preach the way he did. Are you sure he didn't have some Baptist training? Somebody in his family had to have been a Baptist minister. Some of the things he said and the way he said them made me feel I was back home in Mississippi sitting on the front pew of Greater Mount Mariah Tabernacle Church. I was looking around to see if anyone was going to stand and shout, even though I did hear a few well-placed *Amens.*

"Oh don't worry, there have been a few Sundays when either by the sermon or the choir a few people have been moved by the spirit. Isn't that right, Craig?"

Craig nodded in agreement, as he read over the new menu at their son's bed and breakfast.

"Look, Sheila, C. J. added your blueberry waffles to the menu."

"I know, dear, I threatened him about it if he hadn't."

"Oh, here he comes now."

Leaning down as he approached the table, their son spoke then kissed his mother on the cheek.

"Hey, Mom, Dad. Oh no, who is this stranger sitting here? I can't believe my eyes. So, Mom talked you into going to church, huh?"

"Hello son, and yes, Carly went to mass with your father and me. She loved it. By the way, when was the last time *you* sat in pew?"

We all laughed as C. J. slowly backed away from the table while saying, "I'm glad you could make it Carly. Let me tell Lorna you are here. She will be so glad to see you. You haven't seen her since the wedding, have you? So what do you think of the place?"

"It's lovely, C. J. This is a beautiful home and a great idea. You should do very well. I told your mother I was going to have it listed in: "The Places to See and Stay" section of the magazines we carry on the airplanes."

Turning to his mother he replied, "See, Mom, it *was* a smart idea to hire her when you did."

"Don't try to change the subject, child, you heard me. Your old buddy Raymond was our visiting priest this Sunday."

Turning to address me, C. J. asked, "So, Carly, what did you think about my old classmate and best friend in elementary school? He was a talker then, and still one today. Did Mom tell you about all the mischief he and I got into when we were kids? The last thing I thought was Raymond Luther Harris would have become a priest. I think he spent more time in Mother Superior's office than her secretary. He was *always* at church on Saturday doing some chore for his penance. I'm glad he's back home to assist at our church. God does have his way of working things out, doesn't he?"

We all replied, "Amen to that."

CHAPTER SIXTEEN

A LITTLE HELP FROM A FRIEND

"Carly, we have been doing this for a little over six months, and every time you get to this point you shut down. You were standing at the window when your boss walked in and you asked her about---"

"Look, Dr. Paulson! I know what I asked Sheila, and maybe I am not so sure as to why, but I can assure you, no matter how I was feeling at the *time*, suicide was not in my mind."

I was standing by the bookcase of my therapist, Dr. Helena Paulson. She was recommended to me by Sheila after that first Sunday I accompanied her to church. It was the sermon Fr. Raymond preached, and even if he was joking, the suggestion he made about seeking professional help aside from getting "spiritual support" brought me to her.

"All right, Carly, if you say so. I have to accept what you are telling me to be the facts. Only you know what is going on in your head. My job is to help guide you in finding out the truth. I can't help you. Only you can do that. Don't be fooled by all the plaques and accolades on my wall thinking I am some kind of miracle worker, no good therapist is. It is solely and completely up to you, dear, to find the answers. I'm here to perhaps give you some clarity on them, that's all. It's obvious you are hurt and angry. Now it is up to you to break through it all and help us get to a resolution. You cannot blame someone else for this. I will allow my patients to have their pity party for only a moment, but then when it is done, *it is done*. Now the questions remains, do you want to heal? Do you want to get past the anger and the hurt? If so, then let's stop the nonsense and start talking about what has brought you here. If not, we can continue for as long as you like in this space. It is your call, your money!"

I laughed as I sat back down in the chair across from Dr. Paulson. She was right. I was hiding and stopping myself from letting go. I was afraid of what I would say and how it would sound.

"Dr. Paulson, do you mind if I call you by your first name, Helena? Only someone very close and dear could read me that way. Perhaps I could make better progress if we were on a friendlier basis."

Dr. Paulson threw back her head and laughed heartily. "Carly, I don't care what you call me."

Looking back over her shoulder at the wall with all her degrees and honors, she continued, "Don't get me wrong, I worked damn hard for all that, and most of it I deserve, but I not here doing this to be called "*doctor*". I love what I do for people. I wouldn't be here if I did not. Life is about choices, and this is what I choose to do with mine. When someone first walks through that door feeling broken and hopeless and then walks out that *same* door believing they are whole and deserving of happiness in their life, *that* is my reward. My greatest joy is when someone says to me, *'thanks, but I don't need you anymore'*."

I asked, "Well, what about those who think they got it all together and then they need to come back. What do you say to them then?"

"I say, *'hello'*, old friend, let's talk. No judgment here. Only *nothing* is infinite, Carly. Life hurts and can send the best of us spiraling out of control. It is up to that person to decide how to handle it. Some can do it all on their own, and then there are others who need someone to give them a *different* perspective. There is never anything wrong with asking for help, but there is something wrong when you *refuse* it knowing you desperately need it. Don't you think? So what is it going to be for you?"

I took a deep breath. I noticed while Helena was talking to me I was folding and unfolding my hands. It wasn't until she reached over and placed her hands on top of mine that I realized I was doing so. Looking into her eyes as she was smiling at me, I decided it was time for me to really start talking about everything. I was ready.

"Helena, this is not going to be easy for me. I am not a stupid or weak person. I wouldn't be here if I did not want help or realize it is going to take maybe a bit more than *giving it to God* to help me. I know there is power in prayer and letting go to God, but if it was that easy than there would be no need for *you*, right? It's like that joke about the drowning man and all the things God sends to help him, but he can't see it because he is so caught up in waiting for some grand miracle to happen that he lets everything that could save him pass him by. May I have a drink of water, or maybe do you have something stronger? I might need it to let all this out!

"The truth of the matter is maybe somewhere in my subconscious the idea of suicide was there that night, but only for a brief moment. I was *so* tired and angry with all that was happening. Helena, my life is based upon lies and secrets. So many people telling me one thing, and then finding out things I have been told are not *so*, or only half truths, or not true at all.

"I was born to a woman so weak and afraid of her own voice, she allowed someone else to speak for her, to control her. She let people take away her *soul* because she was too afraid to say, '*No you can't! This is mine*'. Then I was sent to live with a woman who had *too* much to say and do with my life. Not just mine, but any and everyone she knew, so much so that I decided I would never, ever let *anyone* have that kind of control over me. It was going to be my choices and my decisions on who I loved and what I had, what I could keep and let go. When I finally get my freedom and could make decisions for my life, what happened? I got pregnant in college, lost my baby, but I recovered. I moved on in life and moved away from the lies and deceits. What happens next? I meet a man, fall in love. What does he do? He lies and deceives me also. Then *death* finds me and he gets a *grip* on my life so much so I am afraid every time the telephone rings. Who will be next? Then I meet a man who changes that for me. A man who for the first time I did not have that gnawing feeling of doubt. I want and accept him for who he is, and all he has to bring to me, and I am grateful for it. I am totally and completely content with him. He does not care about my position, money, or past. Probably, this too may be taken from me."

I stood up from the chair and walked back over to her bookshelf, picking up a figurine of an angel looking down over a person whose face is in their

BRENDA L. WATERS

hands as if they are crying. It felt small and light in my hands. I placed it back on the shelf and turned to her.

"Helena, you have to understand how hard this is for me. I swore to him I would never talk about this to anyone. Only his sister and I know the truth."

Helena looked up from her seat and smiled at me.

"Be assured, Carly, whatever it is you are saying to me right now, no one, not even a court of law, can make me disclose this. You go to a Catholic church, right? When you talk to the priest, just as he is held by the church's laws not to reveal what is said in confidence, so am I. I just don't wear a collar."

I smiled and sat back down.

"His name is Raphael, and he is working undercover with the FBI to infiltrate some family in the Mexican drug cartel. He calls me when he can or sends messages to me from his sister when they speak, which is not often. We, that is Sara his sister and I, don't always know where he is or where he is going. So when I hear from him I feel as if I can *breathe*. He has a little girl, and he loves her with all his heart. Knowing this gives me confidence he will do everything he can to return to her safely. Raphael lost his wife when Isabella was very small, and I know he does not want her to grow up without both a mother and a father. His sister is taking care of her with his parents in Miami while he is away. He and I met under unusual circumstances. He was the detective that busted my boyfriend, who I thought would be my future husband, in a huge drug raid in Texas. I have to admit, when I first saw him, I was interested, but I did not think it could go anywhere, especially under those conditions, plus he had a child. He obviously felt differently, because that first time we met, he gave me his card with his personal phone number.

"Now any other time if a man did this to me, I would have thought that would have been really *tacky* and threw away the card, but there was something different about him. I really can't explain it." What I do know, is I *love and trust* this man and I want a life with him and his child."

I smiled and said, "You know something? This is the first time I have said those words out loud. I haven't even said them to him, even when he tells me he loves and misses me. As I told you, so much happened in such a short period of time; my uncle dying while my cousin and I were visiting him in Chicago. The same night my, mother was brutally attacked and left for dead. Her assailant has never been caught because she refused to help the police in any way. I am so *angry* with her and the way she lives her life and how I am sucked up into it. She doesn't even care how much she hurts her son, my brother, who only wants to reach out to her and love her. Wow! I guess I said a boatload, haven't I? You're right, I have been holding back, denying myself to face the truth."

Dr. Paulson stood up from her chair and while walking toward me, said, "Carly, you made a great breakthrough today. We have a lot of work to do, but I am sure you are on the right road to recovery. For now take time and reflect on today. Think about how you felt letting it go, and we can move forward."

Glancing at her watch, she said, "I will see you next Thursday at the same time. And remember, it is all up to you."

"Thank you for everything, Helena. I will see you next week. Good night."

My telephone rang, and I knew something wasn't right. It was two o'clock in the morning. My heart was pounding so loudly I could hear it in my ears. When I answered, I was right. It was Raphael's sister, Sara, calling. She asked if Raphael's contact, Agent Sheffield had been in touch with me. Apparently Raphael *was* missing. Agent Sheffield had not heard from him in several weeks, and this was not the plan. He was to contact him every week to update him on the movement of the organization. Raphael was good at making contact with the agency without blowing his cover. Apparently he had made some headway into this particular crime family. No one had seen or heard from him. He knew Raphael contacted his sister and sometimes me against the FBI wishes, but he felt it was under control. Apparently *my* home phone and his parents' are *bugged*. They know when and how long we talk and what is being said. They knew he had not disclosed anything to us about the operation, so they felt he was keeping his word. Even though Agent Sheffield was trying to be distant and cool, Sara could tell by his conversation he was disturbed.

To makes matters worse, she spent the hour before she called me trying to get Isabella back to sleep. Isa woke up crying and screaming, "Papi is dead." There was nothing she could do to console her. Isabella saw her dad in her dream lying face down in alligator-infested water.

BRENDA L. WATERS

"Sara, I have not seen or heard from the FBI. This does not mean he is dead, no matter what Agent Sheffield is saying or the dream Isa had. We just have to remain calm and patient. Raphael is too smart to get killed, and he would never leave his daughter. He is coming back to all of us. We just need to pray." Before we hung up we promised each other we would stay strong and call if either of us heard anything.

It was becoming too much for me—big, strong, invincible me. I felt my mind slipping away. Everything was falling apart. I had lost too much and buried too many people. I cried and screamed until there was nothing left. I told myself, *if I can survive Helen Dodson Watkins and her evilness, if I can survive Ethel and her madness, than I can survive anything.*

CHAPTER SEVENTEEN

GOD BLESS THE CHILD

As Taylor was driving to Atlanta's Hartsfield Airport to meet her aunt, Ethel, her thoughts were racing!

"I must have been out of my mind. What was I thinking when I came up with this wild idea? If she calls me one more time from that damn plane, I swear. If she is driving me this insane I can only imagine what she is doing to those poor flight attendants. This is all Carly's fault. If she hadn't joined that church, where she is getting baptized tonight, I would never thought to surprise her with a visit from Ethel. Why did she agree to come? Why did *I* offer to fly her here? I swear this is the last time I am going to do any act of kindness for a *long* time, especially on my dime. Now it's pouring down raining. God, I hope the flight is on time, because I have so much left to do before Carly's ceremony."

Rounding the corner to baggage claim, the traffic was heavy, as usual, at the airport. Several police officers were out in the middle of the street blowing their whistles and directing traffic. She cursed underneath her breath as one cop would not let her pull over so she could wait for her aunt. There were several signs posted telling drivers they could only stop to

BRENDA L. WATERS

let people out. No Parking, No Waiting. Now she would have to exit the airport and drive back around.

"Oh wait, there is that good-looking police officer *I* met last week in the club." She sped up and honked her horn. He was standing in the middle of the street right where she wanted to park. She jumped ahead of a car pulling out, almost clipping the car's fender to get his attention. Stopping where he was standing, she lowered her window.

"Hi, I thought that was *you*," she said. "How *are* you?"

The police officer peered into the car, and when he realized it was that fine woman he met at the club, the one wearing that really tight black dress and those stilettos, he forgot where he was and what he was supposed to be doing. The biggest smile appeared on his face as he leaned into her car.

"Hey, it's you. I'm still *waiting* for that call."

"I'm sorry, I have been *so* busy, but it must be divine intervention for me to be here to pick up my aunt and here *you* are. I really hate I can't wait for her right over *there* and will have to drive out and get back into all that traffic. I know it shouldn't be long because I called and her plane just landed. She should be down here in no time. You know what I mean?"

He knew exactly what she meant. He smiled as Taylor shifted her weight in the car, which caused her skirt to rise just a tad bit higher on her thighs.

"Do you think you could let me pull over and wait for her? She really hates to fly, and I know she is going to be a *basket case* when she gets off that plane. Trust me, you might have to arrest her if I am not here when she comes out from the baggage claim area."

"For you, I can do that. Pull over there by the orange cone and wait, but if my captain comes out, you are going to have to move your car right away, okay."

"Thank you … ah, what was your name again?" Taylor asked.

"It's Stewart, and here is my card *again*."

He reached inside his rain slicker and pulled out his business card and a pen. He wrote something on it and handed it to Taylor as she smiled and blew him a kiss.

No sooner did she park then out the door came Ethel with a porter carrying her bags. She was wearing his ear out. All Taylor could see from her rearview mirror was her mouth moving a mile a minute. The look on

SO I WAS TOLD

that poor man's face told her he was *really* sorry he waited on her. Taylor popped her trunk and got out to meet her aunt.

"Taylor, thank *God* it's you. If that plane had not landed soon, I was going to open one of those doors and jump. That was the worst flight of my life, not to mention those snotty stewardesses. Where has customer service gone? I mean, they knew how upset I was about flying alone; I told them when I first got on the plane. Do you know they would not answer when I pushed my call button? They even threatened to have the pilot come out if I did not stop calling them."

As the baggage handler loaded Ethel's luggage into Taylor's trunk, he looked at her and rolled his eyes upward as if to say, "She is all yours now, lady."

Taylor thanked him and gave him a twenty-dollar tip. He smiled and tipped his hat. It was the least she could do for the aggravation she knew he had to endure with Ethel.

"Taylor, why do you have such a small car? I can barely get inside this thing. What is it anyway?"

"It's a BMW, Ethel, and it only has two seats because that is what I wanted. One for me and one for my purse! How long are you planning on staying? I counted one too many bags for a weekend."

"Oh, Taylor you have always been so *dramatic*. I used to tell you, you should have been an actress. *Everything* is so exaggerated."

Taylor pulled from the curb, but not before she rolled her eyes at Ethel and cursed under her breath. At least she was smart enough to put her up in a hotel and not at her home for this little surprise. This trip was going to bankrupt her with all the tipping she was going to have to do to compensate for the abuse these poor people were going to endure.

"Look, Ethel, we will be at the hotel in no time. You can order room service, get a *drink*, and chill out until I come and get you tonight."

"That's an excellent idea, Taylor. After what I have been through, I need something to calm my nerves. If it wasn't for my daughter, I would have never agreed to fly. You know how I feel about that. Why couldn't I have taken the train to get here?"

From the way Ethel was carrying on about her flight, you would have thought she traveled Trans-Atlantic to get to Atlanta, instead of her one-and–a-half-hour flight from Chicago.

BRENDA L. WATERS

Pulling up to the Marriot Marquis hotel, Taylor parked and was met by the doorman. He opened the door and greeted Ethel with a smile.

"Welcome to the Marriott Marquis. I will have the bellman get your bags. The front desk is straight ahead and to your left. I hope you enjoy your stay."

"Dear man, after what I endured getting here, I can assure you I plan on it. Which way is the bar?"

After one drink, Ethel felt relaxed. She headed to her room to freshen up before Taylor return to pick her up. She had not seen Carly since her grandmother's funeral, and they did not part on the best of terms.

The church was dark and quiet as Carly stood at the altar. She arrived early to reflect and think about this night. It had been a long journey for her to become Catholic. The months of preparation and discussions often times made her question if she was making the right decision. Was this the right thing for her? As she walked to the baptismal pool, she could hear the water gurgling and flowing from the spout as it splashed into the basin. She stepped up, and sitting on the edge, dipped her fingers into the cool water. She felt a calmness come over her as she remembered the words Father Patrick spoke to her about baptism and accepting her new life in Christ.

Smiling as she looked into the water, Carly knew she had made the right decision. With Sheila by her side and Taylor there to witness, she was ready.

The sanctuary light came on, and out walked Father Patrick. He was carrying his lectionary and chalice for the altar.

"Hello, Carly. You're here early. Is everything all right? Is there something you need?

"No, Father, I'm fine. I just wanted some quiet time before my baptism. If I hadn't said it before, I want to thank you for all you have done to help guide me."

Father Patrick smiled. "This will be a blessed night for you Carly. Oh, by the way, in case you were concerned, I will turn the heater on so the water won't be too cool when you get in. Are you planning on staying here until the service?"

"No, Father, I'm leaving. See you tonight."

SO I WAS TOLD

Later that evening, I stood before the altar with many of my friends and church members who were there to witness my baptism. Sheila was standing by my side as my sponsor. Holding my hand, I could not tell who was more nervous or excited, she or me. I looked for Taylor amongst the congregation, but could not find her. She was supposed to be sitting next to me in the front pew. I was afraid she would be late and miss my baptism. Knowing Taylor, if it wasn't because of a man, it more than likely was because she could not decide what to wear. I couldn't worry about her now because Father Patrick was speaking.

"Church, tonight one of our elect will enter into these waters and from them will arise anew, just as our Lord did from his earthly tomb. Carly Collins, please come forth." After a few more words, he smiled and whispered to me, "Welcome to your baptism." As I knelt before the church with him pouring water over my head, he said, "I baptize you in the name of the Father, the Son, and the Holy Spirit, Amen!"

As I stood drenched from the baptismal waters poured over my head and body, I heard the sound of applause and bells ringing. Father Patrick helped me from the pool, and Sheila handed me a towel. As I wiped my face and turned to face the church, my heart skipped a beat. Catching my breath, I saw not only Taylor in the front pew smiling, but standing next to her was Ethel, my mother. *She* was here! I could see the tears in her eyes as she nodded her head and smiled. She gave me a tiny wave, and like those around her, began to clap.

Father was right; perhaps this was not only *my* new beginning, but maybe a fresh start for Ethel and me. I smiled and waved back. Looking out at all the smiling faces and seeing many wiping tears from their eyes, two familiar faces caught my eye. I recognized them from the many photographs they sent. There in the church was Sara and Isabella. They came to be with me on this special occasion. I had hoped they could make it when I extended the invitation. Sara, being a Catholic, knew what this moment meant to me. There had been so many phone calls and letters exchanged to comfort us as we waited and wondered if he was all right. Holding onto unshakeable faith he would return to us. They were all here for me. Truly God had blessed me, his undeserving child.

CHAPTER EIGHTEEN

BEGINNINGS

Sara called, it's uncanny how much she reminds me of her brother. The ease in which we developed a friendship was surprising. Ever since Raphael disappeared, she and Isabella have been my rock. Isa prays every night for her father's safe return. I felt a lump in my throat and my eyes began to tear when Sara told me she asks God to watch over me as well. Since the death of Isabella's mother, Sara said she has not included anyone other than family or her pets in her nightly prayers. It made me smile to know I was important to her also. As I sat on my balcony watching the sunset, hearing this made me feel better. Wiping the tears from my eyes, I felt in my heart Raphael was still alive; out there somewhere.

"Sara, I don't know what to say. Please tell Isa how much it means to me that she keeps me in her prayers."

"Carly, I want you to know it came as a shock to me as well when she asked God to watch over you. We had just finished reading a story and I told her it was time for *lights out*. Usually this brings on, 'Please, Tia Sara, just one more story. I'm not even sleepy yet, just one more, please.' But this night she said okay, got on her knees in the middle of her bed, and started praying. She started out with the usual, 'God, bless Abuelo and Abuela,

211

BRENDA L. WATERS

Daddy, and Tia.' When I expected her to ask him to watch over Stink and Loco, her pet gerbils, she continued, 'Please God! Bless and keep Carly, so Daddy will have a reason to come home to us.' I was speechless. She reached up, grabbed me around the neck, and gave me one of those kisses she and her father used to share. It felt as if a ton of weight had been lifted off my heart. After that, she laid her head on the pillow, told me goodnight, and went to sleep. I told my parents what happened and they just smiled and told me to listen to Isabella, children know. They have a special place in God's heart and unlike us *grown-ups*, they listen when God speaks. They felt he had spoken to her about Raphael and she knows he was alive. Agent Sheffield did tell us other agents in the field reported they believe he is still alive from the bits and pieces of information they were receiving. With this bit of news, even though it did little to help, it gave me a glimmer of hope. If only I could hear his voice, how great it would be.

"Carly, I need to tell you something, Sara continued. After Lonnie died, I didn't think my brother was going to make it. Isa was quite young, and though he was a good father, my sister-in-law did everything for that child. Raphael was taking classes and studying day and night to make detective, so when he was home, it was like he wasn't there. All he did was eat and barely sleep before he was back out the door at work or in class. When she died, Raphael felt so much guilt about not being there for her. Don't get me wrong, they loved one another, but there was some strain there for a while. After her death, he wanted to give up his dream of moving up in the department or becoming an agent for the FBI, but I would not let him, nor would my parents. That's when I decided to leave Louisiana and take a teaching position in Dallas so I could move in and take care of them. At first he did not want this, but when he realized how difficult it would be for him to try to raise her alone, he relented. It didn't matter anyway, because I have just as much stubbornness in me and *no* was not an option. I love Isabella as if she is my own."

I understood how she felt, because just in the short time I got to know Isa, she found a place in my heart. I too wanted to protect and love her.

Sara continued, "When my brother came home from work one night, I noticed something different about him. He was happy, almost giddy. Trust me, I was very concerned, because usually he would come in the house and go straight to his room and the shower. Not this day; he came in and kissed

SO I WAS TOLD

me on the cheek as I was getting dinner ready. He grabbed Isa from the table while she was practicing her writing, picked her up, and swung her around the room, tickling and kissing her all over. My parents and I looked at each other and didn't know what to say. After he put Isa back at the table, he walked over to Mami and Papi and hugged them both. He told me dinner smelt delicious and he left the room to take a shower. He promised to take us out for desert afterwards.

"Carly, you could have knocked me over with a feather. My parents too were in shock. They sat there with their mouths open and just looked at each other. We all busted out laughing. We didn't know what to make of it. We had no idea what had gotten into my brother. He had been so withdrawn since his wife's death. It was all about his work, his studies. He even stopped going to church with us. There was always some excuse. I think my brother was angry with God for what happened to Lonnie. He loved her very much. That night after he put Isa to bed, he was sitting in the kitchen studying. I could not go to bed without finding out what had gotten into him. I think my parents were too afraid to ask—they were just grateful he was his old self again—but I knew there was more to it than that.

"I asked him straight: 'Who are you, and where is my real brother?'

"Raphael laughed out loud and then became very serious. 'Sara, do you believed in *love at first sight.*'

"'Is this some kind of joke?'

"I could tell by the look on his face he was not kidding. So, I grabbed a cup of coffee pulled up a chair and told him, '*Spill, and I mean* tell me everything.'

"That was the first time I heard your name. He told me everything, how he was waiting there at the airport to pick you up to question you about his case. He said the person in custody had given him a description of you, so he had some idea of what you looked like, but he was not prepared for what happened. When he saw you exit the airport doors, at that very moment he knew. Raphael said he sat in his car and watched you while you looked around for a taxi. His palms began to sweat, and he felt nervous. These feelings totally caught him off guard. They were emotions he did not know how to explain. He would not tell me all the details of the situation, but he did tell me it was serious and a very big case. His future was riding on it, and he did not want any mistakes. I hate to tell you this, but I do know

213

there was another cop on the plane to make sure you got on board and made it back to Dallas. That much he did divulge.

"Anyway, when he got the signal from the police officer on the flight it was you, he was going to leave the airport and tail you back to the precinct, but something came over him. He was not going to let you get in the taxi; he had to be next to you. It was against protocol to do so, but he took the chance anyway. He had to act quickly when he saw the taxi pulling up. Raphael jumped out the car so fast he could not remember if he turned off the ignition. When he said this I nearly spit out my coffee. Just the idea of my big brother acting like a schoolboy with a secret crush had me laughing so hard. He said he tried his best to act cool when he approached you, but all he could do was think about how beautiful you were and what a fool this other man was to hurt you. I don't know what he meant by that, but he assured me it was not physical harm. He was certain you were not involved from the information he had, but he had to question you regardless. My brother was relieved when you agreed to ride to the precinct with him. He gave you some stupid excuse about a squad car being dirty."

I laughed when Sara said this.

"Well, Raphael said the more you talked the stronger his feeling grew. He knew it was crazy because he didn't know you or anything about you except what was pertinent to his case. What really broke him was when you found out the person they had in custody was there at the station. He told me how you cried, which made him really angry. It took all he had not to go down the hall and beat the hell out of whoever had caused you such pain. He knew then it was much more than a beautiful woman who caught his eye. I have to tell you I had not heard my brother talk like this about another woman, not even his wife. Please don't misunderstand, I loved my sister-in-law, I was just so shocked to hear him speak this way about another woman. I thought my brother had given up on the idea of someone else. He only talked about his future with Isabella and all the things they were going to do. He never talked about or mentioned another mother for her. When we tried to fix him up with someone, he would find a reason not to like the person. He usually would storm out the door and tell us to mind our own business. He was just fine with his life and the only woman in it was Isabella. He owed her that much."

My conversation with Sara was making my heart grow heavier for

Raphael. My emotions were on a roller coaster as I listened. Hearing her tell me how her brother felt about me only confirmed the reality of what I felt for him. It was comforting to know his feelings were real and only made me wonder where we would be today if life had not thrown a curveball into our relationship. Isabella's acceptance of me in his life touched me more than I imagined. Just as she was about to continue, the other line "clicked" in for an incoming call. As much as I hated to suspend the conversation, I knew I had to take it. The office was sending over a package for me to review, and I told the courier to contact me when he arrived. I assumed it was him.

"Sara, hold on for a minute, a call is coming in, and I need to take it. I won't be long, so don't hang up."

"Hello!"

"Carly, it's Missy. I hope I haven't caught you at a bad time. Momma wanted me to call you as soon as she heard."

"Hey Missy, what is it? Is Rayne all right? Has she had another stroke?"

"No, no Carly, Momma is fine. She's doing really well with her physical therapy. She's getting some feeling and usage with her arm and legs. The doctors anticipate she should recover well after her stroke. They said it was a good thing I was home that day when it happened and acted quickly. Her speech is still a little slurred. That is why she wanted me to call you."

"Thank God, Missy, I was scared to death when I heard your voice. What's the matter, why did she want you to call me?"

"It's your dad, Carly. Porter had another heart attack, and they don't think he will make it. He is in the hospital, and they got him on life support. They want to do surgery, but they need to get him stabilized. I could not get all the details, but I was standing next to Jessie when it happened. You remember Jessie, don't you? Porter's youngest son. I ran into him at the grocery store when he got the call. It was his sister, Leigh Ann, and she was in the emergency room with Porter. She said she found him on the bathroom floor. When I came home, I told Momma, and she thought I should call you in case he doesn't make it. You know this is his second or third heart attack. They put in that pacemaker the last time, but Porter didn't listen. He didn't want to stop the drinking and smoking them nasty cigars. No matter what the doctor or anyone else tells him, he just keeps

BRENDA L. WATERS

on doing it. That was one of the things Jessie and I were talking about. I'm really sorry to have to call you with this bad news."

I didn't know what to say to Missy.

I knew their intentions were good, but this was Porter Williams, after all. Yes, he was my biological father, but there were no memories for me to draw upon, no father-daughter relationship. Never once did he reach out to me or tell me who he was. Just as he was never spoken about in my home, I am sure the same occurred in his. My relationship with the Williams family was silent and distant. Aside from what Ethel told me about my conception and birth, that was the *only* time a discussion of Porter Eugene Williams happened.

"Missy, can I call you back? I have another call holding on the other line. Thanks for calling me about Porter. If something else happens, call me, no matter what time of day. Give you mother a kiss and hug for me. If she or you need anything, let me know. I really need to go, thanks for calling. Goodnight!"

Returning to my conversation with Sara, I tried to sound as if what I had been told meant nothing to me, yet my stomach was churning, my pulse increasing. I did not want her to hear the concern in my voice.

"Sara, I am so sorry for that. I thought it was the office, but it was someone from home. They were calling about my father. He is in the hospital. He's not well and they are afraid he might not make it."

"Oh Carly, I am so sorry to hear this. Are you going to go home to see about him? You know we can postpone the trip with Isa until things get better or you know something."

"By the way, has she figured out where she is going for her birthday?" I asked.

Laughingly Sara replied, "No, I think the secret is pretty safe. Believe me, she has tried everything under the sun to get me to tell her. Like her father, when Isa gets something under her skin, she will not let it go. My niece has even tried to bribe Papi to tell her, but my father, for once, has been able to keep a secret."

I told Sara nothing was going to stop this trip to Disney World we planned for Isabella. "Sara, thanks for the concern. It's not that I don't care about him, it's just I don't really *know* him. I only know what I have been told. We never had a real relationship. If I said more that two words to him,

216

that was two words too many. I do feel sorry about his condition, though. I told Missy, the daughter of the woman who cared for me when I was a child, to keep me informed. If the time comes for me to go home then I will, but for now, me being there is not going to change the circumstances. As a matter of fact, it might only make them worse. I don't know how much his family knows about me. There was only idle gossip when I was a child, but who knows the truth now. This trip for Isabella and your family is very important to me, even more so now after all that you told me. I never wanted children or thought they would be a part of my life, but since I have gotten to know Isa, my feelings about children have changed. I really want to be a part of her life. I want to be there when her father returns."

"I do understand Carly, and I am grateful for that. Well then, we will go on as planned. Again, thank you for this vacation. I don't know who is more excited, Isa or my parents. Good night, Carly, and I will keep you and your *father* in my prayers. I know you will make the right decision."

After we hung up, I got up and walked into my living room. I stood there and looked around my home and all the beautiful things in it. I was proud of what I had accomplished in my life with or without a father, but I knew nothing could replace the emptiness I felt at that moment for not having one in my life. This was not going to be an easy night, regardless of how I felt about Porter. I entered into my bedroom and went to my walk-in closet. I stood there looking at all the clothes, purses, and shoes, neatly arranged and stacked, but it was not what I came for. What I was seeking was buried deep in the corner in a box. It was an old scrapbook and family album I'd had since I was a child. It was worn and ragged around the corners. Glue and aged yellow tape kept it together, along with a faded red satin ribbon I tied around it. I placed it on my bed and got up to go to the kitchen to pour a glass of wine.

Returning to my room, I sat on the bed, taking a sip of my wine. I opened the book on my life and those in it. There were the pictures of Ethel when she was a young woman, the ones I use to stare at for hours when I found out who she was. There were pictures of Grandfather, Uncle Nate, Aunt Martha, Grandmother Marie, Haley, Ginger, and Helen; pictures of the women who shaped and influenced my life, for the better and worse. Photographs of me as a little girl, a teenager, my high school and college graduation, and the letter I wrote to Ethel begging for her help and the

BRENDA L. WATERS

truth, returned to me with the red ink correcting my grammar and spelling, but never answering my questions. Reading this brought back all the anger and hurt I felt as a child when I found out the truth not only about her, but about the man now lying in a hospital fighting for his life, my father.

I kept many pages of pictures of friends in school, my accomplishments, all the things important to me. I stopped on a page, picking up a photograph I know I had seen many a time, but this time I saw something perhaps I forgot or just did not want to remember. It was a picture of Aunt Ginger at the family garage. She was standing next to a car, and there was a man standing next to her. He had a cigarette in his hand. He was in the door of the car with one hand on the roof smiling into the camera. It was Porter Williams. This was the only picture I had of him. I took the picture from the album and sat there looking at it. He was a handsome man, but there was something about him that made me uneasy. Maybe it was what I knew of him or the look in his eyes. The photograph was in black and white, but his eyes were piercing. Why I had this picture and where I got it I could not answer. I placed it back into my book, closing and tying it back with that worn-out satin ribbon. I placed the book on my nightstand. Laying back on my pillow, I closed my eyes to all thoughts and images that were beginning to fill my head. Who is this man, and why was I beginning to cry?

CHAPTER NINETEEN

PORTER

It was the hottest part of the day, and the sun was beaming down on ol' Benjamin Johnson's head. It was the fourth pair of shoes he had buffed and shined since he opened his stand half past ten that morning. All he could think about was getting these Johnston and Murphy's done so he could relax with a nice cold drink. Unlike the shoe shops with all the machines to buff and shine, ol' man Johnson still polished the way his daddy taught him as a boy. A good piece of cotton cloth, Kiwi polish used with a stiff boar's hair brush, and a little spit mixed in with some *elbow grease* could polish and shine a pair of shoes as good as any machine. It was the better part of the afternoon, and his client was admiring the work he did when he looked over his shoulder at the store and all the commotion inside. Handing him two dollars for the shine, the customer commented, "Sure is a racket inside Coleman's store today. Sounds like someone is having a good time. Maybe I'll poke my head in to see what it's all about."

Old man Johnson took the money and was going to give change when the man waved him off and said, "Keep it."

"Ah, yes sir, it sure do sound like some commotion to me. Thanks for the tip. Same time next week for you, sir?"

219

BRENDA L. WATERS

"Yeah, Johnson, same time. I'm going to collect my money on that game you bet me on. I think you gonna lose that one, buddy. You have a good day now, hear!"

With that he stepped down, took a look at his shoes, and walked away with his newspaper tucked under his arm. Johnson looked up toward the sky, not a cloud to be found, only the hot scorching sun and the bluest Mississippi sky as far as the eye could see. He looked around and saw no one on the street, at least not a pair of shoes that needed the dust buffed off of them. The closer he got toward the door, the louder the sound of laughter and coughing became.

"Ooh ooh wee! Man, it is hotter than Satan's balls out there."

Bobbing his head up and down, he apologized to Cristan Coleman when he realized she was in the store.

"Oh, excuse me, Miss Cristan, I didn't know you were here. You didn't hear this old fool say anything, now did you, young lady?"

Cristan smiled and shook her head as she walked to the freezer to get her push-up ice cream before she left the store. As he passed Cristan, he shouted out to Samuel Coleman.

"Coleman, give me one of them nice *cold ones* you got over there in that freezer. I sure could use one; man, my throat feels like it's on *fire*! Samuel stopped what he was doing and handed him the coldest beer he could find.

Boy that was good", he said as he halfway emptied the bottle. "There ain't nothing like a good ol' malt liquor to take the heat and dust out of a workin' man's mouth. What you boys in hear *hooping and hollerin'* about? I could hear y'all all the way out in the street. So did Mr. Murray. He was going to come in here to see fo' himself what the heck was goin' on."

As he walked toward the men, Charlie Simpson told him they were laughing at Porter over there telling another one of his fairy tales. This time it involved him and that Collins girl, Ethel.

"What about *him* and Ethel?" Johnson asked as he finished off the last drop of beer in his bottle, looking inside to see if there was just another drop he could suck out. Placing the bottle in the trash, he took a seat on one of the empty stools at the counter.

"Go on, Porter, go on and tell Johnson what you was telling us. Let's see if he thinks you full of *you know what*, like we do?"

220

Looking around the store and at the men, Porter answered him, "Look, no disrespect to Johnson, but it ain't none of his business. What I was saying was in confidence, understand? It ain't for gossip or discussion, Charlie. I don't care if you believe me or not, I know it's the truth. I was just trying to explain what I knew to Sam, that's all."

"Oh, so now it ain't for discussion. Well I thinks that what peoples say when they know they ain't really telling the truth, or *maybe* something ain't all as it seems. You can trust Johnson; you're a trustworthy man, ain't you, Johnson? Well if you ain't gonna tell it, then I will. Porter said he and that Collins girl were *lovers*, ain't that right, Porter? Oh yeah, let's not forget about how *she wanted him, had to have him, blah, blah, blah!*"

Repeating it again with the chiding way Charlie was retelling it made the men laugh louder; only Johnson wasn't laughing at what Charlie was saying. He slowly got up from the stool, looked around at all the men with his furrowed brow, and shook his head. He stared at Porter for a long time as if he didn't know who he was. Then he spoke with barely a whisper, "Boy, is what he sayin' true? Did you *get* with that gal?"

Porter, becoming increasingly angry at the men laughing at him, turned and replied, "I told you before Johnson, it ain't none of your business. Fat Charlie told *you* cause he just jealous no woman wants his fat nasty ass, that all. But if you need to know, yeah *I fucked her* it's true, why? What's it to you? You her daddy or something?"

"No son, I ain't her daddy, but *yours* might be. Don't you know whose daughter that gal really is? She ain't no blood to Haley Collins. Hell no man, her real momma was Marie Collins. That's the woman your daddy was with. The one he wanted to marry before your mama, but his family wouldn't let him, when he was a young man. Don't you know any of this? Boy, that gal might be your *sister*. Her momma was pregnant when she went back to her husband after they said she and your daddy broke up. Everyone believed that was why Collins killed her. She was suppose to be pregnant with your daddy's baby *again*, not her husband's!"

You could hear a pin drop at that moment; there was no more laughter. All the smiles left everyone's faces, and the tears falling down cheeks from laughter dried up. Sam stopped slicing the meat for the deli display, and the men who were sitting on the stools next to Johnson slowly eased off of them. Charlie Simpson's mouth fell open as he looked at Porter.

BRENDA L. WATERS

Porter took a step toward Johnson and asked him to repeat himself, "Say that again! She is who? Who is her father? You must be out of your damn mind, Benjamin Johnson! There is no way in hell that girl and I are related. What kind of sick, fucking joke is this? You are one crazy old man to even think something like that."

Johnson took a step back from Porter. He realized he had said too much.

"Porter, why would I make somethin' like that up? Look'in here, my Ma'dear was the cook in yo' family's house for a *long* time befo's you were even born. I was just a boy, but I remember her comin' home and tellin' my momma all the stuff that wents on in yo' house. How yo' momma and daddy fought and argued over his foolin' around, especially with Maria Collins."

Porter could feel the rage as tiny beads of sweat formed on his upper lip. He could feel the blood rushing through his veins as he became angrier. This was a lie, a lie, and this old man would pay for telling it. He lunged at him, grabbing his shirt and pulling him close to him.

"Shut up, you old fool, shut your damn filthy mouth. It's not true, you hear me, it's not *true*. I ought to break your neck for what you said. *It ain't true!*"

Porter had Johnson in his grip with his fist pulled back to hit him as hard as he could. Sam jumped over the counter to grab him when he saw all the other men step back. He knew if he did not do something to stop Porter, he would have killed the old man. He knew Porter ever since he came to town, but he had never seen the look in is eyes as he did at that very moment. He believed Porter would have kept his word and killed Johnson right there on the spot.

"Porter, man, stop, you'll hurt him. Look at him, man, you are scaring the shit out of him. Let him go, Porter, let him *go*. This ain't nothing but some woman's gossip. Don't listen to that mess. If you want the truth, go home and ask you daddy, but don't do something you will regret over some bullshit like this. Don't no one here believe this man! Johnson just talking out his head."

Grabbing Porter around the shoulders, he pulled him off Johnson and slung him back against the counter. He turned to Johnson and told him to leave the store.

SO I WAS TOLD

"Get out of here Benjamin, go on. You had your say, now go, before this Negro kills you."

Johnson grabbed his shoeshine box and ran past the men to leave out the back door. It was at that moment Cristan Coleman raised her head out of the cooler to see what all the commotion was. She turned and fell back against the ice cream freezer when Porter Williams ran past her, his face contorted and cursing as loud as he could. It scared her so badly she forgot all about wanting the ice cream. She had never seen a man that angry before. Her father ran after Porter out the door, almost knocking her over. By the time he stepped outside the opened door, Porter was long gone. He stood on the sidewalk for a moment before he walked back indoors. She looked at her father, who shook and lowered his head, telling all the men to leave; the party was over. He told Cristan to go home as well. Cristan had no idea what happened, but whatever it was, it was worth telling her mother all about it. She sure was glad she brought her father's lunch that day even if it was to spy on him and Bernice Campbell.

Porter's legs could not get him away from Coleman's grocery store quick enough, but no matter how fast he ran, what Johnson said to him played over and over in his head. He had to find out the truth. There was only one place he could go for that, and it was *home*, to New Orleans.

Even though he had taken this drive before, on this occasion it felt like the road would never end. Playing the radio did not help. He was hoping it would be a distraction from the thoughts racing through his mind. Memories of his childhood were returning to him as if it were yesterday, and he was that little boy standing in the door as his mother yelled and screamed at her husband to tell her the truth. He was too young to understand what was being said, but he knew his mother was very upset. Tears were flowing down her cheeks as she paced back and forth in front of his father, who was standing at his desk. When she took her vows of *for better or worse*, she never contemplated the worse would come to fruition. The children were young, and Eugene Porter Williams thought if he moved them far away, then perhaps they would not be scarred from his decisions and the choices he made.

Porter was seven years old when he overheard someone crying and screaming from his father's library. He was running down the hallway to

223

BRENDA L. WATERS

catch up with the new puppy, which had his mother's shoe in its mouth. He suddenly stopped running and slowly walked to the library door, which was partially open.

"Please, Eugene, for the sake of my sanity, you have to tell me the truth. Is it possible you---?"

"Millicent, please get a hold of yourself. I have told you the truth. It is done, you hear me, done. I am not going to discuss this anymore. Am I not here? Have I left you? What more do you want? You know how I felt about this from the time we were married. You knew the story, but you married me anyway. We have built a life together. I have given you the children you wanted and this beautiful, fine home, and now you are coming to me with more gossip and foolishness. For God's sake, the woman is *dead*."

"This is not over, Eugene, not over at all. We will continue to discuss this and you will answer me. I don't care how many times you have to tell me. Until I am convinced, you will tell *me*", his mother cried.

It would not be the first nor the last time Porter heard his parents argue and fight, usually ending with his mother crying, and his father walking out the door. Each time this happened, it tore away the bond between Porter and his father. How could he treat his wife that way? The more hurt and sadness he saw in her eyes, the more he swore he would make his father pay, someday. Whenever his father wanted him to go right, he would make a point to go left. His mother was his only saving grace. When his grades faltered and trouble seemed to follow him like a shadow, it was his mother who bailed him out every time. He barely made it through high school, and because of a favor and who his parents were, he was accepted into the college in which his father attended. By his junior year, he was out the door. He was far more interested in drinking, gambling, and the pretty girls on campus than his grades. His father finally had enough and sent for him to come home. It was the last time Porter Williams would step foot into his father's house. The two men could not live under the same roof together. Every day was a challenge to the household's sanity with the endless battles of arguing and fighting between father and son. Porter hated his father. No amount of pleading and begging from his mother or sister could help the situation; it was too far gone.

The night Porter was arrested for almost killing a man over an illegal card game was the last time he spoke to his father. It was his father who

SO I WAS TOLD

bailed him out, and a sizeable donation to the judge and his charity, kept him out of jail. There was only one condition his father asked. He had to leave town and never come back. He had shamed and disgraced his family for the last time. It was an agreement Porter accepted gladly. He packed his things that night and drove away. Some might call it *poetic justice,* or perhaps it was fate, that put him in the path of Helen Watkins and her niece, Ethel Collins. He had heard of the Collins, the Hendersons, along with other bourgeois black families his parents knew and occasionally socialized with. If it wasn't for his car breaking down as soon as he reached Madison and pulling into the Dodson garage, he doubted if their paths would have crossed. Ginger was there that day going over the books and started a conversation while he waited for one of the mechanics to repair the overheated radiator and broken fan belt. She knew he was new in town. He looked restless, like he needed a place to lay his head and some money in his pockets.

She was tired of driving her father around on his errands, and definitely tired of being the lap dog for Helen, especially for her stupid monthly bridge party with her *uppity girlfriends.*

"So, how are long you planning on staying in Madison? Think you might like a job and a place to stay?"

Ginger kept her small house in town before she moved back in with Helen to take care of their ailing father. He accepted her offer on one condition—that he also could work on some of the cars that came into the shop. He was good at it, even though he did not have any formal training. It was his passion as a boy tinkering around with cars and their engines.

While he was talking to Ginger, Helen and Ethel drove up. Ethel had just gotten a new camera and was taking pictures of everything in sight. She took one of Ginger and the man standing next to her aunt. That was the first time Porter Williams saw Ethel Lee Collins, and he liked what he saw.

It was late when Porter arrived at his parents' home in New Orleans. The long drive gave him the opportunity to reminisce about his life. The house and grounds looked the same. His mother's flower bed of wild iris, and marigolds were in bloom. Looking around the yard, he remembered as a boy how he and his sister picked and ate the wild berries when they were in season. Now here he was after all these years, after swearing never to return.

BRENDA L. WATERS

The room was dark. If all things held true, he knew the precise moment his father would enter the study to pour himself that last drink of scotch and maybe light one of his forbidden cigars. Eugene was warned after the first heart attack about smoking and drinking as well as his diet. Heart disease ran on his side of the family. His mother even dug up a part of her famous flower garden to plant fresh vegetables so she could prepare them for their dinners. She oversaw his every move to ensure he would live a long and healthy life, but she could never win the battle with his smoking, drinking, and *his women*. It was because of the latter that his exiled son was home sitting at *his* desk, drinking *his* liquor in the dark. Porter heard the chime of the clock in the hall. He knew at any moment his father would walk through the door.

Eugene had no idea anyone else was in his home except for his wife, their daughter, and her family visiting from France. He walked into his library, turned on the light, and was startled to see *him* sitting there. His first instinct was to reach out to his son, but his pride outweighed that desire. It was his house, and he was the man in charge, his son had to understand the rules when he needed his care or finances. When money is given, you have to dance to the tune of the piper. That was a lesson drilled into Eugene's head from the time he could remember as a young man growing up in his father's house. It was the reason *he* gave up the only thing that mattered to him—his Marie.

Staring at his son, Eugene spoke in a stern voice, "What are you doing here, boy? I see you have made yourself comfortable in my chair and drinking my good liquor. How did you get in here, and what do you want?"

Porter snickered and raising his glass to his father in a salute, he answered, "Good to see *you* too father. It's nice to know some things have not changed. You would think in these dangerous times, you would at least lock those French doors; then again, I assume, since you are the all powerful and mighty Eugene Porter Williams, no one would have the audacity to come here and do you any harm, isn't that right, *daddy?*"

Porter took a sip of his liquor and grimaced as he swallowed. His voice became louder as he eased himself out of his father's leather chair. As he proceeded around the desk, he held onto it to steady himself. The liquor went down smoothly as he felt that warm rush coursing through his veins.

226

SO I WAS TOLD

"You might want to rethink that, old man. Things have changed in the past few years, or are you not aware of it living here in your palace?"

"Keep your voice down, Porter. Obviously you are drunk or damn well on your way. Do not wake your mother or your sister, who's here visiting with her family. They don't need to know you are down here making a drunken spectacle of yourself. So hurry up and tell me why you are here, and then get the hell out."

Looking at his drunken son, he shook his head and smirked while continuing, "No, better than that, let me guess. I assume you are in some kind of trouble and need my money to bail you out. If that is the case, you drove a hell of a long way for nothing. So I hope you enjoyed the long drive and my liquor. Don't waste your time or mine. Get out now! I'm going to bed, and when I get up in the morning, I better not find a trace of you here, do you understand me? I will not have your mother upset to know you snuck in here in the middle of the night rambling through our home, disrespecting me. Leave, Porter, leave the same way you came, sneaking in like a common thief. You are right, no one in their right mind would come in here on me, they fear and respect me too much; unlike *you*. Goodnight and good-bye!"

He turned from his son as he walked toward the door, Porter spoke up. "Nope, things have not changed one bit, no sir! You are still the same cold-hearted bastard you have always been. Just because you own half this county and got money pouring out of your old fat ass, I guess you still think you can just run over any and everyone who gets in your way. You think someone always wants something from you, like you never needed anybody in your whole pathetic life. Who in the hell do you think you are? *God?* There is just one twist here, *Dad.* Unlike Mother, who you would never answer her question when she would beg you, you are going to answer mine. Who was the *whore* Marie Collins, and is her daughter my *sister?*"

His father's hand stopped and rested on the door. If Porter blinked, he never would have seen Eugene take that deep breath. It was almost as if someone had kicked him in the stomach and he was trying not to show it. He slowly turned around and walked over to his son.

"What did you ask me?"

Porter knew he struck a nerve. He could see it in his father's eyes and the change in his voice. "You heard me clearly the first time; I don't need to repeat myself."

BRENDA L. WATERS

It had been a long time since anyone said her name, especially to his face. When she was spoken of, she was always referred to as "she" or "her" or "you know who I am talking about," as if her name was sacred and should not be uttered aloud. It had been so long ago and he put her memory out of his mind. He knew about the rumors, of course he did, he had to live with them, but like all rumors, they eventually died away, or so he thought until now.

"Well, are you going to answer me? I told you I'm not like mother. I want to know. I didn't drive all this way for the scenery. You are going to tell me or I *will* bring the roof down on this house. Now if you want to put *your wife* through all this, then so be it, but I will get my answer."

His father did not say a word to him, but he could tell he was visibly upset. He stood there staring at him as Porter noticed the large vein beginning to protrude down the right side of his neck, and his jaws firmly squared as his back teeth clenched. If he was ten or fifteen years younger, Porter knew his father would have laid him flat right there on the floor of his library, but he was an old man now and he could not win that battle. He watched as the moisture came into his eyes. His breathing became labored as he tried to control the anger and fury welling up inside of him. He stepped toward his son, almost standing toe to toe.

"How dare you come into my home, the home you disrespected and *shitted* on when I gave you everything. There was nothing I would not do for you, but you only cared about yourself. You did not give a damn about me or your *mother*. Here you stand like a simpering coward, not even man enough to come into my home with dignity and respect through the front door, and you have the gall to ask me about ... I don't have to tell you a damn thing about my life and *who* was in it. The question is not who do I think I am, but who in the hell do you think you are! Now get out before I throw you out."

Porter bent over and laughed. He then stood up and began to clap, becoming louder and louder as he grew angrier and angrier.

"Evidently, you did not understand what I said. I ain't leaving until I get my answer. Now who was the little *bitch*, and did you screw her and give her a baby, not *one* baby, but *two*? From what I understand, her husband got tired of raising *your* bastards and killed her for it. Now don't get me wrong, because if she was anything like her daughter, than I can understand *why* you just had to get into them drawers, but *I* want to know, is Ethel Lee Collins related to me, is she *my sister?*"

SO I WAS TOLD

Porter screamed loud enough for lights to start coming on in other parts of the house. His father yelled back. He could feel the tension in his chest, the tingling sensation beginning to trickle down his arm. He knew what was happening.

"How dare you speak that way to me. You know nothing about her and what I sacrificed." He went to raise his hand to slap Porter, but instead he grabbed his chest and fell into his son's arms. He could not breathe. He felt pain before, but not like this. Falling into him, his weight brought them both down to the floor. Eugene could feel the life seeping out of him, he was not going to make it. As he fell, he looked into his son's eyes, the last person he knew he would ever see.

A fine mist was falling as they lowered Eugene Porter Williams into the ground. Many people came to pay their respects. His business associates from over the years, clients, employees, friends and family all came to say their final good-byes. There was not a dry eye at the service except Mother's and mine. I felt it odd she did not cry at my father's funeral, but rather was very stoic and serene. She was there to console Jackie. After all, she was my father's pride and joy. So as I stood there looking down into the ground as he was lowered, I couldn't help but wonder if my little sister held me responsible for his death. No amount of reassurance from her or mother could ease the doubt I felt. Even his cardiologist could not fully ensure our fight did not prematurely lead to his death. Dr. Richardson said his heart was fragile. With his unwillingness to change his diet, stop the smoking and drinking, his family's history of heart disease, he was guaranteeing an early death.

The minister spoke the following words, "We are here today to honor a man who loved his family and his community. Death does not take away what this man meant to all of us, so as we lay him to rest let us remember Eugene Porter Williams, the life and legacy he leaves for all of us to cherish."

Father's attorney, Nicolas Dauphin was present at the graveside carrying his briefcase. He told mother it was our father's wishes to read his last will and testament immediately after he was buried. If we all could meet back at the house in his library, he could carry out the request of his client and good friend. Driving up the winding path to our home sitting beside Mother, I

BRENDA L. WATERS

noticed how warm and calm her hands felt. Occasionally she would glance toward me through her veil, squeeze my hand, smile, turn, and resume looking out the window. I tried to imagine what was in her mind at those precise moments. Was there sadness in her heart or relief that a man who cheated on her religiously, and possibly sired children other than her own, but left her filthy rich, was now dead? She loved him, faults and all, no matter how many times she cried, begged, and he disappointed her. Only her love for Jackie and me could possibly be any stronger.

As we gathered into the library for the reading of Father's will, Mother tried to keep the conversation around the room light. There was a heavy cloud of sadness and curiosity why he wanted his will read so soon. Nicolas took a seat at father's desk and began to read his last will and testament. No one was surprised when he left Jackie her sizeable trust, one for each of the grandchildren, along with his art collection and prize stable of race horses. The bulk of the estate, with his business holdings, money, and the family home, was left to Mother. We were surprised when Nicolas handed me a letter written in his handwriting for me to read either aloud or alone. I was instructed it was my choice. I decided to share whatever it was with the family. It read:

> Dear Porter,
>
> My good friend and counselor, your godfather, Nicolas Daupin has been instructed to give you this letter upon my death and burial. I instructed Nicolas the reading of my will was to occur immediately after I was laid to rest to avert any prolonged mourning or concern over each and everyone's inheritance. By now you heard what I left your mother and sister, the two women I loved dearly, though at times was remiss in my exhibition or demonstration of the deep and abiding love and respect I held for them. No amount of material wealth could ever replace the love one can have and share for another. In my life, I truly understood the need for love and had the experience of such love, though life and circumstances can thwart the ability to express that love. Much was the case for you, my son. I loved you deeply, though your life and the choices you made disappointed

me more so not for my concerns, but rather for the path I knew would befall you. With this in mind, I have changed the circumstances of my will, your inheritance, to reflect this decision. It was always my passion and desire for you to lead this family in my demise, not only as a comfort for your mother and sister, but also for the people who so faithfully and respectfully have worked and served our various business enterprises to ensure the wealth and comfort of our family. I had been blessed with loyalty and respect in the business community and had hoped you would continue in the footsteps of your grandfather and me in the legacy of these vast enterprises. Unfortunately, this did not occur. Your life and actions in it only made me realize you did not want nor held the same aspirations and beliefs in the magnitude of my dreams and hopes for your future.

With this in mind, I had no choice but to *disinherit* you from any birthright you may feel was due you as my one and only legitimate son. My fear for you and the responsibility of this enormous burden would be the squandering of all this family has worked to achieve, leaving your mother and sister to shame and despair. I have instructed Nicolas to ensure any inheritance originally left to you written prior to the revision of this will be left to your mother, Millicent Alise Fitzgerald Williams, to bequeath to you in her accord upon her death. I do so with a grave heaviness upon my heart, for I know you are disappointed with my decision. Son, I conclude with this passage I read the night I decided to make this change to my will. My prayer, I hope, is that unlike your Father, it can make you a better man. I love you, son.

Your Father,
Eugene Porter Williams

"For what does it profit a man to gain the whole world, and lose his own soul"(Mark 8:36).

BRENDA L. WATERS

No one knew what to say. I folded the letter and handed it to Mother. She did not say a word. Jackie attempted to speak, but I raised my hand to silence her.

"Now don't act surprised. We all know how the old man felt about me and my life. So, Mother I guess it will be upon me to prove I am a *good son* if I am to receive what is due me, is that right? Well, I am telling you now I came here for one reason only, to find out the truth, just the truth, but he couldn't even do that. I don't want his damn money. I have been getting along just fine without it. I know what you all are thinking; I deserved what he did to me. Porter, the bad, undeserving son who came home and killed his father doesn't deserve anything."

Before I could finish, Mother stood up and asked everyone to leave the room. She needed to have a talk with her son in private. Jackie left out with Nicolas. As they closed the doors to the library, Mother did something I had never seen her do in my entire life. She walked over to my father's liquor cabinet, took out his favorite decanter of scotch, and poured two glasses. She handed me a glass and told me to sit down, she needed to talk with me.

"Porter, I know you are hurt and feel to blame for your father's death. You are not responsible, I am. You see, I knew your father never loved me. He asked me for a divorce many years ago, but I would not do it. I loved him and thought if I stayed I could change his mind and his heart. I knew every time he looked at me or tried to love me I was only a reminder of the greatest mistake he ever made in his life. It was a mistake that slowly killed him every day of his life, until *she* died. Even then, I don't know if he came to accept his decision or if he felt defeated in it.

The night you came home, I heard you and your father arguing. I was not asleep as he thought. For many years your father and I have not shared a bed. I usually retired before he did so I would not have to witness his drinking, smoking and coming home from wherever or with whomever he had been with. It was the dance we played. I accepted it to stay in this marriage. You see, divorce was not an option for me. I loved him from the time he came into my home when he was sent to Boston to attend college. I never knew the circumstances until after we were married and I had you. By then there was no way I was going to let *her* have him. He loved her passionately."

"Your father knew how much I wanted children, and with love or not,

SO I WAS TOLD

gave you both to me. After your sister was born, the rumors started again about your father and Marie Collins. I tried not to listen to the ugly things that were being said or acknowledge the pity I saw in people's eyes when we were out, but I knew the love he held for her was strong, undeniable, yet I fought for him, fought hard. I held my head high and let people know regardless of how they felt about my marriage, I was still Mrs. Eugene Porter Williams, and would remain so until I died. Porter, you need to know this, and perhaps it was my short coming not telling you sooner, but I never in a million years ever thought this would affect you. I don't want to know what happened between you and this young woman I heard you ask your father about, Marie's daughter, but I can assure you she is *not* your sister."

She could tell by the look on my face, I had no idea she knew about this. Mother never uttered a word throughout this ordeal. Even after the ambulance came and took him to the hospital, she never came to me and said she heard the entire fight that night. Not once as she made the arrangement for the service and burial did she let on she knew what transpired between us that night. She took a sip of her drink, grimaced and continued.

"Don't look so surprised, son. Didn't you ever wonder why I never had anymore children after Jackie was born? You used to ask me all the time for another little brother or sister so you and Jackie could have someone else to play with. There were times when you were so sad when I told you it was not possible, that God only gave me you and her. I watched you, as you would blow out the candles on your birthday cake, knowing full well what you wished for each and every time until you were too old to believe in such things.

"When I was pregnant with Jackie, your father came home from his overseas business trip. He was very sick, so sick we had to place him in the hospital. You probably have forgotten about this since you were so young. Because of the virus and fever the doctor said he became sterile and would never father anymore children. It was a good thing I had my son and a healthy baby on the way, because there would be no more unless we adopted. Marie Collins could not have become pregnant by your father with Ethel or the child she was carrying when she died. Jackie was the last child he would make with any woman. Your father knew this, and so did I. Aside from his doctor, we were the only ones who knew, but Eugene did not care that Marie was pregnant with her husband's child again the last time he saw her. He

BRENDA L. WATERS

wanted her, and if that meant he would raise this child as his own, then he was willing to do so. That was how much he loved her. My husband, what did or did not happen in my marriage was no one else's business; so I chose not to disclose this information to anyone, regardless how much they felt I was a fool to stay with a man who was allegedly having all these outside children. I knew the truth. Yes, he may have loved her, wanted her, but he was not fathering her children. God took care of that. So if his punishment was to remain in a marriage where he could not have what he wanted, then so be it. My love was strong enough for you children to pull me through. I will tell you this, whatever happened between you and this young woman, you are no blood relation to her. It's not physically possible. Do you love this woman, son?"

When she asked me this, my hands turned to ice. The night I was with her flashed into my head. Love was not what I felt for her, but rather some sick need to control and dominate her. I could not look Mother in the eye to answer her.

"No, Mom, I don't. It was not about love. I know I did wrong. I knew it when it happened, but there was something in me that could not control it or stop it. I was consumed by her."

"Porter, what about your own wife and family? Didn't you once think about them? Don't you love your wife and children? I will be truthful, it was a shock when you told us you were marrying a woman so much older than you with children, someone so beneath you and your upbringing. It hurt your father, but it was your choice, not ours. Now to hear you cheated on her breaks my heart, son."

She stood and placed her glass on top of the mantle over the fireplace, turned, and looked me in the eyes. "I can't blame you entirely for the decisions or actions of your life. Your father and I are partly to blame. Our marriage was not the best example of what one should be, but I stayed because I loved you children and did not want to take you away from him. You have to know regardless of how he felt about me, he did love you. It was his foolish pride and arrogance that kept him from being the man and father he needed to be. I know you acted out because of the way he treated me, because of the things you witnessed and overheard, but it was my decision, my burden, not yours."

I did not want her to shoulder the ugliness of my life, so before she

SO I WAS TOLD

finished I spoke, "Look, Mother, you cannot make any more excuses for the way my life has turned out. I was a disappointment to Dad, and to you. I know that, but it was if I could not stop it. I hated the things he said and did to you; the women and his philandering. Jackie and I both heard the gossip and saw the way people would look at you, at us. When we were old enough to understand, I swore I would never make a day in his life happy on my regard. I knew what I was doing. I felt if you were not strong enough to hurt him then I would. I don't hold you to blame or fault you. I knew you loved him. I just never could understand why, but thank you for telling me all this. You have to believe me, that was why I came home that night. I had to know the truth. I did something I regret, no matter how much I tried to act as if it was no *big deal*. I destroyed a young woman's life for my selfishness and pleasure, and I don't even know why I did it. When I heard she could have possibly been my sister, I felt sick and repulsed with myself. I understood the shame Dad must have felt about me. I sunk low, Mom, rock bottom for what I did. I guess it would have served me right if I found out she was my blood."

Mother walked over to the sofa and stood over me. She cupped my face in her hands. "Porter, you are a grown man with a wife and family. If you learned nothing from my love and devotion to you, I am sorry for that. It's not me you need to make things right with, it's your *soul*, son. You have to make this decision. If the life you had with your father and I had anything to do with the man you became, then I am sorry for that. The tragedy of life is not the mistakes we make but rather not recognizing and correcting those mistakes before it is too late."

She kissed me on my forehead and walked out of the room, leaving me alone with my thoughts and the picture of my father mounted over the fireplace looking down on me.

CHAPTER TWENTY

HOME

Two weeks and three days after speaking with Missy, she called to inform me that Porter had passed. His children decided to remove him from life support when the doctors advised them there was no chance of recovery. At that time, no funeral arrangement had been finalized. They were still trying to contact family members and friends.

Missy asked, "Carly, would you like me to call Ethel?"

"No, I think it would be best under the circumstances if I told her myself."

"Well, are you planning to attend the funeral?"

I thought that was a peculiar question. The man was my father after all, or so I had been told.

"I am really not sure at this time, but I will get back with you."

Missy replied, "I will let you know when the arrangements have been finalized."

I had mixed fillings and didn't exactly know what I wanted to do.

He and I never exchanged more than a few words in my entire life. After he quit working for my family, I was told he left town for a while, leaving behind his wife and children. By the time he returned, I had graduated

BRENDA L. WATERS

from high school and was in my first year of college. His wife died shortly thereafter. Some said he was a changed man but was still known for his drinking and gambling. I guess some habits are just harder to break. As for the women, he never remarried, but he had plenty of them around.

After the call ended, I contacted Ethel and told her what happened. She fell silent for a while, so I had to ask to make sure she was still there.

"Ethel, are you still there? Did you hear what I said?"

"Yes, Carly, I heard."

"Well!"

"Well what? What exactly do you think I should say or do? The man is dead, period. What are you concerned about? To be truthful, Carly, I have no feelings on him dying. I closed the book on that chapter many years ago, and I have no intention of revisiting it, dead or otherwise. Thank you for calling and telling me this, but what I am more concerned about is your feelings. What are you going to do?"

"I don't know, I know what I should do, but I don't know if it is right."

"Baby, if you are concerned about my feelings, don't be. Regardless of how you got here, the man was your father. You have to make that decision on how to deal with his death. Whatever you decide is fine with me; all I am telling you is don't waste a whole lot of time on it. The man wasn't worth it. Kiss Taylor for me and tell her to call her mother, *please*. Martha is driving me nuts! Talk to you soon, sweetheart, and Carly, I mean it; don't lose any sleep over this. Goodnight!"

The call ended, but I wasn't so sure I would be able to sleep, regardless of what she said.

The next day, Taylor and I were having a late lunch eating sushi at my favorite restaurant in Midtown. In between bites, she wanted to know for the umpteenth time if I was going to attend the funeral. Missy called and told me the service would be that Saturday.

"Are you going or not?"

"I haven't decided."

"Why not? Aren't you the least bit curious on what is going to be said about you? Don't you want to know if you are going to be in the obituary, along with all those other children of his? Wait, you are now an heiress. I know that would be reason for *me* to go, not to mention the look on that

238

SO I WAS TOLD

cow Leigh Ann's face when she finds out you really are his child. Girl! That would be priceless. Look, if you need support, I will cancel my hair and nails this weekend and fly with you home. How's that for support?"

"Taylor, you are *so* generous, but I haven't decided. Seriously, I don't know what I should do. I did not grow up with the man in my life. Why should I be there in his death?"

Taylor put down her chopsticks and became serious.

"Look, Carly, I know this is not easy. There is no way it possibly can be. The man raped your mother, or so *she* said. You had no relationship with him or his family. It's bad, no doubt, but then again, he was your father. You knew who he was. Yeah, it may be asking a lot for you to do this, to forgive him, but you have to do this to move on. Close the book; end of story. I'm serious, Carly; I will go with you to the service and be there for you. I know *your* mother is not going, right; and we know for sure *my mother* is not going. I think she hated Porter Williams more than your Mama. You know, I never asked her why she did not like him. You think maybe she and him had something going ..."

I stopped Taylor before she finished her thought.

"Taylor, you are crazy. I am beginning to wonder if there is not something seriously wrong with the women in this family. We know for sure both our mothers are a bit off. I hope it is not wearing off on *us*."

We both laughed and finished eating our lunch. The topic changed, but I knew I had to make a decision. There was Sara and Isabella to think about. I had made a promise to that little girl to spend time with her and her family. I knew they would understand if I could not make the trip with them. The accommodations were arranged with or without me, nothing had changed, but then everything had. I did not want to disappoint Isabella. She was old enough to understand death and what it meant, but to a child there is nothing like a promise being broken. We were leaving mid-week with me meeting them in Orlando. Sara told me her bags were packed and by the door. Even her parents had gone out and bought things for the trip. Everyone was ready and happy to go. I heard Taylor talking, but my mind was elsewhere.

That evening I decided to stay late at work. I did not want to go home and think about what I needed to do. I couldn't imagine what difference it

BRENDA L. WATERS

would make if I did not attend the funeral. Putting down my pen, I turned my chair and gazed out my window. I could see the red lights flashing in the tails and wings of airplanes in the night's sky. I noticed the lights in the buildings across the street turning on and off. I wondered how many people were really there working or doing like I was, hiding out because of not wanting to go home. I decided to call Sara and let them know what had happened, what I decided.

"Hello, Sara, this is Carly. How are you?"

"Carly, your ears must have been burning. Isa and I were just talking about the trip. She is so excited. Every day she has been putting a big red X on her calendar."

Sara asked, "So are you packed and ready? I still can't believe you have gotten these accommodations for us at Disney World. I have to admit, I am impressed with us having our own guide. Thank you again for this. What time are you arriving Thursday?"

"Sara, my father has died, and I am calling because the funeral is set for this Saturday. After work on Friday, I am taking the last flight out to Mississippi for his burial on Saturday morning. I did not want to call you until I had made a decision on what I was going to do. I know this is a disappointment to you and Isabella. I had promised to spend time with her, but now this. I am so sorry. I promise I will make it up to her."

"Carly, you don't need to explain. Look, my parents can take Isabella to Disney World. Would you like me to come to the service with you? I can always fly to Orlando afterwards and still have the rest of the week to be with them. With all that is going to be going on with her and my parents, I don't think she will miss us too badly. She will be a little disappointed we are not there with her at first, but I know once she sees Mickey Mouse and the Magic Kingdom, we will be the last thing on her mind. Right now you need a friend. I can tell in your voice this was not an easy decision. I think it is very kind of you to want to bury your father even if you did not really know him. I am glad you made this decision, Carly. Forgiveness is difficult, but you can never heal and be happy until you do. If my brother was here, I know what he would do. He would be there for you. Since he is not, I would like to be."

"Sara, you don't know what that means to me. Thank you, but it is not necessary. Taylor is going to be there with me. If I didn't have that board

SO I WAS TOLD

meeting on Monday, I would still try to make it, but I know it would be impossible. I think this might have something to do with me taking over Sheila's position. She has been grooming me a long time to replace her. She sort of hinted to me before she left this evening that a big announcement was about to be made."

"I would have loved to see her face when she found out she was spending the night in the princess castle. Please tell Isabella how sorry I am. Take plenty of pictures. I will talk to you when you get back home. Just enjoy the trip, and if you need anything, please call me on my cell phone. Good night, and give Isabella a kiss for me. I'll talk to you soon."

Thinking about the bags I too had packed by the door, I realized how disappointed I felt not being able to go with them. But attending Porter's funeral was something I needed to do for my peace of mind.

I awoke just as the wheels were touching down on the runway. I must have dozed off while reading my magazine. My dear cousin Taylor had decided to fly a day ahead of me. No amount of wishing and praying brought me sleep the night before. I was dead tired in mind, body, and spirit. The flight arrived on time, and the car was there to meet me. I closed my eyes for what I thought was just a few minutes, and the next thing I knew, the car was no longer moving, and the driver was opening the door in the driveway of my house. I could see lights on the inside and wondered if Rayne had come with Missy to see Taylor.

"Ms. Collins, we have arrived."

Stepping out, I slowly walked up the drive to a home I had not visited since I laid my aunt to rest. Uncle J.D. was now deceased, along with so many of the people who lived here. The house was left to Ethel, who wanted nothing to do with it, so I became its sole owner. What possessed me to keep it, I could not honestly tell you. With all the unpleasant memories, you would think I would have sold it. Yet, it was my home, the home I was born into and the house I left to become the woman I am today. This house molded and shaped me, it defined me for so long, but no more. Walking into it only made me feel stronger to know I did not let it defeat me. I think this was the reason Ethel did not want it. It defeated her, consumed her. When she realized Aunt Helen left the house to her in her will, she allowed Uncle J.D. to remain in it as long as he wanted until he died. I turned the key into

241

BRENDA L. WATERS

the lock and pushed the door open. It was still as heavy as I remembered. Walking into the foyer, I looked up to see the beautiful crystal chandelier sparkling in the ceiling, the Dodson chandelier. I heard movement in the kitchen and called out, "Hello, is anyone home?"

From the swinging kitchen door out walked Missy, laughing hysterically and wiping her hands on a dishtowel.

"Hey, Carly, I told Taylor and Ma'dear I thought I heard a car pull up. I had the back door opened. How was your flight?"

Walking up to me, Missy was almost as big as her mother was when she took care of me. It wasn't a surprise she became a nurse working in labor and delivery. She was going to school to become a midwife. Her mother trained her without the formal degree, but Missy wanted the credentials to go along with the knowledge her mother gave her. With open arms, she hugged me tightly.

"Good, how are you? What in the world were you laughing so hard about? Let me guess."

"Girl, your cousin is a nut. She had Ma'dear and me rolling in the kitchen while I was doing the dishes. Come on back, I can warm something up if you are hungry."

Walking into the kitchen, Rayne was at the table in her wheelchair. Aside from the slight paralysis, she had not changed. Her hair was speckled with white, but her face did not have a line in it. No one would believe she was as old as she was. She was still my Rayne. I could see the moisture in her eyes as she tried to speak. Rushing over to her, I embraced her and kissed her cheek. She raised her good arm and embraced me. Slowly stroking my hair and looking into my eyes, she spoke with a slight slur, as a result of the complication from her stroke, but I understood what she said.

"Hey baaabie, I'm sooo gladd you home. Step baaackk and let mmee look at you. So beaaauti-full."

"Thank you, Rayne, you are looking good to. Missy told me how much progress you have made. I am so proud of you. You are going to be back to your old self in no time."

Rayne smiled and told me to sit down. Turning to Missy she told her to feed me.

"Miiissy, gettt her something to eeeatt. She is soooo sskkkinny, needsss

242

some meat on herr bones. She and Taaaylor, both are going tooo disappear. That's why they ain't gooot no husbandd. Too skinnnny!"

We all laughed and shook our heads. Nothing about her mind had changed; she still was trying to fatten me up after all these years.

I awoke to the sound of birds chirping outside my window. Looking over at the nightstand, the clock said it was 7:00 a.m. I could not remember the last time I slept this late. I was usually up before sunrise. Missy put her mother to bed shortly after I arrived then rejoined Taylor and me in the kitchen. Heaven knows what time we all went to bed. We laughed and talked about old times in Madison. Taylor told some of the most hilarious stories of her brother and sister visits during their summer break to Mississippi. Being raised on the west coast with her siblings, Taylor thought we were the most backward people she had ever encountered in her life. Who in their right mind ever heard of putting salt on a piece of watermelon? Taylor swore her mother sent her south so she could fatten up before she returned for the school year. When she was home, she did good to get a bowl of cold cereal in the morning before she left for school.

Who knows what time my head hit the pillow? For one small second with all the laughter and talk, I forgot why I was home. It seemed as soon as I closed my eyes all thoughts left my mind. I don't even remember dreaming.

Rising and standing at the opened window, I could see the dew burning off the grass. I thought of Raphael, as I did most mornings. At that precise moment, a breeze out of nowhere blew across my face, sending goose bumps down my arms. As I turned from the window, the smell of fresh-brewed coffee wafted through the house. There was nothing like the smell of a good old country breakfast. It had to be Missy, midwifery was not the only skill she inherited from her mother.

I remember standing at the same mirror looking at myself as I dressed for my Aunt Helen's funeral. Here I was today many years later doing the same for a man I barely new. Like the others, I would be present to send him to his final resting place. They all had died and gone, taking the answers to my questions with them. No more secrets to tell, no more lies to hide.

BRENDA L. WATERS

I heard the front door open and the voice of our driver downstairs. Taylor walked into the room as I placed the strand of pearls around my neck. My grandfather John Henry gave them to Marie when she gave birth to Ethel. On my sixteenth birthday, he gave them to me to wear at my cotillion, as he did Ethel when she had hers. They were left to me when he died.

Standing beside me checking her make-up and hair, Taylor asked, "You ready? The limo is downstairs. Missy and the driver are putting Rayne in the car. Don't worry; I'm here for you. I got your back just in case that bull Leigh Ann and them other heifer sisters of hers tries to start anything."

Laughing while patting her Chanel shoulder bag, Taylor said, "I got my jar of Vaseline and mace right here in my purse. I would suggest you put on some studs instead of those diamond hoop earrings you got on. Ripped ears can be messy."

I nudged her with my shoulder. "Taylor, I swear you are crazy. You are the only person I know who can take a solemn occasion and turn it into the comedy hour. This is not going to be world-class boxing or the wrestling match of the century. We are all too *old* for that kind of nonsense."

She turned to me and said, "Hey! We *are* talking about the Williams family. I remember them when I would visit you during the summer. I'm just saying you got to be ready, that's all. You're walking into enemy territory here. Don't forget they now have to split the goods *ten* ways, not *nine*. Just saying, that's all!"

Stepping from the dresser, I turned to Taylor. "Come on, I don't want to be late and be the last one to walk into the service."

I took Taylor by the arm, and in her usual sarcastic tone she said, "After you, heiress!"

We arrived at the church as people were walking inside. Mr. Coleman was there with his wife. I thought to myself how the years had aged them both. Cristan was walking behind them with, I assume, her husband and children. The boy looked just like her and stood a good foot over her head. There was a little girl holding her hand, but she looked like the man walking behind them. Charlie Simpson was standing outside the door. He had lost so much weight I almost did not recognize him. Missy said he was recovering from cancer, which would explain the weight loss. She said he almost did not make it. If it wasn't for Bernice Campbell, now Mrs. Charlie

244

SO I WAS TOLD

Simpson, he might not have pulled through. She took good care of him and nursed him back to health. Just as we were being let out in front of the church, four black stretch limousines arrived and pulled in front of our car. Parking in a row one behind the other, the drivers exited and opened the doors simultaneously, as if it was rehearsed. Out came the children of Porter Eugene Williams. The boys exited first turning and helped each sister out from the oldest to the youngest. I saw Jessie in his military uniform help his older sister Leigh Ann out of the car. Some faces I did not recognize, so I assumed they were either the spouses or close friends of the family. They were all dressed in black and most wearing sunglasses. Taylor said, "They looked like a herd of black angus cattle being pulled from them cars."

Missy yelped and laughed out loud. Rayne shushed them and told them to be respectful of the deceased. I watched as each of them walked inside. Jessie stood back and held the door for them all. Before he turned to enter, he looked back and smiled in my direction. Removing his military hat, he walked inside. Taylor nudged my arm as we walked behind Missy, who was pushing Rayne up the ramp for the disabled.

The church was nearly full, with the five front rows on both sides of the casket full of family and friends. We found a seat several rows behind the family. I noticed a few people turn and look at me, quickly turning back when I gave them eye contact. There were heads leaned together, with nods and shakes in whispered conversation. The choir was singing a song I remembered from my childhood. His mahogany casket was draped in a full spray of white gladiolas and carnations with green foliage and ivy. There were several standing sprays with golden sashes, along with potted plants and flowers surrounding his casket. The minister came forward from his seat, and the funeral began. While he was eulogizing, I noticed something was happening in the pews ahead and across the aisle. Pieces of paper were being read and passed from one person to another. Taylor and Missy noticed it as well. When the paper reached the oldest Williams daughter, a loud gasp rang out. I could see her mouth the words *no way* to the person who handed her the note. Fingers were raised to pursed lips for silence. Her head slowly turned sideways, with her eyes wide straining to look my way. When our eyes met, I smiled as she quickly turned her head, but not quick enough for me to see her face was flushed with surprise. Taylor covered her mouth to suppress laughter. Rayne's wheelchair was in the aisle with Missy sitting

245

BRENDA L. WATERS

next to her, but instead of listening to the minister, they were eyeing me. They also noticed the disruption and were trying to gauge my reaction.

The service ended, and the casket was carried out by his grandsons, who served as pallbearers. The family followed. Leigh Ann and her sisters were being helped by leaning on the arms of either a husband or their brothers. There were tears falling throughout the funeral procession. The cars were lined up outside, awaiting family to enter while the casket was being placed inside the hearse. Missy wheeled Rayne out of the church while several people came over to greet her. Taylor started to rise, but sat back down when she realized I did not move. I sat there looking at the picture of my father on the obituary. There was no mention of my name. I guess this would be another secret taken to the grave. I folded the obituary and placed it inside my purse. Taylor touched my arm and asked, "Hey, are you all right? Do you want to sit here for a while?"

I turned to her and with a faint smile. I knew it was time to go. Ethel was right; the final chapter had been read.

"No, no, I'm ready to go. I came and did what I said I would do. I buried my father and all the secrets along with him. I'm good. Let's go!"

Rising, Taylor and I walked out the church doors. Stopping and looking back, I realized it was all over now. I watched as the ushers were removing the flowers and sprays from the church to be taken to the gravesite. The sun was high, the sky was blue. I could hear the sounds of various birds chirping, and several squirrels were chasing one another as they ran up and down the great magnolia tree outside the church. It was a beautiful day. I could see them placing the coffin inside the hearse as people were speaking to and walking toward the grieving family. Jessie was helping Leigh Ann inside the limousine, along with his other sisters.

Taking a deep breath, I walked down the stairs of the church, noticing, as I descended each step, that people stopped talking and turned in my direction. Then I noticed a young couple walking toward me. I could tell by their attire they were not from here. By the time I reached the bottom step with Taylor, they were standing in front of me. The young woman smiled and extended her hand as she stepped forward. The young man stood back, but with a smile on his face.

"Excuse me, but are you Carly? I am Gillian, and this is my brother Francois Rene. She spoke with a slight French accent. We are the niece and

SO I WAS TOLD

nephew of the deceased's. It was nice of you to come. My cousin Jessie told us who you were. I am sorry we had to meet under these circumstances. Have you spoken to the rest of the family? Are you coming to the burial site?"

Before I could answer, Taylor stepped forward and introduced herself.

"Hi, I'm Taylor, Carly's cousin, and you are *who?*"

The young woman explained again who she and her brother were, and how Jessie told them when they were in the church who I was.

"Oh, so Jessie told you about *Carly*, did he? Well, did he say anything to the others?"

The young man stepped forward and hugged me, kissing me on both cheeks. He greeted Taylor in the same fashion. He stepped back, next to his sister who was in conversation with Taylor. Little did I know someone was watching this reunion happen. It was Cristan Coleman. Out of nowhere, she appeared at my side.

"Carly, is it you? I told my husband it was you. You remember Anthony Allen, don't you? That's him over there with our kids. I told him I had to come over and say something to you about your *fa*..... I am so sorry about his death. You could have knocked me over with a feather. I told them ... What I mean is I had no idea you would *come*. It's not like you and he..."

Before she finished, I spoke up, "Cristan, it's nice to see you. You have a lovely family. I'm not surprised you and Anthony married. You were together from day one. Your daughter looks just like him; your son has his height, but your face. I saw your parents inside. Your dad looks like he is taking this pretty hard."

"Yeah, he is. You know he and Porter were friends forever. After he left, I think it kind of broke my dad, really hurt his feelings. Things just were not quite the same after Porter found out about ..."

Realizing she was about to say something she shouldn't, she stopped, yet her eyes said something else. She was up to something, but what?

"Oh, well that's just old news."

Stepping back, she held me by both arms.

"You look good, really good. The best thing that happened to you was leaving this *hick* town. You really made good with your life. I mean, I am happy here with Anthony and my family, but you really did something with yourself. I bet your mother and them are real proud of you."

Her husband called out to her. "Cristan, come on. It's hot, and I am ready to go."

She turned and waved him off, turning back to me she asked as she turned in the direction of the Williams family. "Have you spoken to any of them?"

Before I could answer, she grabbed me by the arm and started pulling me toward the limousine, where Jessie was standing talking to an older man, perhaps a friend of his father's. The man then leaned into the car and waved to the people inside. Standing upright, he walked off while patting Jessie on the shoulder. As Jessie turned to enter the car, Cristan called out to him. "Jessie, wait. There is someone here to see you. It's Carly."

Jessie stepped out of the limousine. When he went to walk toward us, a hand reached out and stopped him. I saw him bend down and speak to the person inside the car. By the time he stood back up, Cristan and I were standing in front of him in the opened door.

He spoke first. "Hi, Carly!"

"Hi, Jessie, I don't know what to say, but ..." He stopped me from continuing. Stepping forward, he said, "Carly, you don't have to explain. I know—as a matter of fact, I know everything. Before Dad died, he told me about you. Can we go somewhere and talk?"

He turned to Cristan and thanked her for bringing me over. Taking me by the arm, we walked off from the car. I turned back to see Cristan's husband, grabbing her by the arm and pulling her away, with her mouth agape.

I snickered and proceeded to walk with Jessie.

"Look, Jessie, we don't have to do this here. I don't want to hold up the procession."

"Don't worry about them, Carly, they can't go anywhere without me. Besides, what's the hurry? I'll be brief."

We stopped, leaned against the magnolia tree and continued.

"You know when we were kids, I used to hear the gossip. There were many arguments and fights over you between my mom and dad. My sisters could be really *catty*, because they were jealous of you. I always thought you were pretty; you seemed not to care what people thought about you. One of the biggest fights I had with my sister Betty was about you and her high school year book. You both were in the same graduating class. Well, someone had cut your picture out, and Betty swore it was me. I never understood why she disliked you so much until I came home before Dad passed. My sisters told me he wasn't doing well. It was the night before he had his heart attack, he and I were sitting on the porch talking and laughing about old times. All of a sudden, he got real serious. He took out his wallet and handed me your picture. I could tell it had been cut out from something. It was a picture you would find in a school book. Then it hit me—Dad had cut that picture out. I looked at it and handed it back to him. He took the picture and told me something I had heard rumors of, but never really knew to be true.

"'Son, you know who the girl is in this picture?'

"'Yes, sir I do. It's Carly Collins.'

"'You know who she is?'

"'Sir!'

"'I said, do you know who she is? Son, she is your sister. She's my child, but I could never claim her. I didn't do right by her or her mother. I'm sorry, but that's in the past. I'm telling you this because unlike them other ones in there, you were the only one that was fair to that girl. I used to hear how your brothers and sisters would talk bad about her, your mother included, but you would always came to her defense, even if it cost you a hit on the arm or a black eye. You were more man than I could ever be. I wasn't man enough to let her know who I was. You know, I don't think I am destined to live long in this world. I did a lot of living when I was young. I made a lot of mistakes that brought me to be were I am today, but I tried to make up for them, all but her. I just never could do that.'

"He looked away for a moment and then continued, 'Jessie, I want you to do something for me. When I die, I want you to tell your sisters and brothers who she is. I don't want her name splattered all over my obituary for them crows and hens in town to talk about her, understand? This is for you all only. Your momma is gone, but she knew before she died. I told her. It was her who did not want you all to know and I respected her wishes. I put her through so much; the least I could do was honor her wishes in death. Well, it will be my time soon, and I am asking you to do this for me. They will listen to you. It might be hard with them older ones, but you give them this picture and let them know what I said, here!'

BRENDA L. WATERS

I promised him I would. We sat there for a while in silence, watching the sun set as the crickets began their nightly call.

Jessie reached out to me and took my hand. "I promised him I would do this, Carly, and I think this would be the best time."

Taking me by the hand, we walked back toward the waiting cars. Everyone was inside, and the doors were closed. I started to wonder if this was a good idea.

"Look, Jessie, we don't have to do this right now. Really, I know what your father asked you to do, and I think it is admirable that you want to honor his wishes, but I don't think this is the appropriate time, *really*. I am okay with the way things are."

Out of the corner of my eye, I could see the expression on Taylor's face. She was in conversation with Porter's niece and nephew, and by this time Missy and Rayne had joined them. I could see her abruptly break away as Jessie and I reached the car.

In two strides, she was at my side as the window to the limousine rolled down. I was close enough to feel the cool breeze from the air conditioning.

"Open the door! I have something to tell you," Jessie ordered.

A voice called out from the darkened car as the door gradually opened.

"Jessie Eugene Williams, what on earth are you doing, and why do you have Carly Collins next to you? Get in this car please so we can go lay our daddy to his final resting place."

Jessie spoke in a quiet, but stern voice.

"*Leigh Ann, shut your mouth. Carly has every right to be here. Dad wanted me to do this, and this is as good as anytime. Carly is our sister, Daddy's child, and there's not a damn thing you or any of us can do about it, so move over and let us in.*"

Before he could finish, a loud, wailing scream came out of the car. It was so piercing and shrill; it scared both Jessie and me. We both jumped back from the car door as we heard the sound. The only person who appeared not to be scared out of their mind was my cousin Taylor, who was laughing hysterically; I thought she was going to pass out. She stepped back from the car, holding her sides while bending over; she leaned on the hood of the car, laughing while tears were streaming down her face. The limo driver opened his door and stepped out, he grabbed the back door handle and pulled it open. The sobs and sound of someone hyperventilating was growing louder. He stood by the opened door and asked if anyone had a brown paper bag.

Jessie turned from me and dove into the car. I heard him tell his sister to *breathe*, stop crying, and *breathe*. A lady with a brown bag reached the car and handed it to him, while pushing me out of the way.

I backed away from the car slowly as Taylor came to my side. We were locked arm in arm as we tried to peer inside. I could see Leigh Ann breathing into the bag as her sisters fanned her and wiped the tears from her face.

Taylor looked toward the heaven and said out loud, "Thank you, Father, I knew you would not disappoint me."

With all the excitement and hysterics, I did not notice the taxi pulling up across the street from the church. The driver exited and walked toward me. Taylor saw him before I did. I could feel her pull away as he approached us. He walked up to me and asked, "Miss, excuse me, but are you Carly Collins?"

He was holding out his hand with his fingers enclosed around something in his palm.

"Yes I am, why?"

"The man in my car pointed you out and told me to give you this."

As he was speaking, he slowly opened his hand to show me my grandmother's ruby ring. I recognized it immediately. Taylor stepped forward and asked, "Carly, isn't that Grandmother Marie's ring? I wondered why it wasn't on your hand lately. What is he doing with it?"

Turning to the driver, she asked, "Who are you?"

Taking the ring from his hand, the sounds and voices around me slowly started to fade away. I could feel my pulse racing as my heart started beating faster. I knew who had this ring and how I was supposed to get it back. There was a lump forming in my throat. I could feel the overwhelming sadness beginning to consume me. Looking into his eyes with the ring in my hand, I asked him, "How did you get this? Who gave it to you?"

He turned and pointed toward his taxi.

"He did, the man in my car. He told me to bring it to you."

Looking around his shoulder, I saw the taxi door open. A body began to emerge. My heart stopped. This wasn't real. I felt as if all the air in my

BRENDA L. WATERS

body had been sucked out. My mind had to be playing tricks on me. I could not possibly be seeing this. I could feel the blood draining from my face, as I stood motionless. I could hear Taylor asking me something, but I could not take my eyes off of *him. It was him and he was here, alive.* It was Raphael, my Raphael, at the taxi door, smiling. As he proceeded to walk toward me, I saw a woman and child step out of the car. The child ran past him and into my arms. Grabbing me around the waist, she hugged me tightly. She took my hand into hers and started pulling me toward Raphael as he walked toward me. Letting go, she ran to Sara and stood by her side. We were standing face to face. Not a word was spoken. He took me into his arms and held me tightly. I could feel the beating of his heart and hear him breathing deeply. He cleared his throat. He pulled slightly from me without letting go.

Leaning into my face, he kissed me, first, on my teary eyes, my nose, and my tear-soaked cheeks. Looking deeply into my eyes, he kissed me softly, lightly at first; then with such intensity, it felt as if my overjoyed heart would explode. Over and over, he kissed me. He pulled me into him and hugged me again. He was straining to speak. His voice was raspy and raw. I could tell he was trying hard to control his emotions.

My head was spinning. How did he get here? When did he come home? What happened to him all this time? Was he all right?

Before I could ask him these questions, he spoke. "Carly, my sweet Carly, you have no idea how I prayed to be able to hold you again. God answered my prayers and brought me back to you, back to all of you. I love *you!* I will never *ever* leave you again, never. Nothing is more important to me than you and my family—nothing. Sara wanted to call to tell you I was home, but I told her I had to do this on my own, my way. *I* had to see your face, to touch you, hold you in my arms. I knew it would be a shock, and I did not want it done over the telephone. I wanted to be here for you. I owe you this and more for all you have done to keep me alive."

He opened my hand with the ring inside.

"You told me I was to return this to you. Having this is what kept me alive. It gave me strength. I wanted to keep that promise."

Taking the ring from my palm, he kissed it and placed it back on my finger.

I held onto his hands. Lowering my head, I closed my eyes and thanked God for giving me this day. I thanked him for allowing me to be born, for

252

surviving all the things I did in my life, all the joys and sorrows, even the secrets and lies, the stories I was told. I thanked him for bringing Raphael back to me, to all of us. Reaching up, I touched his cheeks and smiled. All the questions I needed answering, all the doubts I ever had about who I was, where I belonged, who I belonged to, disappeared. They no longer mattered.

Someone standing behind us cleared her voice as she put her arm around me.

"Hi, I'm Taylor and you *have* to be Raphael." Looking at me with the biggest smile on her face she continued, "I heard so much about you. How did you know we were here? Talk about timing."

Raphael released me and hugged Taylor.

"I've heard about you as well. Sorry we had to meet under these conditions, but I just got back and had to come. I hope I am not intruding, but my sister told me where to find Carly. I had to see her, you understand!"

"Oh honey, *you* can intrude all you like. I understand and approve. Don't worry about this and these people here."

She turned and hugged me.

"Well, I guess I don't have to ask if you are going to the graveside, do I? What's that saying; let *the dead bury the dead.* I think them folks over there can handle that. You got far more important things to do right here. Besides, I think there is a little girl over there who you promised a trip. I'll explain everything to everybody. I know they will *love* this. You know, if Uncle Nate was here he would have told you that corny cliché about life, lemons, and lemonade. Well let me be the one to tell you, that little girl standing over there, and that fine man next to you is all the sweetness you are going to need. No go on and get out of here, *I got this!*"

Taylor kissed me on the cheek and hugged Raphael before she left. Leaning into me, she whispered, "*Girl,* if it was me he left, I would have jumped off your damn balcony."

Matthew 7:7-8

"Ask, and it shall be given you; seek, and ye shall find; knock, and it shall be opened unto you: For every one that asketh receiveth; and he that seeketh findeth; and to him that knocketh it shall be opened.

Manufactured By: RR Donnelley
                     Breinigsville, PA USA
                     February, 2011